SUZANNE FORSTER

The Arrangement

MIRA®

ISBN-13: 978-0-7783-2426-3
ISBN-10:   0-7783-2426-5

THE ARRANGEMENT

MIRA and the Star Colophon are trademarks used under license and registered
in Australia, New Zealand, Philippines, United States Patent and Trademark
Office and in other countries.

www.MIRABooks.com

Printed in U.S.A.

This book is dedicated to my mother, who breathed her last on February 2, 2006, and who, despite tremendous physical challenges, managed to come through it all with her dignity, her compassion for others and her lively sense of humor intact. Every life should end so gracefully.

Rest in peace.

Edith Mary Stephenson-Bolster
1916–2006

Prologue

Andrew Villard couldn't remember when he'd last closed his eyes. Waves pounded his sixty-five-foot sloop like fists, hammering his senses as mercilessly as they hammered the hull. This wasn't just a storm at sea. It was an assault on his world. He was searching for a body, his wife's—and God help them both, he had to find her alive.

Andrew had a life most men would have killed for—enough wealth to wield influence, enough power to attract privilege. In a world split between winners and losers, he had won big. But as of seventy-two hours ago, his streak was over. He was a murder suspect. *Prime.*

Lightning ripped a hole in the black-and-blue sky. Wind lashed Andrew's hair. He hugged the mast, bracing as another wave crashed over the bow. He'd hired a small crew so he could be free to search. He had an experienced skipper at the helm, as well as a crewman who had already reefed the main sail and trimmed the storm jib to help stabilize the boat.

His wife, Alison, had disappeared at sea three days ago. The sun had gone down, and they'd been heading back to port when a squall had blown up. Andrew had gone belowdecks to hunt for life preservers that weren't in the cockpit locker where they should have been, and while he was down there, something slammed into the yacht almost hard enough to capsize it. By the time he got back on deck, a storm was raging, and Alison was gone.

Searching for her had been virtually impossible. He'd been alone on a big yacht in the dark with a fierce storm blowing. High winds had driven him back into port, where he'd radioed the Coast Guard, but their search of the coastline had yielded nothing. They'd found no trace of her, even though they'd continued searching until last night, when gale-force winds had made them call it off.

Andrew had been out in the storm every day since she vanished, but that hadn't stopped the Coast Guard from questioning whether it was an accident. They'd gone over his boat, seen the damage and called in the county sheriff's office. It was no secret that sailing was Andrew Villard's passion. In his twenties, he'd been part of the team that raced Lasers for the summer Olympics. Andrew knew the waters, was a seasoned navigator. He was too good to lose someone at sea.

A team from the sheriff's office had searched his sloop, *Bladerunner,* and they were treating him like a suspect. They'd found the damaged lifeline and the scuffed deck. It was only a matter of time until they'd find the insurance policy. And there was the tragic way his ex-fiancée had died. The media had made sure everyone knew about that. It was hailed as more proof of the Villard Curse.

If he didn't find Alison, he would be charged with

her murder. Tomorrow or the next day. Soon. He would be arrested.

The bow rose and crashed down. A wall of water knocked Andrew to the deck and nearly ripped him away from the mast. When he dragged himself back up, he couldn't see any sign of his crew. Dread sent him crawling toward the cockpit, where he spotted the pilot crouching and clinging to the wheel. The other man had taken shelter in the doorway of the pilot house.

"Come about!" Andrew shouted, gesturing to the man at the wheel. "We're heading back in."

He saw relief on both men's faces and knew he'd done the right thing. This was his desperate mission, not theirs. He had no right to endanger their lives.

Another wave lifted them into the air. They were sailing like the *Flying Dutchman* when the crewman began to gesture wildly. "There!" he bellowed, pointing southeast. "The rock reefs. Look at the reefs!"

Andrew couldn't see what the man was talking about. The reefs were obscured by mist, and before he could get back to the mast, the *Bladerunner* had sunk into another deep trough. Water poured over them in sheets, but as they rose again on a crest, Andrew could see that the seas to the southeast were less wild. The storm seemed to have moved past them, heading out to the Pacific.

He spotted a white speck in the black claws of the reefs. As they headed toward it, Andrew forgot all about the danger. The waves were still heavy as they neared, but he was mesmerized by what looked more and more like a human body. The yacht's engines roared to life, helping turn the boat into the wind.

Andrew didn't have to instruct the pilot. He knew exactly what to do.

As they came within range of the rocks, Andrew realized that it was a body, a woman, either unconscious or dead. She wasn't impaled on a reef as he'd feared. She was floating on the surface, nearly naked. It looked as if the clothes had been ripped from her body, probably by the force of the storm. But somehow she'd gotten caught on a large piece of driftwood.

She was battered, too. His gorge rose as he saw that there was little left of her face but bloody pulp. He could discern what might be her mouth, her nose, but other than that, she was virtually unrecognizable. The driftwood may have kept her afloat, but it hadn't kept her from being dashed against the rocks.

Andrew and the crewman rushed to lower a lifeboat. Moments later they climbed down the ladder and pushed off. But even when they were close enough to pick her up, Andrew wasn't able to identify her. Her injuries were a grisly sight, but he couldn't take his eyes off her. He thought he'd seen her move her hand. Was she alive?

As he freed her limp and bleeding body, he saw that she'd been snagged on the driftwood by a delicate gold wristlet—Alison's birthday gift. Andrew didn't know whether it was relief or horror that made him shudder. His wife had been found.

Andrew was ready to rip the No Smoking sign off the hospital wall. Every time he turned around that plaque was in his face, reminding him how badly he wanted to smoke. He'd quit his pack-a-day habit over a year ago, having no idea how desperately addicted he was. Desire had finally begun to wane in the last couple months. Now it was back with a vengeance—and this sign was a constant reminder, lest it slip his mind.

At the moment he was the only addict pacing the floor of Providence Saint Joseph's VIP lounge. A concert promoter by profession, Andrew knew all about such lounges. Celebrities required green room treatment wherever they went, and that included hospitals. This one had a concierge during the day, free coffee, gourmet snacks and flat screen TVs. It also had sleeping quarters, but Andrew was too wired for that. He could only guess what had earned him VIP status. Maybe the ten thousand dollars he'd donated to the hospital benevolent fund.

He checked his watch. It was 6:00 a.m., and he was waiting for an update on Alison's progress. She'd been in surgery twelve hours, and Andrew had heard nothing since three that morning, when they'd told him she should be able to resume a normal life, but it would take several more hours to reconstruct her face. He'd also been warned that this would be the first of several surgeries.

Thank God he'd insisted she be Medevaced to Saint Joseph's. He'd called from the yacht on the way back into port, and there'd been an ambulance there to meet them. The paramedics had taken her directly to the trauma center at San Diego General, but after it had been determined that she had no serious internal injuries, Andrew had arranged for her to be transferred to Saint Joseph's, where the reconstructive surgeons were the best in the world.

The trauma center's surgeons could easily have repaired the broken bones in her body, but he knew it would take virtuosos to put her exquisite face back together.

Alison's face. Andrew could see it so clearly in his mind, fine-featured and fair, the Rapunzel of her generation, which happened to be X. She would rather have lost a limb than her looks. As beautiful as she was, she was also deeply insecure and sought constant reassurance, which may have explained her crazy dreams of superstardom, and her belief that Andrew could use his connections to make those dreams come true. It wasn't the only reason their marriage had fallen apart, but it was one of them.

A flash of blue in Andrew's periphery caught his attention. A young female plastic surgeon, still garbed in scrubs, came through the waiting room door and approached him. Andrew recognized her as one of the operating room team.

He couldn't read her expression. Obvious exhaustion masked whatever emotion she might be feeling. And doctors weren't supposed to telegraph those things, anyway. Alison could be dead, and this doctor's face would show nothing more than professional compassion. Right now, he didn't even see that.

"How is she?" he asked.

She wiped her brow, and he saw the bloodstains on her sleeve.

"It's delicate work," she said, "but it's going well."

Andrew felt light-headed, probably from relief. "She's going to be all right?"

"As you know, the worst damage was to your wife's face," she told him. "We've reset her jaw and reconstructed her nose. She'll need more surgery in the future, possibly several operations, but there's a good chance we'll be able to restore not just the structure, but the character of her face."

"You're working from the pictures I gave you?" Alison had been nearly unrecognizable, even after they cleaned her up, so Andrew had described her at length and given them the wallet-size pictures he carried, most of them close-ups of her face. His hobby was boat design, precision work that made him very aware of details.

"Yes, from the pictures." She smiled, seeming pleased despite her obvious fatigue. Her expression said that this was a victory for medicine, and for her personally. "We've even managed to remove what was left of the birthmark on her throat," she said proudly.

"The birthmark?" Another wave of light-headedness caught Andrew, rocking him back on his heels. The room got very bright, and he didn't realize he was staring at the doctor until he heard her calling his name.

"Mr. Villard? Are you all right?"

"Yes, fine." He forced himself to smile at her as if everything *was* fine, but he was still unsteady. He kneaded his forehead, warding off the threat of a blinding headache. "It's been awhile since I slept."

"We won't be much longer."

"I'll get some coffee," he said, aware that he sounded out of breath. It *had* been several days since he'd slept, and he was exhausted. If he was acting strangely, that was the reason. And it was the only reason he was going to give, especially to this doctor.

1

Alison Fairmont Villard opened her eyes reluctantly. She was in her own bedroom, but the first moments of consciousness still brought bewilderment. Andrew had insisted she recuperate at his home on Oyster Bay in Long Island, but it wasn't being on the east coast that confused her. Each day since the accident had started with a realization that felt almost physical, as if she had to grasp her mind and wrench it to this new time and place, to a world she actually knew very little about. And yet more about than she wanted to.

Her amnesia wasn't as total as the doctors had thought. She remembered nothing about being battered against the reefs and nearly drowning, nothing about the plunge into the raging ocean, but she could remember just enough of what had happened before that to be terrified by it.

Those flashes of memory acted like a spotlight that could blind you to everything except its beam. What she recalled now were the harrowing moments. Everything else was hidden in the surrounding ring of darkness.

Maybe it was the pills. She took them to sleep and to keep the dreams at bay. Whether night or day, when she swallowed a tiny blue pill, she was transported to a cool, safe place, a shaded tropical lagoon, her mind free of clutter and turmoil. She slept in innocence, like Eve before the apple.

Her fingers clasped the small battered loop of copper attached to her charm bracelet. It was an ugly stepsister compared to the other delicate gold charms, but she was relieved to find it still there. She'd reached for it so often it had become a reflex. An embarrassing tic. But the brush with death had made her superstitious, and the old copper penny ring had literally saved her life when it snagged on a piece of driftwood. Its protective powers had been tested.

She rolled to her side and sat up, not bothering to cover her nakedness. There was no one to see her, anyway. She and Andrew didn't share this beautiful suite where she slept her life away, and as far as she knew they never had. Before the "accident," which was how they now referred to it, they'd lived in his Manhattan apartment. Here, in his much larger estate on Oyster Bay, their rooms were in different wings. Different rooms. Different lives.

She had almost no interaction with her husband these days, except occasionally to discuss a social or business event that he wanted her to attend with him, and there had been very few of those. In the first weeks after the accident, he'd spent hours with her, filling in the blanks of her life with him, as well as her life before him. He'd shared as much as he knew of her past, but it was what he'd told her about their relationship that made her realize they'd been on the brink of a divorce before the accident—and Andrew didn't seem to have any desire to reconcile now.

He didn't even seem to like her, which made her feel strangely empty and resentful, even though she wasn't entirely sure how she'd felt about him before. He'd refused to go into the intimate details of their relationship, which had left her both curious and suspicious, but mostly, lost. How was she supposed to pick up pieces she didn't have?

They were together now only because of the agreement they'd made—and that was strictly business. Once she'd recovered enough to lead her own life, such as it was, he'd left her to it. That was how he wanted it. What she wanted didn't seem to enter into anything, though to be fair, he had asked her about that once.

What do you want to do with your second chance?

Her answer had surprised him. She told him she didn't remember asking for one.

She rose and stretched, using her arms and feeling the ripple come from the base of her spine. Her listlessness was replaced by a vague sense of guilt as she considered the state of her bedroom and what she could see of her sitting room through the connecting arch. Clothing had been dropped here and there; books and magazines lay about.

Had she always been this sloppy? Maybe she was rebelling against *his* need for order and organization. He'd called home once when he was away on a trip, and had her search for some papers in his study, which was next to his bedroom. She'd been amazed at the precision of his life.

She didn't feel precise. She felt messy.

"What you are is a zombie," she murmured, startled at the husky tone of her own voice. Part of that was from the surgery and the rest was the way she'd always sounded, apparently. "Do something," she said. "Anything other than sleep."

She started for the bathroom, thinking she might shower and dress, perhaps go to the kitchen and find something to eat. It was late morning, and she probably should have been hungry, but she rarely had much of an appetite, especially for the organic food that Andrew preferred.

He had someone come in twice a week to clean and do the grocery shopping, but other than that they had no staff. He'd let everyone go shortly after he brought her home from the hospital. He'd had concerns about prying eyes and the tabloid press, but they would have been interested in her only because of him.

He'd made a name for himself in the music business, not just for the high-profile events he organized, but for the talent he'd discovered. And it didn't hurt that he was the personification of tall, dark and dashing. Years ago he'd been engaged to one of his own finds, a pop princess named Regine, when she'd drowned, apparently rather mysteriously, in their swimming pool.

Another accident. The women in Andrew's life were prone to them.

The media had tagged it the Villard Curse, but Andrew wouldn't discuss it, except for a few paltry details that Alison could have read in a newspaper. His mother had been a rising star with the New York Opera when she'd suffered a freak accident during a rehearsal. She and Andrew, who was a teenager at the time, had been living with her mentor, the opera's artistic director, and Andrew had stayed on with the director after she died, rather than disrupt Andrew's schooling. His parents had divorced when he was a baby, and his mother had desperately wanted him to have culture in his life. No one had objected, least of all Andrew's father, who'd moved to the wilds of Wyoming and had a family of his own.

When Alison had pressed for details about Regine, Andrew had startled her by lashing out. Apparently the loss was still too painful, but it had been five years. He'd told her not to ask about Regine again, but he'd alluded to a love triangle, of which she, Alison, had been one of the points. Alison had no recollection of that at all. It was her mother, Julia, who'd come between her relationship with Andrew when Alison was eighteen. As far as Alison knew, Andrew's association with Regine had been strictly business up to that point, although it did turn romantic after Alison and Andrew parted. Things quickly became serious between he and Regine, but she was dead before they could marry.

A year after that Andrew had secretly married Alison…and now this.

Her spine rippled again, a shiver this time. She lived with a vague sense of dread that never left her, except when she forced it away. Were there men who found it easier to dispose of women than to leave them? They would have to be patholotical in the extreme, and she didn't want to think about her husband in that way. She was still rattled and disoriented. Right now there was nothing to anchor her, no touchstones, but that would change.

The large sage-green-and-white bathroom soothed

her as she stepped barefoot onto its cool limestone tile. The mostly glass-and-steel house had several levels, domed skylights and was built on low, rolling sand dunes. It was one of the few modern structures in Oyster Bay Cove, and Andrew had kept the decor inside as light and natural as the shores and the sea outside.

As she entered the shower stall, the charm bracelet jingled on her wrist. She never removed it these days, even to bathe. Doing so made her feel too vulnerable. A chunk of her life was gone and the details of her past were confused and fuzzy, but she had a sense of herself as an adventurous person before the accident. Some might even say reckless. Now she was in constant search of ways to protect herself. She kept a marble paperweight on the nightstand next to her bed and a kitchen carving knife in the nightstand drawer, just in case.

She turned one of the knobs on a sleek stainless steel panel, and warm water began to mist from above. Possibly her favorite part of the bathroom was the rain forest showerhead. Standing under it, she really did feel as if she'd been caught in a tropical cloudburst.

When she came out of the shower moments later, wrapped in a bath sheet, she sensed that something was different. But as she walked through the room, still dripping, she didn't notice anything out of place.

As she entered the sitting room, she saw that an envelope and a handwritten note had been left on her writing desk. The embossed envelope was made of pale blue linen as soft and slippery as silk. It was addressed to her, but it had been opened and the contents read. She knew because of the note from Andrew lying next to the envelope. He'd written just two sentences and signed his name with the usual slashing capital *A*.

Alison, there's no way out this time. We have to go. Andrew.

Alison pulled the matching blue stationery from the envelope and read the entire page in one gulp, as if it were a single sentence. Nerves, she thought. The kind that made you eat too fast and caused the food to ball up in your stomach.

My darling daughter,
   Your silence is breaking my heart. You will be twenty-eight soon, and though no invitation is needed because this is and always will be your home, I'm extending one so that you can understand how desperate I am to see you again.
   Please come to Sea Clouds and celebrate the occasion of your birthday with your brother and me. Of course, Andrew is invited, too.
   I long to see you.
   All my love,
   Your mother

Alison's breath had gone dry in her throat. Invitation? It was a summons from her mother to appear. She'd known this was coming, but that didn't make it any less a disaster. Andrew had been holding her mother off since the accident. He'd said he was doing it to protect Alison, to give her time to heal and prepare, but Julia Fairmont had extended an olive branch. She wanted to see her one and only daughter, and no one could protect Alison now.

She had visions of putting the pricey stationery through a shredder and grinding it into a pile of slivers. But she didn't have the nerve, even for a symbolic act of defiance. It felt as if she'd lost control of even the smallest details of her life. She was a chess piece being moved around by master players, one of whom was her husband.

The letter was just one example. It was addressed to her, but Andrew had opened it, read it and told her how they were going to respond, even though the decision had to do with *her* life, *her* family—and should have been her choice. He believed it was time to repair her relationship with her mother, and even though it was part of the arrangement Alison had made with him, she hated the thought of going back to Mirage Bay under these circumstances.

She had only agreed because of personal reasons that were deeply important to her. Those reasons were also why she stayed in this house and put up with Andrew's interference. Unfortunately, she'd had to take him into her confidence, because she would need his help when they got to Mirage Bay. But this wasn't the right time for her to go.

Her mother's invitation almost certainly had something to do with the fifty-million-dollar trust that would have come to Alison on her twenty-eighth birthday, if she hadn't decided to walk away from the family wealth and marry Andrew. Julia Fairmont had been apoplectic. She'd cut off all contact with her daughter for four years, and according to Andrew, it was mutual. Alison had made no attempt to repair the rift.

But last February, in a fit of remorse, Alison had talked him into wintering in Mirage Bay so that she could make amends to her mother. Earlier that year, Andrew had shipped *Bladerunner* back to the West Coast manufacturer for modifications, so they would have his beloved sloop there as well.

It might have worked if her mother hadn't brutally rejected Alison's overtures—and if the weather hadn't turned nasty, whipping up a storm that had sent Alison into the drink. But now, suddenly, all was forgiven. Her mother wanted her back. Something about that didn't feel right, and Andrew's ultimatum only added to the pressure.

It bothered Alison that he'd come into her room while she was showering. Or possibly while she was sleeping. It wasn't the first time. On at least two other occasions while she slept he'd left evidence of his presence. A door ajar, a note, like today.

It wouldn't have surprised her if he'd wanted her to know, so that she would never feel totally safe, even when she slept. Her pills took care of that, but he didn't know about the pills. The doctors and nurses who treated her had quietly refilled her prescriptions and given her samples over the months.

At times she felt like a hostage in this house, which had disturbed her to the point that she'd looked the word up online and learned the dynamics of hostage taking. A captive's resistance—and her will—could be systematically undermined by randomly invading her privacy. When a person's most basic boundaries were violated, anxiety levels spiked—and had the paradoxical effect of making the hostage more dependent on the one who had the control.

Her first reaction had been to deny it. Andrew hadn't been undermining her. He was protecting her. He'd saved her life. But eventually, she'd had to admit the truth. She had no idea how many times he might have slipped in without her knowing, no idea what he might have done while he was there—and just the thought had made her want to take another pill. She would probably become an addict before she figured out how to regain some control of her life.

Her walk-in closet was the size of a small bedroom. She could have been shopping in a boutique, there were so many choices of what to wear. She grabbed the same outfit she'd worn yesterday, a pair of white shorts and a black tank top. Hard to go wrong with shorts on a July morning at the beach. If the clothes were a little roomy, it was because she hadn't yet gained back the weight she'd lost during her ordeal.

Her hair was still wet from the shower and would curl into flyaway waves if she let it dry naturally. What she *had* decided to let go natural was the color. In defiance of Andrew's wishes, she'd let the blond grow out until it had begun to look ratty, and then she'd dyed it. Now it was almost completely grown out to a rich doeskin brown, and it was the one thing that made her feel like her own woman.

She clicked her blow-dryer up to High. This was the part of her morning ritual she liked least—blow-drying, styling, makeup. None of that had any appeal for her—and who was she going to see, anyway? She lived in the same house with a man she hadn't seen a trace of in over a week. The odds of an encounter were slim. Maybe she would just grab an apple from the refrigerator and go for a walk on the beach.

She turned off the dryer without using it and slipped it back in the wall holder. Her husband's apparent surveillance didn't make sense. He was the one who'd insisted they live separate lives, except for their social obligations. They'd both agreed there would be no physical intimacy, so it wasn't her fidelity that concerned him. And yet he seemed to feel the need to keep tabs.

She should have challenged him, but that was a battle for another day. She couldn't expend the energy now. Nor could she make this trip to Mirage Bay. She needed more time. She hadn't even been able to master the piano lessons he'd insisted she take. She was supposed to have been a good player once, but the lines and notes were a foreign language now.

Still, mixed in with her suspicions and the strange brew of emotions she felt toward Andrew was some gratitude. He had saved her life and for that she owed him, but he was asking too much. And she had already decided how to handle it.

"Andrew, are you there? What am I supposed to do about all these open concert dates?"

The frustrated voice of his trusted assistant, Stacy, yanked Andrew's attention away from the graph paper on his drafting table. He turned his head to the speakerphone, where he could hear her sharp sigh.

"Once you have McGraw, Crow and Alvarado confirmed," he told her, "you can lock in the remainder of the U.S. dates. Be sure you tell their people we're not taking special orders. *All* the proceeds are going to charity. The performers get carrot sticks and tap water."

"Seriously? *Tap water?*"

"Seriously." Andrew rubbed the graph paper with his thumb, as if he could massage away any resistance. He'd awakened with the impulse to create something, and that hadn't happened in a while. He assumed it would have a hull and a sail and move through water. Sailboats were all he'd ever designed, and all he sketched now, but so far, this one was eluding him.

"Andrew, are you still there? Christina Alvarado's people won't talk to me. They want to deal with you directly—or she won't do the gig."

"In that case, she's going to be the only world-class American pop artist missing from this benefit. Tell her people that Rock Rescue will be bigger than We Are the World. If she wants to blow that off, it's her choice."

"I can't call Christina Alvarado a *pop* artist!"

"Stacy, you're losing sight of the bigger picture. This is for charity. The stars are invited. Their egos aren't."

He advised her to breathe and then he gave her his usual pep talk about megastars in need of tough love. He finished by reminding her that he'd hired her because of her moxie. What he got back was another sharp sigh, to which he responded, "Whatever you do you have my complete support," and hung up the phone.

He pushed back from his drafting table. Stacy could handle the Alvarado camp with both hands tied behind her back. She just didn't know it yet. You couldn't always accommodate. Sometimes you had to push back. Sudden fame and wealth turned too many young celebs into brats and bullies, and their publicity flacks followed suit. When that happened, nothing worked except an ice bath of reality. Everyone was expendable. It was a sad by-product of the American Dream.

Andrew's home office had a wall of louvered windows that looked out on the white sands and cresting surf of the Atlantic. He crossed the room, cranked open every one of the panels and felt the balmy sea breezes feather his eyelashes and lift his hair. He breathed in salt and the fresh scent coming off the dune's green-and-gold grasses.

As the summer heat permeated the room, and the blue endlessness of the ocean blinded him to all but its brilliant sparkle, he wished that he were out on the water. The yearning was almost palpable. He needed to sail. He hadn't done that since Alison's accident six months ago.

The *Bladerunner* had already been in Mirage Bay when they had gone back last February. Andrew had sent her out there for some modifications to the hull, and then after the accident he'd left her there, dry-docked for repairs. Now, he realized it was just as well that he hadn't brought her back. He wanted the sloop there when he and Alison returned, even if he decided against taking her out.

Sailing wasn't the same now. A darkness shadowed even the thought. He'd become almost as insular as she had—the strange, silent woman in the other wing of the house. For some time now, he'd been backing away from his business, turning more and more responsibility over to Stacy, but that was intentional. He'd also largely withdrawn from the social circuit. It was awkward going out alone. There were always the questions about Alison.

Interesting how all roads led back to her. He couldn't seem to get her out of his thoughts, but maybe that was to be expected. She was at the core of the mystery that dominated his days. Possibly, she *was* the mystery.

His stomach rumbled and he glanced over at the plate he'd left on the built-in counter and cabinets he used for work space. It was an array of summer fruit and a whole-grain croissant that he'd forgotten in his quest to be creative.

He went to the refrigerator that he stocked with juices, fruits and raw vegetables. He'd naturally gravitated toward healthier food since quitting booze after Regine died. He'd never been a falling-down drunk, but every day it had seemed to take more and more to lubricate his inane conversations with the celebrity crowd and their entourages. He'd drunk his way through too many lunches, bullshitted through too many dinners and award show parties.

Garbage in, garbage out. It all sounded the same. One day he'd lost track of his messages and called the wrong hot new rock star. He'd congratulated her on an award that she'd lost to a feuding competitor. She'd filled Andrew's ear with obscenities, which had struck him as funny. He'd dropped the phone and laughed until he cried, and when he'd gotten up to freshen his drink, the liquor bottle was empty.

It had seemed like a sign.

Now, Andrew's goal was to hand over as much

as he could of the concert promotion business to Stacy. They were reorganizing so that the bulk of it could be handled out of his Manhattan office, and the rest he could deal with from wherever he happened to be, including here in Oyster Bay. Stacy would have to hire more staff, which would raise the overhead, but that was fine. It was time he needed now, not money.

He grabbed a bottle of carrot-and-pineapple juice and walked over to his drafting table, still thinking about his new sketch. That's where it seemed to start and end these days, with the sketches. He never got to the building, never even got to the design, though that was his first love.

The walls of his office were lined with photographs and paintings of classic boats, most of them crafted of wood, and to his mind, works of art. Today's serious racing yachts were built with man-made materials, and though their lines were beautiful and their speed breathtaking, they lacked the soul of their graceful forebears.

He set down the juice unopened, picked up his pencil and drew in the hull with a couple of strokes. It was coming now. She would be small, fast and graceful, a sloop. Like *her.*

Once again, his mind went directly to Alison, like a car heading into a curve and driving off the road. How could you not think about a woman who slept naked in a cool dark room, shades drawn, even during the day?

He'd gone there to talk at various times, but she hadn't answered the door, not even when he pounded. He'd let himself in and found her in bed, entwined with the sheets and stretched out like a nude in a painting.

At times he could have sworn she was sleeping with her eyes open, like a sphinx. He never quite knew what to make of the strange creature he'd fished out of the sea, but he could not make the mistake of falling under her spell and wrecking himself on the rocks.

Someone had tried to frame him by making his wife's accident look like murder. Posing as him, they'd taken out a two-million-dollar insurance policy on Alison a month before her accident. All the arrangements, including the results of her annual medical exam, had been handled by fax and phone, and it could just as easily have been Alison herself doing it. Voices were easily disguised on the phone.

Just days before the accident, he'd told her he wanted a divorce. Their prenuptial gave her a million dollars for every year of marriage if he initiated a divorce, and nothing if she did. Without blinking an eye she'd asked for the money. He'd had it wired to the account she indicated, and forty-eight hours later, she'd disappeared off his boat.

It was enough to make a guy think. The wife he's about to divorce vanishes with a nice chunk of change and he's prosecuted for her murder? It was a tidy bit of revenge, if that's what the wife had in mind. Of course, it had backfired.

"Andrew?"

Her voice always startled him. It wasn't Alison's. But then, how could it be, he reminded himself, after all those operations?

He looked up to see her standing in the doorway of his study, lithe and tan in her white shorts and flowing, slightly wild, dark hair. She held a note in her hand. Good, he thought, she'd found it.

She was up, walking and talking.

She wasn't sleeping like the sphinx.

Good.

2

She glanced down to see if her breasts were properly exposed in the plunging wrap top. Her fringed skirt hit midthigh, which was baby stuff on this street corner. Most of the girls' fannies were falling out of their clothes, and some of the flesh was disgustingly jiggly. Not a pretty sight in broad daylight. At least *she* was toned. And she'd known enough to wear a skirt, the working girl's uniform. Short skirts weren't just sexually suggestive, they were efficient.

A sleek silver Porsche pulled to the curb. Not very discreet of the silly bastard, she thought as she walked over to the passenger door. The window zipped down and the baby-faced thirty-something driver checked her out.

"I was looking for a blonde, younger and stacked," he said.

"Aren't you lucky." She gave him a flirty wink and pulled off her silk scarf, exposing platinum-blond curls that would have done Gwen Stefani proud. It was a wig, but this guy wouldn't care. He just wanted to get his apples picked, and that meant serving up as much of his particular fantasy as she could manage.

Young wasn't an option. Stacked, she could do

something about. She cupped her breasts and pushed them up, bending toward the car window. *Silly bastard,* she thought as she saw his salacious grin.

"Get in," he told her.

She barely had the door shut when he peeled out, leaving a streak of smoking rubber behind them.

"The perfect place," he announced as he turned onto a deserted side street a couple blocks up, and parked. The grin reappeared as he unzipped his pants and made himself readily available.

"Knock yourself out," he said.

Cheeky little SOB was going to pay for that remark, she promised herself.

He continued to laugh and joke as she worked him over, pleasuring him with her hands and her mouth until suddenly, he wasn't laughing anymore. He was begging her to stop. Of course, she redoubled her efforts, and within seconds he was squealing like a baby pig.

"Damn, woman, let me at you," he gasped.

He reached for her in his apparent ecstasy, and she shoved him away. "No intercourse! We agreed."

"Yeah, but I need to get off again. That's how freaking hot you are, Julia."

"Don't call me by my name!"

"Oops, sorry." He pointed past her nose, gesturing toward the badly maintained public park they'd pulled up next to. "There's a park bench. Let's check it out."

"You're not sorry."

"You won't be either, sugar. Get your sweet ass on that park bench. I'll make a cushion out of my coat like the hell of a guy I am."

Moments later, Julia was sitting on the bench,

spread-eagled. She tried not to scream with pleasure as he mounted her with the agility of a gymnast. He could have been doing push-ups. His hands were braced on the back of the bench as he leaned over her and pumped ferociously.

Moans of ecstasy gurgled up in her throat, but she didn't want him to know he was giving her the most intense sex she'd ever experienced, the little bastard. She'd refused to let him penetrate until he put on a condom, but that's where her common sense had ended. Here she was, in a public park on a bench under a tree, and she probably wouldn't have cared if the park patrol had driven up.

"Say I'm the man," he sputtered, "tell me I'm the man! Say it!"

She got the words out, and his face contorted. "Oh, my God," he whispered. "Oh, Jesus!"

Julia gasped as he pulled out abruptly and ejaculated all over her breasts, soaking her wrap top as well as her skin. That, she wasn't so thrilled about. He could have waited for her, like a damn gentleman. But that thing he'd told her to say might come in handy.

She managed to clean up the mess he'd made with a hanky she'd tucked in her bra. In her mind the perfect square of fine lace separated her from the role she had to play in order to get what she'd come for, so to speak. She realized how sordid the situation would look to anyone who didn't understand what was at stake, but she knew the truth, clung to it. This wasn't an illicit afternoon tryst for her. It was a quest, and he had what she sought, the holy grail.

As soon as she had her feet on the ground and her skirt back where it belonged, she made her pitch.

"Okay, we did your damn fantasy. You got what you wanted. Now, when do I get what *I* want?"

He was still engrossed in putting himself back together. "You're pretty good, but not *that* good. I'm going to need another session or two, or three."

"Jack Furlinghetti, you dirty rotten liar."

"Hey, I'm an attorney, aren't I?" He laughed uproariously and then reached over and caressed her lips with the pad of his thumb. The sound he made was the hiss of escaping steam. "You've got nothing to worry about," he said.

Julia was steaming, too, and not just from the sex. She damn well better not have anything to worry about. She'd specifically requested him because she thought he was young, gullible and would do her bidding. She didn't want to be wrong about that.

"I'm not going." Alison stood in front of Andrew and ripped the envelope into shreds, letting it fall to the floor like blue snow. "I'm not ready to deal with this yet, and you know it."

He could hear the force in her low, shaking voice. She was putting on a good show, lots of bravado, but underneath it all she was afraid. He'd counted on that.

He set down his pencil, unscrewed the juice bottle top and took a drink. "Don't be dramatic. No one's forcing you to go back to Mirage Bay."

"Your note said we *had* to go. We couldn't put it off any longer." Her stare accused him, and that was no small thing from this woman. Her eyes were a deceptive baby-blue that turned into blazing fire opals when she got upset.

"Alison, don't be ridiculous." He rose from the stool. "It's your family."

"Exactly. It's my family. They eat their young." Her bracelet jingled as she caught the battered copper charm in her fingers. "I'm not ready."

"We're never ready for some things—marriage, children, major surgery. But we screw up our courage and get them done. And afterward, we're glad we did."

"Andrew, please, you know them. They'll crucify me."

"It's your mother, your brother."

"And they both hate me. My mother's been furious with me since I walked away from the trust fund my grandmother left me—and married you. What she can control she hates. What she *can't* control she hates more."

"And your brother?"

"Bret's had it in for me since birth. I was the oldest and the favorite, and he was desperate to dethrone me."

He gave her an encouraging nod. "Congratulations. That's you and Bret to a tee. You remembered it perfectly."

Her headshake was suddenly weary. "I can't remember anything, especially when I'm frightened. My mind goes blank. I may not know what silverware to use. What if I make mistakes at the dinner table? I'll be humiliated."

She was still rubbing the copper loop between her fingers. It was a dead giveaway of her nerves, and as she brought the loop to her lips, he spoke up. "I've asked you to take that thing off the bracelet. It isn't one of the charms I gave you, and it's sure to be noticed."

Her head came up, defiant. "So what if it's noticed? I added it myself, and it's brought me luck. I'm not removing it."

The desire to exert his will was strong, but he told himself to let it go for now. He had bigger battles to fight. "No one in Mirage Bay is going to humiliate you," he said. "I'll handle that."

"Really?" Sarcasm invaded her tone. "How?"

"Leave it to me. I've held your family off until now. You'll be fine. I'll be there with you."

He'd blocked Julia's attempts to see Alison when she was in the hospital, explaining that her presence would be too much for her fragile, recovering daughter. Julia had backed off, seeming to understand, but she'd also become more insistent with every passing month, and she wasn't going to be put off any longer.

Andrew made it a point not to look at the cabinets behind Alison, specifically at the locked drawer where he'd put the missive he'd received earlier that week. "I accepted your mother's invitation," he said, his tone harsh. "It's been six months. It's time."

"You shouldn't have done that." Tears welled, glittering like fire. "You had no right."

He turned away from her, not wanting to be swayed by the agony swimming in her gaze. Her eyes got to him when nothing else could. Except for the dark hair, she looked uncannily like the Alison he'd known before the accident. But that woman he could resist. This one was different. Her fears were real, persuasive. Hell, they were heartrending. And somehow, on rare occasions like this when she broke down, she managed to get to him, no matter how expertly he steeled himself against her.

That was why he stayed the hell away from her.

As he waited for her to compose herself, he realized that she was up to something else. The plate with the breakfast he hadn't eaten sat on the counter just behind her. In his peripheral vision, he could see her pilfering pieces of the fruit and stuffing them in her mouth like a starving child. He wasn't sure she even realized what she was doing.

He turned, catching her as she crammed three of the orange sections into her mouth at once. She froze at the sight of him. Her knees seemed to buckle. Heat flushed her cheeks and she gulped hard, apparently swallowing the entire mouthful.

"Alison? If you're hungry—"

"No, it's not that. Sometimes I panic and forget myself." Her eyes took on that anguish again. "Do you see?" she said. "Do you see now? I'm not ready."

He did see, but there wasn't much he could do. They had to go. Julia was extending an olive branch after four years of silence. Alison's accident had been the catalyst for Julia's change of heart. She'd wanted to see her only daughter, the child she nearly lost, but this was much more. She'd invited them to stay at Sea Clouds, the Fairmonts' compound on the cliffs near Mirage Bay.

The three-story Mediterranean mansion had been in the family for generations, but had been used primarily as a vacation home to escape the harsh East Coast winters. When Julia's husband, Grant, died, she'd begun spending more of her time at Sea Clouds, and now it was her permanent residence.

Andrew needed this opportunity. If Julia rescinded the invitation, he might not get another chance to enter that house, up close and personal with the Fairmonts—one of whom he suspected had set him up for a fall.

Andrew used the smallest key on his chain to unlock the drawer. Inside was the six-month-old edition of the Mirage Bay newspaper he'd found in his P.O. box yesterday, rolled up and bagged in plastic. He'd been having the Mirage Bay paper mailed to him since Alison's accident, but this edition wasn't courtesy of the newspaper's subscription service. This was personal. Someone was calling him out.

He unrolled the paper and laid it on the counter. Alison had just left in a huff and he didn't expect her back, but he'd locked his office door all the same. If she saw this, he would never get her on the plane to southern California. The paper's date was February third, and the lead story was about her disappearance from *Bladerunner*. But the article had been marked up by whoever sent it. Words had been circled with a permanent marker to create an ominous message, clearly intended for him.

I know what you did. Soon the police will, too.
You won't get away with it this time.
How much are your secrets worth?

It smacked of a blackmail attempt, but the sender hadn't given him any contact information. Andrew couldn't risk dismissing it as a bluff. He had plenty to hide and too much at stake, and the sender seemed to know that.

He picked up the plastic casing the paper had come in and examined the mailing label. It didn't have the newspaper's logo, which added to his theory that a private party had sent the paper, and if not for the blackmail aspect, Andrew would have said it was Julia Fairmont. He didn't think it a coincidence that her invitation had arrived within days of the newspaper message, and she had more reasons than most to want him out of the way.

He'd come between her and her only daughter, and even if Julia didn't buy the media hype about the Villard curse, she undoubtedly had some concerns about Alison's safety. She might also think he was trying to use Alison to get his hands on the fifty-milliion dollar trust fund.

How much are your secrets worth? The clumsy attempt at blackmail brought Bret Fairmont to mind. There'd be no other reason for Bret to expose him, certainly not to protect his sister. There was no love lost there. Unfortunately, the blackmail aspect opened the field up to suspects Andrew might not even know. Anyone could have seen something, heard something, although why would they wait all this time? And the second line must refer to Regine, which meant the sender knew something about his past. But then, who didn't?

He put the paper back in the drawer and locked it, but he was still mentally embroiled in the quandary. What *were* his secrets worth? Christ, there wasn't enough money.

He passed the drafting table on his way to the windows. For some reason, the bright blue horizon called up a vision of the first time he'd met Alison, twelve years ago. He'd flown to the west coast to live out his dream of commissioning a sailing yacht from Voyager Yachts, one of the country's foremost luxury boat manufacturers. Andrew had no idea that Voyager had been owned by Grant Fairmont while he was alive, or that the exclusive marina had been one of Alison's hangouts.

She'd been there that day, flitting like a butterfly around the shipyard, a shapely sixteen-year-old in a bikini, flirting madly with the college boys from the rowing club next door. She was underage and too young for Andrew anyway, but that didn't stop her from flashing him a melting smile every chance she got.

He saw a lot of her over the next year as he commuted between the coasts to watch the sailboat's progress, and eventually Andrew realized he was smitten. His intentions were serious by the time he slept with her, but when she took him home to Mama, everything changed. No one was good enough for Julia Fairmont's daughter.

Andrew continued to see Alison anyway, even after *Bladerunner* was done and had been shipped back to Oyster Bay. On her eighteenth birthday he gave her the bracelet adorned with musical charms to encourage her singing aspirations, only to have Julia demand he take it back. She also offered to write him a check if he would name his price. He'd refused the bracelet and the money, but he'd ended the relationship. Julia had been right. He wasn't good enough.

It was the last time he saw Alison until she moved to Manhattan the following year to attend Julliard. By that time he was involved with Regine, his protégé, and Alison's unexpected visit to the rooftop apartment where he and Regine lived was not a welcome surprise. But Alison had sworn she only wanted to meet Regine, that she was a huge fan.

Andrew stared out the window, looking hard at the horizon.

Who'd sent him that threat? And what were they trying to accomplish?

He'd even asked himself if the sender could have been part of Alison's plan to frame him, if there'd ever been such a plan. Maybe the accomplice had decided to finish the job, with or without her. That seemed like a stretch, but Andrew had to pursue every lead—and he was going to start where it had all begun, in Mirage Bay—whether Alison was ready or not.

His first shot put a gaping hole through the perp's heart. Bullet number two drilled right between the thug's eyes. And then, just for good measure, Special Agent Tony Bogart shot the guy's balls off. It was the wrong order. If you were going for a quick, efficient kill, you aimed for the head first. Targets shot in the head did not shoot back. But Tony was letting off steam. This was his release valve for the pressure cooker of law enforcement. Better than taking it out on live suspects, which was frowned upon by the brass.

Another perp sprang up before Tony could eject the spent magazine and jam a new one into the .40 Glock semiautomatic. The thug came straight at him, howling like a banshee. The clip jammed.

Tony flicked his head and sweat sprayed like raindrops. With a hard snap of his wrist, he Frisbee'd the gun at the target carrier system in the ceiling. It hit the drive motors and gummed up the works, stopping the paper assailant in his tracks.

Laughing, Tony pulled a .45 caliber pistol from his thigh holster and blew the bastard away. Four holes in his forehead. Just call him Mr. Efficient.

The target carrier was dead, too, but Tony wrote it off to the cost of doing business. This was a private range, and the owner knew Tony was good for the repairs, but probably wouldn't charge him. The law enforcement gig still got him a few perks. Maybe he'd donate the Glock to Goodwill. He didn't give second chances to guns—or women—who screwed him over.

He holstered his pistol and grabbed a towel to mop his brow. He'd stopped using Quantico's firing ranges. The Bureau took a dim view of their agents killing the equipment, and they'd started docking his pay. Anyone else probably would have been disciplined, but Tony was this year's top gun. Even outside law enforcement circles, he was known as the agent who'd tracked down Robert Starr, a cunning and deadly Unibomber copycat. He'd also been key in averting another Waco-like tragedy in a religious cult in Oregon.

Yeah, the Bureau loved Tony Bogart these days, so much so that they'd just put him on six weeks' administrative leave and strongly suggested he take anger management classes. And all because he'd been working his ass off trying to convince them to admit him to the training program for the Bureau's elite crisis response team.

CIRG, the Critical Incident Response Group, was roughly the equivalent of the army's Special Forces. Tony had the physical skills, but lacked the temperament, according to the psychologist who'd evaluated him. She'd diagnosed him with *intermittent explosive disorder.* And why? Just because he'd taken offense at some of her snide and insinuating questions and called her a free-associating bitch? She'd accused him of having a flagrant disregard for the rules. Ha. When was the last time she'd danced to the tune of a submachine gun's bullets? The rules were great until they got you killed.

In his whole life, Tony had only wanted a couple things really badly—and he'd been denied both times. CIRG was one. A woman from his past was the other. He'd grabbed for the gold ring twice, and it had been snatched away both times. But sometimes fate threw you a bone, even years later, and it looked like he might have another chance at the woman.

He grabbed his bag of gear and stuffed the towel inside.

She would never know what hit her.

After ten years of "stellar service," according to his performance reviews, Tony was taking an enforced leave of absence. The only good news was that it coincided with an opportunity that was deeply personal. For the last two weeks, he'd been receiving anonymous messages on his cell phone, informing him that he had the wrong suspect in the unsolved murder of his younger brother.

Butch had died a grotesque death six months ago of multiple wounds from a pitchfork, and Tony had vowed to bring the monster who killed him to justice. In his last voice mail, the snitch had been kind enough to reveal some vital information about the crime, and Tony had finally decided it wasn't a hoax.

Tony banged out the door of the firing range and into the muggy Virginia heat. Tonight, he was on his way back to Mirage Bay to catch a cold-blooded murderer. He just had time to drop by his apartment, take a quick shower, grab his already packed bags and catch his flight to LAX.

He was looking forward to this trip, and not just because it was a chance to avenge his little brother. Butch had always been a nasty piece of work, a big tough kid who enjoyed pushing his weight around, and Tony wasn't surprised that he'd had enemies. Butch had deserved a good pounding, maybe more than one, but he hadn't deserved to die.

Tony had that other score to settle in Mirage Bay, and thanks to his voice-mail snitch, he might be able to get two birds with one bullet. He liked complicated cases and dealing with clever psychopaths. In this case, he might just have both.

He certainly had no other reason to revisit the town where he'd grown up. He had no family there now. He and Butch had lost their mother in a freak accident that may have been suicide. She'd driven her car up a freeway exit and into oncoming traffic with her two young sons in the back seat. Nobody could explain why she'd done it, although postpartum depression was suggested. She'd been killed instantly. Tony and Butch had been protected by seat belts. They hadn't suffered a scratch. The scars were all internal.

Their father had raised them, though not well. He'd tried to exert control over both his sons, but in different ways. He'd used brute force on Tony, who'd been openly defiant. Butch, he'd spoiled with bribes and overindulgence. After Butch's murder he'd moved away, probably because the memories were too painful. Tony had already left years before to become a G-man, only to be rejected for not having a college degree. He'd stayed in Virginia, found himself a night job, attended school during the day, doubled up on his coursework and reapplied two years later, degree in hand. After the Bureau's traditional thirteen weeks of training, he'd been on his way to amassing one of the most impressive records of any rookie agent in years.

His fervor to be a Fed had shocked everyone who knew him. He'd shocked himself most. He didn't like kids or dogs. He was admittedly antisocial. And in school he'd been voted most likely to end up in San Quentin. None of that had changed, but he had excelled at catching criminals and deviants, the more deviant the better. Maybe because he knew how they thought.

The collar of his cotton shirt was damp with sweat by the time he got to his car. He was looking forward to California's dry heat. He wondered what the odds were that anyone or anything in the sunshine state was looking forward to his visit.

Bad. Really bad.

A smile compressed his lips again. This was going to be a good trip.

3

Alison paced her bedroom, the cell phone pressed to her ear as she listened to the incessant drone at the other end of the line. No one was answering. She'd been trying at various times of the day and night for the last two weeks, but no one had picked up, and that worried her terribly. She didn't know what she would do if something had happened to the one person in Mirage Bay she actually cared about.

She couldn't tell whether the phone was out of service, accidentally unplugged or no one was home, but she couldn't wait any longer for the answer. None of Andrew's arguments had been as powerful as this one, unanswered phone call.

For her, Mirage Bay was hell on earth, a watery graveyard where all her ghosts' demons lay in wait. But like dream monsters, ghosts and demons had to be confronted or they would give you no peace. When you ran from them, they howled at your heels for eternity.

Like about ninety percent of the men in America under thirty with computers and Internet connections, Bret Fairmont had a special affinity for cyber porn. He preferred the video streaming sites, but unlike most other aficionados, he made no attempt to hide his dirty little habit. He liked to leave it on the screen for the whole world to see, and his mother in particular.

He had fantasies of her going as white as the diet pills she popped, and nearly choking on her own revulsion. Not that it was ever going to happen. She was a beady-eyed barracuda beneath the facade of perfect manners and designer clothing. But just once he wanted to see his mother fall to pieces. He could hardly imagine anything better.

Sad, Bret, sad. How old are you now? Twenty-five going on two?

He yawned and stretched, deeply encased in the belly of the backyard hammock. As he gazed up at the boughs of the giant sycamore overhead, boredom burned through him. Lethargy had its own special kind of ache. He'd been lying around all morning in a T-shirt and swim trunks, sipping iced lattes, and he had no plans to do anything else.

He knew how she hated sloth.

And speaking of Julia Fairmont, where was the prize bitch?

You're a sick man, Bret. A sad, sick man. Why the hell do you hate her so much? She's never done anything to you....

But when he closed his eyes he could see the disdain that hardened her beautiful face when she looked at him. It never left him, that look.

Except wish you didn't exist. That's all she's ever done.

His laughter tasted like an old ashtray. It didn't hurt

anymore when she blew him off. He felt nothing. Maybe deep down there was a vestigial flicker of outrage, but on the surface, he was as cold and bitter as she was. He didn't give a fuck what she thought. Why should he?

"Bret! Where are you?"

That was her, probably calling him from one of the balconies. Her shrill voice made him flinch. He hadn't done that since he was a kid. Her tone told him she was pissed, but he'd expected that. He'd missed the job interview she'd arranged for him this morning, blown it off totally.

"Bret? Why don't you answer me?"

He saw her coming, striding across the rolling green lawn in her crisp capris, sleeveless blouse and bejeweled sandals. He threw an arm over his eyes, pretending to be asleep, though he still could see her.

Apparently his silence got to her, because when she reached him, she did something totally unexpected. She grabbed the edge of the hammock with both hands and upended it, dumping him onto the ground.

He hit with a thud. "Hey! What the fuck? I'm never going to get these grass stains out of my trunks, *Mom*."

She held up the letter in her hand. "I have important news, and it concerns you."

"You're dying, and I'm going to inherit everything?" He stood up and brushed himself off.

"Don't be an ass," she said. "Your sister's coming to visit, and I need you to help me get ready."

Her voice *was* shrill. It was shaking, but she wasn't angry. She was nervous, he realized. Shit, this was a dream come true. Julia Fairmont was cracking.

As he stood there, taking in his mother's agitation, it dawned on him what she'd said. "Alison? She's coming here?"

"Yes, and I want to do something really special. I didn't think she'd accept my invitation, or that he'd let her come. This is my chance to win her back, Bret."

Bret's legs went weak. He felt sick to his stomach, but somehow he managed to speak. "She's married, in case you hadn't noticed."

"He *stole* her. You know that as well as I do."

"Stole her? She walked away from a damn fortune to be with him. What don't you get about that? She *chose* Andrew."

Julia's expression was glacial. "He's coming with her, and if you won't help me get ready for their visit, you will at least be here. I just spoke with Andrew on the phone, and he assured me that she's anxious to see you."

It could not possibly be true that Alison was anxious to see him, but Julia had reverted to her polite mode, and Bret played along, even though inside he was still queasy enough to vomit.

"So, I assume she's recovered?" he said.

Unconsciously, Julia used her thumb to center the large emerald-and-diamond wedding ring set she never took off, even though her husband had been dead for years. The ring wasn't about marital devotion, however. She wanted the exquisite stones to show because they represented everything she wanted her life to be and wasn't. Anyway, that was Bret's theory.

"He said she's shaky," Julia said, "but that's to be expected. She's been through hell, and who knows what's happened to her in the last six months. He's never let me speak to her, the bastard."

Bret didn't doubt that his mother wanted Alison back in the family fold, but he questioned how deep her concern actually ran. She'd always favored his sister, even to the point of seeming obsessed, a stage mother's fixation with her impossibly beautiful child. Sometimes Bret wondered if Alison was Julia's second chance—but at what, he didn't know.

But he was only guessing. This could also have something to do with the trust fund that was supposed to have gone to Alison. Julia never told her black sheep son anything, so he had no idea what her real motivation was.

"I'll be here," he said, more to get rid of her than for any other reason. "Now, can I get back to my nap?"

Bret had nothing more to say about his long-lost sister. This felt way too much like watching the sci-fi channel. His mother was coming unglued. He'd been waiting years for this moment, and it had nothing to do with him. It was all about his sister. That was fucked up.

Julia glanced at her watch. "Didn't you have an interview this morning?"

His smile was quick and bitter. She never failed him. "It was a marketing job, Mother. I don't do marketing."

"You don't *do* anything." She was madly rubbing the ring with her thumb. "It's embarrassing, Bret."

"For who? I'm not embarrassed." He had actually held down jobs, modeling mostly. Nothing that met her standards.

"No, obviously not," she said.

Her face had already turned into a mask of indifference. Apparently she didn't even care enough to hold him in contempt. He wanted to laugh, but the pain in his chest had the fiery heat of a twisting knife.

She stormed off, taking the letter with her, and he fished in the pocket of his trunks for his cigarettes.

He lit one, took a deep drag and held the smoke in his lungs. If he went through enough cigs, got black lung and started coughing up blood, would she notice?

He knew the answer to that. He could disembowel himself in the living room in front of her, and she wouldn't flinch unless he dirtied the carpet. And he was probably as much to blame for that as she was. He'd been taunting her for so long she refused to take the bait anymore. He was the disease, and after years of exposure, she'd developed an immunity.

He sank down, sitting on the tipsy edge of the hammock with his bare feet on the ground. He gave his head a good shake, thinking it might make his curly blond hair look messy rather than adorable. He tried hard to look scruffy and unkempt, but sadly, he was as perfect as she was. Their family was a Ralph Lauren ad, and only he seemed to know how ugly the reality could be.

The hammock creaked under his weight. This really was absurd. He was a quarter of a century old. He needed to get some balls, pack his bags and get out of this place for good. He was rotting here. The flies were circling his head.

"Fuck." He let out a moan as helpless as it was savage, and flopped back into the netting, staring through the tree branches at the cloudless blue sky. Yes, he ought to leave, but how could he now that his

sister was making an appearance? He was as deeply suspicious of her motives as he was his mother's. He and his sister shared some things in common besides their looks. There was always something they wanted, always an agenda. And then there was her husband. Bret had only defended Andrew Villard to annoy his mother.

He reached down for his iced latte glass and saw that it had tipped over. Either the grass would enjoy a growth spurt from all the caffeine, or it would be dead by tomorrow. As he picked the glass up and rolled it in his hand, he let his mind roll along with it. Yes, his mother could count on him to be here. The opportunities Alison's visit presented were just too good to pass up.

"Alison, the car is here. Are you ready?"

Andrew's voice came to her from the foyer down the hall. She was standing in front of her dressing room mirror in her underwear—a white lace camisole and panties that seemed strangely alien on her lean, boyish body.

She studied her reflection, trying to imagine how her family would receive her when it was such an ordeal for her to look at herself. The surgeons had performed a miracle. All the scars were cleverly hidden, and her features looked remarkably natural, even though some areas of her face were still numb and dead to the touch. Her smile wasn't quite right, but she so rarely smiled.

She ran a finger down the bridge of her nose and over her glistening lips, trying to make a connection to the image she saw. It was uncanny how much she looked like the woman in the snapshots Andrew had given the surgeons. Except it was an illusion. She'd been stitched together from so many disparate parts, she didn't feel like a whole person.

The world might see loveliness, but the net effect for her was Frankensteinesque. Often, in the dark of the night, she felt vaguely monstrous, and at times her husband looked at her as if that's exactly what she was.

"Alison?" he called again. "Can I send the driver up for the bags?"

She wasn't dressed and her bags were lying open on the floor, empty. She'd given up on packing an hour ago, thinking that if she took a break to get herself dressed and ready, she might be able to finish. Everything about this trip was overwhelming. She wasn't even sure what clothes to take.

The driver was coming down the hall, and she couldn't seem to move. She touched the charm bracelet, the penny ring. *Get some clothes on. Cover yourself with something.*

Her walk-in closet had racks of beautiful clothes, but they were all baggy on her reed-thin frame. Even the shoes didn't fit. She tried to concentrate on the vast array of clothing. It was coordinated by color, type and season, but her mind wouldn't focus. The dressing room seemed to be growing darker, though she knew it was her eyes. She was shutting down, not the lights.

"This is too much for you, isn't it?"

She looked up, surprised to see Andrew behind her. He was a shadow in the mirror, more spectral than human. What struck her was his tone. She'd picked up an unexpected hint of concern. She had to admit that he'd done everything he could to make this trip easier for her, including arrange for a private charter so they didn't have to deal with airport lines and security.

Still, she avoided his direct gaze, not knowing what she might see there. She couldn't bear disdain, and pity would be worse. They'd never had a perfect marriage, and had been on the brink of a divorce when the accident happened. People might assume this was a new start for them, but nothing could be further from the truth. It was an arrangement, and a fairly cold-blooded one.

"I don't...I can't seem to pack." She almost laughed, it was such a ridiculous understatement. She couldn't seem to breathe, either.

"I'll help," he said. "Can you finish dressing?"

"Yes, of course."

"Good. You do that, and I'll get your bags packed."

"You know what I need to take?"

Irony darkened his smile. "I have a pretty good idea. It's the middle of summer in Mirage Bay, too."

When she didn't move, he laid his hands on her shoulders and squeezed, apparently intending to re-assure her. But she was too exposed, and he so rarely touched her that a chill settled in the pit of her stomach. Fear. It was an emotion she'd learned to heed the way an animal heeds a dangerous scent. But she wasn't going to let it—or him—control her.

She looked up at him. "Cheating death was hard. This is harder."

"Family reunions? You'll be fine."

"I don't know what they're expecting." Frustration rang in her voice. He was patronizing her again, managing her like one of his clients. He'd coached her so thoroughly that she'd memorized his pep talks. *You have transient amnesia and can't be expected to remember anything but bits and pieces of the past. There won't be spotlights and interrogations, so don't make it hard on yourself. I've already told your mother how difficult this is for you.*

He bent to pick up her white silk kimono, which was lying on the floor where she'd dropped it. "You're not the same person," he said. "How could you be? They'll see that immediately."

She took the robe from him before he could help her with it. Once she had it on, she turned away and tied the belt. He didn't care about her, not really. He was fixated on finding out who'd tried to frame him for murder. That was the reason he'd given her for returning to Mirage Bay, but she had a gut feeling there was more to it. He wasn't telling her everything.

His voice came to her, low and restrained. "We need to behave like we're married, Alison."

She glanced up at his reflection. He used the mirror to make eye contact with her, and she found it hard to look away. There wasn't a hint of revulsion or pity in his eyes. He was razor-focused, curious and very aware of her, much like any man interested in a woman. But it was all part of the illusion, the arrangement.

"And in love," he said. "People will expect that much."

She knew it was true. Everyone would be insatiably curious, her family most of all. But she didn't know how they were going to do it, or whether anyone would be convinced. It would require acting skills beyond either of their ability. Would anyone believe they were the same passionate, overheated couple who couldn't keep their hands off each other?

Tears rolled down Julia Driscoll Fairmont's cheeks as she plucked the downy hairs from above her upper lip. One by one, she extracted the barely visible offenders, leaving an occasional spot of blood. But the sharpest sting came from the errant nose hairs that dared to protrude from her aristocratic nostrils.

Her esthetician would have been happy to do the honors, with much greater speed and far less pain. But that would have defeated the purpose. It wouldn't have calmed Julia's nerves the way plucking did.

For the last half hour, she'd been sitting at her vanity, balancing a hand mirror and her surgical tweezers—and wincing with every extraction. She was probably adding a wrinkle for every hair. She had heard physical pain caused the brain to produce endorphins that could become addictive, but that wasn't her problem. She wasn't a pain junkie. If anything, her obsession with plucking was in large part thanks to her dear departed mother.

Eleanor Driscoll had been named for Eleanor Roosevelt, and she took that responsibility very much to heart. From her teens, Eleanor Dee, as everyone called her, had been an activist. She'd thought of herself as a modern-day crusader, which included defending society's downtrodden wherever she found them.

Eleanor Dee believed in volunteerism and self-sacrifice. She was against self-indulgence in all its forms, including drinking, smoking and, of course, indiscriminate sexual behavior. Sadly, her daughter and only child, Julia, had failed her on nearly all counts, and in the most disgraceful and embarrassing ways.

"Mea culpa," Julia muttered. At forty-nine, she was still riddled with guilt and would be until the day she died. Only her mother and devoted husband knew what she'd done all those years ago in her twenties, and they'd taken her secrets to their graves. Julia had tried to atone. She'd lived an exemplary life…well, until very recently. But she had raised her two children and become a pillar of the community, as all the Driscolls and Fairmonts had before her. Still, none of that was sufficient penance for the damage she'd done. Nothing would ever be.

So, yes, she was guilty. But she was angry, too, and not just at herself. She was still seething at the way she'd been failed back then. That was the reason Julia plucked and winced. There were times when she wanted to yank out every hair on her body. She was ridding herself of the infidels who'd broken her heart when she'd had a heart to break, the ones who'd betrayed *her*.

She went after her eyebrows next. This wasn't plucking. It was cleansing, and if the pain was some kind of penance for her sins, at least she was inflicting it on herself.

With a sigh, she put down the tweezers and studied her pensive reflection in the hand mirror. Was that spidery thing on her cheek a broken capillary?

Another wince. Another wrinkle.

The mirror landed on the granite countertop with a clink. Even her scalp hurt from sitting so long in an unnatural position. She had no time for this. Her daughter and son-in-law were arriving tonight, in a matter of hours, and she wasn't prepared. Her house was perfect, and her assistant would help serve drinks and hors d'oeuvres. Even Bret was mysteriously cooperative. Everything was as ready as it could possibly be. But she, Julia, wasn't prepared.

Her black silk halter dress was displayed on a molded hanger in her dressing room. As she entered the room, she took in the dress's simple, elegant lines, aware of how it would set off her stunning diamond brooch and drop earrings.

She should have been looking forward to this evening, but what she felt was foreboding. She knew it wasn't possible, given what Alison had been through, but that hadn't stopped Julia from imagining her daughter exactly as she'd looked when she left: lithe and carefree, luminous as summer itself. Alison had a quality greater than mere beauty. She had magic. And if Julia could have put her in a time capsule and kept her the golden debutante forever, she would have.

It was a mother's fantasy, and probably a selfish one, but she only wanted to keep her daughter safe— and protected from predators like Andrew Villard. Just because Alison wasn't dead didn't mean the man hadn't tried to kill her. Julia's suspicions were so strong she'd hired a detective to investigate him— and learned several disturbing things.

She'd never understood why someone with Alison's advantages had thrown herself at a man like Villard. She'd had some crazy dream of being a pop idol, but Villard had never intended to help her with that. Julia probably knew more about him than Alison ever would.

As Julia dressed, she couldn't help but wonder what her own mother would have thought of this strange homecoming party. It had taken a massive heart attack to bring Eleanor down, but she'd lived to see her granddaughter publicly defy her mother's wishes and run off with a sideshow impresario.

Yes, Eleanor had seen it all—and blamed it on Julia's lack of parenting skills. She'd also threatened to invoke the morals clause on the fifty-million-dollar trust that would have gone to Alison on her twenty-eighth birthday. But Eleanor had never made her wishes known to the family's estate attorneys, and technically, the money might have gone to Alison, if she hadn't turned her back on it.

Julia hadn't been so lucky. Eleanor had also imposed the morals clause on her, two decades ago, making it impossible for Julia to collect a dime of that same fund when it was supposed to have come to her on *her* twenty-eighth birthday. And now the money was sitting in a trust account, controlled by lawyers.

"You were a heartless bitch in so many ways, Mother," Julia muttered. "And I'm becoming just like you. You must be so proud."

Fortunately, Julia had never needed the trust money. Her husband, Grant Fairmont, had made his fortune in the yachting industry and left everything to her when he died. Still, Julia wasn't content to leave that much family money in the hands of attorneys who were extracting hefty fees for doing what amounted to nothing. It wasn't right. It wasn't even American, and Julia had already started taking steps to correct the error of her mother's ways.

Eleanor was probably sitting up in her grave and howling.

Julia snorted and cupped a hand to her ear. "Louder, Mother, I can't quite *hear* you."

4

"What have you done to your hair?"

They were the first words out of Julia Fairmont's mouth as she flung open the doors of Sea Clouds and gaped at her estranged daughter.

Alison reached for and found Andrew's hand, grateful to have him beside her. The woman terrified her and always had. Evidently there were going to be no hellos, no welcome homes, no hugs. Alison wouldn't have been comfortable with that, anyway, but this was very strange.

"They shaved my head," she explained to her mother. "It grew out this way, darker, so I left it."

Julia still couldn't seem to believe it. "But you've always been a blonde."

Alison touched her dark waves. "Not always. I started lightening it several years ago."

"Yes, and I assumed you would go *on* doing that."

Alison felt Andrew's hand tighten, as if to tell her she was doing fine. But they were outside, flanked by the marble columns of the grand portico, and Alison wasn't certain her mother was going to let them in the house—or that she wanted to go in. Julia's black halter dress was stunning, and her long dark bob softened her angular features, but her face was pale and masklike. She had on too much makeup, or maybe it was too much Botox. Something was wrong.

"Do you dislike the color that much?" Alison asked. She wondered what her mother thought of the blue silk shantung capri outfit that Andrew had helped her choose.

"It's just so *popstar*. Not you at all." She shot Andrew an icy glance, as if it was all his doing.

"Oh! Is this your daughter and her husband?" A younger woman appeared in the doorway behind Julia. Her round pretty face was wreathed in smiles as she edged beside Julia to extend her hand.

"I'm Rebecca, Julia's assistant. Nice to meet you both! How was your trip?"

Andrew stepped forward to take her hand. "Andrew Villard," he said, "and the trip was fine, thank you. This is my wife, Alison, of course."

Alison and Rebecca exchanged nods. It would have been awkward to reach around Julia, who was still peering at Alison as if she were trying to piece her together like a puzzle.

This was exactly what Alison had feared. Worse.

Rebecca gently took over, whispering something to Julia, and then inviting Alison and Andrew in. "You must be exhausted," she said, beckoning them to follow her into the mansion's breathtaking pink marble foyer. "Did you leave your bags in the car? I'll be happy to get them, but first can I fix you something to drink? Lemonade or a wine spritzer? It's such a warm day."

"We're fine," Alison told her. "We picked up some iced tea at the airport."

Julia seemed to have found her voice. "Rebecca can unpack for you, if you'd like."

"That's very kind, but I can handle the bags." Andrew gave Alison a glance. "We would like some time to freshen up."

"Of course." Julia nodded to her assistant. "Rebecca, show them to their room, would you? The second floor, facing the mountains."

"Oh, Julia, did you forget? The guest room on the ocean side is all ready for Alison and Andrew."

"My memory's just fine, *Rebecca*." Julia's tone was as sharp as her glance. "I'm sure they'll love the mountain view. Show them up, please."

She and Andrew had just been downgraded, Alison realized—and Julia was making sure they knew it. They hadn't been here five minutes. *Unbelievable.*

"Oh, by the way," Julia added, "drinks are at seven on the terrace. You remember, Alison. We always gather on the terrace before dinner." She looked searchingly at her daughter. "You will join us, of course."

Alison didn't know anything about drinks at seven. She just wanted to run. Somewhere in the murky depths of her memory, she could hear demons howling.

"That was terrifying," Alison whispered, speaking more to herself than to Andrew. "She looked like a mannequin in a window display. Has she always looked that way?"

Rebecca had just left them in their suite of rooms with a cheery reminder about drinks at seven. Alison found her to be effusive and overly helpful, but then anyone would have seemed effusive compared to Julia.

The suite was actually a combination bedroom and sitting room, which opened onto a balcony with wrought-iron railings. To Alison's eye, everything about the room was soothing and beautiful. The palm trees and elegant cane furniture created a cool garden of tranquility.

Andrew had gone over to check out the liquor cart, a wheeled brass-and-leather showpiece that was probably an antique. It was weighed down with crystal decanters, all filled a variety of expensive and exotic spirits, of course. Julia Fairmont's hospitality was legend. So was her bitchiness, apparently.

"Do you think she's changed her mind?" Alison asked. "Is she going to ask us to leave?"

"No, she has her reasons for wanting us here, just as we have ours." He glanced over at her. "You can't have forgotten what your own mother looks like. We went through the albums. I showed you the pictures."

"I *do* know what she looks like. That's the point. She's changed. Didn't you see it?"

"*You've* changed. You scared her half to death with your wild-ass hair." He laughed and picked up a slender decanter that glowed amber in the waning light. "How about something to drink? Sherry? It'll calm you down."

"Ugh, I'd rather drink mouthwash." Alison sat on the edge of a wicker chaise near the bed and tried to envision the many faces of Julia Fairmont, the ones she remembered and the ones she'd seen in the snapshots. But the masklike image never left the screen of her mind. It hadn't seemed to bother Andrew, but for Alison it was too stark and disturbing to be dismissed.

To calm herself, she began to mentally rehearse some of the other details she'd conjured up about her mother, with a lot of help from Andrew. Julia had never worked outside the home, but had made a career raising money for various charities. She was allergic to cats, but not dogs, and had an aversion to the color red. Her musical tastes were highbrow, but she was addicted to reality television. And almost nothing had seemed to ruffle her except the sound of crying babies. Alison had no idea why, but a wailing infant could make her mother tremble and slam doors to block the sound.

There was more, but none of it came readily to mind. She still slipped into a fog at times and couldn't remember anything, especially when under stress.

"Was she always that statuelike?" she asked Andrew. "She didn't look quite real. You'd think she had the surgery rather than me."

He started to say something, but Alison stopped him. "Why did we come, Andrew? She doesn't want us here. She acted like we were avian flu carriers."

Alison had caught the horrified flicker in her mother's eye, even if he hadn't. She could only guess what it meant. Maybe all wasn't forgiven, and she and Andrew had been summoned for some kind of confrontation. Or her mother was repulsed because Alison really did look as strange and different as she felt.

He picked up a fifth of scotch and examined the label. She watched him, aware that he no longer drank alcohol.

"You *know* why we're here," he said.

His voice had taken on an edge that prompted her to change the subject. "I love this room," she said, "but the house… It's huge and bewildering. I'm not sure I could find my way back down to the foyer."

"Julia mentioned on the phone that you wouldn't recognize the house. She's totally redone it since you were here last. I forgot to tell you that, sorry. It's been pretty chaotic."

As if by way of apology, he brought her an aperitif glass of something pale pink. She sniffed and then took a sip. Definitely not sherry. It tasted like strawberries.

"Julia is nervous, too," he said. "Couldn't you see that? She *wants* you here. She never stopped trying to see you after the accident."

"Yes, but why? It's not as if we were close in any normal mother-daughter way. Is she still angry with me? Is she curious? She has plenty of money, so this probably isn't about the trust that was supposed to have come to me…unless she wants me to promise in writing that I'll give up my claim."

"Would you do that? The money was yours. It was you who decided to walk away from it. You could always change your mind."

"And start another war? No, I can't do that."

Did he want her to go after the money? Was that the real reason they were here? She buttoned up the light cardigan she'd slipped on over her capri outfit, but not because she was cold. It was to hide the warmth spreading over her skin. When she was nervous she broke out in hivelike splotches on her chest and face.

"Let's talk about something else," she said.

He knelt next to her chair. "Alison, your mother almost lost you. She hasn't seen you in four years. Give her some time."

"But she invited us. At least she could be civil." She touched her face. "Do I look that horrible?"

"You're stunning. Maybe she's jealous."

Stunning? She could feel the red heat crawling up her neck. Soon the brilliance would invade her face and make her look like a burn victim. It had been a day of nasty shocks, and this was one more. Since the accident, Andrew hadn't given her any reason to think he found her attractive, other than an occasional polite reference to her hair or her outfit.

Now, suddenly, he was dishing out compliments, and her mother, who'd always been so proud of her daughter's beauty, was acting like she was a leper. It was too much.

Andrew rose and left her on the chaise, taking off his linen sports coat with the ease of someone who'd always worn fine clothes and took for granted the cachet they lent the wearer. She could still conjure up a mental picture of the first time she'd seen his face. Somehow he'd come into her line of sight, dark and striking in a white sweater that contrasted beautifully with his coloring. Undoubtedly, she'd seen the dark eyes first, framed by the tanned, strong face. But she couldn't seem to remember exactly where the sighting was. A harbor somewhere, possibly on the bow of the *Bladerunner,* with a beautiful blonde on his arm.

The image reminded her that one of her goals while in Mirage Bay was to get a look at his boat, without him or anyone else around.

"Are you up to unpacking?" he asked. "I can do it if you'd like to lie down for a while."

One bed. She shot a glance at the lovely swirls of the white iron bed with yards of sheer veil draped from the canopy frame. It appeared to be at least king-size, but there was just one. That was going to be awkward. Sharing a room was going to be awkward, too, even in this spacious suite.

"I'll unpack," she said, "but maybe I will lie down for a few minutes first." She sounded formal, stiff. She always sounded that way with him. Why couldn't she relax? What did she think he was going to do to her? Realistically, what?

She'd barely completed the thought when he came across the room, drawing something from the pocket of his slacks. "This is for you," he said, handing her a small, black-velvet jewelry box.

She opened the lid to the most beautiful earrings she'd ever seen. The pink, emerald-cut diamonds sparkled so brightly they were almost painful to look at. Pale-yellow diamond chips surrounded the large center stones.

"Why?" she said, looking up at him.

"Because you wore diamonds everywhere. I thought you might wear them to dinner tonight."

"They're exquisite."

"Alison, so are you."

She sucked in a breath. "Why are you doing this?"

His shrug suggested that it was no big deal, but his gaze was focused on her face, intent on her eyes and her startled mouth—especially her mouth. Her stomach dipped and her pulse was quick, hot, crazy.

"You remember," he said. "You even wore them to bed—and nothing else."

She could feel heat flare to the tips of her ears, scorching her face. "Amnesia comes in very handy at times."

She set the velvet box on the end table next to her, a clear rebuff. What looked like generosity on his part was beginning to feel like something else to her. Was this one more insidious attempt to control her, right down to what she wore on her earlobes?

"The earrings are yours, regardless." He casually changed the tone of the conversation. "I'll use the bathroom first, if you don't mind. I'll take a quick shower and be out of there."

Her heart pounding, she watched him go to the valet stand, open his suitcase and take out his shaving kit. It wasn't going to be easy getting ready with just one bathroom. They could take turns with their showers, but where were they going to dress? She hadn't seen any dressing rooms.

"I'm going to hang my suit to steam out the wrinkles while I shower," he said. "Shall I hang your dress?"

She agreed, aware that he knew exactly which dress she was going to wear because he'd packed her bag. It felt strange watching him go through her things, knowing that she'd granted him access to her dressing room and allowed him to pick and choose what she should take. She hadn't thought about it at the time, but now it made her feel vulnerable.

He unzipped her garment bag and drew out the ankle-length black jersey gown that appeared shapeless on the hanger, but clung to every curve on the female body. It looked particularly good on a leaner figure like hers.

Once he'd disappeared into the bathroom, she breathed a sigh of relief and took advantage of the time alone to make a quick cell phone call. She keyed in the same number she'd been calling for days, but again got no answer. Concern weighed heavier on her heart with every attempt. She was going to have to rely on Andrew's help, after all. Promising herself she would come up with a better plan, she turned off the phone. Right now, it was too risky to go herself.

She took a furry, animal-print throw from the back of the chaise and went to lie on the bed. Sleep had been her escape since the accident, but she couldn't imagine drifting off in this situation. She had pills with her, but if she took one now she'd never wake in time for dinner.

The shower came on full force in the next room. He'd left the door partially open, probably for ventilation. Clearly, he was more comfortable with their accommodations than she was. But that didn't stop her eyes from going straight to the crack in the door. Only the sink and mirror were in her line of sight, but that was enough to present what seemed like an irresistible opportunity.

Moments later the water abruptly stopped and the shower door banged open. He appeared at the sink, which allowed her to see him lather up and shave. He'd knotted a white bath sheet around his hips, and her eyes were unavoidably drawn to the knot. But his arms were the sexiest part of his body. She could have watched the play of his triceps, the ripple of cords and veins, for hours. God help her. This was not the distraction she needed.

She closed her eyes, but the memories came flooding back, anyway. She remembered so vividly when she'd first become aware of him in the periphery of her life, the wild infatuation and hero worship, the falling in love from a distance and never believing it could be reciprocated.

Was this the same man she'd felt all those things for? If she couldn't answer any other question about her life, she wanted the answer to that one. She wanted to know if he'd hurt the other woman in his life—and if he meant *her* harm.

Her feelings for him were massively conflicted. She flinched when he got too close, yet a part of her still wanted that, and she couldn't explain why. Or maybe she could. Maybe what she missed was the slow-burning dream, the wondering what it would be like with him. She wanted the Andrew Villard she'd fallen in love with from a distance.

Tony Bogart printed his name in block letters in the motel's guest registry. He was in Mirage Bay unofficially, but he had no desire to hide his presence or his intentions. He wanted people to know he was investigating the murder of his brother—and possibly a second murder associated with his brother's death, though he had no actual proof of that yet, just a telephone tip from his anonymous snitch.

"I got a room with a partial view of the water, special for you," the aging female desk clerk said, sliding an old-fashioned brass door key across the counter to Tony. Disco music throbbed at low volume from the clock radio on the rusting metal file cabinet behind her.

"You gonna want more than one of these?" she asked.

The woman's too-quick smile revealed a missing back tooth and skin like fine red fishnet, yet she wasn't above flirting. Her wink sent a flash of annoyance through Tony. She wanted something, probably a tip, but she'd done nothing to deserve that except BS him, and badly at that. Tony despised lazy con artists. They insulted their mark's intelligence.

"I worked at this motel when I was a kid," he said. "Every room has at least a partial view. Most have full views."

"Yeah? You worked here, at the Sand Castle?" She turned the registry around to read it. "Tony Bogart?"

She tilted back, inspecting him with a gimlet eye. "Are you related to Vern Bogart? I went to high school with him."

Tony nodded. She'd made no excuses about the view. That got her points for being ballsy. "Vernon is my dad."

A quick, sly grin appeared, as if she were remembering. "Your dad was a handsome man," she said. "Tall with real narrow hips, and sandy-brown hair, cut close to his head, a lot like yours. Nice pair of ears, too. A man's got to have good snug ears with short hair."

She tapped her long sparkly fingernails to the theme from the movie *Flashdance*. "What's Vern doing with himself these days? Probably married with a pack of grandkids. How about you? You married?"

She cocked an eyebrow, and her sexual boldness made Tony feel sick to his stomach. But she was clearly a long-term local, and might know something. No harm letting her think she was seducing him while he pumped her for information.

"Dad moved away a few months ago," he said, "after my brother, Butch, died."

"Butch Bogart? That kid who got himself stuck with a pitchfork was *your* brother? The whole town was talking about that. Happened last winter, right? Hotter than hell that day, Santa Ana winds, electrical storms?"

"Stuck *seventeen times*," Tony corrected. "Not very likely he did it to himself."

"Oh, right, sorry." She wrinkled her nose. "How awful for Vern—and you, too."

"Yeah, well, life goes on. You do the best you can." And sometimes you make a mess of it, like Vernon Bogart had, but Tony didn't feel like telling this woman that his father had failed miserably with his children. He'd been too hard on Tony, probably because of the grief he couldn't express, and too soft on Butch. He'd coddled and overindulged the latter to the point that Butch didn't think anyone else's rules applied to him.

"Did they find out who did it?" the clerk asked. "The last I remember they thought it was that local girl, Marnie something. She vanished, right? Did they ever find her?"

"Not *yet*." Marnie Hazelton had been everyone's prime suspect back in February, but Tony wasn't so sure now. He had another lead, but he still had every intention of hunting down Marnie. Last February, he'd paid a visit to Josephine Hazelton, the crazy old lady who'd raised Marnie. She sold vegetables and odds and ends at the flea market, and people seemed to like her, but Tony's gut had told him she was holding back. So he and Gramma Jo would go another round as soon as he was settled in.

After that, he had a social call to make on a cheating ex-girlfriend. *That* should be interesting. What Tony didn't have was a solid motive for any of his suspects, except that his brother had been a classic bully who enjoyed harassing anyone weaker than he was, women as well as men.

"You tell your dad I asked about him," the clerk chirped. "You never said whether he was married or single."

"Single since my mother died over twenty years ago. He's not the marrying kind."

"Well now, that don't matter. Don't need to be married to have a cup of coffee, as far as I know."

Tony nodded, trying to be polite, which was more than his dad would have been. Vernon had never cared about anything except riding hard on his two boys and fly-fishing on a river, any river. He wouldn't have given this toothless floozie a second look, but then, he probably wouldn't have given Pamela Anderson a second look. He wasn't a big fan of the fairer sex. He thought women talked too much and did too little. "Whiny, conniving liars, all of them," he was fond of saying.

The clerk shut off the CD player. "I wonder if I knew your mother. She probably went to school with Vern and me."

"Mind your own fucking business." Tony's voice dropped to a whisper. He brought his fist down on the counter with enough force to knock over her empty coffee cup. "There is *nothing* you know or need to know about my mother."

The clerk's eyes widened. She stepped back from the counter, eyeing the phone that she'd just distanced herself from. "I didn't mean nothing. I was just being nice."

Tony flashed his agent's badge. "You and I are

going to be fine," he told her. "Just make sure I get fresh sheets once a day. Fresh, not flipped—and don't ever mention my mother again."

5

Alison was swishing with peppermint-flavored mouthwash when she heard a tap on the bathroom door.

"Can you help me with this tie pin?" Andrew called to her.

She gurgled for him to wait as she spat out the stream of blue, then blotted her mouth on a towel. With nothing on but panties, she grabbed her dress off the hanger on the door. A bra wasn't possible because of the halter-top cut of the gown, but at least it should be quick and easy to slip into.

"Did you say something?" He knocked again.

Before she could answer, the door opened, and there he was, forcing her to turn away and quickly shimmy into her dress. She pulled the material up and tied the jeweled halter strings. No time to do up the back.

"What do you need?" she asked, tugging various things into place as she turned around.

He seemed amused at the speed with which she was moving, twisting and tying. "Can I help?" he asked.

"It would *help* if you'd respect my privacy."

"I thought you said to come in."

She heaved a sigh. "Just tell me what you want. I need to finish getting ready."

"This." He pointed to the onyx tie bar that hung lopsided on the diagonal pinstripes of his tan-and-white tie. "I'm going cross-eyed trying to get it straight."

"You don't look cross-eyed." She gave herself a moment to look into his eyes and wonder about the soul that resided in those dark windows.

"Did I buy this tie for you?" she asked him.

"No, it was a gift, but not from you."

"Good," she murmured, "otherwise, I would have been questioning my taste."

"What's wrong with my tie?"

She stepped back, ignoring his mock indignation. "The tie bar is straight. Now, let me see the whole look."

She twirled her finger, and he turned around, his smile sardonic. "Do I look fat?"

His sand-colored blazer and slacks looked fabulous, as always. He was a meticulous dresser no matter what he wore, but the dark shimmer of intrigue that resided in his eyes, and his windblown hair, banished any notion of fussiness. He could have been a blood-and-guts hooligan on a soccer field, except that his sport was sailing. Instead of scars, he had a year-round tan and a certain unkempt elegance.

She straightened her bare shoulders, trying to hold the dress in place. The halter ties had loosened, and the back of the dress was gaping open.

"Let me help you with that."

"No, I'm fine."

"Don't be silly," he said, a stern note to his voice. "Turn around."

She did, and felt his fingers purling down her spine as he fastened the buttons. She steeled herself against any desire she might have to shiver—and prayed the splotches wouldn't return. But the featherlight contact was wildly stimulating, and no amount of control could stop her pulse from becoming fast and thready.

Was this why he'd chosen the dress? So he could help her with it? If so, it must be part of the happily married couple act—and he was damn convincing. No one watching them would have known that before this trip he couldn't stand to look at her, much less touch her.

The buttons went down to the small of her back. When he'd done them all, she turned and saw that he'd taken the gold mesh belt off the hanger.

She was still vibrating as she reached for it.

He didn't release it. "You didn't buy the tie, but I did buy this dress," he said. "And I insist."

"You bought the dress?" She knew nothing about that. He must be talking about before the accident. "I really am able to dress myself," she said. "I can handle the belt and the rest of it, thanks."

He touched her hair, and she froze. "Don't."

"Don't what?" he said.

"Don't kiss me, don't even think about it. It's not happening."

The look of disbelief on his face gradually transformed into a faint smile. "Actually, I *was* thinking about it."

"Well, think about my knee kissing your balls. Think about that."

The belt hit the floor. "What the fuck is wrong with you?"

She touched the sink to steady herself. For a

moment it was hard to breathe. What *was* wrong with her? She just couldn't do this. She couldn't casually play this lover's game, and she hated that he could. None of this was affecting him the way it was affecting her. He wasn't vulnerable, wasn't shaking inside the way she was.

"I came here with you," she said. "I agreed to that, but I never agreed to make out with you."

He nodded slowly, as if he was just coming to understand some things about her. "You don't even want me close to you, do you?"

"I guess it must be hard for you to grasp that a woman exists who wouldn't want *you* close."

"Jesus, Alison, I'm just trying to get clear on *what* you want."

"Don't take it personally," she said. "Let's do what we came to do and leave this place. I don't want to be here."

There was a moment when she thought he was going to say something, do something besides pick up the belt and drop it on the counter.

"You're calling the shots," he said as he left the room.

She shut the door behind him, wondering why she couldn't have talked to him in civil terms, why she'd had to be so cutting. And why she was so angry still. The solution was simple. If they had to act like lovers in public, that was one thing, but there was no reason to keep up the pretense in private. She didn't want sham intimacy from a man who was pretending not to be repulsed by her.

It was five after seven when Alison and Andrew walked out onto the terrace off the living room. The slate deck swept out over the ocean, and in the distance the horizon was as silvery bright as the setting sun.

The terrace was beautiful, almost beyond Alison's ability to describe. Billowing ferns and banana trees shaded the wrought-iron furniture and the ornamental arches. Fountains splashed from deep pools of mosaic tiles set in swirls of blue and green. But Alison had no idea whether she was supposed to remember it or whether it was part of her mother's massive renovation.

Only Rebecca was there to greet them, and she seemed flustered as she rushed over. "Julia's running a little late," she explained. "Can I get you a pisco sour? We're having Peruvian food tonight, and the sours are luscious. They're made with grape brandy and lime juice."

"Make mine a virgin," Andrew said.

Rebecca looked surprised, but he didn't explain.

"Make mine a double," Alison said, surprising her again.

As Rebecca went over to the bar, she gestured toward a granite-topped sideboard laden with bowls of seviche, colorful salsas and platters of mussels and other seafood. "Help yourself."

Andrew waited, letting Alison go to the sideboard by herself. They hadn't spoken two words since their face-off in the bathroom. Silence was the norm in their relationship. She'd even thought of it as a conspiracy of silence, but they rarely fought, and that had put a different edge on things. She had no idea what to expect, but she wasn't backing down.

She tried a chunk of braised grouper with some

spicy salsa that brought tears to her eyes. Luckily, Rebecca returned quickly with a tray of drinks. She served Alison a foamy, pale yellow sour, and then gave Andrew his virgin. The sour tasted like limeade with a donkey's kick.

"How do you like the terrace?" she asked Alison.

"Breathtaking." Alison went to admire a graceful iron crane that was taller than she was. "This sculpture in particular. I wonder where my mother found it."

Rebecca hesitated. A nervous smile surfaced. "Oh, but that piece isn't actually new. It's been in the family for years, I believe. It may even be an heirloom."

Alison gasped. "Oh, of course. I must be conf— Everything's so different."

Andrew wandered over and looked at the sculpture from another angle. "Why does it remind me of the iron piece in the foyer?" he said. "Does Julia collect Oriental cranes?"

"Well, yes, she does." Rebecca set down the tray of drinks and helped herself to one. "Her mother did, too, I believe."

Alison shook her head, embarrassed. "I should know these things. I still get confused."

Rebecca's smile was gently reassuring. "Well, no wonder. It's amazing you survived such a terrible accident."

Andrew broke in again, explaining that Alison suffered from a condition called transient amnesia. "But it could all come back to her in time," he said. "We're hopeful that it will."

"Ah, yes, how very convenient."

The sarcastic comment came from the terrace doors,

where Bret Fairmont stood, looking flushed and disheveled. Alison didn't know if it was a fashion statement or if he'd been in a scuffle, but he looked a mess. His hair was a blond rag mop, and his jacket was off-kilter.

He squinted at her. "My God, look what the tide dragged in. Is it really my long-lost sister? Rebecca, get me a drink. Chop chop!"

Look what the tide dragged in. It was a terrible joke. Delayed shock seemed to paralyze everyone there.

Alison and Andrew said nothing. Bret leaned against the door frame, as if to steady himself. Finally, Rebecca moved, going to the bar to get his drink, which was the last thing he needed.

"You must remember me," Andrew said. He boldly walked over to shake Bret's hand. "I'm the guy she married."

Bret glanced at Andrew's hand, but didn't take it.

Andrew slapped Bret's arm rather vigorously and continued to make conversation. "What did you mean by 'how convenient'?"

Bret's eyes took on the gleam of a hungry rat's. "Oh, nothing, just thinking how convenient it would be to have an unreliable memory."

Alison brought the sour to her lips, wincing at the sudden pungency of the lime. She could tell by Bret's behavior that he was drunk, but it was hard to believe anyone would put on such a pathetic display. If she'd had any doubts about the abject hatred she and her brother were supposed to have felt for each other, she could put them to rest. He was an obnoxious boor, and he'd obviously had it in for her since he was old enough to say her name.

What was it he'd called her when they were growing up? *Alisuck.* How mature.

"I see we're all here. Isn't that wonderful!"

Alison turned as her mother walked onto the
terrace. She'd changed into a silk Emilio Pucci print
in bright pink and turquoise, and her mood seemed to
have lightened with it.

"Forgive me for holding things up. Does everyone
have a drink?"

"As a matter of fact, I don't," Bret said.

"You look like you've had plenty, Bret," Julia said
sharply. "Sit down and sober up."

Bret's bloodshot eyes widened. He looked good and
rattled, but got himself to the nearest chair and sat
down.

Alison caught the twinkle in Andrew's eye. Was he
thinking the same thing she was? Possibly the dragon
lady of Sea Clouds had some redeeming qualities.

"Alison, don't you look beautiful. I love what
you've done with your hair."

Julia sounded pleasantly surprised as she walked
straight over to her daughter and embraced her. Alison
tried to relax in her mother's arms, but affection was
the last thing she expected after the front door fiasco.
She'd worn her hair up, thinking it might make a
better impression, and evidently it had.

Clouds of expensive perfume swirled around them
as Julia stepped back and clasped Alison's hands. A
smile softened the angles of her face, but Alison's in-
tuition was working overtime. She could sense the
crackling tension. Julia was as anxious as she was.

Alison also caught a whiff of alcohol mixed in with
the perfume, and it wasn't her own drink.

Somehow, just knowing this very formidable woman was nervous allowed her to relax. But it also made her wonder what flaws her mother's seeming quest for flawlessness might be hiding. She was known in the society pages as a fashion maven, but Alison had never thought of that as a cover until now. The makeup and designer clothing seemed more extreme than before, and she couldn't shake the notion that Julia Fairmont was slowly transforming herself, whether intentionally or not, into something resembling a department store mannequin.

"Alison isn't the only who looks beautiful tonight," Andrew said, coming over to them. He offered his hand, and Julia hesitated only slightly before taking it. She was clearly making a supreme effort to be cordial.

Andrew sounded as if he meant it, and Julia smiled, to Alison's great relief. Maybe this wasn't going to be a nightmare, after all. Only Bret hadn't risen to the occasion. He'd ignored his mother's time-out and left the chair to storm into the house. Interesting how the rebellious little brother routine made him appear much less sinister.

"Here you are," Rebecca said, bringing Julia a brandy sour and a plate of assorted appetizers. "Try one of the mussels and see what you think."

Alison excused herself and walked to the edge of the deck, which overlooked a charming cove of sapphire water, thirty feet below. Beyond that the Pacific stretched like an infinite edge pool. At high tide, the waves crashed thunderously against the rocks, but now all was calm.

Julia came and stood next to her, holding the stem

of her glass with perfectly manicured fingers. Her emerald-and-diamond wedding set glowed in the waning light.

"The view doesn't change," Alison said, "but this house has. It's beautiful."

Julia shrugged as if it was nothing. "I could hardly improve on the view, but the house needed attention. It hadn't been redecorated since you and Bret were small."

That would have been over twenty years ago. "I don't remember," Alison said, "but I can't imagine it being more beautiful than this. You've preserved the classic lines, but made it look fresh."

She hoped that was what Julia wanted to hear. She'd begun to understand the plight of Anastasia, who was either a total fake or the rightful heir—and not even she had known which.

"Alison, look what I found."

Alison turned to see Bret coming toward her, carrying framed family photographs. He had two, which he held up as if for show-and-tell. He seemed to have miraculously sobered up.

"Do you remember where this was taken?" he said, pointing to what looked like an enlarged snapshot of a lighthouse on a lonely promontory. He even turned so the others could see it.

The scene didn't look remotely familiar to Alison. Andrew was standing by Rebecca, watching the Fairmont family reunion. Alison gave him a covert glance, but he shook his head. He couldn't help her this time.

"Sorry, I don't," she said.

"You *don't?*" Bret pretended to be shocked. "Let me guess, transient amnesia? Sounds like a bum with a bad memory."

Alison didn't respond. He was baiting her. His eyes gleamed when he was pleased with himself, and they were gleaming now. He'd been suspicious of her since he arrived this evening, but Alison didn't have it in her to deal with his sniping tonight. Being under attack like this was what she'd feared most.

"Let me see that." Julia snatched the photograph from Bret, pried off the backing and drew the picture from the frame. She read the date on the back.

"This picture was taken on *your* trip to the British Isles, Bret. It was the summer you graduated college. I put the date and place on the back when I had it framed." She glowered at him. "Apologize to your sister. She doesn't recognize the place because she was never there."

Bret's shrug was nonchalant, but Alison realized he'd been trying to pull one over on her. Thank God she hadn't taken a wild guess. He wasn't just out to test her. He was trying to trap her.

"Oops, my mistake," he said. "How about this one? The little prodigy couldn't possibly forget her big recital, could she?"

Bret held up the other photo. It was of Alison at the baby grand in the living room of this house. It was her sixteenth birthday, and she was probably playing *Für Elise,* the only piece she'd ever committed to memory.

Alison had the oddest sensation as she stared at the picture. It felt as if the dead places on her face were spreading to the rest of her body, and she was going numb. This really was too much. He wasn't going to stop until he'd reduced her to rubble.

Julia let out a hiss of frustration. "Bret, your sister

nearly died from head trauma, and she didn't come home to play the piano for your amusement. Now give me that picture and stop badgering her."

Bret handed over the picture. "I guess you're right. You never liked her playing, anyway."

"I didn't say that!"

"You said it to anyone who would listen. You said it to her, isn't that right, Alison? Mom never thought you had any talent."

"Drop it, Bret," Julia said threateningly.

Bret had some kind of comeback, but Alison wasn't listening. She slipped around and left them arguing as she went into the living room. She saw the baby grand against the windows of the far wall, and her pulse quickened.

A moment later, she sat down at the piano and stared at the keys. The blood pounding through her heart made her hands shake. Her head buzzed so loudly it blurred her vision. She could barely distinguish black from white.

She placed her hands on the keys, an octave apart. She pressed one key and then another, trying a chord or two, but nothing was coming back to her, nothing at all. She could hear the music playing in her head, but her fingers didn't know what to do. They couldn't make the connection.

She closed her eyes a moment, straining to remember, fighting, but her mind was empty. There was no point. She started to get up, and then glanced back at the keyboard. Her hand hit the keys in frustration. The noise jarred her, but her fingers opened and began to move. It didn't feel as if she was making conscious choices, but something was happening. She hit one wrong note after another. She winced and grimaced and tried again, and gradually it came, one tentative note and then a second. Soon she had a recognizable melody. *Für Elise.*

She didn't play it well, but she played it, and when she looked up, the entire family was there, watching her. Julia, Andrew, Rebecca, even Bret. Andrew was the one who started the applause.

6

Alison lay awake in the dark, unable to believe that she was sharing a bed with her husband. He was lying on his back, as quiet as she was, but he wasn't sleeping, either. It was too still. Not even a breath could be heard. And yet electricity crackled in the space between them. She could almost hear the noise it made.

That was why he hadn't moved, and neither had she. Not even to roll over and look at the clock. She was afraid to do anything that would force him to speak or in any way have to acknowledge his presence in this bed with her. God forbid they should touch.

Within the veil of their private world, they were separate agents. If anything was holy, it was the distance they'd created between them. They rarely even communicated beyond the necessities of their arrangement…and Alison found it a totally desolate existence.

She had never understood her feelings for him, but tonight it was impossible to deny that she had them. The potent mix included awe, intense curiosity and rampant doubts and fears. She was also attracted to him—what woman wouldn't be struck by his dark, poetic mop of hair and deep-water eyes? How could she not want to know what his mouth would feel like on hers? But sex was not part of their arrangement, and if that wasn't entirely satisfactory to her, it should have been. She'd insisted the relationship be platonic. She'd been as adamant about that as he had, but her reasons had probably been different than his.

Of course, she hadn't anticipated sharing a bed with him, or that he would suddenly turn into the white knight who would protect her from her big, bad family. She was appreciative, and that was the problem. Positive feelings were starting to outweigh the negative ones, which made it hard to keep the feelings in check.

Attracted? Yes. Wildly.

She touched her face and felt the familiar heat creeping up her throat. Thank God it was dark. No one could see this. No one could hear the blood rushing through her heart or see how difficult it was for her to swallow.

No one knew her pathetic little secrets.

They both slept restlessly, and perhaps it was inevitable that they would come into physical contact. Sometime before dawn, Alison brushed his arm with her hand. It was an accident, but he rolled toward her, and their eyes came open at the same time.

She knew instantly what was happening. And by the hitch in his breathing, he did, too. It was the dark of night and no one would know. Maybe they would pretend not to know themselves that they were about to take this further than a touch, much further.

It was dark. A dream. It didn't count.

He moved over her and she rose toward him. His hand slid beneath her and his mouth came down on hers. She was engulfed by that one act, a kiss. It was softness, warmth and dinner wine. It was their first.

What changed everything was the sigh in his throat. There was no return from that sigh. Was it pleasure or anguish?

His thigh brushed hers. His hand was on her breast. Every touch was new and terrifying. She was torn between conflict and yearnings. She wanted to be taken, possessed. Penetrated. *Please.*

Her stomach clenched with anticipation. She saw herself raking his flesh with her nails and pulling his hair. She wanted to be the object of his awe, as he was hers. But she didn't trust him—or anything about the situation they were in. This wasn't just a kiss in the dark. It was an act of sweet desperation, of surrender, and he already had too much power.

He bent to her again. She could feel the heat of his breath, hear his noisy heartbeat, but somehow, he stopped before their lips met.

"What's wrong?" she whispered.

His voice dropped low. "This wasn't supposed to happen," he said. "It won't again."

He turned and sat on the side of the bed. Alison was dizzy with disappointment. She couldn't pretend it was anything else. Where did he get that kind of willpower? And who had he been kissing? The woman he married or the one transformed by plastic surgery? She wanted urgently to know, but told herself it was better that they weren't intimately involved, safer. There was too much conflict and confusion between them.

She was well aware that there were times he couldn't bring himself to look at her, perhaps like right now. And there were times when she wished he wouldn't look at her, because he couldn't hide the suspicion, even revulsion, in his eyes. When had he begun to hate her? she wondered. Had he always felt this way?

She rolled over, away from him. The wall between them was so high it couldn't be scaled, and yet she knew she wouldn't sleep. There would be no peace. Thank God she'd brought the pills with her. She had to do something to obliterate this new and painful awareness of her bed partner.

Alison heard chimes ringing as she stole through the beach house, wondering where everyone was on this hazy July morning. Andrew had left earlier for a walk on the beach. He hadn't asked her to come with him, and she would never have suggested it. She was still reeling from last night's rejection. There'd been no discussion of what he'd done, except in the privacy of her own mind, where she had come to a decision regarding Andrew.

He had preyed on her vulnerabilities for the last time.

Aware that the chimes were still ringing, she lifted her head and sniffed the air. Was that coffee she smelled? After dinner last night, Julia had taken her and Andrew on a tour of Sea Clouds, including the new family room downstairs. She'd told them Rebecca, who had her own room on the third floor, set out a continental breakfast in the family room each morning.

Alison realized that must be where everyone was now. But she was lost in the huge house—and those damn bells wouldn't stop! She couldn't tell if it was the phone or the door, but the chimes crescendoed as she entered the foyer. A dark form was silhouetted against the etched glass of the front doors, and she assumed it was Andrew, back from his walk.

She opened the door, exasperated. "You don't have to ring," she said. "You're part of the family."

But it wasn't Andrew standing there.

"Oh, sorry." The man's tigerish hazel eyes and predatory stare brought a flutter of recognition to Alison's stomach. He hadn't changed at all. His fine features had always made him look sinister rather than sensitive. No pretty boy, this one. "Tony *Bogart?*"

He couldn't seem to take his eyes off her hair. "I've never thought of you as anything but a blonde," he said.

Alison felt like a lab specimen the way he was scrutinizing her. She'd slipped on a cotton sundress this morning that was quick, easy and cool, but it showed some skin, and already he was making her regret her choice.

"This is my natural color," she said, deciding not to explain any further. He must have heard about her accident, but she doubted that was why he was here. She fervently hoped it had nothing to do with the secret past that she and Tony Bogart had shared over a decade ago. Against her parents' wishes, they'd hung out together during her family's stays in Mirage Bay. They'd been teenagers at the time, but their rich girl/poor boy relationship had probably been doomed from the start. It had ended for good when Tony discovered there was another man in her life. He'd actually been trying to propose to her in a local restaurant when Andrew walked in on them. Alison could only imagine how humiliating that had been for Tony. Shortly after that, Tony had packed up and left town, and that was the last contact they'd had.

"Have you moved back home?" she asked, changing the subject.

"I live in Virginia now," he said, "near Quantico. I'm back in Mirage Bay on personal business."

"Quantico? That's—"

He nodded. "FBI headquarters. I'm a special agent."

Of all the careers she'd imagined for Tony Bogart, FBI agent wasn't one of them. Right now he was standing on the porch in ripped blue jeans and a black crewneck T-shirt, looking more like the rebel he'd been when they were younger than a lawman. He was holding something in his hand that looked like an eight-by-ten photograph, but she could only see the back.

"Are you visiting your father?" she asked.

He raised an eyebrow. "Obviously, you're not gifted with second sight. I'm here because of Butch's murder. You must have heard about that?"

Alison prayed her skin wouldn't catch fire again. She knew about Butch's case in detail. She'd gone through Andrew's office when he was away on a business trip, trying to find out more about her mysterious husband and the life he led apart from her, and she'd found issues of the Mirage Bay newspaper that had dated back to her accident.

The discovery hadn't surprised her, after she'd thought about it. Andrew had a personal interest in the yachting accident and its investigation. Butch Bogart's murder had occurred the same day, so it was heavily covered, too. But Alison had found the newspapers stashed in a garbage bag inside a hassock that was also a storage unit, as if Andrew had intended to hide them. That had given her pause. Everyone knew it wasn't the crime that got you into big trouble. It was the cover-up. But what did he have to hide?

She'd read the papers carefully before returning them to their hiding place, and then she'd added the question to her growing list of questions about Andrew, and filed it away. She'd never said a word.

"I did hear," she said, "and I'm very sorry about your brother." The right tone of sympathy evaded her. "Did you come to see Bret? Or Julia?"

"I'm here to see you, Alison."

"Me? Why?"

"You don't know? The local paper's abuzz with the news that you and your hubby are here in Mirage Bay for a visit. I thought someone should come by and welcome you back."

Alison couldn't imagine how the local paper would know about their visit unless Julia had told them. Apparently the woman thrived on fanfare, and one way or another, she was going to make a social spectacle out of this visit. Alison hoped it didn't backfire in all of their faces.

She glanced at the photograph in Tony's hand, but couldn't see what it was. Surely not a picture of her and Andrew.

He flipped the photograph over, handing it to her. Alison's stomach rolled as she took it. She pushed his hand away as he reached out, possibly to steady her. "What is this?" she asked, but she knew. It was Butch Bogart's mutilated body, a crime scene shot.

"There's a new lead in Butch's case," Tony said. "I thought that might interest you."

She swallowed back nausea and held out the picture until he took it. "Why would Butch's case interest me?" She really didn't understand what he was doing. "According to the newspapers, they named a prime suspect. Marnie Hazelton was supposed to have killed your brother, and then vanished. Have you found her?"

"No, Marnie hasn't been found—and I never said she wasn't a suspect. But since you brought her up, let's say our murderer *is* someone other than Marnie—just for the sake of argument. Where were you on February second while Butch was being disemboweled with a pitchfork?"

"I was falling off a *boat* in a storm, Tony."

He smiled, finally, matching her sarcasm. "Right, you went into the drink around six in the evening, according to your husband. The county coroner findings say Butch was killed that afternoon."

Alison took a step back—and spotted Andrew hovering in a doorway that Tony couldn't see from where he stood. What was Andrew doing? Her heart began to pound. She felt spied upon, cornered—by both of them.

"Alison?" Tony pressed a hand to the door and stopped her from shutting it. She hadn't even realized she was about to.

"You can't seriously think I had anything to do with what happened to Butch," she said. "Why would I want to kill your brother?"

When he said nothing, she rattled on, unable to stop herself. "The only viable suspect is Marnie Hazelton. Everyone knows that. The night Butch died, she was spotted on the cliffs by LaDonna Jeffries." Alison touched the penny ring on her bracelet. "Marnie jumped, didn't she?"

The Mirage Bay newspaper had done an extensive profile on Marnie, attempting to unmask the strange child-woman. Rumors were rampant that she'd committed suicide. She'd often been seen swaying on the edge of Satan's Teeth, the jagged rocks at the end of the jetty, as if she were listening to someone no one else could hear.

The article had said every village had its tormented outcast, and Marnie was Mirage Bay's. Even at twenty-two, she was a wary, half-wild little thing that no one could get close to except her friend, LaDonna, and her Gramma Jo, who wasn't her real grandmother at all.

Josephine Hazelton sold fresh fruit and vegetables from a cart alongside the road and was known in town as the produce lady. If you gave her some extra change, she'd read your palm, and if asked about Marnie, she would swear that she'd found her as a baby, in a creek near her house that emptied into the ocean. The infant had been swaddled in blankets and floating downstream in a willow basket, like Moses in the Bible.

Even Butch's friends had been interviewed for the article, and every one of them believed Marnie had killed him because he'd made fun of her disfigurements. Her face was off-kilter. Her eyes didn't line up right, and her smile twisted into a grimace, on those occasions when she did smile. She also had a ruby birthmark that emerged from the nape of her neck and crept around her throat like fingers, as though trying to strangle her.

Marnie's macabre looks had made her a target since earliest childhood, and when the town's fear and loathing became unbearable, she'd taken to hiding. But Butch and his ilk had hunted her down for sport. He'd teased her so mercilessly many people believed she had reason to kill him, except that Butch was the most feared linebacker on the high school team. It took a pile-on to hold him down, and Marnie was no bigger than a mosquito.

She'd had a body, though. The article had quoted locals who'd sworn she'd had the breasts of a Botticelli *Venus,* lithe limbs and a firm bottom. Alison remembered the references word for word. The boys from town all knew about Marnie's figure because she'd loved to soak in the tidal ponds on her gramma's property—and she hadn't worn much beyond what God gave her.

That's what had started the other rumor—that Butch had seen her bathing and tried to force himself on her, and Marnie had stopped him with the pitchfork. Brutally, viciously stopped him.

And now, for some unknown reason, Tony Bogart thought Alison had something to do with that monstrous crime?

She angled a glare at him. "What is this lead you have? If you're going to accuse me of something, you'd better be able to back it up."

"I haven't accused you of anything. I asked you a question that you haven't answered. Where were you when my brother died?"

A door hinge creaked and Tony stopped talking. He looked beyond Alison, searching the foyer, where the sound had come from.

"Villard, is that you?" he said. "Come and join us. I haven't had a chance to congratulate you on your marriage to our fair Alison."

Andrew stepped out of the shadows. As he came over to the door, Alison watched the malevolence seep into Tony's expression. He truly hated Andrew—and probably her, as well.

Andrew's voice was cold. "To what do we owe the pleasure?"

"You should know," Tony said. "You were listening to every word."

Andrew strode over to the other man as if he were going to get physical. Alison almost wished he would. Someone needed to back Tony off. Andrew wasn't trained in deadly force, as Tony must have been, but he was several inches taller.

"My wife is off-limits," Andrew told him. "I don't care what agency you're with, if you have something to say to Alison, you go through me first."

Nothing moved except Tony's trigger finger. It twitched, as if he was firing a gun. His smile was as cold as his eyes.

"How did you get through the gate?" Andrew asked.

"Someone was kind enough to leave it open."

"Then you won't have any trouble getting out."

"None whatsoever." Still smiling, Tony excused

himself with a tip of his head. As he strolled down the marble expanse of the grand portico, he called over his shoulder, "I hope this wasn't inconvenient for either of you. Have a nice day."

Andrew shut the door, and Alison sank onto the nearest settee. Her legs felt weak, but she shook her head, refusing his hand when he offered it.

"We should go down to breakfast before the rest of them come looking for us," he said.

Alison couldn't even think about food. The image of Butch's mangled body kept coming back to her.

"There you are!" Julia came into the foyer, looking fresh and immaculate in a white crocheted slacks and top. "If you want something to eat, you'd better hurry. Bret has almost finished off the almond biscotti."

She walked over to Alison and touched her cheek. "Are you all right, darling? Your face is red. Are you coming down with something?" As she talked, Julia glanced around the space. "Was someone just here? Bret thought he heard voices. This foyer is such an echo chamber."

Alison pulled away from her mother's touch. "It's not a fever," she said. "I have a skin condition, probably a reaction to all the surgery. I can get something for it at the drugstore."

Julia seemed to approve of that idea. "Your little BMW convertible is still in the garage. It's the only car Bret hasn't wrecked," she added dryly. "I'll get the keys for you."

Julia pressed the back of her hand against Alison's forehead, apparently not convinced that she didn't have a temperature. A moment later she was off in search of car keys.

Alison fanned herself with her hands to cool her skin—and looked up to find Andrew staring at her.

"What the hell was that about?" he asked, his voice harsh.

"You mean Julia?"

"No, Tony Bogart."

She shook her head. She didn't know. She truly didn't know.

7

Tony gave the key of his rental Corvette a gentle turn, and soft jazz music oozed from the speakers. Eyes closed, he rested his head against the seat back. Jazz had always reminded him of women. It was sensual and complicated in a way no other music was. Good jazz relaxed him and cleared his head. Bad jazz taunted and irritated. It confused. But it all reminded him of women.

He'd locked in his favorite FM stations when he picked up the car so he could have what he wanted at the touch of a finger. He'd also programmed a shock jock and a bellicose political commentator for entertainment value. For the amount of time he spent in a car, he wanted some perks. Corvettes were pricey, but the agency wasn't paying for this trip, he was—and he'd coveted a Vette since high school, like every other speed-crazed teenage male of his generation.

Tony was still parked across the street from the gates of the Fairmont compound, within easy eyeshot of the grand portico and the front door. He needed to think, and this was the perfect place to do it. If it made the rich folk nervous to have him parked outside their front door, too fucking bad.

Alison looked good in bright red blotches, anyway. A couple more wouldn't hurt her. Abruptly, he switched the music off and rolled his head, stretching his neck. He wouldn't have thought it possible that she could look more beautiful—or that she would ever have turned her perfect golden locks into something dark and wild. Jesus, what a vixen. Her eyes were big and soulful, her mouth a work of pure, unadulterated sensuality. They'd called her the ice princess when she was a teen. He wondered what they would call her now.

He still couldn't think of her as Alison Villard. But at least he'd stopped seeing her face on the targets in the firing range. He was no longer obsessed with the trust-fund babe, his pet name for Alison in the old days, but the thought of her with Andrew still rankled. The smug bastard probably thought he'd just faced Tony Bogart down.

Make that *stupid* bastard, Tony amended. He'd been keeping tabs on Villard for a while now, which was how he'd learned about their trip to Mirage Bay. He'd called Villard's assistant, pretending to be a rep with a Fortune 500 company that wanted to sponsor a charity concert. She'd volunteered that Andrew and his wife were taking a trip to southern California on personal business. The local newspaper item had confirmed their destination as Mirage Bay.

He glanced over at the house. He had a reasonable view of the grounds through the iron bars of the fence. Alison's bedroom window was around the other side. He could remember climbing the trellis and scrambling inside to be greeted by her wearing nothing but a sexy smile. She was hot, and she knew it. What had pissed him off was the way she'd amused herself with him until someone better came along, and then dismissed him like he was a joke.

He'd known he was losing her when she started making excuses not to see him, and then when she turned eighteen she'd begun to travel on her own, making trips to the Fairmont's apartment in New York. Tony had seen her hanging around with Villard in Mirage Bay, but she'd sworn he was just a sailing friend, and Tony had believed her. He'd figured the problem was that he, Tony, had nothing to offer. Desperate, he'd convinced her to meet him at a local restaurant, and he'd poured out his heart. He would go to college, make something of himself. He wanted to marry her.

She'd thought he was joking, and her laughter had cut him apart. Worse, there'd been no chance to explain himself. Villard had walked in and Alison had called the man's name with an excitement she couldn't conceal. Tony had seen it instantly. They were in love, or at least she was.

The bitch had cheated on him. She'd laughed at him for his feelings and his dreams. She was probably still laughing. He'd sworn to get her for that.

Was she sleeping in that bedroom with her husband? The man everyone thought had killed her? Tony was still suspicious about her miraculous return from the dead. Fucking convenient that was, especially for Villard. He might be on death row now if Alison hadn't come floating to the surface.

Men like Villard lived a charmed life.

And so did she. Or had. Once upon a time.

All that was going to change.

Tony pulled his cell from the belt clip and dialed his voice mail. He'd already listened repeatedly to the anonymous snitch's messages, but there was always the chance he'd hear something he hadn't heard before. A clue to the snitch's identity. A hint at the motive for the calls.

The first tip had come in as a voice mail message, which Tony had saved. After that, he'd inserted a modified subscriber identity module, otherwise known as a SIM chip, in the Global System for Mobile Communications slot on his cell. The spy-tech gadget, which he'd learned about during his FBI training, had allowed him to record conversations and permanently save each call. But right now he was only interested in the last message.

He touched a key to play it back.

"The police got everything wrong," the whispering voice said. *"Two people died on February second. Marnie Hazelton didn't kill Butch. She was murdered, too, and then framed for killing him."*

The caller went silent, and Tony remembered thinking the call was over. But the real motive had been to create anticipation, he'd realized.

"Mirage Bay's real monster is an old friend of yours," the voice said. *"Alison Fairmont Villard is the double murderer. She did them both."*

Tony clicked off the phone. He didn't smile, but he wanted to. He had a very personal stake in this case, and he hadn't told anyone yet, including local law enforcement. Considering how they'd handled the investigation so far, he didn't trust them with information this vital. He had more work to do first. With the tipster's help, he hoped to break this case before he told the cops anything.

Unfortunately, the tipster had never once mentioned motive. No one would be able to make a case against Alison without that, and Tony had no idea what her motive might be. No idea in hell. That's why he was here.

He closed his eyes, imagining the face of the woman he'd just confronted. The accident hadn't made her less beautiful, but it had changed her. He'd watched her throat blotch and her hands shake like anyone else's. That could not have happened to the pre-accident Alison. She'd been above it all, supernatural. Now she knew what it was like to be human, and breakable.

She hadn't walked the same earth as everyone else. She'd floated on a cloud of perfection. Her whole family had. And if Tony couldn't have been the one to bring her down, he was glad something had. Maybe there was some justice for those born less fortunate than Alison Fairmont, which was almost everybody.

By southern California standards, Mirage Bay was neither an upscale beach town like La Jolla or a funky art enclave like Laguna Beach. There were no brick streets lined with fashionable boutiques, no monogrammed awnings or oceanfront hotels with five-star restaurants and expensive art in the lobbies.

Despite the skyrocketing value of California coastal property, the town had managed to stay small, dusty and decidedly unglamorous. Kids drove from all over to surf the mostly gentle waves, and on weekends, small gangs of rough-and-ready marines from Camp Pendleton took over the main beer joint and pool hall.

"Beach shabby chic" was how one L.A. restaurant critic had described the local ambience. Alison wouldn't have used the word *chic* in any context, although the weekend flea market did boast fresh-grown organic produce, a variety of handmade items—and Gramma Jo, who was something of a legendary local fortune-teller.

And Mother Nature had been good to Mirage Bay. Cliffs and tidal pools abounded. The towering palms were said to be over a century old and planted by the Franciscan missionaries. And of course, Sea Clouds, the Fairmont compound, was considered one of the most beautiful pieces of real estate in the area.

For serious shopping, you drove to La Jolla's famous Prospect Street or farther south to San Diego, which was rich with malls. It was her mother's favorite way to while away an afternoon, but Alison had never been a power shopper. She'd had another preoccupation back in the days when her family had come to Mirage Bay each winter. Alison had had a secret yearning for fame and fortune, for love and attention. She'd desperately wanted to be a rock star, to put it mildly.

Thank God her needs were much more basic today. All she wanted to do was get to the drugstore, which sat between the supermarket and the dry cleaners in a busy strip mall that was the town's main hub. She'd had to wait for Tony Bogart to drive away before she could leave. He'd sat in that ridiculous Corvette, parked outside the gates, for nearly two hours. It was an obvious attempt at intimidation, but rather than have him following her around, she'd decided to outwait him.

She'd also been debating whether to make a side trip,

but had talked herself out of it. The risk of being seen was too great, especially with Bogart skulking around. She'd taken Andrew into her confidence, and he'd promised to help her find out why her phone calls weren't being answered. For now, she would have to trust him.

Alison was relieved not to find the store crowded as she slipped inside and walked straight back to the aisle where the topical cortisone cream was shelved. In most drugstores, the shelves were periodically re-arranged, supposedly to confuse the customers and keep them in the store longer, but not in Mirage Bay. Nothing ever changed here.

Until six months ago, when everything had changed.

Alison had claimed her skin condition was surgery-related, but she'd actually been using the cream for years. The rash had nothing to do with her many operations, but that wasn't something she could easily explain, so she'd used a convenient excuse. Near fatal accidents, multiple surgeries and transient amnesia were all very handy for explaining away just about anything.

She picked up one of the tubes and read the ingredients. Not the brand she normally used, but close enough, as long as it was effective. This was the worst reaction she'd ever had, probably because her nerves were shot. The encounter with Tony this morning had left her shaken, even though she'd been trying to convince herself that he was only baiting her, payback for the past. It was still hard to believe that he actually worked for the FBI.

"Oh, sorry, I thought you were someone else."

Alison felt a hand on her bare arm and veered away. She hadn't realized the comment was meant for her— or worse, that the young woman gaping at her was LaDonna Jeffries. If the town had a gossip, it was LaDonna. She was the last person Alison wanted to see right now.

"Oh, did I frighten you?" LaDonna said. "It's just that, except for your hair, you look a lot like someone who used to live around here. Alison Fairmont? Anyone else ever tell you that? We called her the ice princess. Funny, huh?"

Not to Alison. LaDonna must not have read the newspaper, which meant Alsion could probably get away with denying everything.

LaDonna peered at Alison, narrowing her eyes and shaking her head. "Wow, you really do look like her. It's almost *creepy*. Sorry, I'm losing it here. Is there something I can help you with?"

"You work here?" Alison could hear her voice giving out. The intense scrutiny made her feel almost ill, especially since she knew this was only the beginning. Once LaDonna spread the word, everybody would be whispering and staring at Alison as if she were some kind of sideshow freak.

"Is something wrong?" LaDonna asked.

"Yes." She began to laugh softly. This was all so absurd, trying to pretend everything was fine, that she and Andrew were fine when they were anything but. Trying to remember—and to forget—and holding so much inside. Sometimes it felt as if she were going to crack like a piñata.

"What is it? Are you all right?"

Hysteria bubbled in Alison's throat. The laughter

turned into a coughing spasm when she tried to quell it. "You were right," she gasped at last. "I am Alison, but it's Villard now. I got married."

LaDonna nodded, apparently absorbing the news. "I knew it," she whispered. "The darker hair threw me off, but I knew I was right."

Nowhere to hide, Alison realized. Open season.

"And you got married," LaDonna said, nodding. Tendrils bounced free of the claw clip that held her curly auburn hair. "I heard about that. You married that hot French guy, huh? Congratulations."

Alison nodded, fighting against her body's need to erupt in some terribly messy way, laughing or coughing. "Thank you, but we were married four years ago."

"Are you sure you're all right?" LaDonna said. "Your voice sounds strange."

Alison cleared her throat. "It's the surgery. It affected my vocal chords."

"Oh, yeah, the accident. You look great, though. No one would know you lost most of your face—or anyway, that's what I heard. Sorry, that must have sounded gross."

Alison just stared at her, helpless. She wasn't about to discuss the devastation to her face. She still felt like a complete freak no matter how good people said she looked. And this one seemed willing to go where angels feared to tread. No sense of boundaries at all.

"Are you sure I can't help you find something?" LaDonna offered. "Please? I can't just stand here and yack, they'll fire me."

Alison realized she was still holding the tube of cortisone cream. She put it back on the shelf behind another larger tube of something else. "I'm looking for hand cream. Where would I find that?"

A smile replaced LaDonna's worried expression. "Come with me," she said. "We're actually over-stocked right now. I like the colloidal oatmeal, myself. It's very soothing, and if you have sensitive skin like I do, it's a must have."

LaDonna shot Alison a pleased look. "Don't take this wrong, but I didn't think people like you shopped in stores like this. I mean, regular old drug-stores. I think it's great. Oh, are you sure you're all right?"

Alison had stopped and clapped a hand to her chest. She was still fighting off what felt like a coughing fit. It burned through her lungs like fire. Maybe she really was sick.

"Excuse me, I need to go," she said, brushing past LaDonna. It was incredibly rude, but if she didn't get out of the store, something terrible was going to happen. She struggled not to cough as she ran.

"What about the hand cream?" LaDonna called after her. "Did I tell you it has colloidal oatmeal? It's great stuff. Alison, are you all right?"

Alison shot through the drugstore door and froze, momentarily paralyzed at the sight of the unfamiliar parking lot.

Where was she?

Mirage Bay, the strip mall in the center of town.

How did she get here?

The black BMW convertible that had once been hers. It was parked not twenty feet away from her. The keys were in the pocket of her dress.

Who was she?

Alison had no answer to that one as she plunged her hand in her pocket and grabbed the keys.

February second, six months earlier

She liked the black water best of all. A leafy canopy of oak trees blocked the afternoon sun, and something about the tide pool's glassy surface seemed to smooth all the imperfections from her reflection. She looked serene and peaceful. It was almost a normal face gazing back at her, not freakish at all. The times she bathed here were like a meditation on her own solemn beauty. For a little while, she was whole.

She was about to rise from the water when a rustling sound caught her attention. She hesitated, crouching down and searching the shadows. A whimper of despair formed in her throat. Someone was watching her. *Him.* She knew even before she saw him step out of the bushes.

That bastard. The sick bastard had found her.

"Ugly *slut*," he hissed at her. He crashed into the shallow pool, black spray exploding in every direction. Slowly, as if in shock, she rose from the water and watched him come thundering toward her. She was naked, dripping.

He was the one who tormented every pathetic moment of her pathetic life. He called her names and crudely groped her. He and his friends chased her everywhere she went, surrounding her like dogs in a pack, laughing and jeering at her disfigured face. Once, they'd tripped her, knocked her to the ground and peed on her, and no one had stopped them.

He had made the whole town loathe and despise her. And now he was going to rape her and leave her for dead. He would have to get rid of her, wouldn't he?

You fucking bastard! I won't let you destroy me!

Tears soaked her face. She couldn't run anymore. Hatred locked her in place. Maybe it was time to die. Time to be free of him—and the crippling shame. He had turned her into a cowering animal.

"Slut," he said under his breath. "You're the ugliest slut I've ever seen."

A pitchfork was stuck in the hard dirt and sand at the edge of the pool. She used it for cleaning out the seaweed and debris. It was her only chance, but it was too far away.

"You're a fucking birth defect," he snarled. "You should never have been born. How the hell did a freak like you end up with a hot body and those incredible tits?"

He lunged at her, but she sank down, evading him. She was fast, but he had brute strength on his side. And animal lust. His jeans were unzipped, his hard penis exposed. She knew what he was going to do, and he knew that she was alone and defenseless. He'd been watching her the entire time.

He threw out his arms like a wrestler, preparing for the takedown. Her mind was running a hundred miles an hour, calculating the odds of getting away. Suddenly he lunged again. She tried to duck, but he caught her by the hair and dragged her to her feet.

It hurt like hell, but she forced herself to relax, to go limp. She waited until he yanked her around and kissed her, and then she slammed her knee into his groin.

He howled with pain and flung her away. They both ended up in the water. Veins bulged in his neck as he gripped her by the throat and held her under. He was going to strangle her! *She was going to die.* She gasped for breath, sucking black water into her mouth and nostrils. It flooded down her throat and into her lungs. Her wild thrashing only made it worse. Within moments, her mind was fuzzy. Everything was as black and murky as the pool.

She lost consciousness, but something brought her back. The pressure was gone. His hands had fallen away from her throat. Maybe he thought she was dead. Her will to live gave her the strength to heave herself up, but she slammed into something solid. It was his body, and she hit him hard.

He went over backward. She must have caught him off guard. As he floundered, she crawled to the side of the pool. But by the time she got to the pitchfork, he was on her again, fangs bared, rearing up like a grizzly bear to finish her off.

She got him in the stomach with the prongs.

He grabbed the pitchfork and ripped it away from her, trying to get free. But the handle hit the ground and dug in. It threw him forward and impaled him like a fish on a spear. His eyes bugged out, and one of his flailing arms clubbed her alongside her head.

That was the last thing she remembered. She must have passed out, but not before heaving him over backward with the pitchfork and stabbing him again and again, seventeen times. They said he'd died of multiple wounds. Horrible wounds. Only a monster could have mutilated a human body like that.

Was it guilt or horror that drove her to flee over a mile down the beach, scale the sea wall and run all the way out to the edge of the cliffs, to Satan's Teeth? Was it guilt or horror that made her plunge into the roiling waters below?

* * *

Alison sat up, breathing hard. Sweat soaked her trembling body. She'd had the dream again. It was coming more and more often and with greater detail each time. Gruesome and graphic detail. Tonight she'd heard him grunt and seen the blood gush from the wounds. She'd felt his body resist the prongs, and the horrible release when his flesh tore.

Her stomach rolled, and she sprang from the bed, knowing she might wake Andrew. She was going to be sick, and she had to get out of the room. She headed for the French doors to the balcony, hoping the air outside would cool her drenched body and slow her spinning mind.

Moments later, as she bent over the balcony railing, breathing deeply, she came to grips with several terrifying realities. It was no wonder she was having nightmares. This was where the nightmare had started. Right here in Mirage Bay, six months and how many days ago? She didn't know. She'd lost track, but that was when her miserable life had taken a fatal turn.

She couldn't stay here, not in this house or this town, and the reason was simple. She wasn't—and had never been—Alison Fairmont.

She was Marnie Hazelton.

8

It was Marnie Hazelton's body that Andrew had found, battered and bleeding from the reefs. He'd assumed it was his wife because of the charm bracelet. He'd had no way of knowing that Alison had lost the bracelet when she'd taken it in for sizing, or that Marnie, who had always secretly idolized Alison's golden perfection and had innocently stalked her like a starstruck teen, had found it.

Andrew hadn't known any of that, but he had known that Alison didn't have a ruby birthmark on her throat, or anywhere. That was when he'd realized it might be the wrong woman in the operating room, but he'd said nothing to the doctors. It was too late, or so he'd told Marnie. All the major work had been done.

The breezes off the ocean were cool, and Marnie shifted gently from foot to foot, trying to warm herself. The rocking motion calmed her. She'd done it since earliest childhood, and her Gramma Jo had insisted it was because Marnie was a gift from the ocean. Gramma swore she'd found her as a baby being rocked by the sea in the wicker basket. She'd also insisted in mysterious tones that the sea might one day call Marnie back.

Marnie had never believed any of it. Gramma Jo loved to tell tales, but the rocking motion did seem instinctive, and she'd always been drawn to the sea, especially when life had seemed hopeless. She'd stood for hours on the cliffs overlooking the ocean, and watched the waves crash against the rocks below, watched and swayed to the eternal rhythms.

Maybe she had actually jumped from the cliffs the night Butch died. Maybe the sea had called her back. She couldn't remember.

When she'd returned to consciousness in the recovery room, she'd told Andrew that she'd killed someone and didn't want to live. Andrew had known immediately that she was Marnie Hazelton. Everyone knew about Butch Bogart's murder and Marnie's disappearance, but Andrew had shocked her with his reaction. He'd not only questioned the reliability of her memory of the incident, he'd made it clear that he considered *her* the victim and Butch the criminal.

"Whatever that bastard got he deserved," Andrew had assured her. "*I* should have killed him when I had the chance."

They'd both known what he was referring to. This was not the only time Andrew Villard had intervened in her life. When she was still a gawky kid, he'd come upon her cornered in a back alley by Butch and his friends. They'd already ripped her blouse, and they were egging each other on. If not for Andrew, she would probably have been assaulted by every one of them.

Butch was big and beefy even then, a varsity wrestler on the high school team, and clearly the ringleader. Most people were cowed by his size alone, but

Andrew had been an accomplished boxer in college. Poor Butch was swaggering one minute and on his butt the next. His friends had scattered like rats from a garbage can.

Andrew had tried to talk to Marnie afterward, but she'd been too ashamed and confused. Why would a man like Andrew Villard take on that bunch of thugs for her? She wouldn't have expected him to look at her, especially compared to a beauty like Alison, who was six years older than Marnie. He and Alison were royalty. The whole town watched them from a distance, enraptured.

"Couldn't sleep?"

Marnie froze. It was Andrew behind her on the balcony. She rubbed her arm, aware of her chilled skin. How long had she been out here?

"A bad dream," she said, surprised at the pang she felt. She didn't want to feel pangs. It was idiotic. She resented bitterly the possibility that some part of her might want a relationship with a man who would actually care enough to ask about her bad dreams.

Impossible. Andrew already knew about this dream. He knew about everything, her darkest secrets.

"It's cold out here," he said. "Should I get your robe?"

"No, I'm fine."

"You're not fine. You're shivering."

She let out a sharp sigh. "I can't stay here, Andrew. I need you to find out what's happened to my grandmother. I have to be sure she's okay, and then…I'm leaving."

"Alison, we didn't come out here on a whim."

"I'm *not* Alison. Stop calling me that!" She spun

around to face him, shaking with emotion. "I hate her—and so do you."

His gaze narrowed, and Marnie wished to God she hadn't said it. Not because it wasn't true. He obviously loathed Alison, but Marnie hadn't been talking about Alison.

"Maybe I have reason," he said.

"Reason to hate her? Well, maybe I have reason to get the hell out of here." She clutched herself, thinking she was going to freeze to death. "I killed him. It was all there in my dream, every gory detail. Butch is dead, slaughtered, and *I* did it."

"I don't believe that. You may have acted in self-defense, but you didn't stab anybody seventeen times. You're not capable of that, which is why you *can't* leave."

She stared at him, defiant.

"You have to stay and prove it. *Alison*," he said softly, emphasizing the name. "You know why we're here. We have a deal, you and I."

Marnie didn't want any part of their deal. She was trying to figure out how to make him understand that when she noticed what he had in his hand.

"Why aren't you wearing this?" He held out the charm bracelet.

"Because it isn't mine." She could barely control the pain in her voice. "Do you have any idea how hard this is for me?"

Six months ago the bracelet had saved her life. Today it was a symbol of her entrapment and her guilt.

"Wear it," he insisted.

She stared at him, burning to refuse. He had refused

to acknowledge her as anyone but Alison. He wouldn't even utter her real name. Marnie Hazelton didn't exist for him, so he couldn't possibly know how hard this was for her. Nor did he care. They had an agreement, and he expected her to honor it.

Why couldn't she? Why the hell couldn't she just do this? The alternative was jail, certainly for her. A life sentence. The death penalty. It all loomed in Marnie Hazelton's future.

Her throat tightened as she took the bracelet from him. But was she angry at him for her predicament, or herself? He had come up with the master plan, but she had agreed to it. He'd never once threatened her.

He'd come to her when she was still in the hospital, recovering from the surgery. Sitting by her bedside, he'd told her that Marnie Hazelton could hide in plain sight. She could assume Alison's identity. He'd promised he would help her. He would coach her and tell her everything he knew about his wife and her history. Marnie hadn't believed it could work, but she and Alison were remarkably close in body type, and Andrew had convinced her she could explain away any changes in her appearance and voice as a result of the surgery. And if she was asked questions she couldn't answer, she could use her diagnosis as an excuse: transient amnesia, caused by head trauma.

Andrew had only had one binding condition: Marnie Hazelton must die so that Alison could live. She had to be Alison at all times, even when they were alone. Even when she was alone. She had to transform to the very marrow of her bones. Otherwise, no one would be fooled, and their plan would fail.

It should have worked perfectly. Marnie was well

motivated, and with Andrew's help she had become an uncanny facsimile of Alison. She'd transformed herself, inside and out, even capturing the watchful Mona Lisa smile that hinted at the mysterious inner workings of Alison's mind. But then the dreams and flashbacks started. The past kept rushing back at her, and despite her condition of no intimacy, she could never have imagined that life with Andrew could be so barren. It felt more like a life sentence than a dream come true.

"The bracelet may have been Alison's good luck charm," she said, "but it's not mine."

"It saved your life."

"And aren't *you* glad?"

The bracelet's charms slipped through Marnie's fingers, glittering like sunlight, even at night. It was eighteen-karat gold, and each charm was a musical symbol, but the only one Marnie cared about was the worthless copper penny ring that she herself had attached to one of the gold links.

She'd had the ring since she was a kid. She and LaDonna Jeffries had been best friends in those days, and they'd often played at an abandoned train station not far from Gramma Jo's house. One of their pastimes had been putting pennies on the track and letting the freight trains flatten them. If the penny was balanced just right when the train's wheels hit, the middle could be punched out without destroying the rim, creating a perfect copper ring.

Marnie had worn her ring home that day, and Gramma Jo had told her never to throw it away. Penny rings not only brought good fortune to the wearer, she'd said, but kept them safe from evil spirits. Gramma had given her a chain to wear the ring around her neck, and Marnie hadn't taken it off once, even while she was bathing, until the chain finally broke.

She'd learned the rudiments of jewelry making from her Gramma Jo, who did everything she could to bring in money, including making and selling agate jewelry at the flea market in town. Marnie had learned many things from her surrogate grandmother, and the most wrenching part of the agreement with Andrew had been losing contact with her. Marnie couldn't imagine what Gramma Jo must have gone through when she learned of her granddaughter's disappearance.

Eventually Marnie had started calling her grandmother's number weekly, just to hear her voice. Marnie hadn't spoken, except to say that she had the wrong number, but even that much contact had reassured her that Josephine Hazelton was alive and well.

"If you hate the bracelet so much," Andrew said, "why didn't you give it back to Alison?"

Marnie didn't feel the need to tell him that she'd kept the bracelet because it had represented dreams she couldn't articulate in those days, even to herself. The sparkling jewelry had symbolized everything she'd longed to be. Not that she'd really held out hope for a fairy tale life like Alison's, but when it had looked as if Alison would never come back to Mirage Bay, Marnie had begun to wear the bracelet, pushed up on her skinny forearm and hidden under her long-sleeved tops. Only when she'd attached the copper loop had it felt as if the bracelet belonged to her.

"You and Alison ran off and got married," she said. "You never came back. When was I supposed to return it?"

"We came back."

"You mean last February? Years later? I would have felt a little foolish returning it then. Obviously, though, I should have."

Andrew shrugged. "I'm sure Alison had forgotten all about the bracelet by then. She had bigger things on her mind."

Like a fifty-million-dollar-trust fund? Marnie wondered. While she was still in the hospital, Andrew had revealed that it was Alison's idea to come back to Mirage Bay. She'd wanted to reconcile with her mother, but Marnie still wondered if it had something to do with the trust fund.

Naturally, she was curious how Andrew felt about the fortune Alison had walked away from. He didn't seem motivated by money. He was wealthy enough in his own right, and he'd already told Marnie that if the money eventually came to her as Alison, he would make no claim on it.

She'd sensed that he was using the trust fund as a carrot to lure her back to Mirage Bay. He wouldn't have insider access to the Fairmont family without her, and there was also the question of who got the money if it didn't go to Alison. If Andrew knew, he hadn't mentioned it. He'd actually said very little about his plan to find out who'd framed him.

"Let's go inside," he said now. "I'll light a fire and get you some cognac."

Marnie shivered. Anything that would ward off the cold sounded good. There was an overstuffed couch in front of the fireplace, with a quilted throw that she could wrap up in. Maybe she could even make him understand that staying here wasn't a good idea.

He stepped back, giving her room to go inside.

Light glowed from the bedroom as she passed him. Fleetingly, she wondered if it made her gown transparent. And if he was looking.

He went straight to the liquor cart and set about preparing her a drink while she curled up on the couch with the quilt. A moment later he offered her a snifter of warm cognac and a cocktail napkin.

She left the bracelet on the table and held the glass with both hands, letting it take the chill from her icy fingers. The mulled cider he'd poured himself was still on the warmer flame, flickering like a golden votive, while he got the fire going. It was a real fireplace with cedar logs, stacked in a heavy woven basket on the hearth. He piled several logs on the grate and lit them.

As the sparks caught and smoke curled up the chimney, Marnie remembered the times she'd stood on the beach and gazed up at the big house on the bluffs, watching wispy ribbons of gray come from one or another of the chimneys. It was a magnificent Mediterranean manse with several floors and ornate wrought-iron balconies, and she'd been completely fixated on what life would be like inside such a grand place.

It was nothing like she'd expected.

Still, she could feel herself relaxing as the logs began to crackle and spit. The bedroom smelled as sweet and redolent as a beach fire. She'd made her own fires as a kid, and slept next to them on the sand with nothing more than a blanket on cool fall nights when the beach was deserted.

Andrew was standing in front of the fireplace with his drink. He swirled the amber potion and brought it to his nose. His lowered lashes made her realize how long they were. When he finally took a sip it struck her as incredibly sexy. So did his pajama bottoms and cotton T-shirt.

A spark of desire startled her. She could feel it between her legs, as hot as the sparks from the fire. What would it be like to have a man like that look at you with heat in his eyes? Now, she was *too* warm. She wondered if he was as unnervingly attractive to all women as he was to her. And if any of them could have helped falling in love with him, as she had. Years ago, as a girl.

No longer. She couldn't let herself be that vulnerable.

"I thought you wanted to know the truth."

"About what happened to Alison?"

"About what happened to Butch."

The cognac went down wrong, burning. "I saw it happen. I heard the gurgling sounds he made. It was grotesque."

"Dreams aren't reality," he reminded her. "They distort reality. You really *don't* know what happened."

He hadn't taken it far enough. Dreams had nothing to do with reality. She'd dreamed of being Alison Fairmont—or at least of having her life—since she'd first set eyes on her. Some of the happiest moments of Marnie's childhood had been spent fantasizing about the debutante who wintered on the cliffs. LaDonna was right. The locals *had* called Alison an ice princess, but Marnie had never believed it. Everything about her had been graceful and glowing. Who wouldn't have wanted to be the golden-haired princess with the silvery laughter?

And who wouldn't have wanted to be married to the dark prince, even if in name only.

"Everything we've done in the last six months was in preparation for where we are now. It's time."

His low voice tugged at her, but she said nothing.

"We were falsely accused, both of us," he added, "and we have a right to know what really happened. We may never get this opportunity again."

She kicked off the throw and set her cognac on the table. "Maybe I don't want to know."

"And live with questions the rest of your life? I don't care what that idiot Bogart says, no one's going to charge you with Butch's murder. You're *Alison Fairmont.*"

Yes, God help me.

"I know you love your grandmother and are deeply worried about her, but are you certain that's the only reason you came here?"

It was a good question. Why had she agreed to *anything* he'd offered, especially taking on another identity? Of course she wanted to avoid prosecution, but what if there was another reason? What if she'd also wanted to live out her dreams and know what it was like to be Alison Fairmont Villard, pampered and privileged wife of Andrew?

Not something to be proud of, but people weren't always noble.

He brought a tray with the cognac and cider as he joined her on the couch. As he freshened both their drinks, she saw the fire's flame reflected in the cognac's honeyed swirls.

"At least you know you didn't kill anyone," she told him. Maybe she could still make him understand. "You don't have painful memories of this place that began the day you were born. You're only here to clear your name. I have no chance of clearing mine. I don't even exist."

"You need *answers*. How else are you going to start making peace with what happened, and move on?"

His conviction surprised her. She had no idea if he really believed in her innocence or was just trying to convince her to stay. If it was the latter, he had an ace he hadn't played. He could use what he knew against her. She was a fugitive from justice. Everyone believed she'd killed Butch. If Andrew was telling the truth, he was guilty only of asking her to take the identity of his wife long enough for him to solve the mystery of her disappearance.

He could swear she'd never told him she wasn't Alison, that she'd fooled him, too. How would she be able to prove otherwise? Or he might admit to knowing the truth, but throw himself on the mercy of the court, saying he hadn't gone to the police because he was trying to protect her.

Andrew rose and walked to the fireplace, seemingly immersed in thought. When he finally did speak, his declaration caught her completely off guard.

"If you don't want to go through with it," he said, "I'll take you back to Long Island, or wherever you want to go. It's your choice. I'll do whatever you want."

"It's that important to you?" she said. "You'd give up your investigation?"

"It's not just the bracelet. You've changed your hair, and you clearly don't want to go through with the plan. You're trying to sabotage this. Maybe not consciously, but you are."

She couldn't deny that she didn't want to be here, but sabotage?

"Marnie."

The resonance in his voice raised the hair on her arms. She couldn't remember the last time he'd called her by her own name. They'd both agreed not to use it again. Just as they'd both agreed to his master plan.

"I want you to stay," he said, "but not for me. I'll do whatever you want."

She could feel herself weakening, but it nagged at her that she was being foolish. There was always the possibility that he was a master manipulator. That he'd killed his wife and was using this visit to ensure his innocence and get the trust fund. His real "plan" might have nothing to do with finding out what had really happened to Alison—and who'd tried to frame him for her death.

Marnie had to make a decision, and either way it would be a leap of faith. She studied the bracelet, its charms glowing like fire.

"I'll stay," she said. "I'll do my best. We have an agreement, and I'll honor it, but I won't do it with blond hair—or with the bracelet."

She sat forward on the couch and put down her cognac. The bracelet was never hers to begin with, and she was giving it back to him now. But he couldn't have all of it. She took the penny ring and angled it against the marble tabletop, pressing as hard as she could. It snapped from the bracelet at the point where she'd fused it years ago.

She would stay, but it had to be on her terms.

9

Julia wondered what vile fantasy she was going to have to deal with this morning as she drove her Mercedes into the parking lot of the seedy motel. She really did loathe Jack Furlinghetti. Look at the risks he was forcing her to take—and for something that should have been hers anyway. At least he'd gone inland and picked a place nowhere near Mirage Bay. Still, she'd had to sneak out of the house right after breakfast, making jokes to Rebecca and Bret about an emergency shopping trip. No one ever questioned Julia's shopping habit.

She'd been worried that Alison might want to come with her, but her daughter hadn't shown up for breakfast this morning, or dinner the night before. Andrew had insisted last night that Alison was fine. He'd said her face was still breaking out, and he'd taken some food up to her room. Julia had planned to check on her this morning, just to make sure that Andrew, control freak that he was, hadn't locked her up like a prisoner. But then she'd gotten the summons and she'd had to move quickly.

Anxiety fluttered in the pit of her stomach as she knocked on the cracked and peeling motel room door.

She'd suggested the Four Seasons, but her much younger partner in crime had insisted on this place, the Luv Shack. She hoped he wasn't into anything too weird. She'd heard about golden showers, flying snakes and three-ring circuses, but she certainly didn't want to experience any of *them.*

"Jack?" Julia didn't know whether to laugh or cry as the door opened. He was dressed in black leather, head to toe. Only a few strategic areas were exposed— his eyes, mouth, lips and his penis, which was fully erect and nodding like a bobblehead doll in livid shades of red and purple. What he held in his hand looked like a riding crop that she assumed was for her. He'd told her to wear a black thong and a sexy black dress.

"Come in, little fly," he said with a lascivious smile.

"You're damn lucky it was me." *You bloody moron.*

The small room looked like a triple X adult shop. There was a circular bed with a gaudy red sateen spread, a mirrored headboard and a pair of furry pink handcuffs on the night table. *Damn bed probably vibrates.* Worse, the room had mirrors everywhere else, including the ceiling, and it reeked of honeysuckle room deodorizer.

"I can see where this is going," she said, indicating his riding crop, "but let's not get carried away, all right? Someone could get hurt with that thing."

His eyes glittered. "Oh, I hope so."

Worse than she'd thought, if that was possible. She could always leave, but that wouldn't get her what she wanted, and Jack Furlinghetti had what she wanted. He held the whip hand, literally.

Just get this over with, she told herself. *Bend over*

and think about shopping. At least she wouldn't be able to see the ceiling mirrors. "Over here?" She walked to a device that resembled a portable pommel horse, with leather straps that were probably meant for the wrists and the ankles.

Grimacing, she flipped up the back of her dress and draped herself over the horse. He would have to strap her in, if that's what he wanted. She braced herself, and her whole body flinched in anticipation. But nothing happened. What was the twisted little fiend doing? Admiring her thong?

She waited for the blows, refusing to say a word.

Finally, she looked over her shoulder and spotted him across the room, bent over the back of the room's only chair. His leather suit had another exposure in the back. There were two cutouts for his buttocks.

"What are you doing, Jack?"

"Have I displeased you in some way?" he asked. His voice quavered. The riding crop lay on the carpet next to him, where he must have dropped it. Suddenly it dawned on Julia what was going on. The pommel horse had been meant for him.

"Displeased, Jack?" she said, putting some steel in her voice. "You'd better *believe* I'm displeased."

It was all over very quickly. She'd only swatted him a couple times when his muscles clenched and he gave a surprised gasp. He dropped from the horse to his knees in apparent shame.

"Look what I've done," he wailed. "I beg your forgiveness."

Julia definitely did not want to look at what he'd done. Evidently it was that most dreaded of male accidents—and she was secretly thrilled. The obnoxious

Mr. F. had a fatal flaw. She turned her back to give him some privacy while he attended to himself. Finding the right disdainful tone was a snap.

"Forgiveness, Jack? I'll have to think about that."

"Will you let me try to make it up to you?"

"I'll consider it, but *only* if you honor our deal."

"I will, I swear, but first I have to redeem myself in your eyes. Let me worship at the shrine of your womanhood, Julia. And if I don't give you more pleasure than you've ever received before, you can punish me in any way you wish."

Could be fun, she thought.

A moment later he was beside her, restored to his domineering persona. He kissed her fingertips and nodded toward the circular bed. "Could I interest you in a hot lunch? Or if you're not hungry, possibly some kitten whiskers?"

"What are kitten whiskers?"

His laughter was positively wicked with delight. "You're about to find out, my reluctant little slut."

Damn, she's beautiful. Andrew forgot everything else but the power and grace of her lines as he made his way down the ramp and onto the dock. She had masts as long and sexy as a supermodel's legs, but when it came to sailing yachts, he was into natural beauty. He couldn't take his eyes off her lean, gleaming silver hull. She was built like a knife blade, and the way she cut through wind and wave took his breath away.

The waterfront cleared his head of clutter like nothing else, and after last night's confrontation with Marnie, he needed a break. The woman was driving him nuts. She lived and breathed her own personal pain, and he had no way to combat that. She didn't know how to compromise. Maybe she couldn't.

So, her hair was dark and wild, and the brace-let...gone.

And she was calling the shots.

Andrew needed a rest. He needed the sea to wash him clean.

Seals were climbing onto the jetty rocks to sun-bathe. You could see their glistening black coats and hear their throaty barking for miles. An outgoing tide coaxed rich, briny smells from the shoreline.

Just for the pure joy of it, Andrew tilted his head back and breathed in, filling his lungs. The midmorning haze had started to burn off, revealing the promise of a sapphire-blue sky, and the gulls were in full flight—all signs that it was going to be a beautiful summer day.

Sun warmed the back of his neck as he walked to the very end of the long dock. The planks creaked with his weight and the water beneath made soft, silky noises. The Mirage Bay Yacht Club was a tiny organization with either a big heart or a need for funds. Andrew wasn't a member, but they'd agreed to rent him the guest berth indefinitely.

He'd decided to leave *Bladerunner* here for repairs after Alison's disappearance. The work had been minor and finished within weeks, but Andrew hadn't dealt with the yacht until now. *Bladerunner* had been dry-docked at the local boatyard until two weeks ago. Now he was glad he'd called ahead and had them put her back in the water.

A speedboat plowed by, churning the water. He

watched the gentle waves rock his own vessel, and felt a familiar yearning. He wanted to take her out again. He wanted to bake in the sun, get burned to a crisp, and taste the salt wind. It was hard to imagine that sailing in Mirage Bay wouldn't be tainted with bad memories, at least the first time out, but it had to be done. Someone was out to get him, threatening to go to the police. He had to have some plausible explanation for Alison's disappearance. One way to do that was to recreate the incident in his mind and see if there was anything obvious that he'd missed.

Fleetingly, he wondered if Marnie liked the water, and then he corrected himself. Not Marnie, Alison—and of course she liked the water. The day his wife disappeared, she'd convinced him to go for a sail, despite the storm blowing in. He'd been questioning her motives ever since.

He'd asked her for a divorce earlier that week, and she'd taken the news so calmly he'd immediately been suspicious. Alison was larger than life, with insecurities to match. She'd never handled rejection well, and he'd expected icy outrage and a series of hysterical scenes, at the very least. Possibly their prenup, which compensated her nicely if he asked for a divorce, had eased her pain, but Andrew had sensed something was up. Alison was ruthless when it came to getting what she wanted and going along with the dissolution meant she wanted something. Somehow, he doubted it was the money. She'd walked away from a fifty-million dollar trust fund to marry him.

She'd even agreed their marriage was a mistake and admitted seeking him out to further her career. She'd hoped he would make her a recording star the way he had Regine. Alison had a pleasant enough voice, but no real musical talent, and she hadn't taken it well when he'd told her, which might explain her calm reaction to the divorce. If she wasn't going to get what she wanted, why stay with him? But he'd given her the bad news over a year ago. It didn't make sense that she would wait this long—and disappearing off his yacht on a stormy night seemed a little extreme.

He'd been engaged to Regine when Alison re-entered his life. She was living in the Fairmont's upper eastside apartment and studying at Julliard, and she claimed to be serious about her singing career. She was also a huge fan of Regine's. She volunteered her time, traveling with Regine when she was on tour, and eventually she became a regular fixture, even in their home. After the freak accident that took Regine's life, Andrew had been shell-shocked and grateful for Alison's compassion—and her companionship. Not love, gratitude. He'd been in denial.

When he'd asked for the divorce, he'd apologized for letting things go as far as they had. But Alison had insisted that she understood. He'd married her on the rebound. Of course she would give him a divorce. All she wanted was one last sail on *Bladerunner.* He'd made the mistake of agreeing, and it *was* their last sail.

With that night still on his mind, Andrew gripped the line and pulled the yacht close enough to the dock to climb aboard. He made his way to the port side bow, where the lifeline had given way. The repairs had removed all traces of the accident, but Andrew wouldn't soon forget the sight of the snapped line. It was the first thing he'd seen when he came up from below.

He'd gone down for life jackets that should have been in the cockpit locker. The storm had blown up out of nowhere and the yacht was lurching violently. Possibly Alison was caught off balance and thrown over the side. It wasn't until later that he discovered she had taken out a large insurance policy on her own life a month prior to the accident—and forged his name to the documents. If she was embittered about the divorce, she'd gone to a lot of trouble to seek revenge, even for a scorned woman, and may have paid for it with her life.

He'd already given some thought to the other Fairmonts' motives. Alison had told him the family trust passed down from mother to daughter. If she was wrong and Bret was next in line, then Bret would have reason to get rid of his sister, and perhaps to frame the most obvious suspect, Alison's estranged husband. It wasn't totally impossible that Bret, or someone else, had stowed away below deck. But that hadn't occurred to Andrew at the time, and he hadn't searched the yacht, even after he brought it back on. Someone quick and agile could have slipped away unseen while Andrew was radioing the Coast Guard. Also, the weather reports had predicted the Devil Winds would blow in that evening, which was why he'd tried to talk Alison out of the sail. The conditions were perfect for a disappearance at sea.

Andrew wasn't sure what Julia might have to gain, but that didn't rule her out. Having Alison dead might clear the way for her to reclaim the trust. And then there was Tony Bogart, her old boyfriend. He seemed to have held a serious grudge all these years, which meant he might have it in for both of them, Alison and Andrew.

Andrew couldn't rule out Alison herself. He doubted she was a strong enough swimmer to negotiate the seas in storm conditions. It would have required an accomplice and some advance planning, but it had been dark enough that night to conceal a small powerboat by the reefs. Nothing would surprise him where she was concerned, even the possibility that she was still alive and waiting to make her move, whatever that might be.

He'd gone through her checkbook, bills and credit card statements, but there'd been no activity since the accident and no evidence tying her to the insurance policy. He'd also gone through her clothing, her purse and her Blackberry. Nothing. But none of that was conclusive. She was plenty smart enough to have planned ahead and covered future tracks. It was easy to get credit cards in a different name, and she'd had accounts he'd never had access to.

All along, he'd been hampered by the possibility of triggering suspicions if he investigated too openly. Back in February he'd met with the insurance agent who issued the policy, but Andrew had known if he pushed for an investigation he would bring Marnie under suspicion of fraud and forgery, and he couldn't risk that. He'd actually had to say that the forged signature on the insurance policy was his own, to avoid a probe.

He'd learned from the agent that the entire transaction had been handled via phone calls and faxes. The man had never met Andrew until that day, but he'd mentioned their phone conversations, which meant whoever took out the policy was either male or had a male accomplice. For some reason, Tony Bogart kept coming to mind. Andrew could easily imagine him trying to kill Alison and frame him, but if it had been Tony, he'd blown it big-time.

Andrew reached into the pocket of his cargo shorts for the keys that would let him into the main salon. If there were any supplies aboard, he was going to make himself a cup of coffee and do a bit more thinking before he headed out to sea. He wouldn't raise the sails today. That was a two-man job. He'd just motor out and back.

It disturbed him that Marnie was having second thoughts, because that raised the question of whether he could trust her. Alison had been a cold, calculating bitch who'd had everything handed to her. Marnie was just trying to survive. She'd never expected to be given anything, which had the paradoxical effect of making him want to give her everything....

Now *there* was a dangerous impulse.

Andrew breathed ice-cold laughter. He couldn't afford to be *that* sentimental. He wasn't even sure he'd meant it when he'd promised to take her back to Long Island. He knew the manipulative power of noble male sacrifice. Women were suckers for it. On the other hand, if she'd taken him up on the offer, he wanted to think he would have done it. He had some firsthand knowledge of what her life had been like, and she didn't deserve any more grief at the hands of some asshole.

The first time he'd come face-to-face with her in the hospital—and later confronted with Alison's perfect, but sterile, features—he'd forced himself to recall the defiance and the courage he'd seen in Marnie the day he'd run off the young thugs who'd had her cornered. It was closer to beautiful than anything he'd ever seen in Alison.

He tried the key, but the lock didn't want to give. Maybe he had the wrong one—or maybe he was distracted. He'd had dark thoughts about the possibility of becoming locked in mortal combat with Marnie. He had to prove his innocence, and she was not only his alibi, she was his ticket into the Fairmont world. Unfortunately, all she wanted was *out* of that world, and even though he could hardly blame her, he needed her. His worst-case scenario was that her real identity might be discovered, or even that she might confess. This trip had thrown her into turmoil, and she was unpredictable, anyway. *Untamed* was probably more apt.

Ironic, he realized. Those were the very qualities that attracted him, and yet for the last six months he'd been trying to reprogram the wildness out of her—and turn her into someone he despised.

Beyond the lap of the waves and the cries of the gulls, Andrew heard a familiar sound. The dock creaked and groaned under the weight of footsteps. The sun was in his eyes as he looked up and saw a silhouetted form coming down the gangplank.

The figure stopped at one of the other moorings, to Andrew's relief. He didn't want to be disturbed right now. Still, he continued to watch the intruder. It appeared the man had stopped to admire one of the yachts, but within moments, he was headed Andrew's way again, slowly and with a certain air of menace.

As the man neared, Andrew realized who he was. Speak of the devil. Tony Bogart.

10

Tony was tempted to thank Andrew Villard for being the easiest stakeout he'd ever had. He'd been sitting in his rental car on a side road at the bottom of the hill when Villard had driven by a short time ago. Tony had recognized the Mercedes SUV as one of the Fairmont stable of cars. Apparently now it was a six-figure loaner. And easily replaced, he thought acidly, like everything owned by the rich. Nothing but toys to be tossed away when they no longer amused.

He'd followed Villard at a distance, staying several car lengths behind. Tony had been waiting since dawn for one of them to leave the Fairmont compound. Unfortunately, it was Andrew. He wouldn't be as much fun to taunt as Alison, but Tony had a little something up his sleeve.

Now, he ambled over the dock's rotting wooden planks, taking his time. Unlike most locals, he didn't have saltwater in his veins and he'd never enjoyed the reek of low tide, but he wanted to give Villard a chance to work up a sweat, wondering what was going on. Intimidating a suspect was something any law officer worth his stripes enjoyed, though most wouldn't admit it.

Fear didn't have its own smell. That was a myth. But fear did have a look. The eyes turned unnaturally bright and the skin ashen. People dried up like slugs in the sun and were forced to lick their lips. Some couldn't even talk.

Tony relished those signs. Few things made him feel more in command of a situation, except the resistance of a trigger against his finger. The sight of a weapon worked wonders on assholes who didn't have the sense to show the proper respect.

He understood life's most essential hierarchy: the law ruled. Even the rich were low on that food chain. Sure, they had fat cat lawyers, but that didn't always get you off in these days of public trials and court TV. Nowadays, everyone had to roll over and show their bellies, and Tony loved nothing better than watching fat cats get skinned.

Villard leaped from the boat and walked toward him. He didn't look like a man ready to roll over. Fine, Tony was always willing to do it the hard way, especially when he was armed and the other guy wasn't. Villard had on khaki shorts, a white V-neck T-shirt and deck shoes. Hard to hide weapons in so little clothing, unless you had a gun stuck up your ass.

Tony came to a stop and let Villard do the approaching. He told himself it was a calculated move, but he had to admit that something about Villard made him uneasy. He didn't have the cold, hard stare of a killer. That was another myth. Killers had wet eyes, like weasels, and they were cowards at heart. But Villard did give the impression of someone who had little more than a passing acquaintance with fear and loathing—and could give a flying fuck about dominance hierarchies.

He'd have to remember not to drop his guard.

"Do you have a boat moored here, or am I under surveillance?" Villard asked.

Tony smiled. "Have you done something that requires surveillance? I'd be happy to hear your confession."

Villard dismissed him with a contemptuous look. "This is a private club," he said, "and somehow I doubt you're a member."

Arrogant asshole. Tony pretended to be apologetic. "The gate wasn't locked, and I just happened to see you down here. I'm staying across the street." He stepped back, shuffling and smiling, as if to leave. "And you did tell me if I had anything to say that concerned your wife I should come to you."

"What about my wife?"

"Well, I wasn't going to mention it," he said, angling a curious look at the other man, "but I couldn't help but notice…"

"Notice what?"

"There's something weird about your wife."

"What are you talking about?"

Tony lifted a shoulder. "You know what I mean. She's different."

Villard was nonchalant. "No one expects her to be the *same*. She's been through a lot."

"Hey, I *knew* the woman, and she's different. She doesn't like to be looked at. She turns her head to avoid it. Alison loved to be admired."

"We're done with this conversation." Villard headed back to the sloop. He began to undo the mooring lines.

Tony strolled along behind him. "You're taking the boat out?" he asked.

"Suddenly, I'm feeling the need for some fresh air."

"Really? I thought it might be the need to return to the scene of the crime."

"There was no crime, Bogart, unless you know something I don't." Villard glanced around at him. "How do we know *you're* not returning to the scene?"

"Me? Why would I want to hurt Alison? I was about to congratulate you on your marriage. Should have done that yesterday. Bad manners."

Villard's disgust was palpable. "Jesus, are you still carrying a torch for my wife? That's pathetic, Bogart. Grow up and go away."

Tony meant to laugh, but nothing came out except an embarrassing squeak. His voice had broken like a teenager's. Rage consumed him. *Stupid fuck.*

By the time Tony had calmed himself, Villard was on his boat and preparing to pull away from the dock. Tony held his tongue, watching as Villard easily maneuvered the large yacht. He looked like a natural, someone who would understand sailing to the point of knowing the currents—and exactly the right spot to dump a body overboard so that it would never be found.

Except that the body was found—and alive. By Villard himself. That didn't compute for Tony, but it was why he'd joined the FBI. He loved a good mystery.

Tony felt his cell vibrating inside the case hooked to his belt loop. He checked the display, saw that it was an unknown caller, and pressed Talk. His snitch's calls came in that way.

"Bogart," Tony said. It surprised him that his hand was unsteady. He'd worked with informants before, but none who had such power over his deeply personal desires. This was Tony's chance for justice on several levels.

"She's killed twice," said the muffled voice in his ear, "and she'll kill again soon. This time she's after someone you know and love."

"Who's killed twice?" Tony asked.

The voice turned scornful. "You already know that."

"You're talking about Alison Fairmont? Who's she after?"

"You already know that, too. Is your hearing going?"

The line went dead, and Tony hit *75, alerting his cell phone service that he wanted the call traced. The service was intended to deal with telephone threats and harassment, but it was the only resource Tony had at the moment. He'd been cut off from the FBI's electronic surveillance operations when they put him on administrative leave.

The caller *sounded* like a woman, but there were many ways to disguise a voice. Someone he knew and loved? Tony had to laugh. There wasn't anybody who fell into both categories, except Tony himself.

His smiled faded as he watched Villard navigate the boat out of the yacht club and turn it toward the reefs. This was getting more interesting all the time. Maybe he should thank Villard for dragging his beautiful wife out of the drink and bringing her home just in time for Tony to get a little payback.

* * *

Whoever designed this house should have included street signs.

Marnie was lost in Sea Clouds, searching for Julia's room. Her skin had finally calmed down, along with her nerves, but it had taken nearly twenty-four hours. Andrew had covered for her, but this morning he'd gone out early, promising to come back with news of her grandmother.

Now it was nearly two in the afternoon, and the house had seemed unusually quiet all day. Marnie had begun to wonder where everyone was, and she was too anxious to sit and wait for Andrew any longer.

She'd decided it might be a good idea to spend some time with Julia. Perhaps they might even find some common ground. But first she had to locate her room. When she'd gazed up at the house as a kid, she'd always imagined it was the second-story room with the huge Palladian windows and romantic wrought-iron balconies, overlooking the ocean. But finding it from the inside was like negotiating a labyrinth.

The second floor had two wings offering spectacular views of both the mountains and the ocean. As Marnie made her way from one wing to the other, she encountered shadowy alcoves and empty guest rooms. Finally, she found a wide hallway with double doors at the end that looked promising.

She had lain awake all night, thinking about the choice she'd made and the bizarre lie she was living. There was no way around that. Obviously, she couldn't tell Julia the whole truth, but at least she could admit her fear that she wouldn't be able to live up to Julia's expectations. That much was certainly true, and something even a real daughter would feel under the circumstances.

But as Marnie approached the double doors, she heard voices inside.

"There's something fundamentally off about her. Haven't you noticed? She's lost in this house. She looks around like she's never been here before."

Marnie moved closer, listening. It was Bret's voice.

"You can't expect her to be the old Alison after what she's been through," Julia said.

"Who said I wanted her to be the old Alison? I hated that bitch—and she hated me. But something's wrong. Doesn't it strike you as odd that she can remember us, her family, but she's forgotten the house where she spent half her life?"

"Bret, don't call your sister a bitch. It's disturbingly low class."

"How do we know she *is* my sister?"

Marnie entered the room and hesitated, wondering what she was going to do when they saw her. Julia sat at her marble-topped writing desk, which faced the balcony, overlooking the ocean. This *was* the room that a much younger Marnie had imagined. From the inside, it reminded her of a palatial villa on the Mediterranean. Spacious and elegant, it seemed to have been designed with columns and arches everywhere. The gleaming marble floors almost made her dizzy.

Bret sat tilted back in a chair, his feet resting on his mother's desk, probably to annoy her. Neither one of them saw Marnie in the doorway behind them.

Julia scribbled notes on the pad. "She'd damn well

better be your sister. I'm planning a belated wedding reception this weekend for her and Andrew. I'm going to tell them tonight at dinner."

Marnie couldn't believe any of what she was hearing.

Bret seemed astounded, too. "You're throwing them a party? I wouldn't expose her to my society friends, if I were you. It would be cruel."

Julia glanced up from her task. "What do you mean?"

"She's an embarrassment. Did you see how she held her stemware when we were all at dinner? That was a 1996 Chevalier Montrachet, and her fingers were all over the bowl of the glass, warming the wine. Alison never would have done anything like that," he insisted. "She wasn't meek and mousy, either. She was a Fairmont, and she acted like one."

Julia set down her pen. "That's crazy. Do you seriously believe that Andrew would bring an imposter into this house? I'd have the police here in a heartbeat, and he knows it. If Alison hadn't turned up alive, he would have been charged with her murder."

Marnie wondered what her chances were of getting out unnoticed.

Bret swung around, as if he'd sensed her hovering. "Were you eavesdropping? What did you hear, you conniving little bitch?"

"I wasn't eavesdropping. I was standing right here, in full view, listening to everything you said about me, you conniving *bastard*."

Marnie fired bullets at him with her glare. She had never liked Bret on principle. He was a snob, and he'd always made it clear by his disdainful manner that he was too good for the likes of Mirage Bay. Many times she'd imagined flipping him the finger, but she'd never thought about walking up and slapping him.

Why not?

Bret didn't even try to duck. Maybe he was too startled as Marnie walked over and cracked his jaw with her palm.

The noisy pop of flesh against flesh was deeply satisfying. Marnie felt fiery heat and knew she'd hurt him. Her hand was stinging.

Bret touched the bright red palm print on his cheek. "You stupid *cunt*," he whispered. "I wish to God you'd drowned."

Julia nearly knocked over her chair as she sprang up. She moved in between her sparring children, as if she was used to refereeing them.

"Bret, don't even think about hitting her back," Julia warned. She grabbed his fist and gave him a push.

He let out a snarl of frustration. "Jesus, are you still protecting her after she turned her back on you? What the hell do you want? *I'm* the faithful son, the only kid who hasn't left you, but do you give a shit?"

Bret kicked over Julia's chair and stalked out of the room. His spitting fury as he stormed past Marnie sent her pulse into orbit. She had to protect herself from these people. That had never been more clear.

Julia went quiet, looking out at the ocean. Marnie had no idea what to do. She shuffled, about to excuse herself, when Julia turned. "Where are you going?" she said. "Come over here and let me have a look at you."

Marnie lifted her head, summoning strength, but

she felt like a stick figure as she walked over and stood in front of Julia. Her camisole and jeans were baggy and ill-fitting. She hadn't had Andrew to help her pick out something this morning. She probably looked like a street person, and she had never felt more like the imposter she was.

"Your outfit is *disastrous*. What were you thinking, putting lace with denim? I don't like those sandals, either. They're too Birkenstock."

Marnie touched her burgundy silk camisole. "Everyone's doing it."

"Everyone's doing what?"

"Wearing lace with denim. You can wear lace with anything."

"So this is a fashion trend? You never bothered following trends before. You've always had my innate sense of style." Julia waved a hand, presenting her own outfit—a navy-and-white sundress with epaulets—as if for comparison.

"I've lost weight," Marnie said. "Nothing fits, and I don't seem to care about clothes anymore."

"Well, that much is obvious."

Marnie's voice tightened with emotion. "He's trying to poison your mind against me."

"Bret?"

"Yes, Bret! And I'm making it easy for him because I'm not right yet. I'm not fully recovered, but—" She stared fiercely at the woman she was trying to reach, aware that some door had closed and Julia Fairmont had shut her out.

"Listen," she said, "if you don't believe I'm your daughter, then say so now, and I'll go. Andrew and I will leave, and you'll never have to see either of us again."

Julia looked surprised, and wary. She went over and straightened the spindly chair, sliding it back into the writing desk. Probably both expensive antiques, Marnie imagined. She didn't know what to make of Julia's silence, but she felt a rising sense of dread as the woman closed her hands on the back of the chair and bowed her head for a moment. She was either distressed by what had happened or contemplating what to do next.

Worse, Marnie had no idea what she actually wanted Julia to say. It might be easier for everyone if she simply told them to leave.

11

Julia turned around, her gaze distant, as if she were still looking out at the ocean. She walked up to Marnie and reached out to touch her.

Marnie flinched, not sure what to expect, but Julia didn't seem to notice her shrinking away. She caressed Marnie's face with her fingertips, traced her cheekbones and feathered her eyebrows, all the while looking at her in an oddly unfocused way.

"Of course you're my daughter," she said. "Have I ever suggested that you weren't? You look just like me. Even more than you did before, I think."

A quick smile softened her expression. It was almost tender, and Marnie felt a strange kind of gratitude welling up. Of course it was relief, but it was something else, too. She hadn't been the object of anyone's tenderness in a very long time.

"Thank you," she said, feeling awkward.

"Don't be silly. Come with me." Julia beckoned her into the bedroom, where there was an elegant three-panel mirror. "Look at the two of us," she said. "The resemblance is striking, don't you think?"

Marnie nodded. She didn't dare say that she barely saw the resemblance at all. They were both brunettes rather than blondes, although Julia's raven color might not be natural—and they shared the same bone structure. She couldn't deny the similarities, but Marnie's expression was perpetually guarded and her naturally wavy hair difficult to control. Apparently she had no fashion sense, while the woman next to her was a Neiman Marcus mannequin. Julia was perfect— makeup just so, every hair in place.

But there *was* something else about Julia's honed features that struck Marnie as familiar. Her stomach churned as she studied their reflections, but she couldn't put her finger on what it was or why it bothered her. Maybe she didn't want to know.

"And there's another reason I know you're my daughter."

"The piano?" Marnie ventured.

"No, the way you fought with Bret." She gave Marnie's hand a little squeeze. "That was my daughter, *classic* Alison. You never did take any shit from your little brother. I can remember thinking I should give the two of you boxing lessons, and let you fight it out in the ring, but I was worried about Bret."

Julia's laughter was infectious. Marnie laughed along, pretending to be delighted, too, but she was also aware of what had just happened. She'd won Julia's support and sealed her own fate. She and Andrew weren't going back to Long Island, at least not immediately.

"We need to talk," Julia said. She led Marnie over to a striped satin chaise, where they both sat. Julia seemed almost giddy as she pulled her closer.

"Now that the cat's out of the bag," Julia said, "and you know about the reception, I might as well let you in on the juicy details. I haven't thrown a big party since the house was decorated, so it has to be exceptional. Everyone will be expecting a smashing affair."

Marnie must have looked as pensive as Julia had moments ago when she was gazing out the window. Marnie dreaded the very thought of the party, but somehow she managed a smile and a nod.

Julia squeezed her fingers again. "It's going to be wonderful," she said, her laughter a bit too bright and bubbly. "Everyone knows you ran off and married Andrew, and that we've been estranged. And your accident was front-page headlines when it happened. There won't be a single regret. They'll all show up, hoping for fireworks."

Wonderful? Marnie began to giggle, too. She couldn't help herself, and somehow she knew Julia wouldn't notice the tinge of hysteria, anyway.

"Guess who has a *hot* new job?" Bret looked up from his gazpacho with a sly smile. He directed the question to everyone seated around the formal dining room table except his mother. Julia, he pointedly ignored.

Only Rebecca smiled back at him, Andrew noticed. And it was a quick, strained smile at that. More trouble was brewing, which came as no surprise. Andrew had spent time with these people when he was dating Alison. It was fair to say they didn't play well together. If given the chance, they'd probably gut each other and sell the vital organs to a body parts broker.

Julia cocked her head at Bret, who was at the other end of the table. "Who has a hot new job?" she said in a withering tone. "Surely no one seated here."

Andrew reached for Marnie's hand under the table. Things were still tense between them, but on their way down to dinner just now, she'd told him about the do-or-die confrontation in Julia's bedroom. He'd been surprised—and proud of how she handled herself, though there hadn't been time to let her know.

His priority had been calming her fears about her grandmother. Josephine Hazelton had won a contest and gone on a cruise somewhere. Andrew had stopped by her cottage and found it locked up. From there he'd gone to the flea market, where an elderly woman who claimed to know Gramma Jo had sworn she heard her talking about the cruise. Andrew had found it odd that the woman had no details. She couldn't remember where Gramma Jo had gone and didn't know when she'd be back, but she was adamant about what had happened.

Marnie had been so relieved, Andrew thought she might faint. Apparently her grandmother had talked about taking a cruise someday. It was a fond dream, and Marnie was thrilled she'd been able to do it. She'd asked Andrew to discreetly keep checking for details. She wanted to know everything, especially when Gramma Jo would be back, although they'd both agreed that Marnie shouldn't visit her. If anyone would recognize Marnie, through gestures alone, it would be her.

Andrew hadn't mentioned his encounter with Bogart at the yacht club. No point worrying her about that yet.

Bret grinned, doing his Cheshire cat thing until the silence grew uncomfortable.

Andrew picked up his water glass. "Who do we congratulate?"

"Could it wait a minute, Bret?" Julia rose, clinking her fork against her water goblet. "I have something to announce. If I could have everyone's attention."

There were only the five of them at the table, counting Julia, but she seemed determined to preempt her son, and Andrew couldn't blame her. From what he'd seen, Bret was the sand in Julia's Vaseline. He lived to embarrass her.

Bret sprang to his feet and held his wineglass high. "No, it can't wait. I've been asked to be a spokesmodel for a line of men's spa products."

Julia's eyes narrowed. "Spokesmodel? Is that like a celebrity who does commercials?"

Andrew could have told her what spokesmodeling was like. It was a lot like a rock star, and he'd dealt with his share of those. Thank God his assistant, Stacy, was handling it now, although he'd already started receiving voice mail messages from her wanting advice and counsel.

"It's like Mark Wahlberg for Calvin Klein underwear," Bret explained, answering his mother. "This is a new line of men's toiletries, and they want a fresh face. They're selling the products in discount outlets like Target and KMart, and I suppose they want the Fairmont name to add a little cachet to their brand." He angled a glance at her. "Nice, huh? I knew you'd be pleased."

"*Discount* outlets?" Julia looked as if she'd bitten into a lemon. "And have you accepted their offer?"

"They want an answer tomorrow."

The way Julia was holding her dinner fork, Bret might not live that long. *Score one for Bret*, Andrew thought. Julia would never want the family name associated with low-end spa products.

Marnie started a round of applause, which seemed to catch everyone off guard, including Bret. Her soft smile made Andrew wonder what was going through her mind. He knew she was relieved about her grandmother, but she was also subtly different since that morning's confrontation with Bret and Julia, as if she'd rediscovered something within herself. She was a fighter by nature. He had faith in her, but it wasn't *his* faith that mattered.

"I suppose congratulations are in order." Julia held up her glass and acknowledged her son with a resigned nod. "To Bret's new adventure."

"Here, here," Andrew said, to the sound of clinking glasses. He hadn't expected Julia to go along with Bret's "hot new job." And maybe she wouldn't. The night was young.

"My son is a hard act to follow," Julia said when they were done toasting him, "but I do have a little something to share. Rebecca and I managed to secure the Dave Matthews Band to perform at the reception— and we didn't even have to use Andrew's services to do it."

Her smile was demure, but her pleasure was obvious. She had just rendered her son-in-law useless.

Bret finished off his wine, his eyes still sparkling. "Tell me this party's not black tie."

"It's black tie," Julia retorted. "This is a grand occasion, Bret. We're celebrating Alison and Andrew— and it's also the first party in our new home, the unveiling, so to speak."

Andrew wondered if she meant the unveiling of something more than the house. He hoped Julia didn't have any other surprises in store, such as publicly exposing an imposter in her household. Andrew was aware that his thoughts had taken a paranoid turn, but he couldn't help but wonder if that was why Julia had so graciously accepted Marnie as her daughter, not to mention him as her son-in-law. Maybe it was all a setup.

As they returned to their first course, Andrew considered his tablemates. Bret was a piece of work. But was he a dangerous adversary, capable of carrying out a blackmail threat, or just a spoiled, rebellious overgrown kid? Andrew had no doubt Bret would make a hell of a model. He had the looks, the refinement, the ski-jump cheekbones. Hell, he was prettier than his sister. Was he also as cold and calculating?

Julia did seem capable of eating her young, as Marnie had warned, but she also seemed to care about them in some oddly desperate way. She'd accepted Marnie almost immediately, and if it wasn't a setup, then perhaps it came out of her neediness for a relationship with her daughter. But it might also have come out of her guilt for having tried to get rid of her.

Andrew almost missed Julia's assistant, Rebecca, who faded into the woodwork with her plain brown hair and cotton dress. She was quiet but bore watching. Dangerous currents had been known to run in still waters. Rebecca was a cipher, and he'd never trusted ciphers. He would have to find out more about her.

Andrew picked up a soft hissing sound and glanced at the ceiling, where two enormous teak fans rotated slowly, their blades revealing a mural of a tropical rain forest with animal eyes peering out of the darkness. Eerily beautiful, they reminded Andrew of his tablemates and the suspicion that pervaded the room.

"What size party are we talking about?" Bret asked his mother. "Do you think the Qualcomm Stadium in San Diego will be big enough for Alison and Andrew's tens of thousands of friends?"

Julia ignored him. "I've kept the guest list small because of the short notice. We'll have fifty for dinner, served in the large dining room, and afterward, dancing in the Chinese pavilion. It's been enlarged and redone."

They hadn't seen the Chinese pavilion on their tour the other night. Andrew remembered the old version as perfect for dancing on a balmy summer evening, but Julia had complained years ago that the pagoda roof and Oriental dragons were dated. He was curious what she'd done with it.

"It sounds lovely," Marnie said. Her smile was bright, but Andrew could hear the tension in her voice. "But I didn't bring anything formal."

"Not a problem," Julia said. "I'll have my personal stylist pick out some gowns and bring them over. You can choose whatever you'd like. Rebecca and I will help, too. We'll make a day of it."

Marnie went pale. "No, really, that's—"

Andrew nudged her foot under the table. She was acting like a poor relation, not the coddled daughter of a privileged family.

"—great." Her voice sharpened. "Maybe some champagne?"

"Oh, lots of champagne," Julia assured her.

Andrew could see that Marnie was still struggling with this to-the-manor-born stuff. A formal reception would test her to her limits, and again he wondered if that's why Julia had insisted on throwing it. He was also aware that Marnie had all but sacrificed herself for him. She could so easily have blown their cover when she was confronted by Julia, and gotten the hell out of this place. At the very least she could have begged off the reception, using her health as an excuse. But she'd done neither. And he owed her for that.

Naked breasts everywhere. Marnie was afraid she was going to be hit in the face by one of them. She was just tipsy enough that her reflexes were shot, and even ducking breasts seemed slightly dangerous.

"More champagne?" the stylist asked, topping off Marnie's glass. "You're falling behind."

Marnie's nod was a little exaggerated. She was sitting on the carpet, stretched out next to Julia's chaise in a real Dolce and Gabana gown of red organza ruffles, and exhausted from trying on dresses for the last hour and a half. This shopping-at-home stuff was new to her, and a little bewildering, but the ridiculously expensive champagne was fun.

Marnie set her overflowing glass on a silver tray that had been left on the chaise. She was already slightly woozy and very loose. However, Belinda, Julia's personal stylist, was right: Marnie was well behind everybody else.

Julia had finished nearly a bottle of bubbly on her own and was going through designer dresses like a runway queen. Rebecca had had several glasses, but she was diluting them with peach nectar and something else that Marnie couldn't remember the name of. Even Belinda was drinking on the job, but she'd been burning off the alcohol's effects by helping everyone with their clothes and trying on things herself.

Marnie was the lightweight in this crowd. She was a novice when it came to haute couture, booze and breasts. So this was an education. None of them was wearing much in the way of underwear. They'd all stripped down to their panties in the first twenty minutes. Bras had hooks. They took too long.

"Isn't this fabulous?" Rebecca said, throwing open her arms to reveal her flouncy, strapless, black satin Balenciaga.

Julia was squeezing herself into a body-hugging sheath that looked as if it were made out of spun gold. The daring slit up the front and the delicate diamond straps created one of the sexiest looks Marnie had ever seen. Breathtaking. She couldn't imagine carrying off such a dress.

"What size is this thing?" Julia demanded, struggling with the zipper. "Have I gained weight?"

Rebecca laughed. "Time to cut the carbs!"

Julia scowled at her. "You're twice as big as I am," she retorted. "Time to start sticking that toothbrush down your throat again."

Rebecca turned pale with surprise, then flame-red. Whether she was bulimic or not, she was definitely angry. Marnie could see it in her eyes, and she understood the impulse. Rebecca wanted to lash back, but wouldn't dare. Julia was too formidable an adversary.

Meanwhile, Julia shimmied out of the sheath and thrust it at Belinda. "Have Alison try it on," she snapped. "She's nothing but skin and bone from all that surgery, and I don't like that red monstrosity she has on at all."

Marnie went very still, wondering if this was going to escalate into a full-scale fit on Julia's part. "I like what I'm wearing," Marnie said, remembering too late that Julia did not like the color red.

"Alison, get off your bony ass and try on the damn dress!"

If anyone knew about casual cruelty, Marnie did. Still, she couldn't believe Julia's outburst. It had to be the alcohol.

Poor flustered Belinda held up the dress. "It looks like it would fit," she said softly, encouraging Marnie.

Julia had wrapped a terry robe around her and was furiously sorting through the rack of gowns Belinda had brought. "This stuff is all wrong," she said. "There's *nothing* here that would work for me."

"You told me to bring the gowns for Alison."

"I know what I told you!" Julia turned on the stylist, her teeth bared. "Alison and I wear the same size—or we *did*. We have the same taste. If these rags don't work for me they're not going to work for her, either."

Apparently no one was safe from Julia's tirade. Marnie sprang dizzily to her feet. "Give me the dress. I'll try it on."

She unzipped the organza gown and yanked it off over her head, not caring whether or not she was doing it right. Or that she was wearing nothing underneath except bikini panties. Fortunately, she had had some experience with nakedness. She'd been splashing around in tide pools all her life. She wasn't used to having an audience of startled women, but she was too furious with Julia to care about that, either.

Belinda hustled over to take Marnie's dress, and

handed her the shimmering sheath. With the stylist's help, Marnie had the new dress on, zipped and hooked in a matter of moments. It fit like a dream, hanging as if it had been made for her angles and delicate curves. The wide-set diamond straps glittered against her creamy skin.

"Wow," Rebecca whispered, as Marnie turned for the other women. The draped bodice was beautifully cut.

"It doesn't suit you," Julia said.

But Marnie had seen her reflection in Julia's panel of mirrors. The gown fit her to perfection. It was a miracle, a spun-gold miracle. And Julia was clearly jealous. Marnie wasn't going to let her run roughshod over all of them, just because she could.

"This dress has my name on it," Marnie stated.

"*Gown,* not dress," Julia corrected. "And it's too *much* gown for you, Alison. Maybe something less vampy, all right? Belinda?"

"I love it," said a male voice from the doorway.

Someone squealed at the sight of Andrew in the entrance, and he pretended to cover his eyes as the women rushed to cover themselves. Strangely, though, even Julia hushed as he walked into the room.

"Didn't mean to crash the party," he said. "I was looking for my beautiful wife, and I heard your voices from downstairs."

His beautiful wife? Marnie's heart hesitated when Andrew caught her gaze. Without a word, she turned, letting the dress curve on her body. Looking at him over her shoulder, she said, "What do you think?"

"Really, Alison, you shouldn't have shown him the gown," Julia interjected. "It could be bad luck."

"We're not getting married," Marnie murmured. Besides, it was too late. He'd seen it already. And boy, had he seen it. Andrew was eating her up with his eyes as if she were a delectable dessert and he was a man with a sweet tooth. Screw Julia. This was the dress Marnie was wearing.

12

Bret jogged down the pier, his leather flip-flops slapping the wooden planks. Madly trying to tuck his shirttail into his walking shorts, he headed toward the small crowd that had gathered around a roped-off area at the end of the pier. A dozen or so kibitzers had stopped to watch a crew set up for what looked like a photo shoot.

His photo shoot, Bret hoped. He was almost an hour late—and probably damn lucky to find anyone still there. Why the fuck hadn't he set his alarm? He'd slept until one in the afternoon. If it hadn't been for the racket from his mother's room, he'd still be flaked out. Who knew a bunch of liquored-up women trying on dresses could make so much noise?

As he approached the crowd, Bret slowed to a walk and smoothed his clothing. The cut-rate ad agency hired by Surfaces, the local men's cosmetics company, had asked him to provide his own wardrobe, so he'd done some summer layering with walking shorts, a striped shirt and a pullover, all in shades of blue, green and khaki.

His tinted aviator sunglasses rounded out a look that he considered perfect for an afternoon stroll on a sunny pier—or for the Everyman who bought his shaving balm at the same place he got his toilet paper.

Bret only hoped the balm's intensely minty smell would mask the dampness filming his body. He'd been told by the ad agency's artistic director, who doubled as their photographer, that they wanted a sporty, windblown look. Shouldn't have any trouble with windblown, Bret thought. He probably looked like he'd been caught in a fucking hurricane.

Bret sidestepped an elderly couple and ducked under the rope. The young, hip, jeans-clad photographer was calibrating his light meter, while an assistant worked on polishing up a coin-operated telescope that was one of the props for the shoot. Painted green, it was completely encased in a bulky concrete frame, apparently so no one could walk off with it.

Bret was supposed to sit at the base of the telescope as he stared out to sea, but he'd already noticed something odd. An umbrella had been set up nearby, and it was shading a man getting his makeup and hair done. Either Bret had been replaced, or he was going to have company in the ad.

"Hey, sorry I'm late," Bret said to the photographer. The man's hands were busy, so Bret greeted him with a friendly little wave—and tried to remember his name. They'd only met once, at a session to discuss this ad, and Bret had realized that they were around the same age. But then everything about Surfaces was young and trendy, except the wealthy CEO, a local businessman who'd made his money on software design and was branching out.

The photographer seemed genuinely startled to see him. He tucked the camera under his arm and squinted at Bret's windblown look. "Hey, man, what are you doing here?"

"Not good?" Bret figured there was something wrong with his outfit. "This is what people wear on these piers. Take a look around. Slightly disheveled, but chic, you know. Neat is out."

"So are you. Out."

Bret lifted his head. "What are you talking about?" He waited for the guy to grin and tell him he was kidding.

"This shoot was scheduled to start an hour ago."

"I know, I had problems. Traffic—"

"Your manager was supposed to have called you."

"My manager? Why? What's going on?" Bret hadn't had time to check his messages. He'd shoved his cell in his pocket as he ran out the door on his way here.

"Look, I'm sorry," the photographer said. "The powers that be have decided you're not the face we need for this campaign."

Bret felt a familiar tightening in his chest. Panic. It was spiking fast and cutting off his air. His voice was sharp with disbelief. "Just because I'm late? It won't happen again. I promise."

"Late's got nothing to do with it. The decision came down from Surfaces's CEO last night. You're *out*."

Bret cocked his head, not at all sure he was buying this. "Bullshit," he said under his breath. "Ben Palmer has been pursuing me for a year. What's this really about?"

"Hey, he found someone else. Get over it."

"I am over it, trust me. I'm *all* over it." *Asshole.*

He turned to go, stopped midstride and whipped around in frustration. "For Christ's sake, man, I'm getting the shaft over nothing. Don't I deserve a little honesty here?"

The photographer scowled and went back to his calibrating. "You didn't hear it from me," he said as he fiddled with the camera. "I heard Palmer got a phone call about you. That's all I know."

Obviously, his meddling mother had bought them off. Bret wondered what it had cost her. Probably she'd called in a favor. She had vast connections through her charity functions to countless VIPs, especially in cosmetics, fashion and show biz circles. Then again, maybe she'd had to screw somebody.

Palmer himself? A squatty, sexually ambiguous billionaire with bad skin? Bret perked up, but only for an instant. He couldn't even squeeze any pleasure from that sordid image of his mother's discomfort. He was so used to being thwarted at every turn it hardly fazed him anymore. It was his birthright. Nothing he'd ever done was enough in his mother's eyes. Nothing ever would be.

"No more questions," the photographer said. "I'm losing the light."

"Bummer," Bret muttered, adding as he turned to leave, "I hope the fucking sun goes out."

Bret was actually smiling by the time he got to the dented family car and unlocked the door. The Infiniti sedan was the end of the line for him. His mother wouldn't let him drive anything else because he was merciless on cars, according to her, and he never had the money for repairs. Shit, if she'd stop sabotaging his life he'd have the money to buy his own car.

Moments later, cradled in the leather bucket seat, he revved the engine and coughed up a wad of laughter. His mother must have jumped on this one with all fours. She probably didn't want him announcing his new job at her chichi party this weekend.

He could feel the anger churning in his gut, but he couldn't be bothered with it at the moment. Fits of temper took too much energy. And in a weird, twisted way, he was pleased. He didn't have time for a half-assed modeling job, anyway. He had bigger fish to fillet.

Poor Julia. She should have let him be this time. She and her darling daughter were going to need one another, because when he got through with them that's all they'd have. Each other. In hell.

The Bull's Head Tavern was a dark watering hole with low ceilings and a massive old-fashioned mirror behind the bar. The place did smell faintly like someone might be pasturing a few bovines nearby. Probably it was the sawdust on the floor and the fumes coming from the overflowing sump in the back alley. But that hadn't stopped the tavern from being one of the most popular after-work spots in Mirage Bay. When it was crowded, people milled around on the sidewalk outside, waiting to get in.

Fortunately, it was relatively quiet when Tony Bogart wandered in around six that evening. He wasn't here to socialize. He had an objective, and he spotted her immediately. LaDonna Jeffries sat at the end of the bar all by herself, absently chipping polish from one of her long, red fingernails, and seeming not the least bit interested in her glass of beer. She probably didn't even realize she was wrecking her manicure. Her focus was on her cell phone, lying silent on the counter, and her gaze didn't waver from it, even when Tony slipped onto the empty bar stool next to her.

She shifted away from him without so much as a look. Obviously, she didn't want to talk to anyone. Not exactly the reception he'd had the last time they'd met. He'd been after the same thing then. Information. But she'd offered up something much different.

He studied her burnished waves and what he could see of her dejected profile. Something was wrong in LaDonna Land. A guy, of course. From what he knew of her, which wasn't much beyond her reputation for being eager to please, it was always a guy. Some people wore their problems like conference name tags. Everything was available, and much too cheaply.

"Excuse me," Tony said. "I'm looking for Alison Fairmont. Have you seen her, by any chance?"

LaDonna flipped open her cell phone and scrutinized the display. As she snapped it closed, she gave him a disdainful glance. "Here? Alison Fairmont? You can't be serious."

Not eager to please tonight, apparently. Tony took no offense, although he thought it was odd she didn't recognize him. Either he'd been very forgettable when they hooked up last February, or she was really preoccupied. They'd never been more than passing acquaintances, except that one time. She was closer to the age Butch would have been than she was to Tony's. But he'd known LaDonna Jeffries by reputation, and she'd definitely known who Tony Bogart was six months ago. She just hadn't taken a good look at him yet.

"Do you know Alison?" he persisted, and fortunately, she couldn't resist. That was LaDonna's problem. She couldn't resist much.

"Everyone knows Alison," she said, "or thinks they do. Some of these idiots around here probably even think she gives a shit that they exist. Maybe she looked their way by mistake. Hah."

LaDonna rolled her eyes and grabbed her cell again, going through the menu, probably looking for the guy's number. Meanwhile, the bartender wandered over, and Tony pointed to LaDonna's beer, letting the man know he'd have the same thing.

The jukebox started to play a country-and-western tune with just enough bluegrass in it to set Tony's teeth on edge. Why did most fiddle music sound like the same thing over and over again?

"So, Alison wasn't nice to you?" he asked LaDonna.

"Coldhearted bitch," she murmured. "She could have bought the hand cream I showed her. Some of us have to work for a living."

"Don't like her much, do you?"

She tapped buttons on the cell's keypad, still ignoring him. "Don't care one way or the other."

"Is she coldhearted enough to kill someone?" he asked.

"Kill someone?" She thought a moment, shrugged and continued with her cell. "We're all coldhearted enough for that."

"What's his name?"

"Who?"

"The guy *you* want to kill."

"What's with all these questions?" She turned her

head and gave him a good hard look. "Jesus," she whispered, "is that you? Tony Bogart! Why the hell didn't you say something?"

She grabbed for her glass. Tony leaped up and caught her wrist before he was wearing the contents like a wet T-shirt.

"What the hell are you doing?" he said under his breath. "Put that down."

Beer splashed as the glass hit the counter. "Bastard," she said, her eyes welling with tears. "How about I kill *you?*"

"*Why?* What the hell is wrong with you?"

"You snuck out of my place without even a note. You slept with me, and you couldn't leave a note when you left? Couldn't call later?"

"You've been angry at me all this time?" Maybe that was *his* number she'd been looking for on her cell, not that he'd given it to her. She'd been too much the fatal-attraction type for him. She hadn't been good in bed, either, although he'd told her she was wonderful. She'd been worried about whether she was fat, and if she was pretty enough. Lots of women had those issues, but LaDonna was *obsessed.* He hadn't been able to get out of there fast enough, and no, he hadn't left a note. But he hadn't figured she'd hold a grudge for six months.

The sleuth in him was taking mental notes, as always. LaDonna Jeffries was beginning to look a little whacked. But just how whacked? he wondered. And what was her snapping point? Everybody had one.

The water-works surprised him. But she seemed to be in genuine pain, which cast more doubt on her emotional stability.

"Let me make it up to you," he said. "You want a fresh beer, dinner? How about we get something to eat, whatever you want."

"What's the catch, Bogart?"

"Nothing. Good food, good conversation."

She glared at him, brushing away tears with her fingers. "That's it? Why don't I trust you?"

Pretty hard to defend himself against that. "All right, maybe a couple more questions? I'm doing some research. No big deal."

"Jesus, they always want something." She stuffed her cell in a pocket of her fabric bag and called out to the bartender, who was waiting on someone else.

Tony figured he'd blown it. She was after her check so she could leave. But when the bartender finally ambled over, carrying Tony's beer, LaDonna ordered the most expensive champagne in the house.

"It's on him," she told the man, pointing to Tony.

Tony shrugged. "Whatever she wants."

LaDonna's pursed lips weren't quite a smile as she sat back and folded her arms. "Okay, ask your questions. Let's get this over with so I can enjoy my champagne."

"You're looking great," he said, letting his gaze flicker over the cleavage pouring forth from her plunging neckline.

She tweaked up the neckline a little, but seemed pleased.

"So," he murmured, "how's life been treating you, other than tonight?"

"Get real, Tony. You don't care about my life. Why were you asking if Alison killed somebody?"

"That *isn't* what I asked."

"You implied it."

"I asked if she was capable. It's the way a G-man thinks. Everyone's guilty until proven innocent. Besides, *you're* the one who said she was cold-hearted."

"Alison, coldhearted?" She snorted. "You used to date her. You oughta know."

The disdain in her voice cut at him, but he was careful not to let her see that. And since she refused to engage in friendly conversation, he might as well get to the point.

"Let's talk about another friend of yours, Marnie Hazelton."

"What about her?"

"You two actually were friends, right? Since childhood?"

She reached into the pocket of her bag for her cell phone, caught herself and stopped. "Why do you ask?"

"Have you talked to her recently?"

"So…this is about your brother, Butch?"

Tony tasted his light beer and grimaced. "Maybe," he admitted. "And let's say I'd like very much to speak with your friend. I might even be in a position to help her."

"Yeah, *right.*"

For a split second, Tony actually considered taking LaDonna into his confidence. If she knew he had another suspect, she might be willing to talk about her friend—and there was so much Tony didn't understand about Marnie Hazelton. Like who the hell she actually was. No one had been able to find any records on her, including the local cops who'd investigated Butch's murder. There were no fingerprints on record, no medical or dental files, no social security number or financial information. She'd gone to local schools sporadically, apparently dropping out when the teasing and harassment became too much. And her grandmother wasn't really her grandmother. Josephine Hazelton had given Tony and everybody else some cock-and-bull story about finding a baby in a basket.

And now *she'd* disappeared, too—the grandmother. There'd been no sign of her yesterday when Tony went out to her cottage.

"Seriously," he said. "I need to talk to Marnie."

LaDonna flashed him a glare. "I don't know where she is, and I wouldn't tell you if I did. She didn't kill anybody, although she had plenty of reason to. Your brother was sick, Tony—"

"That makes it okay to stab him seventeen times?"

"In my book, it does—and I hope he suffered."

Tony took a long drink of beer, giving himself time to mull over the fact that LaDonna had just given him a motive. He'd never seriously thought of her as a suspect, and for some reason, he still didn't, but this was getting interesting.

Damn screeching fiddle. There it went again. He glanced over at the jukebox and fantasized how it would explode when he emptied his pistol into its howling guts. That calmed him immediately.

"If it wasn't Marnie," he said evenly, "then who killed Butch? You must have a theory on what happened."

The bartender brought their champagne, poured them each a glass and left the bottle in a dripping bucket of ice on the counter. LaDonna took a healthy slug of the bubbly. Apparently she liked champagne better than beer.

"I'm sorry, but who *wouldn't* want to kill Butch? He terrorized everyone, even his creepy friends. Maybe they ganged up on him."

Tony tried the champagne and decided to stick with the lousy beer. He wondered what the bubbly was costing him. Sour shit. It tasted like bad ginger ale. "What about Gramma Jo?" he asked.

"The old lady? She'd never hurt anyone."

"Not even to protect her child? Okay, then, who?"

She started listing people who might hate Butch—a transient he'd beaten up for the fun of it and nearly killed; a neighbor whose dog he'd shot because it yapped all night. "What about you, Tony?" she said, a sneer in her voice. "Your brother was the first one to rub it in when Alison dumped you. I heard he and his friends were laughing themselves sick at the idea of you proposing to Goldilocks and her thinking it was a joke."

Tony's guts twisted. "He was young and stupid, a kid."

"He was an ass." She set down her glass. "Like I said, *everybody* hated him."

And Tony was starting to hate her. There was no love lost between him and his brother. Butch had fucked him over but good, but that was Tony's very personal business. No one got to slander Butch but him.

"I have to go," she said. "I'm dating a guy, a *really* nice guy."

Tony laughed. "You mean the one who was supposed to meet you here?"

"He'd be here if he could," she snapped. "He probably has car trouble."

She slid off the stool and hesitated. "I really thought you'd be different, you know. I didn't think a guy who'd been dumped would be so quick to dump a girl. Like…you'd know how it feels, and you wouldn't want to do that to anyone else."

She stared him straight in the eye, as if she had the moral high ground and he was the sleaze. Tony had no answer for her. He turned back to his tasteless beer and let her have her parting shot. Quite a temper on Mizz LaDonna. She'd all but bared her teeth at him. Made you wonder if a woman like that could get mad enough to kill somebody.

He heard her stalk away, but didn't bother to look up. He hadn't learned Marnie's whereabouts, but he'd done something more important. He'd planted the seed about Alison, and as much as LaDonna didn't like him, she didn't like Alison more.

13

"To my one and only daughter, Alison, who is more beautiful tonight than I've ever seen her, and to her dashing husband, Andrew, who's not so bad himself."

The well-heeled crowd tittered politely as Julia Fairmont raised her glass, first to the heavens, and then to Alison and Andrew, who as guests of honor were sitting at a flower-strewn table with the Pacific Ocean as their backdrop. All of the dinner courses except dessert had been served, and the food had been plentiful and delicious. Champagne and caviar, filet mignon and lobster. Now it was time for toasts, and after that, more champagne and dancing.

"May many more blessings rain down on their wonderful union," Julia said, "such as grandchildren, perhaps? It has been *four years,* you two."

The tittering turned to laughter, and Marnie actually found herself blushing, but not for the obvious reasons. Julia's seemingly heartfelt toast had caught her totally off guard, especially the reference to grandchildren, which was the last thing she expected to hear. It had to be for the guests' benefit. Julia wanted everyone to know what a loving, accepting mother she was.

The last several days had been focused entirely on party preparations, and Julia had monopolized nearly every minute of Marnie's time. She'd clearly intended some mother-daughter bonding, but she may have had another goal as well. She'd managed to slip subtle comments about Alison's relationship with Andrew into many of their conversations, quietly insinuating that he might be a dangerous man, and Alison might have something to fear.

Are you at ease around him? Is everything all right between you? Of course, I'm sure he's never touched you in anger, Alison, but do you worry that he might?

Obviously, Julia still harbored doubts about Andrew's motives. She hadn't come out and said she believed he was responsible for Alison's fall from the yacht, but she'd put it out there, probably to see what her daughter's response would be.

Marnie had deflected Julia's questions by saying how grateful she was for Andrew's care and devotion while she was recovering. She reminded Julia that he'd saved her life, and Julia had let it go—but now here she was, all smiles and gushing tributes. One would think *she* wanted to have Andrew's babies.

"Here, here!" someone called out.

Champagne flutes were lifted, and more voices chimed in with good wishes. Marnie reached for her own glass, but caught herself. One of the first rules of social etiquette: you don't toast yourself.

Andrew clasped her fingers and brought them to his lips, as if she'd been reaching for him. It was a nice save. She smiled and met his gaze, aware that her face was still flushed, but then who wouldn't be from all this excitement? She'd worn the pink diamond earrings that Andrew had given her on the evening they'd arrived at Sea Clouds. It had seemed important to shake off her doubts and make a gesture that said they were united, side by side, in this room of virtual strangers.

The crowd applauded, calling for more toasts. Marnie wasn't quite sure what was expected. Andrew picked up his flute and rose to answer the clamor. He turned to Julia first, thanking her for the beautiful occasion she'd created, and then to the crowd, expressing gratitude for their presence and for his many blessings, which included, of course, his wife.

He spoke in low, modulated tones with just the faintest European inflection, and Marnie was aware of the pride she felt. If he had a dark side, it only seemed to add to his allure tonight. The black tie attire made him seem *more* virile rather than less. If anything about him was dangerous, it was his hypnotic ease. He was as much at home with this fancy crowd as he was in the fairy-tale atmosphere Julia had created for the party.

The Chinese pavilion was an open-air pergola the size of a small ballroom that had been designed as part of the house's ground-floor terrace. It overlooked the ocean, and Julia and her party planners had turned it into something magical and palatial. Oriental lanterns had been replaced with crystal chandeliers, and thousands of miniature lights draped the wisteria boughs hanging like garlands from the tiled roof. But the most striking light came from the glowing horizon, which was wreathed with the vibrant reds and purples of the sunset.

Backlit by the blazing sky, Andrew turned to

Marnie. "I can hardly improve on my mother-in-law's tribute to my wife's beauty, but may I also say that I love the gown Alison is wearing tonight—almost as much as I'm going to love taking it off her after you nice people leave."

It was totally inappropriate, but the crowd broke loose and roared. Marnie didn't have to pretend to be flustered, but inside she was humming. All week long she'd been dreading this affair. She hated being the center of attention for any reason. She always had, long before she became Alison Fairmont. But tonight it felt as if something had inoculated her against the dread. She was immune, beyond making any more silly mistakes, and even if she did, it seemed these people would accept her, anyway.

She actually felt a little bit drunk, though she'd only had two glasses of champagne, and she hadn't taken any sleeping pills since she'd come to Mirage Bay. The pills made her groggy and forgetful, which would have been especially risky tonight. Who knew what the guests, all friends of Julia's, might say and do? Who knew what the *family* might say and do?

"If I might be allowed to make a toast?"

The man who stood was short in stature and stocky, but strikingly handsome in his formal white dinner jacket. Julia had briefed Marnie before the party about all of the guests, but in particular she'd mentioned Jack Furlinghetti, one of the family's estate lawyers. When she'd brought him over to her during cocktails, Marnie had been hyperaware of his curiosity and his scrutiny. It was obvious that this introduction was important, especially to Julia.

"May you lose your hearts and keep your heads,"

Furlinghetti said, generating another laugh, "and may your children have very rich parents."

The attorney hadn't even taken his seat before someone else spoke up. "Does the black sheep get to toast the happy couple?"

Bret was already headed toward the dais. Marnie saw him moving through a path created by the tables, an open bottle of beer in his hand. But he wore immaculate black tie, like everyone else, and he looked clear-eyed and sober, more sober than Marnie felt, actually. And he'd been remarkably restrained all through dinner. She had kept an eye on him until she'd been distracted by all the pleasant commotion of the evening.

Julia gave the combo a signal to start playing, and the keyboard player launched into one of the songs from a list that Marnie had chosen as favorites of hers and Andrew's. The small group of local musicians had been hired by the party planners to fill in until the Dave Matthews Band was scheduled to arrive, which was after the dinner and the toasts. Soon, Marnie hoped.

Meanwhile, Bret walked over to the observation deck that served as the bandstand, and took one of the mikes from its stand. "Now I won't have to yell to be heard," he told the startled guests. "I know my mother wouldn't want that."

The keyboard player glanced at Julia, taking his cues from her.

Julia's thumb worked against the huge emerald-and-diamond on her ring finger. The glint in her eyes was frightening.

"Be quick, Bret," she said, smiling and pretending to be amused. "It's time for our guests of honor to dance."

She nodded to the musicians, who continued to play softly.

"My sister, Alison, should get everything she so richly deserves—"

The combo surged into a chorus, and the music swelled, muffling the rest of what Bret had to say. But Marnie was close enough to hear him and her blood went cold.

My sister, Alison, should get everything she so richly deserves—and I plan to be there when the bitch goes down and takes that fucking French loser with her.

It was hard to believe he could hate Alison that much. But many people did, Marnie realized. Tony Bogart was an avowed enemy, and Julia's feelings for her daughter were clearly ambivalent. Even Andrew had not been able to hide his revulsion at times. The list of people who may have wanted to do Alison harm was growing. And perhaps they still wanted to.

She felt Andrew's hand brush hers and realized he'd heard Bret, too.

She pulled away, confused. There were too many realizations rushing at her. All of Andrew's attentive behavior could be a way to keep her here, carrying out his plan, whatever his plan actually was. Maybe she shouldn't trust him, either. Throughout her life, Marnie had been the object of hatred and a target of violence. She'd blamed it on her facial deformities, but today she had the face—and the life—of a woman who was beautiful and privileged, and yet the hatred was every bit as intense. And the real Alison may have been a victim of violence, too. Could more be far behind?

"Come with me," Andrew said, taking Marnie's hand.

"Where are we going?" She found it hard to keep up as he tugged her with him down a back stairway that led to a lower deck. Her high-heeled sandals clattered and clacked, but there was little chance anyone could hear her. The party in their honor was going full blast in the Chinese pavilion. The Dave Matthews Band had arrived as Bret finished his toast. They were into their first set now, and everyone was clapping and singing along, thrilled by the presence of rock royalty.

"We're leaving before I kill someone," Andrew said.

"Bret?"

Andrew's smile was fleeting and dark. "How did you know?"

"I heard what he said."

"Foul-mouthed little punk. Somebody should discourage him from spewing filth by ripping out his tongue and stuffing it down his throat—and I'll volunteer."

Marnie wanted to laugh, but getting down the steps in high heels took her full attention. In retrospect, Bret's toast didn't seem all that sinister to her, considering that he was always mouthing off about something. But this time he'd said it at his mother's fancy party in front of guests. At least they hadn't heard his childish name-calling.

Andrew tightened his grip on Marnie's hand as they came to the bottom of the stairs. The lower deck extended from the family room where Rebecca served continental breakfasts each morning, but now the entire area was dark. The only light was a motion detector that came on as they stepped onto the deck.

Marnie carefully picked her way across the slate tiles, still holding Andrew's hand for support. "Do you think Bret suspects the truth about me?" she asked him.

"He may suspect, but he doesn't know. It's Alison he hates, not you. She's a threat to him in some way. Maybe it's just sibling rivalry, but I think it's more."

Marnie lowered her voice. "Like what? Do you think Bret had something to do with Alison's disappearance?"

"If he did, that would make her *re*appearance an incredible threat, wouldn't it?"

"But how could he have? Bret wasn't on the boat, unless he stowed away, which seems unlikely."

"I don't know *how,* but I'm going to find out."

Marnie shivered as they walked to the deck's wrought-iron railing. "Alison seemed to attract darkness," she said. "I'm getting the feeling she had *many* enemies, and that this is a very dangerous place."

Andrew took off his tuxedo jacket and draped it over her bare shoulders. He squeezed her arms before he released her. "Let me worry about Bret, all right? Tonight's a celebration, and you shouldn't be thinking about any of this. I'm glad you wore the earrings. They're stunning on you."

She nodded, aware that he'd cleverly changed the subject.

"Are you warm enough?" he asked.

"Fine."

"It's a beautiful night."

He gazed down at the waves crashing on the rocks below, but Marnie couldn't join him. The thunderous sounds echoed inside her, and she averted her eyes. Suddenly she was filled with fear, and it seemed to have come out of nowhere. The waves were triggering flashbacks, one after another, images that had been buried for months. Distorted faces loomed in her mind, calling to her.

No, she couldn't look down. She couldn't even think straight.

What was this? Was she reliving all those hours she'd spent teetering on Satan's Teeth, telling herself how much easier everything would be if she jumped? Back then she'd stared at the deafening waves for so long, she'd seen faces, heard voices. She'd gone a little crazy.

Had she finally jumped that night? She couldn't remember. The dream about Butch had brought the violence back to her in vivid detail, but everything after that was still gone.

She was gripping something between her fingers, and she realized it was the fabric of her dress. She'd pinned the copper ring to the inside of her gown near the diamond strap, and her hand had gone there automatically to touch the good luck charm.

She turned away from the railing, hoping to stop the flashbacks. But the mist from the salt spray assailed her. All of her senses were tuned into the past now, and she couldn't shut them off. She could even smell the piercing perfume of the scrub pines on the cliff.

She looked up at the deck above, where music and energy pulsed, wondering why she couldn't be a part of that life, of any life where happiness was possible. She'd never allowed herself to get caught up in self-pity. Even with the hand she'd been dealt, self-pity had seemed as pointless as jumping off a cliff. But apparently she still harbored hopes for something better. She wanted happiness. A heart that wasn't ravaged.

What were the odds?

Something drew her gaze higher, to the deck on the third floor, above the party. That level was dark, too, but for a second, it had looked as if someone was up there. Either Marnie's senses were still jumbled or she'd seen someone—a woman peering over the side, down at her and Andrew.

But no one was there now, and Marnie didn't even know why she thought it was a woman. It was too dark to see anything but a vague silhouette.

"Are you all right?" Andrew asked.

She gave him a quick nod. If she'd spoken, he would have heard the tremor in her voice. She had to calm down. She was overreacting to everything, see-ing things that weren't there.

"I'd like to go," she said, drawing his coat around her.

He cupped her elbow and they started to walk, slowly, with Marnie wobbling in her heels. If tonight was her test, then as of right now, she felt like a big fat failure. She couldn't even walk without help.

"Let go of me," she said. "I can do this on my own."

He released her and stopped in apparent confusion. "What's the problem?"

Marnie kept going. She didn't feel like explaining herself. And she wasn't going back to the party, either. She'd had enough excitement for tonight.

But she hadn't taken two steps before Andrew shouted something. She turned to see him lunging at her, but there was no way to avoid him. His hands hit her chest with shocking force, and Marnie was literally lifted off the ground. She fell backward and tumbled into the railing.

She hit the iron bars and crumpled. The world seemed to explode. But the thunder she heard was not crashing waves. Marnie had no idea what it was as sharp, fiery objects bombarded her, cutting her skin and stinging her eyes. The pain was excruciating.

Something hit her temple and gashed it. The blood nearly blinded her. She could taste it as it filled her mouth, and her screams sounded strange and strangled. But that was all she could do—crouch and scream and cover her head with Andrew's coat.

14

Marnie heard him coming at her and braced herself against the railing. The voice shrieking at her to protect herself blocked out everything else. *Don't let him near you! Keep him away!* All those years of being terrorized had taught her how to fight for her life.

"Stay back!" She struck out at him with the spike heel of her shoe.

Andrew dodged the slashing four-inch heel. "What the hell are you doing? I'm trying to help you."

"You tried to push me over the railing!"

"No, I was pushing you out of the way."

"Out of the way of *what?*"

"That." He pointed to the shattered base of what must have been a huge clay planter. "It fell from the third floor balcony."

She struggled to sit up and clear her head. She could see what was left of the pot now. There were broken pieces of clay all around her, some of them large. Planters that size didn't fall all by themselves.

"I saw someone on the third floor," she said. "I think it was a woman."

He looked up, but there was no one there now. "Jesus," he breathed.

He whirled back on Marnie, and she braced automatically; she couldn't help herself. She was like a delayed stress victim in situations like this. Her survival instincts were swift and primitive, even though she'd begun to realize that he couldn't have done it.

"It could have cracked your skull," he said. "I pushed you out of the way. Why in hell would I want to hurt you, Marnie? *Why?*"

She sagged against the railing. He had a point. She was much more important to him alive than dead, which might make him the only person she actually could trust. But what a twisted reason to have to put your faith in someone. Her mind was still whirling. She'd just begun to feel safer with him, and now she was beginning to question everything again, especially this trip to Mirage Bay.

It had felt like a pragmatic move. She could have left him when she'd recovered enough, and started over again somewhere, but she hadn't. She'd known that she could never go back to her life in Mirage Bay, not with Alison's face and a murder charge if anyone discovered her real identity. But she'd needed to make sure her grandmother was all right. And maybe she'd wanted to believe Andrew's story that he'd been framed—and his promise that he would find a way to prove them both innocent.

Staying with him had seemed like her best option when she'd thought everything through. People who looked like Alison Fairmont could not easily disappear. Marnie could have melted into the forest and lived on nuts and berries. She could have blended with street people or hidden out in a trailer park, but not Alison. Marnie didn't know how to be Alison on the run. She would have been a dead giveaway.

He knelt and touched her forehead where some of the clay shards had hit her. "You're covered in blood," he said.

"I'm all right. You need to go look for whoever did it."

"And leave you like this? No way." Apparently the noise from the party had drowned out the sound of the crashing pot. No one had even looked over the railing to investigate.

He took his tuxedo coat and used it to blot her face. She let him do it because she couldn't see what needed to be done—and she wasn't sure she could have controlled herself. A strange inner tremor had invaded every muscle, every motor nerve.

"I'm taking you up to our room," he said, "and once I'm convinced you'll be safe there, I'm going to discover who did this."

"It's Alison, right? Someone's trying to kill Alison?"

"I don't know what they're trying to do, but I'm going to find out. And meanwhile, let's keep this to ourselves until I've had a chance to look around."

Marnie was happy enough to keep quiet. An attempt on her life at her own belated wedding reception seemed like the ultimate degradation. The last thing she wanted was all that attention focused on her. And it was important now that she have time alone to sort through all of it—from Julia to Bret to Tony Bogart to this—something she should have been doing from the beginning instead of sleeping her days away and avoiding the reality of what her life would be like when she finally came out of the closet as Alison.

Alison, she reminded herself. The attempt had been made on Alison, not Marnie. That was where she had to start.

At least she knew it wasn't Andrew. He'd been right here with her. Although, if she wanted to let her mind run amok—and why wouldn't it in a situation like this?—she could come up with a plausible explanation for Andrew having set the whole thing up.

It had been *his* idea to leave the party and come down here. What if he'd planned the attempt so that he could push her out of the way and once again be the hero? What was it now? Three times that he'd saved her?

She touched the copper ring again, wondering what it would take to make her feel safe now. "I'll go back to the room," she said, "but I want a gun."

Marnie leaned toward the bathroom mirror and gently worked at the gash on her temple with a warm, soapy washcloth. She'd already cleaned the rest of her face, which was a bloody mess from this wound on her head, but it was the only real injury she had. It didn't look deep enough to need stitches, but it would take a while to heal. Meanwhile she could cover it with her hair. She was lucky that Andrew's coat had protected the rest of her body from the flying shards of clay.

Andrew watched her in the mirror, wincing as she dabbed away at the dried, caked blood.

"Go easy," he said, "or you'll have a scar. Want me to help?"

"Yes, get me a gun."

His wince became a grimace. "No guns. People get hurt when guns are involved."

"People get hurt when giant pots are dropped from balconies. You're the one who said it could have cracked my skull."

She left the rag in the basin and grabbed a tissue from the box on the vanity. "Someone tried to kill me."

"No, they didn't."

She barely got the tissue to the oozing wound. "What?"

"Someone's trying to scare you, not kill you." He folded his arms and gave her a look that was patient and forbearing. "Dropping planters on people's heads isn't an efficient way to dispatch an enemy. In fact, it's sloppy, and no self-respecting murderer would bother."

"And *you're* the expert on self-respecting murderers?" Marnie's heart had begun to pound. Why was he acting like this was no big deal? "Why would someone want to scare me?"

"To see if you'll turn tail and run. You don't have a lot of fans around here, even among the immediate members of your family."

"It wasn't Bret, if that's what you're suggesting. I saw a woman."

"Can you describe her?"

"No, but I'm certain it was a woman." Unfortunately, Marnie couldn't tell him why she was sure. She didn't know herself. It was one of those lightning bolt realizations that left you with knots in your stomach because you couldn't back it up with details.

She looked at the tissue, which was soaked with blood. "Why haven't you gone up there to look for her?"

He pulled another tissue out of the box and handed it to her. "Because whoever did it is already gone. They were gone before we got back to this room."

If he was trying to reassure her, he was failing miserably. She kept thinking he was downplaying what had happened because he was somehow involved, but that possibility made her sick to her stomach. And she didn't understand how it would benefit him to have her killed, or even to scare her. It made no sense at all.

She had to put that kind of craziness away and start thinking more rationally. And most of all, she had to calm down instead of giving in to her worst fears. She was probably overreacting because she'd given up too much control to him. Dependence was a terrifying thing when you grew up believing people wanted to hurt you, and she had let herself become very dependent on Andrew Villard.

"You're probably right," she said, "but it's still a crime scene, and someone should check it out. If you're not going to, I will. She may have left clues that could identify her."

"I'll go, but I want to be sure you'll be okay here. Can you handle that cut by yourself?"

"Of course. All it needs is a bandage."

"Good. I'll tell Julia you're not feeling well, and ask her to make our apologies to the guests. I'd ask Rebecca to bring you up some tea, but there'd be too much explaining involved."

"I'm fine," Marnie insisted.

"Okay, I'll lock the room when I leave, and take the

key with me so I don't have to disturb you when I get back. Why don't you take one of those pills that help you sleep?"

She nodded, though she had no intention of taking a pill. "I could do that," she lied.

"I know you're frightened, and I'm not trying to downplay what happened. But I don't want you to obsess about this. I don't think we're dealing with a killer. I really don't."

She nodded again, wishing he would leave. "Right, me either." She fumbled through the medicine cabinet, looking for the bandages.

He touched her shoulder, hesitated, then gave it a quick squeeze. "Don't make me the bad guy," he said with a sigh. "I'm trying to help."

He seemed to know he wasn't getting through to her—and perhaps he even understood the impossibility of doing so. When she heard the lock turn over and click, she walked to the bathroom door to assure herself that he'd really gone. And then she let out the tension with a few choice words.

"Get the frigging hell out of this place, Marnie, while you still frigging can."

She drew back her hair and studied the earrings he'd given her, their beauty so exquisite it gave her a premonitory chill. She did not want to become another statistic, another victim of the curse that seemed to stalk the women in Andrew Villard's life. Alison had disappeared from his boat, his fiancée had drowned in his pool, and when he was a kid, his own mother, an opera singer, had been injured by stage rigging during a rehearsal. She'd gone into a coma and died.

That was too many accidents to be coincidental,

and yet that would probably be what he maintained.
She'd only asked him about it once, and he'd warned
her not to bring it up again. He'd clearly thought she
was accusing him of something. But she'd read the
clippings about Regine in the newspapers she'd found
in his office—and Julia had told her the rest.

*You did know that every woman who's loved him
has had a terrible accident, didn't you?*

Andrew moved quietly through the dark hallways
of the third floor. He didn't expect to find anyone, but
there was always a chance someone from the party on
the floor below might wander up. He doubted that
anyone had heard anything. The band had been playing when the clay pot hit, but things were pretty quiet
now. They were probably taking a break, and people
at these things tended to wander, looking for bath-
rooms—and places to have sex.

There was also the chance that someone might
have noticed that he and Marnie were missing, like
Julia. There were plenty of reasons to be cautious. He
hadn't been on the third floor until tonight, and didn't
know his way around. He and Alison had not been
welcome at Sea Clouds when they'd come to Mirage
Bay in February. They'd taken a vacation rental instead, and spent time on the boat. But Alison had been
preoccupied with trying to make contact with her
mother, who'd seemed reluctant even to take her calls.

He'd gotten to know his way around the house
when he and Alison were dating, and she'd invited
him on visits, but the third floor had been unfinished
then. Now it appeared to be as beautifully decorated
as the rest of the house, but largely unused. He'd

already discovered two guest rooms and a workout room as he moved quietly through the dark hallways, but the next room he found was the one he decided to search.

The old-fashioned billiards room was paneled with burnished mahogany walls and high ceilings. Tiffany lamps and wooden ceiling fans dominated the decor, but more importantly, this room opened onto the balcony where Marnie had said she'd seen someone at the railing.

Once outside, Andrew moved slowly toward the railing, cutting arcs across the stone deck with his penlight. He couldn't search the way he wanted to without drawing attention to himself, but at least there was no security to worry about. He'd convinced Julia it wasn't necessary to hire guards for tonight, that the band would have their own bodyguards.

But right now, the group was on a break, and the party was showing signs of slowing down.

Andrew's penlight picked up something bright. He knelt for a closer look. The faux amethyst looked like a gem that might have fallen off a piece of costume jewelry or summer clothing, possibly even a sandal. It was definitely something a woman would wear.

He picked it up and slipped it in his pocket, glad he'd found it before someone else did. He wasn't telling anyone, even Marnie, about this bit of evidence, if that's what it was. And once he'd finished here, he would go down to the ground floor terrace and clean up the mess from the broken pot.

He didn't want to give Julia any reason to call the police or feel she needed security for the house and grounds. He had plans of his own, and security guards would very much get in his way.

15

"Good grief, Rebecca!" Julia exclaimed. "How many calories do these apple croissants have?"

"Calories? I'm not sure. They're sugar-free."

Rebecca stopped putting the finishing touches on a plate of fresh fruit and picked up the package of croissants to look at the label. But Julia wanted to look for herself. She set her coffee mug on the bar where Rebecca was laying out breakfast, and snatched the package out of her hand.

"Sugar-free?" Julia pulled her reading glasses from her gamine bangs and propped them on her nose long enough to skim the ingredients list. "The calories aren't in the sugar. They're in the fat. Look at this—three hundred and fifty calories a serving. That's *one* croissant. I can't eat these things, and you shouldn't be eating them, either."

Marnie stood quietly by the windows, a steaming cup of black coffee in her hand. Watching Rebecca's reaction was painful, and Marnie burned with the need to defend her. Embarrassment crept up the assistant's pale throat in a crimson tide, the color so vibrant it reminded Marnie of California poppies.

Marnie palmed her coffee mug, relishing the satisfaction it would give her to empty it on Julia's over-bearing head. But she couldn't do anything that reckless this morning. She wasn't even supposed to be here, having breakfast with her "family."

Andrew had already dressed and gone by the time Marnie woke. He'd left a note saying he was taking care of the business they'd discussed, which Marnie assumed meant tracking down last night's assailant. He'd also made it clear that he expected her to stay in their room and avoid the rest of the family. She could say she was still recovering from her illness of the other night, but he didn't want anyone to know about the falling planter.

Marnie turned her gaze to the terrace beyond the windows. All traces of the clay pot that had shattered on the slate surface were gone. Andrew had cleaned it up last night. He'd said so in the note. He hadn't missed anything, really, and perhaps she should have been glad he was willing to go to so much trouble. He was determined not to let anything get in the way of his mission, not security guards or the police or even Julia's concerns—and part of his mission was proving Marnie innocent of Butch's murder. She really ought to be grateful—and cooperative.

But she hadn't been able to silence her own concerns. She wasn't ready to call them suspicions yet, but this morning, she'd needed to get out of that bedroom lockup and have a look around for herself, talk to the family, get a feel for the general mood of things.

Because of their bizarre alliance, Andrew had become her only point of reference, and she desperately needed another touchstone. She was too isolated, and he was too powerful. She had no idea how his investigation was going or whether he'd made any progress in her case. He didn't talk about it, and she hadn't been able to bring herself to question him. Maybe she didn't know the right questions to ask, or even feel she had the right to raise them. Somehow she had become his coconspirator in the ring of silence they'd created.

She could see the possibility of a kindred spirit in Rebecca, but Marnie would have to be careful there, too. She'd been picking up mixed signals from the woman since the beginning, especially where Bret was concerned. The two of them might even be aligned against her in some way, although that seemed a little too paranoid even for Marnie.

She brought the mug to her lips and blew to cool down the steamy brew. The coffee smelled delicious, but was still too hot to drink.

She had taken care to use makeup to mask the tiny abrasions on her cheek and throat. She was lucky there weren't more marks. The cut on her temple she'd covered with a clear bandage, and fluffed her hair over it. If anyone noticed, she was going to say she'd left the medicine cabinet door open and had run right into it. Keeping it simple was important, especially when you were lying through your teeth. She hated lies, and yet she was living a beaut, wasn't she.

Fortunately, no one had noticed anything amiss this morning, and there hadn't been a word said. Julia's main concern was whether her first party since Sea Clouds's makeover was a success.

"Nothing looks good this morning," Julia said, turning up her nose at the array of food. "I ate too much last night, dammit. Did you like the food, Alison? I hope that isn't what made you sick."

Marnie looked up, just realizing Julia was talking to her. "The food was wonderful, and so was the party. If anything, it was too good, too much excitement for a shut-in like me."

She had been reassuring Julia of that since the start of breakfast. *No, Andrew and I didn't leave because we weren't having a good time. I was getting a headache, and we thought a breath of fresh air might help. Yes, the Dave Matthews Band was a huge hit. Best party ever, really.*

Julia reached for the plate of fruit, grabbed her coffee mug and brought everything to the large wrought-iron table, where she picked through the melon slices and pineapple wedges, finally deciding on an enormous red strawberry.

"Come sit down, Alison, and have some fruit. Would you rather go outside? We can eat on the terrace."

"Not dressed for the terrace," Marnie said, indicating her bare shoulders. The halter-top sundress was one of the only things in Alison's closet that actually fit her. "It looks breezy out there."

Julia's nose wrinkled. "Are you sure you're all right? You don't look quite up to snuff. Is that makeup you're wearing?"

Marnie's fingers flew to her cheek. "Just a bit. Thought I needed a little color."

As Julia studied her, Marnie had a realization. She didn't understand how it was possible that Julia hadn't recognized that this *wasn't* her daughter, her flesh and blood. Marnie remembered reading somewhere that mothers could identify their child's T-shirt simply by smelling it, the bond was so powerful. It was biochemical, instinctive. A mother knew her child. How could Julia not?

Marnie's gut was telling her that something was terribly wrong with the Fairmonts. Julia was a self-involved nervous wreck, Bret was a rebellious mess and probably a borderline alcoholic, and Alison... well, Alison wasn't around to be observed, but if she'd done any of the things that Andrew suspected, she might be the most dysfunctional of the bunch.

Marnie had been an avid reader as a kid, but she'd had no money for books, so she'd read what Gramma Jo brought home from the library, which were all hard-core true crime books. If it was about a serial killer or a psychopath, it was right up Gramma's alley. Marnie hadn't really understood the predilection, but she'd learned a lot, and she remembered reading that sociopaths and psychopaths often had attachment issues. They weren't able to empathize with others and form normal bonds. No one really knew why. Some of them had been abused as children, but not all.

Marnie wondered if it was possible for a family of great wealth, breeding and social stature to have attachment issues. Now that she was living with the Fairmonts, her answer would have to be yes.

"I toasted some bagels," Rebecca said, apparently trying to atone with a plate of sliced bagels she offered Julia. "They're low-fat and so is the cream-cheese spread."

"Thank you, Rebecca, but I didn't ask for a *bagel*." Julia's tone was withering. "I suppose you'll have to eat them yourself, but maybe that was the plan?"

Marnie was about to break a fingernail on her coffee cup. She walked over and took the plate from Rebecca.

"I *love* bagels," she said. "And maybe I'll have one of those croissants, too. No, that's okay, Rebecca, I'll get it. You've done enough."

Marnie shrugged for Julia's benefit, as if to say what's a girl who likes to eat to do? She headed for the coffee bar, where Rebecca had retreated in confusion.

Marnie picked up a sparkling clean coffee mug and waggled it at Rebecca. "Can I get you some coffee while I'm here?"

Rebecca looked as if she didn't dare respond.

Julia sniffed and set down her melon wedge, apparently no longer able to eat in the presence of such idiocy. She took her coffee and walked to the window where Marnie had been standing.

None of this came as a great surprise to Marnie. Andrew had told her—and she'd witnessed it enough first-hand—that despite Julia's airs in public, she could be an incredible bitch in private. In a bad mood, she swore like a sailor and rained insults on whoever had set her off. Unfortunately for Rebecca, she seemed to be the usual target. She couldn't seem to do anything right. And neither could Bret, Marnie had noticed. Clearly, though, Alison was different. Despite having been banished for marrying Andrew, she had some kind of exemption that Marnie didn't understand.

Andrew swore he didn't understand it, either. And he wasn't sure that the real Alison ever had. It was a troubled and deeply complicated mother-daughter bond.

Marnie returned to the table, an apple croissant in hand.

"I need a workout after all that food and booze last night," Julia said. "How would you girls like to come to the club with me this morning? We'll pedal our asses off and everyone will feel better. "

She smiled brightly at both Marnie and Rebecca, apparently prepared to forgive them in exchange for some self-flagellation in the gym. No doubt it would also be a great chance for Julia to show off her prowess on the equipment.

Marnie bit into the croissant and actually spoke while she was chewing, determined to be more repugnant than Rebecca could ever hope to be. "Sorry, can't," she said. "I need to borrow the BMW to get some errands done."

Julia managed a graceful shrug. "Of course, darling. The car is yours whenever you want it. You know that. How about you, Rebecca? A workout would do us both good, yes?"

Marnie took another quick bite. Otherwise she might have told Julia how to do her evil self some good.

Rebecca's smile was sheepish and apologetic. "I'm expecting a call from your accountant this morning. There's an inquiry from the IRS that can't be put off. But I'll use the third-floor gym later. I've been working out up there lately. Thanks for suggesting it."

At the mention of the third floor, Marnie had the sudden awareness that she could be in the room with the culprit who'd dropped the planter. Her gut had told her it was a woman, and although there had been many female guests at the party, these two lived here and were intimately familiar with the third floor.

Somehow, she couldn't see Julia resorting to dropping pots. She must have more effective ways to deal with her enemies, like insulting them to death. And Rebecca was hardly the nefarious type, but who knew?

"Yummy bagel, Rebecca, thank you," Marnie said, making a point to pick up her dishes as she left the table, hoping in vain that Julia would get the hint that Rebecca was her assistant, not her slave.

As Marnie set the dishes next to the sink, she wondered what Andrew might have found on the third floor, if anything. She'd pretended to be asleep when he came in last night. A silly move, she realized now, but she'd still been mired in her own suspicions about him at the time.

This morning, he was gone, but she would make a point to ask him about it. She'd also go up herself for a look around. She could always use the excuse that she wanted some exercise. But for now, she had other plans. She was venturing not just out of her room, but out of the house. Andrew seemed reluctant to talk about his investigation, so Marnie had decided to do some reconnaissance on her own, starting with the main reason she'd agreed to come back to Mirage Bay.

What Marnie remembered as she got out of the car was the heat. It had been brutally hot and dry that February afternoon. The air had smelled of scorched creosote from the fires in the hills, and the devil winds had stung her skin with burning sand.

But the lush oak glen behind her gramma's cottage was cool and dark and mossy green, and the tidal pool was as slick as a mirror. Only one spindly creature, a daddy longlegs gliding across the surface of the water, disturbed the eerie calm.

The tide wouldn't be high enough for bathing until that evening, but Marnie couldn't wait. She was going to float on her back like a seal. She stripped off the thin linen shift she wore on blistering days like this, and then realized she might not be alone—

The sound of a car door banging shut brought Marnie back to the present. She had shut the door herself. She was home.

She slammed her fist to her chest, and tears welled, despite her fierce attempt to hold them back. She had thought she would never see this place again. The old cedar-shake cottage she'd grown up in still looked as if it was about to slide off its foundation. The front porch was several inches lower on one side, and the overhang sagged in the middle like a canvas awning. Termites, probably. They'd been eating away at the place for as long as Marnie could remember.

But the cottage could have been a pile of rotting wood and it would still have been beautiful to her, still a monument to the best and purest moments of her childhood. Nothing had changed since she'd left. Except her. She used to be pure, too.

She had agreed not to meet with her grandmother, but she hadn't said she wouldn't visit the cottage, and there was no one here now.

Marnie started for the porch, dust billowing around her sandaled feet. The morning air already had the smell of a hot day about it. The baking sun had turned the surface of the clay path to powder, and the wooden porch was creaking before she'd stepped foot on it. Marnie loved hot summer days, even when they dried you up like a raisin.

She hesitated at the sound of a sudden burst of

laughter coming from inside the cottage, but it didn't sound like her grandmother. As Marnie stepped onto the porch, she saw that the front door was ajar. Had someone broken in?

She burned with outrage. What could Gramma Jo possibly have that anyone would want? She was old and poor. It infuriated Marnie that the most vulnerable became targets simply because they were the least able to defend themselves. There was something horribly twisted about that.

She wet her lips, weighing her options. She couldn't do anything crazy. Her grandmother might be in there with the intruder, but Marnie didn't think so. Someone was taking advantage of Gramma Jo's absence.

She crept across the creaky porch to the door. Shock rolled through her as she peeked through the narrow opening and saw a man and woman in a heated embrace. The man's back was to Marnie, which concealed both of them as they kissed and writhed against the back wall. They had their clothes on, but that wasn't going to last long. He was unbuttoning her blouse and she was tugging hard on his belt loops, trying to get his pants down.

Marnie was now certain her grandmother wasn't there and the intruders were taking advantage of that. But they weren't robbing her family home. They were turning it into a cheap motel.

She banged on the door frame. "Hello? Anyone home? Josephine Hazelton?"

A mad scramble ensued inside. The woman squealed and began buttoning herself up, and the man shot out the back door and was gone before Marnie could get a look at him.

She banged again. "Hello? Who's there?"

She thought the woman might try to make a run for it, too, but a moment later the door swung open. All her clothing was buttoned now, but the amorous intruder did not even have the decency to look sheepish about the situation she found herself in. The smile on her face was defiant, and Marnie was stunned when she saw who it was.

16

"LaDonna Jeffries? What are you doing here?"

"Excuse me?" LaDonna struck a haughty pose when she saw who it was at the door. "I could ask *you* the same question."

Marnie reminded herself that her friend from years past thought she was dealing with Alison Fairmont, whom she obviously didn't like. Marnie caught the insignia on LaDonna's untucked blouse and realized she must be on a lunch break from the drugstore. It gave all new meaning to the phrase hot lunch.

"I came to see Gramma Jo," Marnie said, thinking quickly. "I heard she makes a natural soap with the herbs from her garden. It's supposed to be good for sensitive skin."

In reality, Marnie *had* been trying to help her grandmother develop an herbal soap before the accident, but she didn't know whether or not Gramma Jo had gone on with it.

LaDonna tweaked her blouse into place. "I don't know anything about that. She asked me to keep an eye on her house while she was gone, and I'm trying to help out. I come three times a week to water her plants."

She was doing a good job of getting her own garden watered, too, but Marnie kept her mouth shut about that. "Do you know when she'll be back?"

"She had to go to the hospital. But that was like a month ago."

"The hospital?" Marnie's voice nearly turned to a squeak. For a moment she couldn't find the breath to speak. "Are you sure?"

At LaDonna's nod, she asked, "Was something wrong with her?"

"She never did say, and I didn't want to pry. She called and asked if I would watch the place, and she told me where the key was. But she acted like she didn't know how long she'd be gone."

There had to be some mistake. "I'd heard she might be going on a cruise," Marnie said.

"That may be what she was telling people. Maybe she didn't want to deal with a lot of personal questions. Actually, I think it was more like a nursing facility than a hospital, but I don't have the name."

"Do you know if she's all right?" Marnie's heart was racing, and she told herself to calm down. Alison would not have been panicking like this over Gramma Jo.

"No, and I haven't heard a word from her. I've been asking around, but nobody else has heard anything from her, either. It's weird, like she just disappeared." Worry clouded LaDonna's expressive brown eyes. "I've been a family friend for years, and I really love Gramma Jo. I wish she hadn't been so secretive about where she was going."

Marnie was grateful for that much. It helped to know that someone shared her concerns, and

LaDonna *was* a family friend. "I don't see her car here. Did she drive herself to the facility?"

The family car had been an ancient station wagon, and in the early days before the flea market, Gramma had parked alongside the road and sold her vegetables and her wares right out of the back. She'd told fortunes in those days, too. Marnie could remember her asking customers for a personal item, which she'd clutch in her palm.

Marnie never knew whether Gramma had the "sight" or not, but some people swore her predictions came true. Gramma should have warned them all about February second.

"I don't know that, either," LaDonna was saying. "One day she was here, and the next day she was gone, but she took hardly anything with her that I could see."

"That is strange." Marnie had been racking her brain, but she wasn't aware that Gramma Jo had any health problems. Of course, grief and worry took their toll on the body, and her grandmother wasn't a young woman. Marnie could hardly bear the thought that this was her fault. She would not be able to forgive herself.

Whoops of excitement drifted up from the beach. Beyond the sand dunes, maybe a couple hundred feet away, a mother with two young children was laying out a blanket, apparently for a picnic on the sand. They all wore their swimsuits, and the kids were dragging inner tubes as big as them toward the gentle surf.

"I don't know what to do besides keep my eye on the place," LaDonna said.

And meet your creepy boyfriend here, Marnie

thought. Her stomach was churning, but it wasn't because of her old friend's sex life. LaDonna had always been a sucker for male attention. She traded sex for love, and wondered why she never felt good about herself, much less loved.

Marnie was worried sick about her grandmother, who'd lived on this patch of land her whole life. It had been left to her by the eccentric maiden aunt who'd raised her, and Gramma Jo had nothing else as far as Marnie knew, certainly not insurance to pay for medical care and hospital stays. There were no other relatives, either. Gramma Jo had married briefly after dropping out of high school, but found she had nothing in common with a young husband whose sole interests were drinking beer and working on junker cars. She'd kept the name, but happily said goodbye to the man. There'd been no one else until Marnie came into her life many years later.

Marnie fought to keep her voice detached when she spoke. "I guess that's about all you can do," she said. "I'm sorry to hear about Gramma Jo. I hope she's okay."

She wanted to say more as she stepped back to leave. LaDonna had shown an appalling lack of respect for her grandmother's home, and Marnie wanted to extract promises that LaDonna would actually water the flowers and lock the place up tight—and most of all, stop turning it into a love shack. But she doubted that Alison would have cared about any of that, and once again, Marnie couldn't take the chance.

Like every obsessed investigator, Tony Bogart had a love-hate relationship with crime scenes. He was intimately familiar with the frustrations of coaxing forensic secrets from a blood-spattered bedroom or a barroom back alley. He'd heard all the analogies to seduction. Probably he'd compared too many of life's frustrations to sex and women, but not when it came to crime scenes.

The allure wasn't about seducing secrets from dead bodies and inanimate objects. It wasn't about the guesswork. It was about the inevitable—the return of the suspect. Tony lived by the age-old theory that the perpetrator could not resist his own sense of horror or triumph or whatever other irresistible emotion had held him in thrall when he committed the crime.

He had to return to the scene to be a witness to his own guilt. Or genius. Sometimes it was to try and undo what he'd done, but every perpetrator came back. Even if he revisited the crime only in his mind, he showed up. Always. They all did. And most showed up in the flesh.

This morning was no exception. Tony had only been hoping for one suspect. He got three, maybe four.

The crime scene was the tide pool hidden on the oak glen behind Josephine Hazelton's cottage, where his brother, Butch, had been murdered. Tony had been keeping an eye on the place since he got back. He'd noticed immediately that it was vacant, and he'd found out from the nearest neighbor that Gramma Jo had been gone for about a month, but the neighbor didn't know anything more than that.

This morning Tony had noticed activity in the cottage, and he'd decided to stake it out long enough to see who was inside. He hadn't been there fifteen minutes when he'd had the good fortune to see Alison Fairmont drive up and get out of her car.

Of course, Alison was already a suspect, but her strange behavior this morning had cemented that in his mind. For no reason that Tony could understand except guilt, Alison stood by her BMW convertible, staring at Josephine Hazelton's ramshackle cottage, and cried as if her heart would break.

Tony was hidden in the glen, near the pool where Butch had been killed. He'd been waiting for Alison to come over to the actual scene, but maybe her guilt was too great for that. Or maybe she'd noticed the activity in the house, too. Alison had never struck him as having a functioning conscience, which was why the tears had surprised him.

He watched her take the steps to the porch, and from there it got even more interesting. Alison had barely knocked on the front door when Bret Fairmont scrambled out the back, trying to stuff his hard-on into his pants, which wasn't easy when you were running.

Not all investigators would have pegged Bret as a suspect, but Tony had no problem making that leap. Having sex in or near a crime scene was one of the weird things some perpetrators did, especially if the original crime was sexual in nature. There'd been no evidence of a sexual assault on Butch, but that didn't mean his murderer might not have been a gay man who'd come on to Butch and then killed him after being rejected. That would make even more sense if Bret were a homophobe who couldn't admit his homosexual tendencies. Tony had no proof that Bret was gay, but a serious investigator thought in terms of all possibilities.

He'd quickly moved to a cover that allowed him to get a better look at the front door, but he'd also cursed himself for not carrying a camera. He'd missed several beautiful blackmail shots. He would have used them to extract information rather than money, but he would have used them.

Apparently Alison didn't see her brother flee out the back. She kept banging on the door, almost as if she was angry. Tony waited for another unzipped male to follow Bret, but it didn't happen that way. Instead, a woman appeared at the front. Women rarely returned to the scene of a crime for sex, but this one just might have.

LaDonna Jeffries? Suspect number three?

It was beginning to look like a high school reunion.

Tony couldn't get close enough to hear their conversation, but he could see the tension in their exchange. LaDonna had her arms crossed and her chin high, the classic defensive posture. Alison looked angry at first, and then, strangely, anxious. Tony knew the two women weren't friends, but he wouldn't have thought them enemies. Watching them, he wasn't so sure.

The conversation had ended abruptly, and Alison had seemed in a hurry to go. LaDonna left moments after Alison drove away. She'd jogged down the gravel road in her Skeetcher tennis shoes, apparently to wherever she'd parked her car so it wouldn't be seen.

Tony had decided not to follow either woman, intending to check out the house instead. But the surprises weren't over yet. Another car pulled up just after he retrieved the key that LaDonna had left under the mat, and let himself into the cottage. Tony ducked out the back door, just as Bret had done.

But Tony didn't sprint for the woods. He glued himself to the outside wall by the door, which he'd left open a crack. And now he was observing suspect number four.

Andrew Villard entered through the unlocked front door and scanned the room, apparently to assure himself that he was alone.

Tony watched him quickly work his way from the living room to the kitchen, going through the drawers and the cabinets, checking the messages by the phone and the notes stuck to the refrigerator with magnets. He used a tissue to avoid prints, which was interesting. But if he was looking for something specific, he didn't seem to find it.

When he disappeared into the cottage's only bedroom, Tony slipped inside and crept to the doorway to watch him. Villard had stopped at one of the dressers, and he was looking at some pictures of Josephine Hazelton and her granddaughter, the missing Marnie. He took a snapshot from the mirror and slipped it into his pants pocket. A small jewelry box caught his attention next. He bent down, looking closely at the box, quickly checked the contents, then slipped it into his pocket, as well.

He wasn't stealing from the woman. No one stole a snapshot.

What the hell was he doing?

He went through the rest of the bedroom, carefully searching dresser drawers, cabinets and closets. A paisley shawl in soft pinks and greens was lying on the bed as if it had been tossed there. He picked it up, but didn't take it with him.

When Villard left the house, he went straight to the

scene of the crime. He made his way around behind the cottage to the oak glen where the murder had taken place. He walked the perimeter of the pool, taking in everything around him. A natural formation of boulders created a path that extended a few feet into the pool, and when he reached the last stone, he knelt and measured the depth of the water with a branch he'd picked up.

Maybe he was trying to recreate the scene in his mind. Tony couldn't figure it out, but as Villard stared at the shiny black water, he looked disturbed, even shaken.

That was when Tony realized that he himself had no such feelings about this place. His brother had died here. Butch had been butchered, yet Tony felt little more than a flicker of irony at the gallows pun. That was wrong. It was sick. He should have been enraged. The victims of violent crime deserved that, even his asshole brother. They deserved justice, and yet all Tony cared about was solving the puzzle, winning the game, getting the prize. Sometimes, he wondered why.

Tony put the soul-searching out of his mind when Villard tossed the measuring stick away and left the glen. Moments later, as the man got into his car, Tony crept through the trees to the side road where he'd hidden the Vette, and waited for Andrew to drive by. Tony wouldn't need to follow closely. The rooster tail of dust would tell him which way Andrew had gone, even when he got to the main road. It would also hide Tony's car from his view.

Tony tailed Andrew to Mirage Bay, where he pulled up in front of the local jeweler's shop and went in. Fifteen minutes later, he came out and walked across the street to a real estate office. Tony could venture a guess as to the reason for those visits, but he would wait until Villard left the area before he confirmed his suspicions.

Of all the visitors to Josephine Hazelton's house that morning, Villard was the only one who had ventured to the actual crime scene, but Tony had to admit that he was the least likely suspect. He was an outsider with no real connection to Butch and no particular motive to harm him.

Butch had more reason to want to harm Villard. A normal kid might have hated the guy because he'd stolen his brother's girl, but Butch had never been normal, although he did once confide to Tony that he hated Villard's guts because Villard had done something to embarrass him in front of his friends. Butch hadn't gone into detail, and Tony hadn't pressed. They'd never been close that way.

As much as Tony wanted to nail the French bastard, he didn't have the goods on him. Not yet, anyway. And there was something far more intriguing about Villard. Tony had had him under surveillance for several days, and with the exception of this morning, he was starting to see a pattern in Villard's movements. The man had an objective, but unfortunately, it didn't make any sense to Tony. Andrew Villard seemed to be investigating the death of a woman who was very much alive.

His wife.

Julia took great pleasure in gazing at her new circlet bracelet as she drove through the light afternoon traffic on the San Diego Freeway. She didn't have to take her eyes off the road because her hands were right there in front of her, and the way the round-cut diamonds caught the sun was dazzling.

She didn't think of that kind of pleasure as bad, although her mother would have. Eleanor would have called it materialistic. But how could it be wrong to take so much pleasure from just one new piece of jewelry? She wasn't bringing home bags of baubles, thousand-dollar designer shoes or Citation jets, even though she could well afford them. It was one bracelet, and it made her happy when so little else could these days.

Julia relaxed her grip on the wheel. Her knuckles had gone white around edges just from thinking about her mother. Eventually she would tire of the bracelet and buy something new and sparkly to boost her spirits, but that might be months, even years from now. She still loved her S600 Mercedes, too, and it wasn't new. She understood value. She'd bought a car that would last.

She spotted the sign for her freeway exit ahead and glanced in the rearview mirror, getting ready to change lanes. As she did she saw the car behind her moving with her. The dark green sedan followed her from the fast lane of the freeway into the middle. Julia didn't think much about it. Southern California freeways were hell in the best of circumstances, and she liked to be in the exit lane well ahead of time.

She was also dreading this afternoon's rendez-vous. She'd gotten carried away at the gym, and she was running late. But that was probably intentional. She didn't like how things had been going with her lawyer, Jack Furlinghetti. He was stringing her along, playing her, and there was little she despised more than being played.

As she got ready to change lanes again, she checked both mirrors, rear and side, and saw that the car was still with her. Curious, she began to pay attention. The sedan took the exit with her, too. The sun was reflecting against the windshield, and she couldn't see the driver, but the vehicle looked like a standard midsize four-door, nothing fancy.

Julia turned right at the exit, and the other car did, too. The sun was coming from a different angle now, silhouetting the driver, and Julia thought it might be a woman. She could see what looked like long hair, although she couldn't make out any details.

When the sedan was still with her at the next turn, she fished her cell out of her purse and, with one hand, keyed in the speed dial code for Jack Furlinghetti's cell phone. She knew he wouldn't be in his office. He was waiting for her in a motel room, hopefully not as sleazy as the last one.

He answered on the first ring. "Where are you?"

He must have seen her number come up on the display. "I'm being followed, Jack. I think it's a woman. It might even be…my assistant."

Julia hadn't realized she suspected it was Rebecca until she'd said it. She glanced in the mirror again, trying to get a better look at the car and the license. Rebecca drove an old Volkswagen Rabbit. It couldn't be her—unless she'd picked up a rental. Julia still couldn't see the driver clearly. Rebecca normally wore her hair up. The color might have been hers, reddish-brown, but with the bright sun, she couldn't tell.

"Lose her and get over here. You wrote down the directions, right?"

"I'm not coming, Jack. It's not safe. We'll have to reschedule."

"You're going to be sorry. I had a surprise for you."

"Really?" Her voice was singsong. Heh heh. Wink Wink. "What kind of surprise, Jack?"

He snickered, and Julia grimaced. Her mother was right; she had no morals. Jack Furlinghetti redefined the word *revolting,* but she was worse. She was encouraging his revoltingness, exploiting it.

"I want an answer, Jack. Are you are going to cooperate?"

"Only if you do. Get your awesome ass over here."

"Apparently you'd like a threesome? You, me and my tail?"

"Is that a trick question?" In a different tone, he added, "Julia, you know what I mean."

"I'll call you back to reschedule," she said, clicking off the phone. Bastard. She would have to find another way to deal with him. Would her mother think her immoral if she strung him up by his balls? Probably not. It might be the first thing Eleanor would heartily approve of.

A horn blared, reminding Julia that she wasn't paying attention to the road. She tossed her cell phone in the passenger seat. They really should pass a law against the nasty things.

When she glanced back at the mirror, the sedan was gone.

Jack Furlinghetti finished off the soft drink he'd gotten from the vending machine in the motel lobby.

He dropped the can in the wastebasket, not quite sure what he'd been drinking. The medication he was on blunted his senses and made everything taste the same, but he'd had a thirst that had to be quenched, and the vending machine had been handy.

The motel room was a disaster, small, stuffy and claustrophobic. Even for a guy with a seedy motel fantasy, he had to admit that this was a challenge. The decrepit air conditioner had wheezed its last almost as soon as he'd turned it on, and the building was about as well insulated as a sardine can.

He sat on the bed and picked up his cell, smiling at the rusty creak of the box springs. He had phone calls to make. It wasn't easy accounting for all the time he'd been away from the office lately. And Julia wouldn't have liked his surprise, anyway. There wasn't going to be any sex today, at least nothing exotic. Just some bad news for the lady of the house. Julia didn't know it yet, but she wasn't getting what she wanted.

His mind went oddly blank as he stared at the cell's keypad, trying to remember his office number. The phone was new and he hadn't programmed it yet. What the hell was that number? He hated not having information at his fingertips.

He reached inside his suit jacket, snagged a packet with two tiny red tablets, ripped it open and swallowed them both without water.

Give yourself a minute. You'll be fine, dude. Superman.

The bed groaned loudly as he got up and walked to the grimy second-floor window. He wrestled it open, looking for a breeze. The parking lot was empty, except for a dented compact car and his silver Porsche, which stuck out like a handful of sore thumbs.

No, Julia wasn't getting what she wanted. And neither was anyone else in the Fairmont family. He wasn't giving control of the trust fund over to any of those desperate losers, no matter what they did. Both Bret and Andrew, the son-in-law, had paid him visits to make discreet inquiries. Jack was a little surprised neither of them had offered him sex. The only one he hadn't heard from was Alison, who had a legitimate claim—and hadn't breached the morals clause. Yet.

Of course, if *she* were to offer him sex...

But there were other, smarter ways to deal with her. He grunted and shut the window, which was nothing but a conduit for the drippy heat.

Now, Eleanor Driscoll, there was a woman after an attorney's heart. That crazy morals clause she'd come up with practically guaranteed that her female progeny would screw themselves out of the money, so to speak. Of course, it could be legally challenged in a heartbeat, but who among the proud and prominent Fairmonts wanted their dirty laundry aired in court? And Jack would make sure it was a packed courtroom and not some closed session with a hired private judge.

Eleanor was quite a dame, and probably as hot as a cherry bomb in her prime. Who else would think in terms of moral clauses except someone struggling to contain his or her own rampant libido?

The office phone number—555-2100—popped into his head, thanks to the pills. One of his clients had been supplying him with smart pills that did everything from jump-start your memory to make you an analytical genius. He hated game shows, but had found himself watching *Jeopardy* and acing the questions before the contestants could hit the button. It was unreal. Of course, it was illegal, too. Not narcotic illegal, just not approved for use by the FDA.

Not that he really needed to be any smarter. The people he dealt with were endlessly stupid. What made being an estate lawyer so easy and lucrative was how efficiently most people, especially the wealthy, fucked up their lives and brought about their own financial downfalls. Jack hardly had to do any work at all.

He glanced over his shoulder at his depressing surroundings. Time to pack up and say goodbye to this dive. He also needed to replenish his supply of pills. He'd found only one packet in his suit jacket. Possibly he'd been taking more than he realized.

17

The misty pink clouds sat like scoops of strawberry ice cream on the lavender hills, and the evening air was heavy with the sweetness of star jasmine. It was cocktail hour at the Fairmont mansion, and Julia and Bret were sipping what looked like champagne cocktails when Andrew joined them on the terrace.

"Can I get you a drink?" Rebecca asked, approaching him with a tray of appetizers.

"No, thanks." He carefully dodged her as he walked over to Julia, who'd taken possession of a chaise longue under a huge Kentia palm.

Whether intentional or not, the slit of Julia's sarong skirt had fallen open to reveal enough skin to make you wonder if she was wearing underwear. And the glazed smile told him this wasn't her first drink.

Bret, on the other hand, looked stone-cold sober as he stood at the railing, his back to the ocean, watching Andrew with a glower.

Andrew's gut tightened. Maybe *he* had better watch for falling pots. Bret was positively malevolent tonight.

Andrew turned to Julia. "Have you seen Alison? She's not in the room, and there's no note. When I left she wasn't feeling well."

Julia sloshed her drink a bit as she set it down. "I have no idea where she is. I haven't seen her since breakfast. Is everything all right?"

Andrew tried to quiet the uneasiness he felt. "Everything's fine. She probably went for a walk."

"At this time of day?"

"People do take walks before dinner."

"Maybe in Long Island," Julia murmured. "Here, we walk after dinner."

"I saw her go," Bret said. "She hit the beach about an hour ago, wandering around like she was in some kind of trance. She's probably halfway to San Diego by now."

"See there?" Julia said, beckoning for Rebecca. "Join us in a drink, Andrew. Alison is fine. She knows her way around."

"Are you kidding?" Bret came off the railing. "She didn't even know her own name. I shouted at her several times, and she didn't look up."

Andrew didn't smile. "My guess is she didn't want to talk to you."

Bret smiled, but it was vicious. "My guess is she *doesn't* know her own name."

"Bret, don't be ridiculous," Julia said impatiently. "Rebecca, I need another drink. And bring something for Andrew."

Andrew looked hard at Bret, trying to size him up. It could just be more of his spoiled-brat routine, the sibling rivalry garbage. But if Bret had figured out that Marnie wasn't his sister, and he intended to try and prove it, then Andrew had one more time bomb on his hands. He could feel the pressure mounting as he weighed Bret's open hostility against Julia's inebriation. Were either of them capable of masterminding an elaborate frame-up scheme? One was becoming more aggressive, the other seemed to be cracking up. It could be either of them.

Rebecca hurried over with a tray of drinks, which Bret neatly intercepted, since Andrew was already on his way to the ramp that led to the stairs to the beach.

"Don't hold dinner," Andrew called back. "I'm going for a walk."

It seemed to take forever to get down the several steep flights of steps, and he found the shore nearly deserted when he got there. This was a public beach that often got crowded during the day, but most people packed up and went home around dinnertime.

The sun was dropping and the breeze getting chilly. To the north, he could see all the way to the Mirage Bay pier, where the neon lights of the arcade were already blazing. To the south the beach wound around the cliffs, and his visibility was limited. Bret hadn't said which way she'd gone, but he'd mentioned San Diego. That was south.

Andrew glanced back up at the terrace. Bret stood at the railing, looking down. Rebecca was right next to him.

Andrew went south.

Andrew was on the path from the beach to Gramma Jo's house when he saw Marnie walking toward him. She was gripping something in her hand, and she'd left the front door of the cottage hanging open. Apparently she'd walked all the way from the Fairmont mansion to get here, which was well over a mile, by his estimation. He'd just made the same trip himself, and he could feel the strain in his legs.

She advanced with her head high and her face stricken. Even the wild dark hair flying around her couldn't hide the raw emotion he saw. She already knew the news he'd been planning to break to her. Her grandmother was gone, but not on a cruise. He'd done enough checking to discover that no one actually knew where Josephine Hazelton was.

But Marnie didn't want comfort. He could see that, too. Pain bristled from her like porcupine quills. It was her barrier. And he had to respect that. He'd always admired her nerve. Another woman might have allowed him to take her in his arms and comfort her, even Alison. But not this one. She would have turned him into a pillar of salt.

She stopped three feet in front of him and held up a shawl that shimmered with rainbow-sherbet hues and was fringed with long white tassels.

"Marnie? What's wrong?"

"She didn't take her wrap with her. She never went anywhere without this."

"That's your grandmother's wrap?"

Marnie unclenched her fingers and tried to smooth the wrinkles from the fragile silk material. The tassels bounced around, getting in her way.

Andrew didn't attempt to help her. This was sacred territory.

"She would *never* have left it behind," Marnie said. "It belonged to her aunt, and she was superstitious that way."

Now she was trying to fold the slippery material into something smaller and neater, something manageable.

"Let's go sit on the porch and talk," he suggested.

"No, I can't."

The dark hair fell away from her face as she looked up at him. Her intensity actually spooked him at times, the wary chill in her eyes, the sullen heat in her mouth. She was wild at heart, frightened—and frightening. But it was the kind of fear that attracted a man, called out to him like the sirens on the rocks, whispering an invitation and threatening to wreck you if you took it.

He felt a stirring in his groin and hated himself for the impulse. He couldn't go there, couldn't even let himself think about going there.

"Something terrible has happened to my grandmother," she said. "She's gone, and she didn't leave any clues, nothing for me to find. Not even a note."

He quieted his voice. "Why would she have left you a note, Marnie? She thought you were dead."

Pain pierced her gaze, but she went on talking. "She told my friend LaDonna that she was going to a hospital of some kind, but I didn't find any record of that, no phone number, no doctor's name."

"Marnie, it won't be that hard to find her. There aren't that many hospitals in the area."

He wasn't sure she'd heard him. She'd tucked the shawl under her arm for safekeeping, and all he could think about was how young she was. Not how young she looked. She *was* young, twenty-two, and seriously inexperienced, he suspected. She hardly looked different than the day he'd pulled Butch and his thug friends off her. But that was Marnie and this was Alison. Alison with Marnie's eyes and Marnie's soul.

It was amazing how a personality could change the face.

"It's one thing to ruin my own life," she said. "I have to live with that and with what I did to Butch. But I didn't ever want to hurt her. She gave her whole life to raising me."

Andrew glanced past her to the house and the small forest of oak trees behind it. He wondered if she'd gone into the glen and tried to face down that horror. It could account for her state of mind.

"It's getting late," he said. "Let's start walking back."

She searched his face, as if seeking something, but with little hope of finding it. Was he to be trusted? Was anyone?

Anguish. Those were the waters she swam in. The despair in her expression made him feel helpless—and Christ, he hated that feeling.

"I'll find your grandmother," he said. "I promise."

Goose bumps rippled down her bare arms. It almost looked painful. She averted her gaze, but began to nod. He wasn't sure why.

"Let's walk," she said.

The light was fading quickly as they walked back, and the beach was nearly empty, except for a few die-hard surfers and some families packing up to go home. It was too late for swimming and too early for beach fires, which made it quiet and peaceful, but lonely, too.

They'd walked probably a mile when she stopped and turned to him.

"Thank you," she said.

"For what?"

"For listening to me. I must have sounded pretty crazy."

"You're frightened and worried. That's not the same as crazy."

"Yeah." She nodded, and they walked a few more feet. He stopped this time.

"I have something of yours," he said. "I'm not sure this is the right time but I think you should have it. I was at your grandmother's cottage this morning. I'd been to the flea market, trying to get more information on her. I talked to several people this time, and most of them expressed concerns about the cruise she was supposed to have gone on. They said she'd been away too long. They hadn't seen her in weeks."

He took the jewelry box from his jacket. "This was on her dresser. According to the writing on the box, it belongs to you. I thought you might like to have it."

He opened the box, and she moved closer for a look at the delicate gold chain inside. It sparkled in the low pink light.

"My grandmother gave me this when I was a kid so I could wear the copper penny around my neck," she said. "I wore it night and day until the chain broke. We never had the money to get it fixed, but…" Marnie took the chain from the box, letting it hang from her fingers. "It's not broken anymore."

"She must have had it done after you disappeared. Apparently she did believe you were coming back."

She opened the clasp, took the battered copper ring from the pocket of her shorts and looped the chain through the penny. "She actually believed the ring would protect me, and at first, I wore it mostly to humor her. Can you put it on me?" she asked, handing it to him.

As he fastened the chain around her neck, he

realized that this was the reason she would stay. None of his promises to exonerate her meant anything to her, really. They weren't persuasive, but this was. She would not be able to leave until her grandmother was found. And Andrew needed her to stay. All of his meticulous planning would blow sky-high without her—and it might blow anyway. He hadn't received another blackmail threat since the first one, but he could feel it coming in his gut. Time was running out.

He needed to focus on that instead of the curve of her neck—and how vividly he could remember the line of that curve as she lay in naked slumber in her perpetually darkened bedroom in Long Island. That was inappropriate right now, and it would be inappropriate later, too, because he'd promised her there wasn't going to be any sex, and himself that there wouldn't be any more thoughts of it.

And she was so goddamn young.

"Why do you let her do it to you, Reb?"

"Do what?" Sweat dripped from Rebecca's brow as she pumped away on the elliptical trainer, ignoring Bret Fairmont as best she could. She grabbed the towel and mopped her forehead, wishing she hadn't stripped down to her sports bra and bicycle shorts. She hated the thought that he could see the rolls of flesh created by the strangling tightness of her shorts.

He was a pig, even when he tried to be nice to her. He didn't understand her life—never would, never could, and probably didn't care enough to bother. That made him a pig.

"Why do you let her take her frustrations out on you?" he said. "Tell her to fuck off."

Right, just like you *tell her to fuck off?*

He was standing in the doorway of the workout room, and Rebecca was on the elliptical trainer facing the windows that looked out at the terrace. She could see him in her peripheral vision, cocky and artlessly gorgeous in his trunks and tank top, but she preferred the view out the window, which was pitch-black oblivion, except for the lights on the terrace.

Bret definitely brought out the worst in her. She'd been raised by strict parents who had taught her to be unfailingly polite, but somehow when he got her alone, he could always provoke her into trading barbs. If only she had the nerve now to tell him to leave her *alone.* She would be changing machines in a minute, which would bring her face-to-face with his insinuating smirk.

Some people could invade your privacy just by being within eyeshot. He was like that with her. He took…liberties.

He would laugh at the word, she knew. *Liberties.* Pig.

"You want some water?" He walked over to the watercooler and poured himself a cup. "You're going to get dehydrated the way you're sweating."

"I want to sweat," she mumbled. "Water weight."

She mopped herself with the towel again, her face, her neck, even her cleavage this time. Let him look. Let him lust over her voluptuousness. The thought would have made her convulse with laughter, except that he actually had lusted once. He'd been a man with a mission. Maybe he only got hot for women who were totally unlike his mother. Some men had kinks that way.

He drank the water and crushed the cup. "You need to be more assertive, Reb."

The wall behind him was floor-to-ceiling mirrors, which seemed to accentuate his height and his leanness. If anything, he might be too lean, in her opinion, but the width of his shoulders saved him from skinniness. They made his torso a lovely elongated triangle.

Of course, the mirrors did the opposite with her body. She could see every flaw—her love handles and her double chin, and now they were glistening with sweat. Ugh.

It took courage, but she got herself a fresh towel from the linen cabinet that she kept stocked, and walked over to her machine, which was next to the water cooler.

"Excuse me," she said, waiting for him to get out of the way. Her heart was pounding so hard she could feel the tick of blood through the veins in her throat.

His smile was sexy, mocking. "That's not assertive."

He meandered over. She thought about standing her ground, but that didn't last when he moved into her space, her breathing space. She was still panting from her workout, and she could feel the heat emanating off her body. He must be able to feel it, too. She was burning up.

She took a half step back.

"You shouldn't let anybody push you around," he said.

He reached out and touched her mouth, fondling her lower lip. For some reason, she didn't move as he trailed his thumb over its fullness. The unwelcome caress ignited a shower of sparks in the depths of her belly.

"Did I ever tell you how much I like your lips?"

"Probably."

He smiled. "If you were more assertive, you wouldn't let me be doing things like this…kissing you when you don't want to be kissed."

She reached up to knock his hand away, but he hooked her wrist and pulled her close. "Kissing the shit out of you," he said, as his mouth came down on hers.

Rebecca's head was thrown so far back she couldn't get her balance. She flailed and grabbed him by the hair. The point was to yank it, and she thought that's what she was doing, but his moans told her that she was encouraging him. And then, suddenly, she *was* encouraging him.

She gripped his head with her clawing fingers, prolonging the kiss. She was moaning, too, and panting, and grabbing at him with her other hand. His back, his hip, his butt. She squeezed his cheek and he nearly crushed her in his excitement. His hips banged into hers, grinding and sliding, and his penis got harder with every rotation.

It all got wild and confusing after that, except that it was perfectly clear they were going to do it. He tore at her bicycle shorts and she tried to help him. Nothing else mattered except getting their pants off, and when that was done, he backed her to the wall and entered her.

Two hard thrusts and she was screaming for more. She wrapped her arms and legs around him, struggling to move with him. But he couldn't hold her, and they slid down the wall and hit the hardwood floor with a bump. Fortunately, she had some padding.

"Mmm, Reb, I love pushing you around," he said, as he rolled her onto her back and entered her again.

"Ouch." Her backbone was trying to saw its way through the floor as he rocked her back and forth. "This isn't working."

He pulled out abruptly and hoisted her to her knees. "I've got a great idea," he said as he tipped her over the nearest workout bench. Before she could get her balance, he was behind her, inside her and thrusting again, thrusting wildly.

"Oh, baby, I love fucking you," he gasped. "Why did we ever stop?"

He barely got the words out before he convulsed in spasms of pleasure. She clung to the bench, trying to catch her breath as he fell on her and embraced her passionately. He seemed happy, but it really hadn't worked all that well for her. It never did.

There was no postcoital cuddling. Bret possessed just enough chivalry to help her off the bench, and that was it. He bent to his ankles and yanked up his shorts. Rebecca still had one leg in hers, but couldn't move quickly. She had spandex and sweaty flesh to deal with.

When she looked up he was zipped up and done. You'd never know he'd just been humping like a hound dog. He'd barely broken a sweat. That made her hate him more. That and the fact that he was watching her struggle to get her damn bicycle shorts back on.

She would have turned away, but that view wasn't any better. She hated those disgusting mirrors. They were a cruel joke of the fitness industry, designed to promote self-loathing and keep people using their equipment. Julia probably loved them, the skinny bitch. Skinny *old* bitch. She kept her age a deep dark secret, but she had to be at least fifty.

"Don't let my mother bust your chops about being fat," he said. "It's none of her business."

"So, you think I'm fat, *too?*"

He shrugged. "I didn't say that. You could lose a couple pounds. Who couldn't?"

"You." She looked him over and sniffed. "You're too skinny."

"Hey, I'm in great shape. Check it out."

He bounded over to a wide pull-down machine, straddled the seat and grabbed the handles above him, but could barely budge them. Rebecca hooted. "I used that machine earlier, and that's the weight *I* lifted."

"I don't need no fucking *masheeen,*" he said, letting the weights clang down. He dropped to the floor and assumed the push-up position, starting with the standard two-arm and then switching to one. She had to admit he was good. She couldn't compete with that.

But as she watched him, she realized that he hadn't paid enough attention to where he'd decided to show off his form. He was doing his macho one-arm push-ups directly below a rack of dumbbells.

"You're the man, Bret," she said.

"You damn right."

Sweat was pouring off him, and he'd begun to strain as she strolled over and looked down at him. She moved around him, as if to better admire him, and then ever so casually, she reached up and tipped the rack just enough that the smallest dumbbell rolled off and landed on his head.

Kathunk. She winced at the sound.

Bret hit the hardwood floor facedown. He groaned and passed out cold. He'd been on his twentieth push-up. Hopefully she hadn't killed him.

She spoke softly to his prone form. "Assertive enough for you, Bret?"

18

Marnie scrubbed the penny ring with a toothbrush until it shone. She'd used a tiny bit of toothpaste, an old trick of her grandmother's, and it seemed to be working. When she was done scrubbing, she rinsed the copper thoroughly in warm water, blotted it dry with a soft towel and put it back on the chain her grandmother had given her.

The feel of it and the deep golden glow gave her a sense of comfort as she fastened it around her neck. Maybe at one time it had even made her feel safe, but right now her concern for her grandmother was too great. Somehow Marnie had to find out what had happened.

She didn't have access to a computer, but she'd spent the evening going through the phone book calling hospitals and nursing homes and asking for Josephine Hazelton's room. Most refused to give out the information because of the new privacy regulations. Marnie got around that by calling back and asking to discuss Josephine Hazelton's overdue account. They were quick to check on that, but none of them had any record of such an account. And, of course, they couldn't reveal whether a Josephine Hazelton had been there in the last month.

Finally, Andrew had made her stop. While she'd been calling, he'd used his cell phone's wireless Internet connection to check the obits in the county papers, going back to when her grandmother had last been seen in the area. But he'd found nothing himself, and he'd insisted that was good news. Josephine Hazelton wasn't dead or hospitalized, so it was just a matter of tracking her down. He'd promised again to do that. He would even hire a detective if he couldn't find her on his own—but only if Marnie would come to bed.

And now that she had washed her face, changed the bandage on her temple, brushed her teeth, dabbed some cream that smelled of lilies around her eyes, *and* cleaned her good luck charm with the spare toothbrush she'd found in the medicine cabinet, there was nothing else to do except that. Go to bed.

Her cool, black satin nightgown hung on the door hook. She shed her clothes and slipped it on, glancing at her reflection in the mirrored door. She'd received lots of compliments the night of the reception, and she was beginning to see what other people saw, the strange beauty, the wariness. They hadn't used those words, but she could be objective because she still didn't see the exquisite face in the mirror as her own.

It was Alison Fairmont Villard's features she saw, but that was starting to change. The more Marnie looked at herself, the more intrigued she became. She could see glimmers of herself everywhere, in the blue eye color that she shared with the real Alison, and in the questioning arch of her brow. But she also found herself wondering who Alison really was. It didn't seem possible that one woman could be as evil and conniving as Andrew and Bret saw her, or as ideal and perfect as Julia did.

But Marnie had idealized her once, too. Almost everyone in Mirage Bay had. Could they all be wrong?

She touched the ring that rested above her breasts, glad to have it back on the chain and not to have to wear the bracelet anymore. But even the bracelet had once seemed like a magical gift, and possibly a sign.

"Bedtime," she told herself. Andrew was already there, and she'd run out of stalling tactics.

She turned off the bathroom light before she opened the door to the bedroom's darkness. In a moment her eyes would adjust and there would be enough moonlight to get to the bed. Sometimes it felt as if she were nocturnal, anyway. Her favorite thing had been floating in the tidal pool on summer evenings. The important thing now was not to wake Andrew. What he'd done today—and what he promised to do—had actually meant something to her. She felt grateful, open, and that was a dangerous place to be.

She slipped into bed and pulled the sheet over her. It was too warm for the comforter, and if she'd been alone there would have been nothing but cool air on her body. She missed sleeping naked. She missed her world.

"Are you okay?"

Andrew's question came to her in the darkness. She couldn't tell if it was emotion making his voice husky, or if she'd awakened him.

"I'm fine," she said.

She heard a click and soft light flooded his corner

of the bed. He sat up and looked at her lying next to him, and the light made her acutely aware of his shoulders and the curve of his spine. Possibly because he wasn't wearing a pajama top. He rarely ever wore them, but she'd tried hard not to notice.

"Are you sure?" he said. "You were in there a long time."

"I was avoiding you."

She could see his surprise. Something had welled up inside her, possibly the need to tell the truth for once.

He took in her black satin gown and the good luck charm and everything else that wasn't covered by the sheet. "Avoiding me? Why?"

"Because it's so odd to be in bed with you. Don't you feel it, how difficult this is?"

"I feel it. I've been trying to remember when I last slept." He rolled his neck and gave a small purring groan.

Marnie felt a tug in the depths of her stomach as she watched him rub his thigh through the flimsy cotton of his drawstring pajama bottoms. Her thoughts flew helplessly to other parts of his anatomy. The thin material played with her imagination, seeming to reveal the way his hip curved into his leg and on down his thigh. Of course the fly had bubbled open. Didn't they always?

Not that she'd had much experience with men's flies. She'd only had real sex twice, and it had been with a sweet, overweight boy with badly pocked skin, who was even shyer than she was. They were both sixteen, but he'd seemed to understand about disfiguration and had needed acceptance as much as she had. They'd been inseparable until Butch and his gang caught up with them. Butch had humiliated the boy in front of everyone and forced him to call Marnie names. Terrified, he'd thrown up all over Marnie, much to Butch and his friends' glee.

Her first and last boyfriend. His parents had been summer renters, and she'd known he would be leaving, but the way he'd shunned her afterward had hurt the most. Maybe, stupidly, she'd wanted him to stand up for her, but she had understood his fear—Butch and his friends were terrorists. And she'd always known he wasn't the one.

The man who had embodied all of her teenage yearnings and dreams was sitting next to her now. And the great irony was that he couldn't—or wouldn't—touch her, either. She was as much a pariah now as she had been back then. Nothing had changed, really.

She watched him massage his neck and imagined what it would be like to give him a neck rub. Her fingers tingled. But she sensed that even a touch would breach the electrical field that separated them—and probably short-circuit the entire house. The tension in the room was thick, charged. It felt like physical weight.

He angled his head around, as though he could feel her interest. "Sure you're okay?"

She nodded, but his gaze had already drifted from her face to her chest. "What are you looking at?" she asked.

"Your good luck charm. What did you do to it?" He leaned over and took the ring in his fingers for a closer look. His skin brushed hers, and Marnie's heart hesitated. Her throat burned with feelings she didn't understand. The anticipation, yes, but the fear?

"I shined it up a bit," she said.

"You smell like lilies."

He seemed to be lingering, drinking her in, and that set off a crazy tug-of-war inside her. She wanted him to stop, but she wanted something else much more. And she had wanted it for so long that the pull was nearly irresistible. She wasn't going to be able to let this go. It was like holding a kite string in a high wind. She'd done that as a kid, and it had felt as if the kite would lift her right off her feet.

Remembering that sensation, the thrill of it, made her ache.

Andrew's leg brushed hers, leaving no doubt that an electrical field existed. Pleasure sprayed like jets from a fountain. When the contact was gone, she noticed the loss of it instantly. Was he feeling any of this? Did he even know what was going on?

Despite her fear of rejection, Marnie touched his hand, sliding her fingers over his. She could hardly breathe, waiting for his reaction. Even that light contact was amazing. It felt as if there were sparks coming off her fingertips. How could he not react?

When he did nothing, it made her deeply curious. What would it take to make this man respond?

He was still bent over her, holding her good luck charm, and she could feel the pulse beat in his fingers and the breath coming hot from his lungs. Whether he intended it to or not, the back of his hand rested on her breast, making her acutely aware of her own heartbeat.

She stroked his forearm, smoothing his dark hair

and savoring the firmness of his muscles. Her nails lightly rode the distended veins and cords.

Had he made a sound? She stole a glance at him and saw a muscle twitch in his cheek. His jaw was tight, locked. He had to be feeling something. His face was beautifully contorted.

She slipped the charm from his hand, and his fingers brushed her skin, setting her afire. It was all she could do not to moan.

"Touch me here," she whispered suddenly, guiding his hand to her breast.

She saw him flinch and couldn't tell if he was pleased or repulsed. *Surprised,* she told herself. *Maybe it was just surprise.* But his breathing was harsh, and his hand dropped away as soon as she removed hers.

He heaved himself up, leaving her there.

"Is something wrong?" she asked him.

"I forgot to take a shower."

Stricken, she nodded. Of course, a shower. She had never felt dirtier.

"I'll be right back," he said, rolling out of the bed.

"Take your time." Her voice had enough edge to cut metal, but she got no response.

He actually turned off the light as he left, which she took as a signal that he hoped she'd be asleep by the time he got back. Not a chance. She lay there, smoldering. Was she really that disgusting that he had to wash away all trace of her? Or was this about him? Was something wrong with him?

Furious, and feeling as if she could bleed to death from so many puncture wounds, she realized how ridiculous their conspiracy of silence was. He might have a need for secrecy, even between them, but she did not.

She threw off the sheet, and a moment later, she was out of bed and following him into the bathroom. She could hear the shower going and see the steam rolling over the top of the stall, but she didn't care. Fuck his privacy, fuck his secrecy, fuck him.

She opened the door and there he was, totally naked. The blue-and-white tiles brought into sharp contrast his dark hair and bronzed skin. His height, his breadth, the darkness that hung between his legs, all of it was beautiful beyond anything she could have imagined. He quite literally took her breath away.

"Marnie?" He reached to turn off the shower.

"Who is it you despise?" she asked him, speaking over the noise of the water. "Alison? Or me? It's all right if it's me. I've been despised all my life, but I didn't expect it from you…and I don't understand."

He looked confused, as if she'd blindsided him. Probably she had, but she didn't care about that, either. She had been shunned and shunted aside too many times, and this man held her future—and possibly her life—in his hands. There wasn't going to be any more silence, not between them.

"It's never been you," he said. "Alison was empty inside, a lovely void. Dead, even when she was alive."

Marnie had never asked him, but she had to now. "Is that why you killed her? Because I'm living in fear that you did."

"I didn't kill her. I don't know what happened. That's why I'm here, Marnie."

He'd had no reaction to her question. She'd seen

no flashes of guilt, anger or contrition. He was unequivocal. "Okay," she said, nodding.

"She was the exact opposite of you," he said.

"And what am I?"

"A hot spark. A life force."

"Then why won't you touch me?"

He flinched again, only this time it wasn't in disgust. It was something else, something hot and anguished. His jaw tightened as he stared at her in the black satin gown that had once been Alison's. Water still poured from the showerhead, flooding him and the stall. He couldn't seem to get it turned off, maybe because he wasn't really paying attention. He couldn't tear his eyes off her. And she saw nothing resembling revulsion in those eyes. It was all lust and desire and potent male need.

"Take that thing off," he said.

His meaning was clear, but he didn't give her time to get out of the gown before he pulled her into the shower with him. Steam roiled around her as she fell into the inferno. Marnie let out a tight little croak of joy as the drenched gown slid to her feet. She flung herself at him, hitting him so hard that they fell against the shower wall together, and then she began to laugh. It was just all so crazy it didn't seem real.

"Jesus," he whispered. He probably thought he'd gotten himself tangled up with a wild creature, something straight from the dark heart of the jungle. And he had. He didn't know how long she'd wanted this. How long she'd had to hold these feelings in check.

She gazed up at him, her head thrown back, her throat exposed and utterly vulnerable. She could hear his low growls of desire, and shuddered as he bent to kiss her mouth. Who was the animal now? she thought, laughing. She couldn't seem to stop.

His body was hot and steamy against hers. Everything was dark and hard, but his kiss was achingly tender. Their mouths melted together, clinging and tasting. Thirsty. Insatiable. And she loved every wet second of it.

She pulled back, and he grasped her arms as if afraid she'd get away.

"You found me in the water," she said. "Now, let me find you."

The scent of lilies saturated the air as she touched his face and his aroused body. He was slippery and slick, and her hands streamed through his drenched hair and down his back to his tightly clenched glutes. God, he was sexy. The water drove her to her knees, and she held him with both hands, like a glass she was about to drink from. He stopped her before she could begin to get her fill.

"That's as much finding as you get," he said. "My turn."

She ended up in the corner, out of the direct spray, as he knelt between her legs and kissed the droplets from her mound. It was excruciatingly sweet having him search out every little bead from the folds and curls of her sex. She arched her back and opened her legs, afraid she would slide to the floor in a heap. The pleasure was so intense it made her want to scream.

"Our turn," she pleaded.

She fell against him as he rose, and he lifted her off the floor by her legs. Their hot, urgent kisses led to urgent love against the wall, with warm water pouring all over them. He pressed her to the tiles, and she curled her arms and legs around him like vines. Their joining was slow and piercingly sweet, yet utterly tumultuous. They were two bodies drowning in water, but Marnie had never known what it was to drown in desire, in physical longing. As he sank into her and sighed, she sank into an ocean of her own need.

The fit of their bodies was tight and fluid. Perfect. Deep muscles clenched as she rocked up and down. Every thrust lifted her, sending her flying like the kite in the wind. But it was the noise that set her free. The throaty groans and gurgles. The sloshing, slapping and splashing. Sex in the shower was rife with distinctly wet, lugubrious sounds that she would never get out of her mind.

And before it was over, she understood what she was facing. Every day with Andrew Villard felt like a terrible risk, but she didn't fear for her life, she feared for her heart. It was one thing to make a deal with the devil. It was another to fall in love with him.

19

Tony heard the phone ring and reached out in his sleep to turn it off. If his dad heard the noise he'd stomp the shit out of him *and* his phone. He'd already flushed one cell down the toilet and crushed the other under a tire of his truck.

As Tony reared up and crammed the cell under his pillow, he realized where he was. He wasn't sixteen years old and back in his old man's house. He was in his motel room, and he'd probably just missed a call from his informant.

"Shit," he snarled, yanking the phone out from under the pillow. He flipped the lid and thumbed the talk button in one fluid motion. "Hello? Hello?"

"Where were you?"

"Right here," Tony said, struggling to get his bearings. His heart was hammering, and he'd been in a crouch, ready to defend himself from his father's flying fists. "It's six in the morning."

"Go back out to the cliffs. You missed something."

Tony adjusted the phone's volume to make sure he got every word the caller spoke. His snitch was at it again, thank God.

"What did I miss?" Tony asked.

"Evidence that will prove I'm telling the truth."

"Evidence on the cliffs? What kind? Tell me what I'm looking for."

"Dig deeper than you did before."

"Dig deeper? What does that mean?"

Click.

The piercing dial tone made Tony scramble to turn the volume control back down. The snitch had hung up. Tony tapped in *75, which automatically reported the call to his cell company's tracing service, but he didn't expect them to be able to trap it. If his caller was smart, he or she was probably using a pay-as-you-go mobile phone, which made tracing virtually impossible. And Tony couldn't call in any of his FBI colleagues on this one.

He rubbed his face, digging into his eyes to get the sleep out of them and still feeling very much like a sixteen-year-old kid. His hands were shaking, and that was death for a marksman. None of this emotion was good. It all had to be kept under strict control, and that was the very thing that eluded him. He wasn't an automaton like one of those Hostage Rescue Team guys he so desperately wanted to be. He got angry and scared and he shook. That was bad. It would ruin him if he couldn't get control.

He got up from the creaky bed, stretched until it hurt and then adjusted his balls through his boxers. He needed coffee, and he was going to have to hit a Laundromat soon or buy some clean underwear. He looked around the room. Damn cheap-ass motel didn't even have a coffee service.

Tony replayed the call in his head as he stood at the toilet and emptied his bursting bladder. Probably the beers he drank last night, which also explained his headache. He needed to find another way to get to sleep, maybe something over the counter. Or a sledge-hammer.

The snitch had said go back to the cliffs. Tony had to assume that meant Satan's Teeth, where Marnie Hazelton was supposed to have jumped. Tony had already been there. Twice, in fact. He'd searched the area the day after Butch's murder, and again this trip. He wasn't a crime-scene technician, but he knew how to look for evidence, and he hadn't come up with anything. So, unless the caller meant some other cliffs, which didn't make sense, Tony had to wonder what his informant was up to. This could be a wild-good chase, and if it was, the con-niving bitch would pay. Tony would find her and throw *her* off the cliff.

The bitch could be a *him,* he reminded himself. Voices were easily disguised.

As he bent over and flushed the toilet, he watched the water surge into a whirling vortex, and his imag-ination supplied a body being sucked down the drain with it. He wanted to think it was symbolism, the body of his enemy, whoever that blight on his life might be, but he wasn't so sure the flailing victim in the suck hole wasn't him.

Something about the position of the boulders bothered Tony. Two of them were propped against each other near the edge of the rocky cliffs, and even though he'd noticed them when he was here before, no bells had gone off. This time he was going to move them and have a look underneath.

Looking under rocks. Could have been his job description.

He scoped out the area visually, aware of the unusually low tide. Satan's Teeth was a natural seawall. Carved by erosion, it jutted out fifty feet from the cliffs above the beach, and the drop to the water below was probably double that. At high tide, he would have been looking down at roiling ocean water, but right now, it was dangerously shallow. A jump from this height at almost any time other than high tide would be certain death.

The beach was deserted, except for a few die-hard surfers. It was too early for people of normal intelligence, in Tony's humble opinion. Even as a kid, he hadn't understood the surfing culture. Most of the wave monkeys were as hopelessly retarded as the movies made them out to be—and Tony had always been a loner, anyway. When he'd gone to the beach, he'd hung out by the pier, a good mile away from Satan's Teeth, to the northwest. That was still the hot spot, but people seeking more privacy often headed toward the cliffs, and Tony didn't want to be noticed by lovey-dovey couples out for an early morning walk. About a mile and a half farther south was Josephine Hazelton's cottage and the secluded glen where Butch was murdered.

Tony had picked worn, scruffy clothes to blend in— jeans, a T-shirt and a windbreaker, but it was already too warm for the jacket. He left it lying on a rock and pulled a pair of latex gloves from the pocket of his jeans. Moments later, as he heaved the second boulder aside, he spotted the sheered rocks. Two of the outcroppings the seawall was named for were broken off.

Satan had two teeth missing, and no one seemed to have noticed.

Tony knelt for a closer look. He didn't even bother with speculation about the various ways this could have happened. It dovetailed too neatly with the calls he'd been getting. Following the snitch's line of reasoning, the boulders were meant to hide the evidence of a fight between Marnie Hazelton and whoever had pushed her from the cliff. The teeth had been broken during the struggle, but Tony knew that even forensics wouldn't be able to determine how long ago that had happened.

It didn't look recent. Not days ago, certainly. There was already a greenish, mossy cast to the broken rocks.

He stayed close to the ground, searching for whatever else he could find. A half-dozen beer caps still looked shiny and new, and some cigarette butts were scattered around, a few with lipstick prints, probably courtesy of the local riffraff, who'd been using the place to party. Anything he found of interest went into one of the plastic evidence bags he'd brought with him, but certain questions nagged at him.

Why hadn't the sheriff's detectives noticed signs of a struggle six months ago? There would have been footprints and damage to the area beyond the broken teeth. The vegetation would have been disturbed, the dirt and rocks displaced.

He was still mulling over those questions as he brushed his gloved fingers over the loose earth and felt something sharp.

Dig deeper than you did before.

He quickly dug free a metal object. It looked like

a woman's hair barrette, but this wasn't the dime store variety. Underneath the encrusted dirt, it was solid gold, inlaid with diamonds and had the initials *A.F.* engraved on the underside.

Tony turned the barrette in his hands. Alison Fairmont. He had no doubt it was hers. She'd worn it back when they were secretly seeing each other. That was before she'd decided it was sexier to let all that honey-blond hair of hers fall around her face. Once she'd gotten the idea of being a pop star in her head, she didn't have room for one other fucking thing.

Laughter caught in his throat, burning. It should have felt better, knowing he was going to make her pay. For everything. But the way his stomach was churning, he felt almost sick.

He put the barrette in its own plastic bag. He could understand why it hadn't been found, if it had fallen off during the struggle and been ground into the earth with their feet. Of course, everything he'd found here, including the barrette, could have been planted for him to discover, but in this case, he wasn't sure he cared. It was evidence against Alison Fairmont Villard, public enemy number one.

As he turned to walk back to the cliffs, where he'd left his rental car, he saw a woman walking up the beach from the other side of the seawall, from the south. At first he didn't recognize her. Maybe the dark hair threw him off, but she seemed to be looking right at him, and as she drew a few steps closer, he saw that it was public enemy number one herself. Alison.

His first impulse was to duck, but it was too late for that. She was barefoot and wearing a billowing dress, and she looked odd, her gaze fixed almost trancelike on the seawall. Even stranger, she reminded him of someone else. It might have been the way she was staring. The sense of recognition was strong, but he had no idea who it was.

He continued to walk toward the cliffs, but her gaze didn't follow him. She didn't even appear to have seen him. She was definitely looking at the rocks, at Satan's Teeth. Talk about returning to the scene. Tony couldn't have asked for better confirmation of his theory.

Tony had already concluded that Marnie was a witness to Butch's murder and had to be silenced, but he still didn't know why Alison had killed Butch. Maybe Butch knew something about Alison and was blackmailing her. Stupid move, but Butch wasn't known for his smarts. More likely Butch had made a move on Alison and she'd fought him off.

Tony focused inward, thinking, imagining the struggle between Alison and Butch. And then it hit him—the only thing that made sense. His brother *had* gone after Alison, but not for sex. For revenge. He'd had to wait a few years for the opportunity, but any amount of time would have been worth it. The Bogart men were proud SOBs. Butch had been defending the family name and Tony's honor.

Tony could easily see Butch taking Alison to a secluded area like the glen to scare her. But Butch had badly underestimated Alison's ability to defend herself. She'd grabbed the pitchfork and gutted him—and Marnie had stumbled on all the bloodshed. She may even have helped Alison. She must have hated him enough to want him dead.

Tony felt vindicated, justified, even triumphant. Would it hold up in court? Tony would make sure it did because it fit Butch's M.O. perfectly. He was just the kind of kid to rip his big brother to his face, and then go behind his back and avenge him. Wouldn't it be something if Butch had died trying to make sure the Bogarts could hold their heads up again.

Julia was trying to figure out how to fasten her new Tiffany diamond circlet bracelet as she came upon her youngest in the kitchen. He was in a very strange position, bent over with his head inside the open refrigerator door. When he came out, he had a bottle of beer in his hand.

It wasn't even ten in the morning.

Julia dropped the bracelet and her bejeweled straw tote bag on the countertop. "Bret, put that away. It's too early to drink."

He groaned, apparently at the noise she was making. As he turned and his face came into view, Julia saw why. One of his eyes was swollen shut, and he had a large, nasty-looking knot on the top of his head.

He pressed the dripping bottle to his eye. "I'm not drinking it. I'm using it as an ice pack, and praying to God it numbs the pain."

"What happened to your head?"

"Ask your precious assistant."

"Rebecca?"

He moved the beer bottle to the knot and closed his eyes. "She'll try to deny it, but she dropped a dumbbell on my head."

"Rebecca?"

"Is there a parrot in here? *Yes, Rebecca.*"

"What did you do to *her*, Bret?"

"What did *I* do? Talk about blaming the victim. Your son could as easily be in a coma as not, and you're questioning his character?"

"Bret, are you saying that Rebecca attacked you unprovoked?"

He set the dripping beer bottle down. "I may have annoyed her, but did *you* try to kill the last person who annoyed you? She's damn lucky I haven't called the police."

Julia had already begun to dig through her purse in search of her cell, but not to call the police. Bret looked bad enough to be in a coma, and he would never seek medical attention on his own behalf.

"You're going to the doctor," she said, keying in the speed-dial code to her cosmetic surgeon. She'd spent a small fortune with that man, and the least he could do was see her son on an emergency basis.

"You're sending me to a doctor?" Bret said. "You don't care what that little bitch did to me?"

"I wouldn't call Rebecca a *little* bitch." Julia sniffed, as if pleased with her own joke, and that seemed to mollify him slightly. "And, of course, I care about you. If I didn't, would I insist you see a doctor?"

What she actually cared about was that he not disrupt their lives any more than he already had, especially with Rebecca, who was a far better assistant than Bret was a son, if Julia was being honest. There was little doubt in her mind what she would have done if she'd been free to play switcheroo right now. She would have sent Bret packing and adopted Rebecca.

"I don't need a doctor," he said. "*She* does—a shrink in a locked ward in the psychiatric wing. What are you going to do to her?"

"I'll deal with Rebecca." Julia was sure there was a great deal more to the story, but she would get the details from Rebecca—and warn her to stay the hell away from Bret. Julia didn't want to think about what Bret must have done to provoke Rebecca that way. She was always so kind and eager to please. Kind to the point that it could get on your nerves, in Julia's opinion, and lately she seemed to be hovering, here, there and everywhere. But still, Julia had little doubt Bret had deserved what he'd gotten.

In a matter of moments, Julia had the doctor's office on her cell and an emergency appointment for Bret later that day.

"Where's your sister?" she said as she hung up the phone.

"How would I know? The way she skulks around I barely know she's in the house. Has it ever occurred to you that she may have suffered brain damage in that accident? She's different. Hell, she's creepy, and you don't even seem to notice."

Julia stuffed her phone back in her purse. "I wonder what I would do if the members of this family ever supported each other. Probably die from the shock. Is there anything a mother loves more than to have her children splashing around in a cesspool of animosity?"

"Maybe we needed better examples, *Mom*."

Julia was torn between killing him and protecting him. This morning, the darker impulse was winning. He hated her, and at moments like this she hated him, too. But she never stopped caring about him. She couldn't help it. Despite everything, he was her child, and blood bonds were powerful. Her mother had adored him, too, though she'd known that to hand him a fund worth tens of millions would have been ruinous.

"I need to find Alison," she said. "I'm taking her and Rebecca shopping this morning. I really wanted it to be just Alison and me, a mother and daughter thing, but Rebecca insisted on coming, for some reason."

Julia picked up her new bracelet, snapped it on and held out her hand, admiring it. She adjusted her wedding rings, lining them up. "Do you think Rebecca might be jealous of Alison?"

Bret groaned out laughter. "What's there to be jealous of? Rebecca has the hots for me."

Julia gave her son a sharp glance. "What does that mean?"

He winced and pressed the cold beer to his head. "She wants me, but she can't have me. I'd *never* mess with the help. What are you going shopping for?"

It didn't escape Julia that he'd changed the subject, but she wasn't too worried. Obviously *little* Rebecca could take care of herself. "Since when do I need a reason to go shopping?"

Bret glanced over at the door to the terrace, and Julia followed his gaze. She was startled to see Alison standing in the open doorway, wearing a loosely fitting peasant dress. Her skirt was wet and her feet sandy, and her eyes were averted. She looked sullen and achingly beautiful, a waif with incredible bones.

Julia's heart skipped painfully. What she would have given to look like that, on any day of her life. Alison was perfection, even when she was trying hard not to be.

The poor child also looked as if she needed a hug, and that wasn't Alison at all. Julia felt a disturbing twinge, almost a premonition. Was Bret right? It was hard to imagine her prissy daughter wading in the surf and letting the wind whip her into this state. Alison had changed in ways that Julia couldn't understand or relate to. But why wouldn't she have? All that trauma and surgery, all that time with her suffocating husband.

Bret cracked the beer and began to drink it. "What the hell happened to you?" he asked Alison.

Julia cut him off. "Are you all right, dear? You do look a bit disheveled."

Alison glanced down, taking in the mess that was her skirt and her grimy feet. It didn't seem to register. "Nothing," she said. "Walking."

"Is there a problem?" Julia persisted. "You and Andrew?"

Alison looked startled. "Why would you ask that?"

"No reason. It's just that I didn't see either one of you this morning for breakfast, and I wondered—"

"Well, stop wondering," Alison snapped. "Andrew and I are fine."

From his vantage point, Bret shot Julia a knowing look. *How's that for creepy?* it seemed to say. But Julia didn't agree. Churlish behavior wasn't out of character for Alison. She'd had a mercurial personality even as a young girl. With family, she'd had a tendency to be high-handed and demanding, as if life owed her something just because she was so beautiful. To the rest of the world, she was the fairy princess, the debutante. Even her adoring grandmother, Eleanor, hadn't known about Alison's darker side.

Both of Julia's children had been adept at hiding their private selves, and maybe Bret was right that they'd learned by example. Julia sometimes felt as if she'd grown up incubating a pack of demons in the dark corners of her psyche, and she wasn't entirely sure who to thank for that. She'd never been abused or grievously neglected. Her mother and father had been preoccupied with their charitable work, but they'd always insisted on quality time with their only daughter, had always drummed their values into Julia's head. It was just that their standards were so impossibly high—and nothing but the best had ever been good enough.

You were a paragon or you were nothing.

Over the years, Julia had realized that the closer she got to paragon status the more she felt like nothing—and the more she felt as if she was living in two different realities, neither entirely of her own creating.

Perhaps she had passed on her own peculiar brand of schizophrenia to her children, because Bret didn't seem to be dealing at all well with reality these days. He refused to see the truth about his sister—and worse, he seemed unusually agitated by her presence. Julia would have been tempted to think this had something to do with the trust that Alison had walked away from, except that Bret knew the money passed from woman to woman on the Driscoll side. He wasn't in the line of succession, and Julia had taken pains to make sure he understood that. She'd even had one of the family's very accommodating attorneys talk to him.

As Julia stood there, looking at her two children, driven apart by their rivalries and yet so alike in stature and temperament, she felt another jolt of apprehension. But this was physical, as if a cosmic hand had reached down, grabbed her by the scruff of her neck and given her a shake.

Suddenly her heart was racing and her thoughts whipping. She could smell fire and hear a child crying. The sound came from somewhere nearby, a baby wailing as if it were dying, and the piercing sharpness of its cries made her blood run cold. Something *was* wrong, and she had caused it. She had allowed herself to look back, like Lot's wife—a terrible mistake. Turning into a pillar of salt was nothing compared to the devastation she had just glimpsed.

20

Andrew's morning had been a bitch. It had started with an urgent voice-mail message from his assistant about problems with a rock concert in Mexico. After he'd returned Stacy's call and put out the fire, he'd taken care of some nagging details that had to do with his own fallback plan. He'd come up with the plan months ago, but had hoped he would never have to use it. Now, he had no choice. Tony Bogart was tailing him.

Andrew had spotted him this morning when he'd left the compound and driven into town. He'd managed to lose him, but he had a bad feeling that Bogart was closing in. Maybe the G-man wasn't bluffing. Andrew had assumed the newspaper threat had come from one of the Fairmonts, but Bogart couldn't be overlooked. If he had evidence, he could be waiting for the right moment to blow the lid off—which meant Andrew had to move. Now.

He'd used up the rest of the morning hunting for a needle named Josephine Hazelton in a haystack roughly the size of San Diego County. Unfortunately, no one had been able to tell him anything more than he already knew about Marnie's Gramma Jo, but everyone had expressed concern.

It seemed she was a loner, well-liked by those who knew her, but close to no one but her missing granddaughter. Andrew had not wanted to be obvious by asking too many questions. He'd already picked up on the avid curiosity among the locals about Alison's condition and her return to Mirage Bay. When questioned, he'd said it was a family reunion, long overdue. But some of the looks he'd gotten had made him wonder what rumors were circulating about the Fairmonts. He knew from Alison that the family had always been fodder for gossip, which was why he might have to hire a discreet P.I. after all. A true missing-person's search was beyond his capability, and that's what this seemed to be turning into.

And then there was the other reason he'd left the house at dawn. He'd needed some time to clear his head and try to figure out what had happened between him and Marnie last night. She'd caught him by surprise in the shower, and maybe his guard had been down. All he knew was it would have taken a much better man than him to resist her.

She'd insisted she was all right afterward, but she'd seemed shaken and hadn't wanted to talk about what they'd done, so he hadn't pushed it. She'd rolled to her side, as if she were sleeping, but he'd been awake all night. Their sex had opened floodgates for him. His body may have been designed to do the penetrating, but something about hers had touched him more deeply than he wanted anything to go. He'd lain there, vibrating, haunted by it.

He needed to let it go now, but he was finding it impossible to get back to whatever "normal" had been for him and Marnie, impossible not to think of her in sexual terms. And neither one of them needed the situation to get more complicated.

As he pulled through the gates of Sea Clouds and parked the car in the grand portico, he saw that Julia's Mercedes and the sedan Bret drove were both gone. The house felt empty as Andrew let himself in. His first stop was the kitchen where he found a note from Julia, explaining that she, Alison and Rebecca had gone shopping, and that Bret was at the doctor's.

Andrew checked his watch. Julia's note said the women would be back later that afternoon, which would give him plenty of time, except that he didn't know how long Bret's appointment might take. It was ten-thirty now, and there wasn't a minute to waste. He had a unique opportunity to search the entire house— and he knew exactly where he was going first.

He reached into the coin pocket of his jeans and touched the fake amethyst gemstone, making sure it was still there. He knew what he was searching for, but that wasn't what had his adrenaline pumping. He'd been waiting six months for this.

Julia's office was immaculate. That was no surprise. Everything else about her was, too, at least to the eye. The decor was similar to the rest of the house—shimmering marble floors with tiles so precisely laid you could barely detect the seams. Palladian doors led to the terrace overlooking the ocean, and everywhere, elegant palms threw fronds that touched the floor.

Her desk was an antique secretary with a glass top that reflected Andrew's pensive expression with as much detail as a mirror. He couldn't imagine getting any actual work done in a showplace like this, but it was clear that she was a busy woman. Her appointment book was tightly scheduled. He also noticed that she'd circled certain months at the top of the pages. The current month, July, then February, April, August and November.

It may have caught his attention because of the circled words in the blackmail note he'd received. A coincidence? He didn't see anything to explain it. Most of the copious notes she'd made in the appointment book had to do with her schedule, but there was something printed in the top margin of the month for July that he didn't understand. The letters *B.C.* were followed by an arrow pointing to the letter *S,* all in caps.

Andrew made a mental note of it and kept looking.

The inner workings of her desk were not immaculate, he discovered. The drawers were jammed with bulging file folders, mostly filled with newspaper clippings of her accomplishments, hard copies of correspondence and financial records going back several years. She also had a collection of Montblanc pens and enough pricey office paraphernalia to open her own stationery store.

The drawers were packed, but not messy. They looked tight, tense and disorganized. Like the woman. Julia did seem tightly strung beneath all the makeup and designer clothes—one twist away from snapping like a watch spring.

Among other things he was looking for self-sticking mailing labels, the kind that were computer-generated. He found a rollout cart, designed to match the desk, that housed a laptop computer and a printer.

No labels, however, nor had he seen any indication since he got to Sea Clouds that Julia subscribed to the Mirage Bay newspaper, but it couldn't have been that difficult to get a hold of a six-month old issue.

He didn't bother searching her equally immaculate bedroom. He went straight to her dressing room, which was part of the huge walk-in closet. He checked her shoes first and found several pairs studded with fake gemstones, but none with a missing amethyst. Some of her clothing also had gemstones glued to the fabric. One casual top had amethysts, but they looked intact.

He turned his attention to the mirrored vanity table, wasting no time on anything else. The drawers yielded nothing but an array of cosmetics and accessories, but the framed mirror had a secret. One of the rosebuds in the lower right corner of the gilded frame was actually a button. Andrew pressed it, and the entire mirror slid up to reveal a home safe.

He was well-versed with the various options of home safes. He had one hidden in the wall paneling of his closet in Long Island, and he'd recommended them to his clients in the music business.

Right now Andrew was looking for any evidence that Julia or someone in this house had been involved in trying to frame him. A copy of the insurance policy on Alison with him as beneficiary was the sort of document people kept in a home safe, but he was no lock pick, and the safes were impossible to open without a combination.

He glanced at his watch, aware that he had more ground to cover and was running out of time. He gave Julia's walk-in closet, her bedroom and her office a last visual once-over. On his way out, he looked again at her desk and her appointment book. He wasn't quite sure what he'd found here, but he was going to commit it to memory for future reference.

Bret Fairmont's bedroom had its share of surprises, but no way did Andrew expect to find a cache of women's clothing in his closet. The room was situated in a second-floor corner of the house that Bret had managed to make darker than doom with light-blocking shades. It could have been a sports bar with all the neon liquor signs on the wall; however, there wasn't a hint of sports memorabilia to be found.

Evidently Bret wasn't a sports fan, nor was he into cars or any of the other things that most twenty-five-year-old males liked, although the computer workstation wedged in the corner against the shaded windows looked as if it was loaded with high-tech equipment.

The room wasn't as immaculate as Julia's, but there wasn't much out of place. Like mother, like son? A scary thought. Andrew did a quick search of the workstation, but found nothing to implicate Bret in the newspaper threat. That didn't surprise him. Bret would hardly have left evidence lying around, knowing that Andrew and Alison were coming for a visit. Time was tight, so he went straight to the walk-in closet, which was also neat and orderly. Dress shirts hung on an upper rack, slacks on the lower. A rotating device displayed belts and ties, and clear acrylic containers held folded sweaters. Even his casual clothes were sorted and stacked—jeans, T-shirts, shorts.

Bret was a mess, but his personal space didn't seem to reflect that.

Andrew searched for a safe first, but came up empty-handed. He had better luck with the hanging garment bags. The second was full of women's clothes. Andrew was looking at frilly dresses, skimpy skirts and tops, high-heel shoes, even women's underwear, and something that might have been a hairpiece. He didn't find anything with amethysts, but Bret definitely had a few fake-gem-studded items in his collection. The first thing that came to mind was that Bret was a cross-dresser, except that one of the blouses had Alison's initials embroidered on the pocket.

Andrew didn't know what to make of it. Were these all Alison's things? Sibling rivalry run totally amok? He checked his watch. He'd been here fifteen minutes, but hadn't found what he was looking for. Maybe there was still time to check out the computer.

He saw the framed posters as he came out of the closet. Three of them hung on the opposite wall, each lit from below by a small spotlight. They looked like print ads, blown up to poster size, and the model in each of them was Bret, looking rakishly handsome and masculine. Apparently he'd been serious enough about modeling to have some portfolio shots taken. It really was impossible to imagine this guy wearing a frilly dress.

Andrew turned his attention to the computer—and discovered another facet of Bret's personality when he touched the computer mouse. The monitor must have been in sleep mode because it flashed on immediately. Andrew's jaw went slack at the pictures on the screen.

Pornography. Hard-core. Women with men, other women, mixed groups, and some very friendly animals.

Andrew clicked on Favorites and the list that dropped from the menu bar was almost entirely of X-rated sites. No wonder Bret kept it dark in the room. He had an Internet porn collection worthy of a true freak. But he'd made no real attempt to hide what was on the screen. Sleep mode meant the screen went dark after a period of time. An accidental brush of the monitor could activate it, or even the vibrations of someone walking into the room.

Andrew tried the workstation's top drawer and found it locked. The second, deeper drawer was half filled with files in hanging folders. Behind the folders were stacks of magazines and videos that looked like a mix of porn and legit films.

Andrew was working with a paper clip to jimmy open the top drawer when he heard footsteps coming down the hallway. The house's marble floors let you hear someone coming for miles, and he was back inside the closet before the door opened. But he'd left the closet door ajar, which allowed him to see Bret enter, kick the door shut behind him and drop his jacket on the nearest chair.

He was sporting a good-size bandage above his temple, and he may have had a black eye; it was hard to tell in the dark room. Andrew was curious how he got the injuries, but he was more interested in what Bret intended to do at the computer.

Alison's brother sat down at his desk and used a tiny key from his key chain to open the top drawer. He drew out an envelope, from which he took several five-by-seven photographs, and then he turned on the desk light, which enveloped him in an eerie halo.

More porn? Andrew wondered, as Bret rolled back in the chair and held the pictures up, splayed in his hand so that he could see several of them at once. Andrew could just make out a naked woman in what looked like graphic poses. He eased the closet door open, hesitating at a loud creak of the hinges.

Christ. There was nothing to do but duck out of sight and pray. The door would creak again if he shut it. If Bret turned around, Andrew would have to talk his way out of this. But when he looked again, he saw that Bret hadn't moved. He seemed oblivious to the noise, so engrossed in the pictures he'd tuned everything else out.

Andrew decided to risk it. He crept up behind him, close enough to see the woman in the photos. His stomach lurched when he saw who it was. The sexy blonde who had her legs open and was pleasuring herself was Alison Fairmont.

Andrew fought back the sour taste of stomach acid. The questions assaulting him were ugly, more disturbing than the photos. Bret was clearly twisted, but what about Alison? Andrew could see that this was a much younger Alison, probably still in her mid to late teens. But Bret would have been younger, too, younger than her. Had he taken these photos himself? And had Alison posed for him?

Bret shifted in the chair. Andrew thought he'd been caught, but Bret's eyes never left the screen. He seemed hypnotized, totally unaware that someone else was in the room. Fighting a wave of disgust, Andrew realized that the little pervert was reaching down to unzip his pants. It was time to make an exit.

* * *

"Oh, look, here's a lovely pinot! Alison, let's have some wine and relax while Rebecca's gone to find those other sizes."

Marnie uttered not a word of protest as Julia poured them each a generous glass of the ruby-red wine. Just moments ago, Marnie had collapsed on one of the dressing room's velvet settees, and she intended to stay there. She really couldn't hold a candle to Julia when it came to power shopping. The two of them had been trying on clothes all morning, and Marnie was ready for a shot of oxygen. Julia didn't even look winded.

At least the shopping was a distraction from the worry about her gramma Jo. Andrew must have been up before dawn. He was already gone when she woke up, but he'd left a note telling her not to go out hunting for her grandmother. He still had concerns about Marnie's safety, and had told her he would do the searching. He'd promised that he would track down her grandmother himself or put a detective on the job.

It was difficult, but Marnie had decided to trust him with the search. She wasn't nearly as worried about her own safety as she was Gramma Jo's, but she didn't want to undermine his efforts—or have Julia get suspicious about what the two of them were doing.

Julia brought a tray with the wine and some appetizers from the light buffet the store had set up in their fancy private dressing room. It was the size of a small apartment, with its own wet bar, fridge, microwave and bathroom. Marnie couldn't get over it. She'd grown up in a house with less square footage than this—and not nearly as well furnished.

"Isn't this fun?" Julia said, sliding the tray between them on the settee. "I can't tell you how happy I am that we found you some things that *fit*. But really, darling, it's time for an entire new wardrobe. Andrew should have helped you with that before you came. Look at you." At Marnie's wilted state, she shook her head. "You've lost your will to shop."

"I'm fine." Marnie took a sip of the wine and sighed. Lovely. Really. She could get used to this. Maybe not the shopping, but the wine, the appetizers and the cushy velvet furnishings.

It did feel odd sitting around in her underwear, but the store had provided silk kimonos to wear while they were waiting for Rebecca to come back with the different sizes. Normally it would have been one of the store's stylists, but Rebecca had volunteered.

Private dressing rooms were a first for Marnie, as were most of her experiences so far as a Fairmont. But she was learning to deal with Alison's life by being quiet and observant, and by following Julia's lead. If Julia loved a polka-dot capri outfit on her, that was the one Marnie chose. If she thought a certain dress needed alterations, Marnie stood on the seamstress's stool and let herself be measured and turned, the garment pinned and tucked.

Flying under the radar. Marnie was used to that. She'd had to do it most of her life, but never like this, immersed in enemy territory.

"Are you having fun?" Julia asked.

There was a hopeful note in her voice, which made it easy for Marnie to smile and say that she was. "I've missed having a mom to go shopping with."

Marnie had actually been thinking about her grandmother when she said "mom," but should she have said "mother"? Did the Fairmonts use words like *mom?* Surprisingly, Julia seemed touched. She tried to laugh it off, but the sparkle in her eyes looked suspiciously like tears.

"I don't think you've ever said that to me before," she replied softly.

Marnie wasn't sure what to do. Julia set down her wine, trying to regain her composure. On impulse, Marnie sprang up and went over to her. They were hugging even before Julia had risen to her feet.

Marnie's only desire was to put her at ease. It was hard for her to witness any kind of suffering, probably because she'd had her own fair share. But Julia was clinging to her, and Marnie didn't know how to comfort her, except to hang on, too. It was so odd. In the enemy's arms, Marnie felt the very real concern of a mother for her child. Julia really did love Alison.

The awareness touched Marnie, but it also stirred guilt about pretending to be the daughter Julia so clearly wanted a relationship with. She was glad to have seen this side of Julia. She wouldn't have guessed it existed, but she didn't want to complicate things by adding to her pain.

Julia pulled back, and Marnie felt a tug of sadness. She wanted something like this, too, a connection with another human being. She missed her grandmother and the comfort that had come from their special bond. This life was lavish, but lonely.

"Sorry," Julia said. Hurriedly, she began to straighten herself, brushing at her hair and rearranging her kimono. She was clearly embarrassed.

Marnie stepped back to give her some room. "Would you like your wine?"

"Yes, please." Julia sat down and took the glass Marnie handed her. When she looked up, she was clearly chagrinned. "That was awkward," she said. "I do apologize."

"Why, for heaven's sake?"

Julia took a deep breath and chased it with a swallow of the wine. She shook her head, as if gathering herself for something. "Let's talk about you, Alison," she said. "Please, while Rebecca's not here. I'm worried."

"Why? What about me?"

"You would tell me if anything was wrong, wouldn't you? You didn't seem at all yourself when you showed up in the kitchen this morning."

"I'm not sleeping well," Marnie said. "It was a bad night."

Julia's gaze was searching. "I know this is going to be hard to hear, but I have to say it. Everyone believed that Andrew tried to kill you, including me. And you can't really blame any of us. There was the accident and the insurance policy, and the two of you weren't getting along. Why were you even out on the seas in that storm?"

Marnie finally understood why Alison and Andrew had been summoned to Sea Clouds. Julia *was* concerned about her daughter's inheritance, and her son-in-law's motives. And if she believed him capable of attempted murder, then her distrust was profound. It was ground zero for Alison Fairmont and her mother, and Marnie was going to have to rebuild from the ashes. Now. The rebuilding had to start this moment, but sadly, it would all be lies.

"Going for a sail was my idea," she said. "Andrew and I *had* been having some problems, and I wanted to be on the water. I thought we'd be able to talk there. He warned me about the storm, but I insisted."

It was almost exactly the story Andrew had told her. Not completely lies, then. "Really, everything's all right," she said imploringly. "Drink your wine and let's talk about something else, anything, that silk jersey wrap dress. Did you like it?"

"No, let me finish. I've been trying to find a way to tell you this since you arrived. Sit down, please."

Marnie did, and Julia continued. "You and Bret will each come into a great deal of money when I'm gone," she said, "but Alison, never forget that you're wealthy now. Your grandmother's trust will be yours on your next birthday. It's been carefully managed by Jack Furlinghetti, one of the estate attorneys, and it's worth considerably more than fifty million now. It's important that you're prepared to handle it wisely."

Marnie was stunned. Andrew had said the trust might still be coming to her, but she had figured the family lawyers would find some way around that.

"Of course," Marnie said. "I'm sure Mr. Furlinghetti will advise me."

"I know you're shocked. I can hear it in your voice." Julia twisted her ring. "I wasn't being honest with you last February. I said you'd breached the morals clause by running away, that you'd blown your chance at the trust. I was still angry and wanted to hurt you. I apologize for that."

Marnie nodded, afraid anything she said could give her away. Apparently Andrew knew nothing about this, either. He'd never mentioned it.

"Alison, do not put the money in Andrew's name. Don't commingle it with your joint funds or give him control in any way—"

"Mother, Andrew has his own money."

"How much? Just exactly what does he have?"

"I don't know. We don't discuss it."

"That's what I thought." Her hand closed over Marnie's forearm. "Alison, I can help you. I have the means to get you out of any situation you're in. I have the means to make *him* go away, just talk to me. Tell me what's he's done, and we can deal with it together."

"He hasn't done anything. Really. Why do you think he has?"

Julia's fingers tightened on Marnie's arm. "You must remember that nasty mess with Regine several years ago. You were there when it happened."

"When *what* happened?" Marnie was stunned. Julia must mean that Alison had been involved somehow. Was she talking about the love triangle Andrew had alluded to? He'd refused to discuss it with Marnie beyond insisting that Regine's death was an accident.

Julia's eyebrows shot up. "When she drowned at his New York apartment in that ridiculous rooftop pool, of course. The police report said you were there that evening, at the scene."

Marnie knew Alison had moved to New York and that she'd been a source of support to Andrew after Regine's death. The tragedy had actually brought the two of them back together, but Marnie knew nothing about Alison's having been there that night. She wondered how Julia could have known.

"You mean the newspaper, right?" she asked Julia.

"How could you have known what was in the police report? They don't make those things public."

Julia drained her wine glass and glanced around as if she wanted a refill.

Marnie snatched the glass away. "Answer me," she said, her voice faint. "How did you know what was in the police report?"

"I hired a detective to check up on Andrew, but *only* because I wanted to protect you. I was terrified he might try to harm you, too." Julia rifled through her tote bag, pulled out an accordian file and handed it to Marnie. "Here's what the investigator uncovered. I never told you because I was afraid you'd hate me for interfering, but your accident convinced me that I was right about Andrew. Look at it, Alison. Dammit, *look*."

Reluctantly, Marnie set down the wine glass and took the file. Inside was extensive coverage on nearly every aspect of Andrew's life. She skimmed the reports of his financial and personal history. If the figures were accurate, he had considerable wealth at the time of Regine's death, but that wasn't what Julia wanted her to see, she realized. There were also old newspaper clippings, and one instantly caught Marnie's eye. It was a story about Regine's death with a huge color picture of the young pop star.

According to the caption, the shot was taken at a concert a month prior to the drowning accident. Petite and elegant in a form-fitting gold lame jumpsuit, Regine waved to the crowd. Her ginger-colored hair was pulled tight against her scalp and knotted in a long, swinging ponytail. Huge pink gems sparkled from her earlobes.

"The earrings," Marnie whispered. She touched

her own earlobe. She'd actually worn the pink diamonds today for the first time since the reception. She'd been hoping to feel their magic again, but what she felt now was horror. He'd given her his dead fiancée's earrings?

Julia pushed back Marnie's hair for a better look at the earrings. Obviously she hadn't noticed them at the reception. Marnie's hair had covered them that night, too. "When did he give you these?" she demanded. "You know their history, don't you? These are the Villard diamonds. They're cursed."

"I don't believe in curses." Marnie was utterly shaken by the thought of wearing jewelry he'd given to Regine. Why hadn't he told her?

"Read the background information on Andrew," Julia urged. "The earrings belonged to his mother. She was an opera singer, supposedly with great promise, but she died in a freak accident when Andrew was a teenager. He inherited the gems and gave them to Regine—and *she* died in a freak accident. Now, you've had an accident, too."

And so had the real Alison. Marnie had been given the earrings *after* the accident, but she couldn't tell Julia. Andrew hadn't said whether he'd given the earrings to Alison before she disappeared, but he'd said she loved to wear diamonds, that she wore them to bed and nothing else.

Marnie tried to quiet the quaking sensation in her gut. It seemed possible that she was the fourth woman in his life to wear the Villard diamonds, and the other women were either dead or missing. That did sound like a curse.

"Take them off," Julia said. "Just take them off."

Marnie removed the earrings and jammed them into her bag.

"Now read the police report," Julia insisted. "Read the whole file. You need to know everything."

"Enough," Marnie said. "I've heard enough."

"Fine then, *live* in denial. You already know the worst. You were there when they charged him with her murder."

Murder? Marnie could hardly breathe as she stared at the papers in her lap. He'd been charged? Marnie hadn't questioned Andrew's claim that Regine's death was an accident. She'd had enough to handle with her own recovery and transformation. Now Marnie had to read the police report. Otherwise, she wouldn't know what Julia was talking about—or the extent of Andrew's lies.

21

Andrew stepped out of the shower onto the marble floor, his body pink and steaming from the vigorous scrub he'd given himself. The first thing he did was check out the light slanting through the bathroom window. The rays were pale, the color of eggwash, but the angle told him it was late afternoon, probably around four o'clock.

The second thing he did was grab a towel from the cabinet. He knotted it around his hips and took another one for his dripping hair. Earlier, he'd dozed off in an overstuffed chair in the bedroom, waiting for Marnie to get back from shopping, but unfortunately, it wasn't her that had jolted him awake, queasy and sweating. A lurid dream of Bret and Alison had sent him straight to the shower, where he'd cranked up the water as hot as he could get it. Everything about that perverted scenario made him feel unclean.

He wanted to believe there was some explanation, but he wasn't optimistic. Bret was clearly a demented little fiend, and Andrew didn't know what to think about Alison. He'd suspected her of many things, but incest and porn weren't among them. Worse, as far as he could tell, the discovery meant nothing to his investigation, which put it in the category of more information than Andrew wanted to know. He couldn't completely dismiss it, though. He couldn't dismiss anything right now.

Andrew finished shaving and was patting on some cologne when he heard someone enter the bedroom. He pulled on a terry robe and went to the partially open bathroom door. It was Marnie, loaded down with shopping bags. She and Julia must have had a productive day.

He watched as she dropped the bags on the bed, rolled her shoulders and clasped her hands in the air, stretching like a dancer after a hard practice session. Tension sharpened her breathing. She wasn't relaxing for the fun of it. She was much too on edge for that. She looked different, too, dramatically different. Andrew's gut clenched as he noticed the ultra short, sleek hair.

It was another long moment before he saw what she'd actually done. The long dark waves were gathered in a knot at the nape of her neck. She'd pulled her hair back and off her face.

He let out the breath he'd been holding. Fuck.

She was changing before his eyes, he realized. She didn't look so young anymore, so impossibly young. Her cropped aquamarine jacket and matching pants were sexy and sophisticated, and her feet were encased in sky-high, pointy heels made of soft, silvery leather. It was an outfit a woman with style and money would have worn. Lots of style and money. He didn't know if that was good or bad.

Good, he told himself. To think anything else would be as stupid as it was selfish.

The dark circles under her eyes told him she wasn't sleeping well, either. Hell, why should he be the only one? On her, dark circles looked sullen and sultry. Even drunkenness and dissipation would have looked good on her, he feared. She wore no jewelry at all except for the gold bangles on her arms.

Still, it was quite a transformation.

And it worked, too. His chest was wire tight.

She discarded her jacket on the bed and began to unbutton her blouse, a delicate white, sleeveless thing with tucks that gave it the look of an old-fashioned slip. The neckline dipped low enough to reveal the swell of her breasts. She seemed to glow there, and he couldn't take his eyes off the soft flesh shimmering in the low light.

For Christ's sake, Villard. Stop her. Now. You let her undo one more button and you're going to be tearing that blouse off her, kissing her wild, hungry mouth and violating her body again. You have things to tell her, and there may not be another chance.

He tried to speak and couldn't. Instead, he cleared his throat.

Her head shot up, and she saw him. "Andrew? Why didn't you tell me you were here?"

They needed to talk, but something in her expression stopped him. It was elemental, a glint of fear and suspicion that caught him totally off guard.

"I hate it when you do that," Marnie said. Her fingers whipped at the buttons of her blouse, doing them up.

Andrew seemed genuinely confused. "When I do what?"

"Sneak up on me like that, watch me. You know what I mean."

Apparently he didn't. He continued to watch her, silent and intent, as if he was dealing with a temperamental animal. The buttons were tiny and infuriating. She couldn't get them done up. Her breath escaped with a low hiss.

Finally, he went to the liquor cabinet and poured a glass of red wine. Marnie couldn't help but notice. She'd still never seen him drink.

"Are you going to tell me what's going on?" he asked.

She stood by the bed, only half done up and painfully aware of her gaping blouse. Why the hell didn't he turn away and let her finish? The question burned to be asked, but her unbuttoned blouse wasn't the real problem, and clearly he sensed that. He knew something was wrong, and as much as she wanted to confront him with her damning evidence, she wasn't sure it was safe.

Would she be a threat to him now that she knew the truth?

He held up the glass, and she realized he'd poured it for her.

"No, thanks," she said sharply. "I've been drinking all day."

"Really?"

"Mm, *really*, it's an important part of the shopping ritual." She pointed to the bags on the bed, wondering if she might still be a little drunk. Maybe that would get her through this. "And it does ease the pain."

He was already filling a second goblet with fruit

juice. It was a deep vibrant red, the color of pomegranates, and it made Marnie thirsty.

"If I know Julia, she paid for everything," he said, stopping long enough to sample the juice. "I hope it eased *her* pain."

It was meant to be a quip, but Marnie had come too close to Julia's pain to appreciate the humor. How odd that Andrew was suddenly the enemy and Julia her ally. Life could turn on you in a second, as casually as a storm blew in. And so could people.

Andrew savored his drink. It might as well have been wine the way he handled it. He bent his head to the rim of the glass, breathing in the fruity notes. He even swirled the ambrosia in his mouth before swallowing. Marnie was reluctantly aware of the sensuality of the ritual. He held the bowl with long, strong, beautiful fingers that could make a woman want to drown.

How well she knew. As did *two other women,* it seemed.

She clutched her blouse, covering herself. It didn't feel safe confronting him here in this room, alone. Crazy as it sounded, she wanted to be where someone would hear her if she screamed. Where she could run.

Marnie's reaction told Andrew what he needed to know. Her concern for her grandmother outweighed anything else that might be bothering her. She'd even forgotten the buttons on her blouse. He hoped that meant she would be open to his idea, or at least to listen. There was only one way to track down a patient with no family who was probably ill and lost in the medical system. Hire an investigator.

"I wish I had better news," he said. "I didn't find her, and it's going to take more time and skill than I have. I'd like to hire someone, but I want to talk to you about it first."

"Hire someone?"

"We need a professional, Marnie. I can't ask the questions I need to without drawing attention to myself, and to you. That's dangerous for both of us. A real investigator wouldn't be hampered by any of that. Plus, he'll have contacts and access to data banks."

"Do you know someone?"

"In the music business, you have to know someone," he assured her. "Rock stars are often in need of discreet assistance, and they want only the best."

She seemed to be struggling with the idea. "No one at the flea market could tell you anything about Gramma Jo?"

"She may not have wanted them to know where she was going. I'm sure we'll find her with the right help."

"You think it's safe to hire someone? It won't get back to Julia or Bret or, God forbid, Tony Bogart?"

"A good P.I. doesn't care about anything but his case, Marnie. He has no interest in juicy details about the Fairmonts. That would be a distraction."

"All right then," she said, releasing what sounded like a sigh of relief. "Is that what you wanted to talk to me about?"

"That's part of it." He was still concerned about her state of mind. She'd been upset about something, but there was no more time to feel her out. He'd run out of options for his own investigation. He was down to the fallback plan, and that's what made this so hard.

The plan involved Alison's disappearance, but it was imperative that he keep those details to himself, even from Marnie. He could tell her nothing, and yet he needed her complete cooperation.

"I'm worried about your safety," he said. "I have been ever since that planter nearly hit you." He came over to sit beside her on the bed. "Bogart has me concerned, too. I thought it was just jealousy. Now I'm not so sure. Marnie, the guy is dangerous, and if he finds out I'm gone, he may come after you. I want you to stay away from him. I want you *here* at the house."

"You're telling me not to leave the house? Ever?"

"Just promise me you won't go looking for your grandmother. It's not safe."

"You think I'm in actual physical danger?"

"I don't know. I just want to be sure you're all right while I'm gone."

"Gone?"

"I have to go to Mexico. There's a problem with a concert down there, and my assistant can't handle it." He could see the suspicion rising in her eyes. Damn, this was going to get brutal. He could feel it.

"What kind of problem?"

"There's been some rioting. The lead singer of the opening act is in the hospital, and I may have to cancel the South American leg of the tour. I'm booked on a red-eye tonight."

"You're flying to Mexico *tonight?*"

"It won't take me long. I could even be back tomorrow." *A white lie,* he told himself.

She was already off the bed, pacing around in her bare feet. He assumed she was worried about the possibility of someone making another attempt on her.

But he could not have been more wrong. He realized that the moment she stopped pacing. Her accusing glare could only mean this was about him.

Marnie went to her purse and pulled out what amounted to the smoking gun. She then strode past Andrew to the liquor cart, grabbed the open bottle of wine and took a slug.

"Listen to me," she said, her voice raspy with rising frustration. "Before you go anywhere we have business to take care of."

"What business?"

She opened her hand to show him the pink diamond studs. "These were *her* earrings. Regine's. I don't want them, thank you."

The diamonds hit the cart's glass top with a soft *plink,* followed by the *clack* of the open wine bottle.

"Those earrings belonged to my mother," Andrew said. "They're all I have of hers that has any real meaning."

"But you gave them to Regine. How could you have given them to *me,* knowing the situation?"

"What situation?"

"How she died." Marnie crossed the room and handed him the rest of her evidence, the police report. "Explain this to me."

His expression turned icy as he saw what she'd given him. "Where did you get this?"

Marnie shook her head. He was the one who'd lied. She wouldn't let him put her on the defensive. "You said Regine's death was an accident. This file says you were charged with her murder."

"The charges were dismissed as soon as my alibi

was substantiated. Where did you get this report? No, don't tell me. Julia, right?"

He threw down the papers and walked over to the fireplace, where a small blaze crackled in the hearth. "She didn't want me anywhere near her precious daughter. Obviously, she still doesn't. Do you think it was an accident that she left out the part about the charges being dismissed?"

"What do you mean by *alibi?* You weren't there when Regine drowned?"

"No, I was there, passed out cold in a lounge chair by the pool. Alison had dropped by that evening to have drinks with Regine, and I knocked down one too many, as I often did in those days."

"What was Alison doing in New York?"

"She was staying at the family's apartment and taking classes at Julliard. When she first moved to the city she called and asked to meet Regine, said she was a big fan. I was reluctant at first, but Alison was persistent and eventually I ran out of reasons not to introduce them. They bonded instantly, partly I'm sure because Alison didn't stop raving about Regine's latest CD."

She caught the cynicism about Alison's motives, but wanted to keep the focus on him. "You said you drank too much that night?"

He nodded. "Regine wanted to swim. She asked me to join her, but I wasn't in any shape. Alison had some phone calls to make, so she went in the house for privacy, and I stretched out on one of the chaise lounges by the pool. The next thing I knew Alison was shaking me. She said she'd found Regine floating facedown in the water."

His hesitancy suggested that he was still shaken by his former fiancée's death. Marnie told him she was sorry, but her voice lacked any real warmth.

He stared into the fire. "She was already gone."

"Then why were you charged?"

"My own stupidity, I suppose. The whole night was a blur. Alison left before the paramedics got there. She had some other dire emergency and I told her to go, but I shouldn't have. I was still out of it. Apparently I broke down and told the paramedics that Regine's death was my fault. They thought I was confessing and called the cops, who hauled me down to the station and booked me. When Alison showed up and explained, the charges were dismissed."

"Alison explained what?"

"She'd been standing by the terrace doors while she made her phone calls. She could see me on the lounge chair, but Regine was out of her line of sight. She told the police I'd passed out and never moved from the chair. A blood alcohol test confirmed that I was well past the legal limit."

Marnie needed a moment to absorb what he'd said. It was plausible enough, but there were still things she didn't understand. "Why didn't you tell me about this?"

"It's not something I enjoy talking about. I *was* drunk when Regine drowned. If I'd been sober, she might be alive. To this day, I feel responsible."

His voice was taut enough to break. She could hear anger and regret.

"You really should let it go," she said finally. "I'm sure I'm not the first to give you this advice. You can't change what happened, and it *was* an accident."

He was quiet for so long that Marnie's thoughts began to race. "Could it have been something else? Suicide?"

"No, Regine didn't kill herself. Someone did it for her."

His head came up, and the angle of his jaw was white, clenched. Marnie knew she should wait, but the questions spilled out anyway. "Someone murdered her? Who?" She answered for him. *"Alison?"*

He nodded. "I was in a drunken haze for a long time afterward, trying to ease my guilt and avoid thinking about it. Alison was right there to help me forget, and at first, I was grateful. It wasn't until after we were married and I sobered up that it dawned on me. Regine was in the way of Alison's grand ambitions, which included pop stardom—and me—as a means to that end."

He exhaled tightly. "She was amoral, incapable of thinking beyond her own needs."

Now Marnie understood the revulsion in his eyes when he looked at her, the barely concealed loathing. He had reasons to hate Alison that anyone would have understood, and he was also struggling with guilt and self-recrimination. Could that tangled mix of emotions have driven him to act on his hatred of Alison?

Marnie's thoughts began to whirl again. Maybe it wasn't Alison's trust fund he'd been after, as Julia had suggested. Maybe it was revenge.

She moved away from him, toward the door. "Some people might call that a motive, Andrew. They might say you were punishing Alison for what you believed she did to Regine. Is that why Alison fell into the sea and drowned? Because she drowned Regine?"

He turned on Marnie, icy and furious. "If I was going to kill Alison, I would have done it that night with my bare hands. She would have been dead the moment I realized what she'd done. I wouldn't have waited five years and pushed her off a boat."

He was enraged. Marnie could feel the heat of it burning through the edges of her fear. She could hear it in his voice. He hadn't done it. Or maybe she just desperately wanted to believe he hadn't, and that was good enough.

She walked over to the bed and sat on the edge, feeling drained more than anything else. Julia may have given her a way out of this, but now that door had closed. She was trapped. She was here, with him—and she was staying.

She bowed her head and let out a sigh.

"Are you all right?" he asked.

"No, I'm not," she said, going quiet. There was no such thing as all right under the circumstances, but she had made her choice, and at least the room had stopped spinning. This was her world. He was the devil she knew.

Finally she asked the only logical question that came to her. "Are you really going to Mexico for a rock concert?"

"Why else would I be going?"

"I don't know, to find Alison? Isn't that what you would do if you thought she was alive? Look for her? Andrew, please, tell me the truth."

Andrew steeled his voice. "Listen to me," he said. "I'm not going to look for Alison. The odds of her being alive are infinitesimal, and we need to concern ourselves with real live threats. We have *plenty* of those. Now, will you let me finish what I need to tell you?"

"Andrew, is this trip about a rock concert or not?"

Her eyes were on fire. Blue fire. She wasn't going to let this go.

"Yes, it *is* a rock concert. I'd bring you with me, but it won't be pretty, and to be honest, I don't want to have to worry about you."

She went quiet, pensive. Finally, a nod. He took it for acquiescence.

"I want you safe while I'm gone," he said. "Can we talk about that?"

Resistance lurked in the set of her mouth. She wasn't convinced of anything, least of all any plan he might have for her safety.

"The detective works with a partner," he told her. "I want to hire them both, one to find your grandmother and the other to keep an eye on you while I'm gone. I've already set everything up. If you agree, a man will show up tomorrow to work on the grounds in place of the regular gardener, and at night, he'll stake out the house. No one will know why he's really here, but you'll have a special cell phone, and all you have to do is press a button if you need him."

"There's going to be a detective here tomorrow? How did you manage that?"

Andrew rubbed his fingers together in the universal gesture of money changing hands. "All I ask is that you don't blow his cover."

"No, of course not." She touched her throat, covering a reddening patch of skin. Another blotch was forming on her face near her jaw, and the distress in her face was obvious. "There was no need to do that, Andrew. It's not me I'm worried about."

"Then, what is it?"

"I have a bad feeling about all of this." She rose from the bed and began to pace again. "Something's wrong."

He frowned. "Can you give me a little more to work with?"

"I don't like the idea of some stranger hunting for my grandmother. *I* should be doing that. And as for you flying off in the middle of the night to a place where people are rioting—well, that's just crazy."

"The P.I. isn't a stranger. He's a professional, and the best money can buy. And I appreciate your concerns about my safety. That's very sweet, but there's no reason. I can take care of myself."

She glared at him. "Sweet? Me? Hardly. I'm not a fortune-teller like my grandmother. I'm not even superstitious, really, but this trip of yours…"

She shook her head, seeming unable to explain herself. Maybe it really *was* him that she was worried about. He wanted to remind her that he'd taken on four strapping young men once, on her account, but she would probably rather forget about that, and he didn't want to embarrass her.

"I was a boxer in school," he said, "at Cambridge, and a pretty good one. I'm well-versed in self-defense, and I'll have a weapon on me."

"What kind of weapon?"

"A pistol, semiautomatic."

"Can you get that on a plane?"

"The gun and I travel separately."

Her brow furrowed. "Is that supposed to be reassuring?"

She stared at him for several long, soul-searching moments, and finally he couldn't take it anymore. It felt as if she were cutting into him with a fiery blade. God, she was intense. She might not be a fortune-teller, but she had an uncanny ability to read him. And she was wise to have a bad feeling about this trip. She was right about that.

To his complete bewilderment, she reached behind her head and unhooked the chain at her nape.

"What are you doing?" he asked. His jugular began to pulse. Never a good sign.

She walked over to him, her hand extended, the delicate gold chain dripping from her fingers. "I want you to take this with you, just in case."

"Your good luck charm? I can't do that. It's from your grandmother."

"Take it, wear it. I want you to. *Dammit.*"

She had that fierce, show-no-mercy expression on her face, but he was beginning to see it as a front for deeper emotions, in this case fear and frustration, even anguish. She really didn't want him to go, and she was struggling with her feelings.

He took the chain. "Thank you," he said, not sure what else to do. "I'll keep it close. I promise."

"Okay, then," she said, her voice going hoarse.

Please, God, don't let her cry. I don't do well when this woman cries.

He watched her closely, praying that she would win her fight against the tears. He really didn't understand what had provoked her to give him the charm. He knew what it meant to her, beyond the connection to her grandmother. It had saved her life.

She sucked in a breath, apparently shoring herself up.

Grateful, he moved to drop the chain in the pocket of his robe, but her hand flashed out and caught his, as if he'd been about to slap a child.

Her expression was fierce again. "I want you to wear it," she said. "The chain is long enough. No one will see it under your clothes. Here."

She took it from him and turned him around. She had him so off guard he didn't think to protest. It was as if a form of paralysis had come over him. He was a Ken doll, unable to move until she lifted his arm. Bizarre. He felt her doing things to his neck, breathing on him and feathering his skin as she stood on tiptoe and craned around his shoulder, trying to see the chain she was arranging.

Her fingers were warm and silky, and her breath trembled a little as it lapped against his hair and face. She smelled of lilies and tangy feminine perspiration. He was nervous, too.

"There," she said, her voice low and oddly breathy. "Now maybe I can relax."

Yes, but could he? When he turned around, she averted her eyes. He tipped her head up to thank her again, and saw the roiling mix of emotion that shadowed her eyes. What in God's name? Pain, fear, desire. They were burning her up. It confounded him.

"I can't let you go," she said. "I'm scared."

His body was in knots. "Jesus, Marnie."

22

It had already gone too far. Marnie wanted to take back what she'd said and tell him to go on his trip. She would help him pack. He would be back before anyone missed him, and everything would be fine. But she couldn't seem to stop herself. *"Stay with me."*

She couldn't stop the shudder that unlocked her frozen jaw or the fire that stung her throat like nettles. She was going to cry.

"Don't go," she got out.

He stood back to peer at her. What was going on? That was the question in his eyes. He didn't seem to know who this poor, pathetic woman was any more than she did. But as he stared at her, his jaw tightened into a knot and his face formed a scowl.

And then a miracle happened. He was the one who lost control. Not tears, nothing like that, but just for an instant, he gripped her arms hard enough to take her breath away. "Andrew?" She hadn't imagined the hesitation in his breathing or the painful twitch in his cheek muscle.

"Shut up." He yanked her into his arms with such force she couldn't speak. "I have to go, but you'll be fine. I have you covered. Nothing bad is going to happen."

Something in his voice told her that he meant every word, but only the first part registered. He would not change his mind about going. There was nothing she could do.

She sagged against him. "Okay then, whatever."

"I'll be all right," he whispered. "I'm coming back for you."

He took her by her shoulders and held her away. "It's true," he said, as if that statement was a revelation, even to him.

Marnie crawled back to him. The entire length of his arms she crawled, clutching and sighing, into the heat of his embrace. His robe had come undone and she stole her way inside it, coming flush against him, grinding her hips into his, aching, reveling.

"Ah, God," she whispered.

She just couldn't help herself.

He groaned, and it was the most erotic thing she'd ever heard. She felt him hardening against her belly, and the pressure sent an urgent thrill through her.

She was so afraid of this man, and so crazy hungry for him. And was that any surprise? All her life she had dreamed of being with him, and now that she had been, he was leaving her, and she didn't know where the hell he was going—or why.

"Whatever we're doing, we need to stop." Andrew's warning turned into a growl.

"Yes, but not tonight. You're leaving and there are no guarantees, Andrew. I need this."

She shrugged out of her jacket, and before it hit the floor they were both at work, unbuttoning her slacks. His reaction was immediate. His cheek muscle wasn't the only thing twitching now. He was aroused, but for a moment, the sight of him took her back. She'd rarely encountered a man in this state who hadn't been calling her names and degrading her. It had almost always been that way. Men like Butch had lusted after her and hated themselves for it.

This was different. He was different.

His robe hit the ground, and he bent over her, hesitating long enough to draw up her camisole and release the front closure of her bra. Her breasts fell free, and he let out a sigh that was heavy with appreciation. There was none of the hesitation of their last encounter in the way he touched her. His hands thrilled her. They were tender and sweetly punishing. His lips and teeth were even better. His white-hot tugs on her nipples made her whimper with pleasure.

"I need to make love to you," he told her. "There are no guarantees, and *I* need that."

She dropped into the overstuffed chair and reached for him as he moved between her legs. The weight of his body sent voltage coursing through her. She couldn't hold still. She couldn't wait. It was insane, but she was already climaxing when he entered her. The pressure of his body moving inside hers created even deeper sensations. It was like a waterfall breaking the surface of a pond and driving all the way to the bottom before dissolving into ripples and bubbles.

Suddenly everything tightened, and Marnie forgot to breathe. He scooped her into his arms and she fell against him, limp and shuddering, still spasming with pleasure. She couldn't move to save her life. She wasn't sure she ever would again.

At some point later when the tremors had quieted, she hooked her arms around his neck and buried her face in his shoulder. She wondered how long they had before he left. There would be no sleep tonight either, but that wasn't a concern. She wanted to feel the heat and solidity of his body and whatever sense of comfort that could give her.

Tomorrow it would all be different. He would be in another country, and she had a plan of her own, although it didn't involve searching for her grandmother. She would let the expert do that, at least for now.

Marnie sat up in bed, startled to see daylight beyond the glass balcony doors. She'd known Andrew would be gone before morning, but she'd thought he would wake her when he left. She slipped on his robe and made a quick search of the bedroom and bath. Apparently he'd had a bag packed. Otherwise, she would have heard him.

She found the cell phone he'd mentioned on the night table, with a note explaining that it had a panic button for the detective, as well as international range and a number to reach Andrew in emergencies. That relieved her mind. She didn't see her good luck charm anywhere, either. He hadn't left it on the pillow, as she'd thought he might.

She touched her throat, aware of the hollow sensation in her stomach. She'd worn the ring since she was a kid. There was no way not to feel naked without it.

As she gathered the terry robe around her and tied the sash, she contemplated what her next move would be. It wasn't quite seven, and the light filling the windows was hazy with coastal clouds. She doubted anyone was up yet. If she acted quickly, she might be able to accomplish her mission while the household was still sleeping.

A moment later, she was downstairs and moving soundlessly through the house, stopping at every window to look out. The landscaping was extensive, despite the mansion being built on a cliff. Rock gardens alternated with terraced greenbelts, and every patio had potted palms, hanging ferns and bubbling fountains. She'd noticed that a small crew came occasionally to do the heavy work, and the rest of the time, one gardener maintained everything.

She was looking for that man.

When she'd covered the entire floor, she stood at the living room windows with a deep sense of disappointment. She'd been hoping to see the man Andrew had said would be here. Maybe it was too early, or the wrong day. She thought he'd said in the morning, but the grounds were deserted.

She was turning away when she thought she saw a sudden movement. A shadow? Had it come from the terrace? It could have been anything, a bird in flight. She unbolted the French doors, glancing around before she slipped outside.

It was getting late enough that someone might be awake. The tide was low, muting the sound of the surf, but Marnie thought she heard another noise, the scuff of shoes on stone.

It sounded as if someone was walking on the terrace below, the one where she'd been standing when the planter fell. She went to the railing to look down, and heard the noise again, only now it was coming from behind her. Her pulse kicked up a notch.

She went straight to the worst-case scenario, and her thoughts careened with indecision. She had no way to defend herself. If she went over the side, it was a twenty-foot drop to the slate tiles below. *Turn and go for his eyes, then run.*

Adrenaline surged. She turned, checking herself only as she registered the asinine grin on his face. "Bret?"

Alison's brother swaggered toward her, eyeing her oversize robe. "If it isn't Ali*suck*," he said. "I see you still like to run around in your bathrobe."

"I thought I heard someone outside."

"So, you just had to dash out and investigate?"

He moved closer, his grin curling into a sneer. He was wearing his usual beach gear—cargo shorts, a tank top and leather flip-flops.

"I have to go." Her voice dropped low, a snarl. He brought out the cornered animal in her. Maybe she ought to tell him what had happened to the last asshole who'd cornered her. "Get out of my way."

He didn't, of course. He purposely blocked her when she tried to go around him. He hadn't touched her yet, but he was daring her to make him do just that.

"Remember what happened the last time you were with me in a bathrobe?" he asked her.

From the way he looked at her, Marnie knew it was sexual, but she didn't dare react. She had no way of knowing what might have happened between him and his sister.

"I was going through a growth spurt," he said. "And you threatened to tell Mom, but you never did. That was the last time you ever tortured your disgusting little brother, wasn't it, Alisuck?"

"I don't know what you're talking about."

"The last time you ever laughed at Bret for being a perv."

She caught a glimpse of the raw emotion burning in his eyes, and knew she had to get out of there. It wasn't sex he wanted, it was revenge. He hated his sister. "Are you going to get out of my way?" she demanded.

"What's the rush? Where's the hubby this morning, off sailing?"

"He was called away on business."

"Really? Nice timing."

Bret reached for the sash of her robe and she slapped his hand away. The son of a bitch thought he was going to expose her? Like hell. She might have to go for his eyes, after all.

"We're playing hard to get?" He laughed and lunged at her.

Marnie dodged him, letting out a shrill scream, but it wasn't just Bret who'd startled her. A man had bounded onto the terrace. He wore rawhide gloves and was dressed like a gardener, but she'd never seen him before.

"Was that you, ma'am?" The man hesitated, glaring suspiciously at Bret. "I heard someone scream."

Bret threw up a hand, exasperated. "Yeah, she screamed. You frightened her half to death. Who the hell are you?"

Marnie rushed over to the man, who was well out of Bret's reach. He could easily have been a gardener. Many of the local landscaping crews wore gloves and wrapped bandannas around their heads. "What's your name?" she asked.

"Diego Sanchez," he said. "I work for Horton Landscaping. Is there anything else I can do? If not, I have some cleanup work on this terrace. The plants need to be pruned."

"Of course, clean up the terrace. I'll get out of your way." She glanced at Bret. "If you'll excuse me, little brother. I'm going inside to put some clothes on."

A cold smile touched her mouth as she made her exit. If she was right, Sanchez didn't work for any landscaping company. Andrew had come through with the detective he promised, which made her wish she could hole up and do what he'd asked—stay safe. But she needed to get dressed and go out, though she intended to be cautious in the extreme. Certain questions had been nagging at her for months, and she'd promised herself if she ever got back to Mirage Bay, she would deal with them. Now, with Andrew gone, might be her only opportunity.

23

By the time she got to the Mirage Bay Yacht Club, Marnie had decided she probably *wasn't* being tailed. She hadn't seen any cars behind her on the way here, and she'd taken some unexpected turns, just to be sure. She'd also been watchful since she arrived, and hadn't spotted anyone lurking in corners.

Still, even as she'd been driving, she'd had the feeling of being watched, and it had stayed with her as she let herself out of the BMW and walked to the gate that led to the docks. It had actually felt like eyes at her back, a cliché she'd never fully appreciated before. Maybe she was still reacting to the way Bret had sneaked up behind her.

If someone had been tailing her, he was the most likely culprit. She'd left Sanchez cleaning up the terrace, so she doubted it was him, if he *was* the person Andrew had hired. And someone had nearly dropped a planter on her head, if that had been intentional. So many *ifs*. Too many. She'd come here precisely because too much was unanswered, and the question on her mind today was what had really happened on Andrew's boat.

She used his key card to open the gate and let

herself in. He kept the card and the yacht keys in a leather case with his watches and cuff links. She'd been startled to find a purse-size pistol in the drawer of her nightstand, along with a note from Andrew telling her it was the gun she'd asked for. The note warned her to use it only as a last resort, and he'd included printed safety instructions and a small box of bullets. It must have been a last-minute decision on his part, because he hadn't mentioned it to her when they'd talked last night.

Marnie had no intention of using the gun. She'd been only half-serious when she'd asked for it.

She was glad she'd worn deck shoes for traction as she picked her way down the ramp. It probably hadn't occurred to Andrew that she might want to see the yacht where Alison had met her fate, whatever it was. But checking out the *Bladerunner* had been a goal of Marnie's since she'd learned about the accident. She'd also become consumed with knowing who Alison really was. The woman whose identity she'd taken was the catalyst for almost everything that had happened in February, and when she'd disappeared the answers had disappeared with her.

Marnie had never been on the *Bladerunner,* or any boat, but picked Andrew's sloop out from the crowd before she got to the bottom of the ramp. Of course, it was the biggest sailing yacht in the club, and moored in the guest dock at the end of the pier, so wasn't hard to spot. And Marnie had seen the vessel before. It had been quite an event when Andrew launched the *Bladerunner* and took his wife out for their first sail in the bay.

Marnie went straight to the bow, where Alison had gone overboard. She knew all the damage had been repaired, so there wouldn't be any physical reminders of what had happened, but she wanted to see the exact spot. She wanted to feel the vibes and see if there was any way to connect with the events of six months ago—a stormy night when Alison had fallen from this boat and Marnie had plunged from a cliff. Had either of them been pushed? Both of them?

She didn't understand why the ocean had taken one of them and not the other, if that was what had happened. One of her grandmother's favorite sayings came to mind as she stared down at the water. *When you give things to the sea, be it trash, woe, prayers or wealth, the sea remembers.*

It had come from an old sea fable, and the words had long haunted Marnie. She'd thought of them as she stood on the cliffs that night, looking down at the boiling ocean. But now, she picked up nothing from the placid waters of the bay. No storms today. The weather was balmy and beautiful. Maybe if the *Bladerunner* had been moving, heading out to sea…

She glanced at her watch, knowing she had to get on with her search. She went belowdecks next, where the only object of interest she found was a photo journal of Andrew's various boating trips. The leatherbound album wasn't lying out, but it wasn't hidden, either. Marnie discovered it under a stack of coffee-table books as she was checking out the volumes in the yacht's library.

She leafed through pages of pictures, reading the detailed captions, notes and anecdotes. It was a labor of love for him, obviously, and apparently the trips were something he'd been documenting since he purchased his first sailboat at age nineteen. He'd been all over the world, to exotic locales like Fiji, Pago Pago and the Virgin Islands, and some of the more recent trips had been taken with Alison.

It didn't surprise Marnie that he hadn't talked about his sailing adventures, considering how little they'd shared during their six months together. What did surprise her was the snapshot of Alison she found toward the back of the journal. It had been blown up to eight by ten, a shot of Alison standing on the bow, barefoot, in a sheer cover-up with a black bikini underneath.

Marnie continued to stare at it for several seconds, not quite sure what was bothering her. Abruptly, she realized Alison was standing where she had just been, at the bow—where Alison was supposed to have gone over the side. Marnie's stomach rolled as if the boat had moved. She turned the page and saw more pictures of Alison—a full page of them in snapshot size. These were different shots, but she was standing in the same place.

Marnie didn't understand. Two pages of pictures of Alison at the scene of her accident, one of them a blowup. Why would Andrew do this? Last night's conversation came back to her. She didn't want to believe he'd pushed her, but he so clearly hated her.

A sense of foreboding gripped Marnie. Another roll of her stomach forced her to put the journal down. She left it under the stack of books where she'd found it, her only thought to go above and get some air. But her foot caught on something as she made her way through the main cabin.

She glanced down at the heavy wooden handle protruding from the oblong hole in the teak drawer. The drawer was a built-in storage unit beneath one of the couches, and the hole served as a pull. Marnie knelt and wrestled the drawer open. The handle belonged to an odd-looking, narrow-bladed saw with jagged teeth.

The kind of saw to cut through a lifeline.

The way her thoughts were going frightened her. She jammed the saw back into the drawer and shut it. The question propelled her toward the stairs that would take her above deck. The hatch door was open, and as she climbed the steps and the cockpit came into view, her heart dropped. She wasn't alone on the boat. While she'd been below, someone had come aboard, and he was the most unwelcome visitor Marnie could imagine.

Tony Bogart was standing in the pit, his hands on his hips, staring at the sweating woman who'd frozen midstep. She could not let him see what she'd just seen.

Rebecca tried the handle of the guest room door, relieved to find it unlocked. Andrew was still out of town and Alison had left early this morning without a word to anyone, so Rebecca had decided to take a chance and check out their room. She hadn't had the opportunity to prepare it for them because of Julia's sudden decision to switch their rooms. The unlocked door might mean the beautiful couple had nothing to hide, but she sincerely doubted it. Everyone in this psycho family had something to hide, especially these two. She just hadn't figured out what it was yet.

She started with the nightstands. People kept their most personal and private possessions right next to them, and it was amazing what they didn't lock up, what they thought was safe just because it was nearby. She'd been working for wealthy families since she was a kid, first as a babysitter, then a housekeeper, now an assistant, and it was better than a degree in psychology for digging up dirt—and for predicting what people were going to do next.

The Fairmonts had been predictable from the beginning, although Rebecca had wanted to believe differently. She'd wanted to believe Bret saw her as someone worth his precious time and interest, and that Julia would recognize her potential. But money had made them all careless—and cruel.

Julia treated her like hired help. Rebecca was used to being dismissed, ignored, even invisible. The wealthy had a way of making you feel as if you didn't exist except to serve their needs, but Julia had crossed the line when she started ridiculing Rebecca for being fat and incompetent. And Bret pretended to be her ally, but he treated her like trailer trash. Even Alison, who'd defended her in front of Julia, had made it look as if Rebecca was some pathetic thing who couldn't defend herself.

Huge mistake. She could defend herself.

A trembling smile crossed her lips and her heart surged with anticipation at the beauty of her plan. Just watch and be amazed, world.

She spotted Andrew's side of the bed by the fancy leather case on the nightstand. It contained his jewelry and other odds and ends, but nothing all that interesting—or incriminating. There was also nothing of interest in the nightstand drawer, just some loose change, a pack of breath mints, airline tickets and a few receipts. Rebecca wasn't sure whether Andrew was the exception to her rule or whether he knew this was the first place a good snoop would look.

Alison's side was a whole different story. Rebecca opened the nightstand drawer and clapped a hand over her mouth when she saw the gun. "There *is* a God," she said under her breath.

She eased the drawer open farther, trying to figure out if the weapon was real. "Shit," she whispered as the bullets and the instructions came into view. *Shit.* This was perfect. They were playing right into her hands, all of them.

Rebecca didn't have much use for people like the Fairmonts. They'd been given every damn thing they had, the money, the social status. None of them had worked a real job in their lives. They bitched about everything and appreciated nothing, especially her. She'd worked hard and killed herself for what? A little bit of praise, a hint of approval?

But this gun had to be a sign that she was doing the right thing. Someone needed to cut the Fairmonts down to size, and maybe it really was supposed to be her. In a way it was justice.

God, she hoped that was true.

"Rebecca? What are you doing in here?"

Bret had the door wide-open and was leaning against the frame, watching her. She had no idea how long he'd been there or whether he'd seen what was in the drawer. It blew her mind that she hadn't heard him, hadn't heard a thing.

"Hey, Bret, you're up early." She took a step toward

him, smiling as if she were actually pleased to see him—and blocked his view of the nightstand. "Alison asked me to clean up while she was out today."

"That sounds like Alison." He rolled his eyes. "Spoiled brat should do it herself."

"Yeah, probably." Rebecca still had no idea what Bret was up to. She edged back until she felt the drawer against her hip, and pushed it shut. "I'll just finish up, though."

Rebecca pulled a dust rag from the rolled-up sleeve of her blouse and wiped down the nightstand, focusing on the table lamp. She kept a cloth stashed somewhere on her person at all times in case Julia wanted a spot cleanup. It happened.

Unfortunately, Bret hadn't missed her attempt to cover her tracks. When she stepped away, he was still looking at the drawer.

After several long seconds, he glanced up at her with an expression of concern. "Maybe you'd better get out of here, Rebecca. You're in enough trouble already, aren't you?"

"What's that supposed to mean?"

"I found your notes. I know what you're up to." An enigmatic smile appeared as he nodded toward the bedroom door and waved her out.

"You're quite a piece of work," he whispered as she brushed past him. "Good luck."

Rebecca began to shake once she was out in the hallway. *Good luck?* She hurried toward the stairs, wondering what he'd meant by that. Was he going to let her get away with it? Did he want her to do it?

24

Marnie patted the pocket of her shorts to make sure the keys to the boat were there. She had to get the cabin locked up quickly, but without making Bogart suspicious. The pictures of Alison had disturbed the hell out of her. The saw was probably a common tool used on the boat, and she intended to give Andrew a chance to explain all of it. Meanwhile, she didn't want a bastard like Tony Bogart nosing around.

"Everything okay?" he asked her. "You don't look so good."

"Couldn't be better," she said evenly, determined not to give him even a glimpse of the anger flaring inside her. He had no business boarding the *Bladerunner*. He might as well have broken into their home, but of course, he assumed she wouldn't dare confront him. No one confronted the FBI, even when they were unofficial.

"I was just getting ready to leave," she said.

She turned her back to him long enough to lock the cabin door. There. Good. Now to get him off Andrew's yacht.

"Returning to the scene of the crime?" he said. "In my experience, only killers do that, not victims."

"Crime? What crime?" She feigned surprise that he would utter the word.

"Excuse me, the *accident*. Still, it must be difficult for you."

"Not at all," she said. "I'm lucky to be alive, and what else matters? I believe in closing the door on the past and moving on. You should try it."

His head snapped up, and his eyes turned mean. Marnie met the visual assault with a shrug. They both knew what it meant. *You got dumped, Bogart. Get over it.*

"Don't flatter yourself," he said, his tone contemptuous. "My interest in the past is limited to seeing my brother's killer on death row, and trust me, I won't rest until that happens."

He scratched his face, rubbing his thumb along his jaw with enough pressure to leave a white crease.

Marnie had hit a raw nerve. The reckless corner of her soul didn't care. No matter what Alison had done to Tony, it didn't justify him stalking and harassing her like this. He was holding her hostage with his accusations, and getting away with it. Marnie was reasonably certain he didn't have the jurisdiction or the authorization to investigate any of the alleged crimes that had happened February second, including his own brother's death. And she was sick of him breathing down her neck. No wonder she'd felt as if she were being followed.

Perspiration trickled down the back of her neck, and the sane voice in her head told her not to provoke him any further. She might have listened, if he hadn't made it personal.

"You weren't even a good fuck," he said, "you know that? I'm not sure why I bothered."

Marnie climbed the remaining stairs and stepped onto the gleaming teak deck. Her breath came heavily, but not from exertion. "What the hell crime are you accusing me of, Special Agent Bogart?"

"What are you guilty of?"

"Wishing I had a gun? Why the hell are you here? You're trespassing. Where's your warrant?"

"What?"

"Produce a search warrant or get off this boat."

"Prove you didn't invite me here," he said.

"You're uninvited. *Leave.*"

She glared at him until he snarled something obscene under his breath, and jumped down to the dock. Only then did she unclench her sweating fists. Andrew had told her to call in case of an emergency. She'd tucked the cell phone he gave her in the same pocket as the keys. She dug it out, trying to remember how to use the speed dial function. He'd programmed his number in, but this wasn't like her own cell phone, and the keypad might as well have been in Greek.

"Do you have the gun? Marnie, did you bring the pistol with you?"

"Stop asking if I have the gun," she snapped, speaking into the cell's mouthpiece. Andrew's soft, gravelly voice yanked at her nerves, pulling them tighter, notch by notch. "What difference does it make? Bogart is gone."

At least the cell phone worked. She'd reached Andrew on the first try, and told him that Tony Bogart had probably followed her to the boat. She'd also told Andrew about finding the photo journal and the pictures of Alison, but he seemed to be avoiding her demands that he explain.

"I had a feeling you might leave the house," he said, "and I wanted to know that you could protect yourself. I wanted to be sure you'd be all right."

She brushed at her forehead, wiping the dampness away. She must be a lovely shade of red by now. "I'll be *all right* when you answer my questions. What are those pictures about? There must be a dozen of them."

His silence made her heart hesitate.

"I was studying them," he said at last, "trying to figure out how she fell. The one I enlarged was taken the evening it happened."

"Who took the pictures?"

"I did."

"All of them? All posed the same way in the same place? Doesn't that seem a little bizarre to you?"

"Not bizarre at all. I searched for every photo I'd ever taken of her in that spot. I wanted to compare them. Marnie, there aren't that many places to take pictures on a sailboat."

Nearly the entire yacht was visible to her from where she was standing in the cockpit. "I've never been on a sailboat before, but I can see plenty of places."

"Either you believe me or you don't. Look again at the pictures taken the evening she fell, and you'll see that each is a different contrast and intensity. I used a software program to bring up the detail. I was looking for evidence."

"Evidence of what?"

"That the lifeline broke or that something was tampered with. Something tangible to explain why she went over the side."

"Evidence that you didn't push her?"

"Yes, exactly, but I didn't find it."

He didn't sound hesitant or evasive anymore. He sounded tired of being accused every time they spoke— and she was tired, too. God knew she didn't like being on the offensive any more than he liked being on the defensive, but she couldn't ignore what was right in front of her. Still, she could feel her suspicions dissolving, and it was almost a relief. Believing him was easier. Living with paranoia and distrust was a bitch.

"What about the saw? I found a saw in one of the storage units."

"What did you do, search the boat? Sometimes you have to cut through tangled rigging, and a saw's the quickest way to do it."

At this point she should either change the subject or apologize. She wasn't ready to do the latter. "Is it dangerous there?" she asked him. "When are you coming back?"

"I'm not the one you should be worried about. The only risk a concert promoter runs is being pissed on by a drunk rock star." He was silent a moment. "Marnie, go back to the house and get the gun. Don't go anywhere without it."

"Andrew, I don't have a permit to carry it."

"So, you'll pay the fine. That's better than being dead."

"Why do you keep insisting that someone's going to kill me?"

"Maybe I'm trying to scare you into being more cautious."

"In that case, save yourself the time. I don't respond well to scare tactics."

"Marnie, Bogart is a mean bastard, and you're no match for him, no matter what you think. He has a vendetta against Alison, and it's not just because she dumped him."

"All of which I already know," she reminded him.

He gave a heavy sigh. "Do we have a deal or don't we?"

"You asked me not to search for my grandmother, and I haven't."

"Will you go back to the house and stay there?"

She thought the boat was rocking, but when she touched the companionway door to steady herself, she realized it was her. She'd been shifting from foot to foot, rocking the way she used to when she was a kid.

"I'm on my way back to the house," she told him. It was easier than trying to explain that she had errands to do first, such as stopping at the gas station for fuel and the drugstore for odds and ends that were essential to civilized life, like feminine hygiene products. Or that as beautiful as Sea Clouds was, she had to get out of there every once in a while or go insane.

She appreciated his concern for her safety, unless it was just one more way to keep her locked down and under control.

"Good. Take care of yourself until I get home. Can you do that much for me, please?"

Something about the tone of the conversation had irritated her from the beginning. She was being patronized, and this wasn't the first time. He'd been doing it since the day she opened her eyes in the hospital.

"Sure." She hung up the phone.

* * *

The strange gasping noises were like nothing Marnie had ever heard. At first she thought someone was strangling, or being suffocated. Sweltering in the midday sun, she stopped to listen. They seemed to be coming from the far side of the house, where there was a delivery entrance off the kitchen.

Marnie had just pulled into the front portico and let herself out of the car. She'd been heading into the house when she heard the sounds. She didn't know whether to be frightened or concerned. Even if it was just someone crying, she was going to be careful.

She was still damp all over, her face flushed and spotty. It had been a lousy day so far, and this weird turn of events didn't bode well. She yanked off her cardigan sweater, tied it around her waist and prepared to investigate. She wasn't anxious to go inside the house, anyway. She never knew what was lying in wait for her at Sea Clouds.

"Hello?" Marnie called out as she moved slowly around to the side of the house. "Who's there?"

No one answered, and the noises got louder. It did sound like sobbing, she realized. She thought about going for reinforcements when she saw a pair of sandaled feet protruding from the recessed entrance to the side door. The gaudy, heavily jeweled sandals were immediately familiar, and so was the perfume. It smelled like someone had broken a bottle of Wind Song.

"LaDonna?"

Marnie discovered her childhood friend sitting on the stoop, bent over and sobbing her heart out.

"Did you fall?" Marnie asked, sitting beside her on the stoop. The pantry and kitchen were just inside the doorway, and she was concerned that someone might hear, but LaDonna didn't look as if she could get up.

"Are you all right?" Marnie asked.

LaDonna's auburn curls bounced as she shook her head. "No, I'm not all right. I'm terrible. I'm going to die."

"Should I call 911? The paramedics? What's wrong?"

"It's your stupid brother. He just dumped me."

"Bret? You and Bret?" Marnie was stunned. Her thoughts flashed back to the morning at Gramma Jo's cottage when she'd come upon LaDonna. It must have been Bret who'd ducked out the back way.

"Is that why you're here? You came to see Bret?"

"No, I was delivering a prescription for Julia. She likes to have her drugs of choice dropped off at the back door."

Marnie felt like a hypocrite for disapproving. There was a time she would have had her sleeping pills delivered, if she'd thought she could get away with it.

"And you ran into Bret?" she asked.

"No, I called him on my cell when I got here, hoping he'd come down, but he went ballistic, the asshole. I'm not supposed to act like I know him. I'm okay for sex, but not the family. Apparently he doesn't want to embarrass your drugged-up mother."

She crumpled in a heap, gasping, moaning, furious.

Marnie had never seen her friend this way. Sadly, she could relate. She'd had a crush on a man who was out of reach since she was a kid. Andrew had never treated her this way, but how could he? He had to make the world believe she was his princess bride.

The tightness in her throat was due to bitterness,

Marnie realized. She really did understand. All her life she'd been not good enough.

She touched LaDonna's shoulder. "Why don't we take a walk," she said. She wanted to get her away from the doorway, where they could talk uninterrupted. There was no telling who was inside.

"Why are you being so nice to me?" LaDonna asked as Marnie helped her to her feet.

"Because I understand about man trouble," she said. "All women do. We're all sisters when it comes to men."

They walked to a corner of the courtyard inside the wrought-iron fence. It was still private, but far enough away from the house.

"Are you in love with him?" Marnie asked, gentling her voice. She couldn't imagine how anyone could be, but it wouldn't help to be judgmental now.

"Yeah, stupid me, I am. But I hate him, too. He treats me like shit, and I probably should be glad it's over."

Marnie was careful not to take that bait. If she put Bret down, LaDonna would most likely leap to his defense. She wanted to be over him, but she wasn't. It didn't happen that quickly, and for some people, it never seemed to. They kept going back to the well long after it was empty.

"Listen," Marnie said, "we all make mistakes when it comes to men. Don't feel bad. Your mistake wasn't in loving him, it was in not seeing that he wasn't good enough for you. You should have dumped him first."

"I suppose." LaDonna sighed, clearly not convinced.

There had been too many heartbreaks, Marnie

realized. Too much rejection. Eventually it wore you down. She searched for some other way to get through to her. She needed something tangible, not platitudes.

"Remember the guitar player you caught with those groupies?" She touched LaDonna's hand. "You dropped him like he was spoiled meat. It's not like you don't know how to cut a guy loose."

LaDonna stopped sniffling and peered at Marnie. "How did you know about Jerry?"

Immediately Marnie realized she'd made a mistake. Alison couldn't possibly have known about the guitar player. LaDonna had told Marnie years ago in strict confidence. It was the sort of thing only best friends shared.

As Marnie struggled to come up with a plausible explanation, she could feel heat flare up her neck. It was creeping onto her face, the blotches that she'd had since childhood. The blotches that LaDonna knew about.

Her old friend stared at her, shock transforming her face. She didn't say anything for several seconds, but she couldn't take her eyes off the blotches, or Marnie. She didn't say anything, but she had figured it out. Marnie could feel it. LaDonna knew who Alison Fairmont really was.

"I need to go," LaDonna said, glancing at her watch. "I have to get back to work."

She began to walk to the pharmacy delivery car, parked just outside the back gate. Marnie hurried to walk with her.

"You know, I think Bret told me about that guitar player," Marnie said. "Someone did, I just can't remember who now."

"Right, sure." LaDonna nodded her head, but never once looked at Marnie. "Thanks for your help. That was nice of you."

Everything she said sounded flat and false, and finally Marnie stopped and watched her get in the car and go. A sense of wild desperation came over her as she realized what she'd done. LaDonna may have been a friend once, but she was wildly indiscreet and possibly the worst person in the world to keep a secret. Marnie was going to have to take drastic measures, and she had to move fast.

25

Tony Bogart paused to look up at the darkening sky. The rising crescent moon reminded him of an ivory elephant tusk, as pornographic as it was white and luminous. He stared at the strange sight awhile before continuing down the deserted beach. He felt like a damn pervert anyway, out walking around in the dark, but it was still warm and humid, and his motel room had no AC.

He needed to clear his head. He wasn't thinking worth shit lately. It felt as if he'd regressed to childhood since coming home. He'd always had good instincts, even before the FBI training, but somehow, he'd managed to lose his target. Andrew Fairmont had disappeared, and Tony had already exhausted every resource available to him to track the man down.

He'd had the Fairmont place staked out for days, but he'd dozed off last night, and this morning he'd noticed the compound's gate open. He'd asked questions down the hill and was just damn lucky that a convenience store clerk leaving his shift had seen Fairmont in a taxi around midnight, heading for the freeway.

Mirage Bay was dead asleep by midnight, even

during the summer. You didn't see a lot of taxis rolling around, so it wasn't surprising that the clerk would have noticed. Tony had been able to trace Fairmont as far as the San Diego airport, but after that the trail evaporated. Tony had taken the risk of using his FBI credentials to get access to airline schedules, including passenger manifests, but had found nothing.

Fairmont had fucking vanished.

Desperate, Tony had gone after Alison, planning to question her about her husband's disappearance, but she'd flipped out and kicked him off the boat before he had a chance. That wasn't like Alison. She might have venomous fangs hidden under that beautiful mouth, but she didn't bare her teeth and snarl like the woman he'd encountered this morning. She wasn't a street fighter, like him, and she didn't make threats when she had everything to lose.

Something was way off with her. Drugs, maybe. Pain pills. With all her surgeries, she'd had the time and opportunity to get hooked. He would have to check that out. It was also bugging him that his snitch had gone silent again—and left him hanging. Tony had tried telling himself that this dead end wasn't his fault; he didn't have access to the forensic expertise he needed. But it *felt* like his fault.

He glanced up as he approached the cliffs, not because something had pulled his attention. When Satan's Teeth came into view you always looked up at the monstrosity. The teethlike outcroppings and the legends about them commanded attention. But tonight it was that strange horned moon, and the way its light reflected off the jagged cliff edge.

Tony was still staring at the cliffs when he saw

something rocking back and forth. It looked as if someone was up there. He strained to see. Was the person dancing, some strange ritual in the moonlight? But then the wind changed, and he caught the screams. It was two people fighting, locked in physical combat.

Women. At least one of them was. The screaming got louder. Rocks tumbled down the cliff, and with every move the figures were getting closer to the edge. He shouted at them to stop, but they probably couldn't hear him over the incoming tide and the noise they were making.

He broke into a jog, heading for the cliffs. He was too far away to do anything, but he might get close enough to identify them. One of the women was slender with long hair that looked dark, but he couldn't be sure The moonlight had turned it silver. His first thought was Alison Fairmont. She was the aggressor, wrestling the other woman toward the edge.

He couldn't see the victim, but he could hear her screams. "I won't tell anyone," she cried out, pleading with her attacker.

Tony heard the pop of what he thought might be a gun, drowned out by shrieks as one of the figures fell to the rocks below. He couldn't tell which had gone over, but it looked like the one being attacked, and she was as good as dead. The tide was coming in, but the water wouldn't have been deep enough to break her fall.

Tony stopped in his tracks, gathering his wits. He had just witnessed a cold-blooded murder. He glanced at his watch, checking the time, and then ripped his cell phone out of the case attached to his belt, and called 911. He would never be able to get to the woman on the rocks, so he headed for the cliffs.

He sprinted away from the water, leaped onto the seawall and then ran back out to the cliff edge. It was some distance, and when he got to the spot where he'd seen the fighters, the long-haired woman was gone. He looked down the beach, but there was no sign of her. She'd had plenty of time to get away.

Tony paused to catch his breath and consider his options. He had almost certainly witnessed a murder, which meant he was no longer off duty. He was now an eyewitness.

"Helluva game." Bret finished off his beer and lined the empty cup up with the others on the table next to his recliner. He wanted another one, but he could feel the booze fuzzing his head. "Can you believe the Padres? They *killed* the Dodgers."

He grabbed the remote to turn off the TV and the TiVo box. His mother's silence made him glance over his shoulder to see what she was doing. She always preferred the sectional sofas in the third row, but Bret liked to be right up front where he couldn't miss anything.

Watching the Padres play was the only thing he and his mother still did together, but she'd flaked out on him tonight. She'd stretched out on the couch and fallen fast asleep, snoozing through the last hour of the game, though she would never admit to that.

"Mom? Are you all right? Did you like the game?"

"Great," Julia said, her voice husky. Her lids blinked open and she quickly sat up, aware that she'd been caught napping. "I must have closed my eyes for a minute," she said. "I'll make some coffee."

"Too much pinot?" Bret knew that would get a snarl and snap out of her. She didn't disappoint.

"Why do you say that? I only had those two glasses." She jerked her Padres jersey into place as she made her way up the long, shallow steps to the crescent bar.

"Then why are you making coffee at 10:00 p.m.?"

"I may stay up and do some work. I'm on the planning committee for the charity gala for the philharmonic again this year."

Yeah, right. He rose and scooped up the cups, proud of himself. There were only four. "How about that triple play by the Padres?" he said as he crossed the room to another wet bar, built into the far corner. Somewhere in those brushed chrome cabinets was a trash receptacle, although he always had trouble finding it.

"Great," she said, "great."

Suddenly his mother was inarticulate. The only word she could manage was *great*. He was pretty sure she hadn't even seen the play, but he was going to torture her with a few more questions, anyway.

"Of course, you saw that inside-the-park home run by Piazza in the seventh inning. It blew off the outfielder's mitt."

"Yes, I saw it. Do I look stupid to you?"

"*Stupid* isn't the word that comes to mind, actually. Piazza sat out the seventh. He twisted his ankle."

"You smart-ass…" Julia took a bag of coffee from the refrigerator and banged the door shut. "I don't know why I watch these games with you. I should have gone to bed like Alison." She was just getting started on a tirade when a thunderous noise stopped her. It sounded as if someone was trying to break down the front door. "What the hell is that?"

Bret's heart nearly slammed through his chest wall. The pounding was loud and insistent. Someone meant business. He left the empty cups on the counter and made a dash for the media room door.

"Bret, where are you going?"

"It's the front door," he called back to her, from out in the hallway. "You stay here. I'll get it."

"Alison, wake up!"

Marnie felt the bed shaking and she heard Alison's name being called, but she was groggy and slow to react. She rolled to her back and saw people looming over her, but she couldn't make out who they were through the heavy veil of sleep. It looked like Bret and Julia.

"What is it?" she said, wondering if she was dreaming.

Bret's face came to within a few inches of hers. "You have to get up and come downstairs, Alison. Tony Bogart is here. He wants to talk to you."

Alison. *She* was Alison. They were trying to wake *her.*

She sat up, still trying to clear her head. She didn't remember having taken a pill, but she'd had this same feeling in the past when she'd tried to wake herself before the effects wore off. Thick and hazy, as if she was walking through a snowstorm.

"What time is it?" she asked.

"It's ten-fifteen," Bret answered.

"In the morning?"

"At night," Julia interjected. "Alison, you have to come down with us. Someone's been murdered, and Tony is talking like he thinks you had something to do with it."

"Murdered?" Marnie looked at them, confused. Her vision cleared instantly. She could see Julia's shock and concern. Bret was pale and still, as if he knew something Alison didn't—and feared the worst.

"Who was murdered?" Marnie asked.

Bret glanced at Julia, but neither of them spoke. That's when Marnie realized it must be someone she knew, someone she cared about.

"Not Andrew?" she said.

26

Alone in the Fairmonts' living room, Tony took full advantage of the chance to have a look around. It was too dark to appreciate the view, but it had to be spectacular—and so was what he'd seen of the house. He'd never been formally invited inside the fabulous Sea Clouds. He'd been Alison's dirty little secret when they were dating. She hadn't minded amusing herself in his sordid world, and being treated like a goddess, but he hadn't been allowed near hers. She probably thought he would soil the furniture.

He almost laughed. She'd been right about that.

There were family pictures on the baby grand, all of them of the perfect family, living the perfect life, beautiful people without a care in the world. The world where he didn't belong, even now. He quelled pangs of jealousy, not for Alison, but for the charmed life she lived—and took totally for granted.

She'd been right about him soiling the furniture. It was going to get good and dirty.

Moments later, as the three Fairmonts filed into their living room, he was sitting on one of the white silk couches, innocently leafing through a coffee table book. But as he rose to acknowledge them, the petty jealousies turned into something else. The Fairmonts looked confused, frightened and defensive—and he was none of those things. Suddenly this was business. He was their equal, and more. He might be their executioner.

He zoomed in on Alison, his investigative brain operating like a camera lens. She was wearing the same outfit she'd worn on the boat that morning, navy shorts, a white polo shirt and deck shoes, but she looked disheveled and disoriented. The navy cardigan was missing, and her clothes were wrinkled and off-kilter.

Interesting. Alison was never wrinkled and off-kilter. And even more interesting, she was holding Julia's hand. Or possibly Julia was holding hers. Either way, mother and daughter had never been close. This was something new.

Tony pulled out his badge and made sure they saw it. He had no authority to investigate this case, but the Fairmonts didn't know that. Only sophisticated white-collar criminals and seasoned crooks knew to say nothing and ask for a lawyer. When most people saw a badge, they talked, and he was counting on that tonight.

He'd just left the local police on the cliffs after telling them everything he'd seen, except the name of his prime suspect. They would figure that out soon enough. Meanwhile, he had a few questions for Alison and family. He almost smiled. This was going to be fun.

Alison stepped forward, and her heavy-lidded gaze slammed into his. She hated him. Good, he could feed off that. Anything but the indifference she'd shown him back in the days when he was a lovesick fool.

"Who was murdered?" she asked.

"LaDonna Jeffries. Someone shot her and pushed her off Satan's Teeth. She was dead before her body hit the rocks."

Tony watched Alison suck in a breath and whisper LaDonna's name. Pretty convincing, he allowed. You would almost have thought she gave a damn.

"I'm sorry if this is inconvenient," he said, using his guardian-of-the-public-safety tone, "but there a few questions I have to ask."

"Sure—" Bret's voice cracked on the word. "Anything we can do to help. LaDonna was a great girl. Why would anyone want to hurt her?"

"A great girl? How well did you know her?" Tony zeroed in on Bret, who actually knew LaDonna inside out.

"Not very well. I did know her, though. I guess you could say we were friends."

Tony enjoyed watching him squirm, as he imagined Alison might have squirmed when she'd been questioned about him years back. Other than that, he had no interest in the pretty younger brother.

"What about you, Alison?" Very casually, he turned his attention to her. "Were you and LaDonna friends?"

"We knew each other," she said.

He continued to focus on Alison, although it was difficult to avoid her ferret-eyed mother, who was still hanging on to her hand. "Do you mind telling me your whereabouts at eight forty-five this evening?"

"I was right here," she said. "I was probably asleep in my room by then."

"She was." Julia chimed in, moving in front of her daughter. "We were all home this evening, watching the Padres game. Alison didn't feel well, and she went up to her room to lie down."

"It would help if you'd let your daughter answer the questions," Tony suggested, again the excessively polite lawman. "How about you, Bret? Were you here, too?"

"All night. We get the games live through our cable service. Did you catch that triple play in the sixth?"

"Not a sports fan," Tony said. "I was out walking on the beach tonight."

He let that sink in, and then continued. "Nobody went out for any reason at any time?"

"No," Julia said, becoming more emphatic, "we were here the entire night. Bret just told you that."

He nodded. "You and Bret were watching the game, but Alison was all alone, right? Up in her room?"

"Actually, I went up to check on her about eight forty-five," Julia said. "She was sound asleep, so I didn't disturb her."

Tony didn't believe Julia for a second. Eight forty-five was exactly the time he'd asked Alison about. Julia was going to try and provide her daughter with an airtight alibi, Tony realized. That was unfortunate.

Bret stepped forward. "Are you here to charge one of us with something? What? Murdering LaDonna? That's crazy."

"That's up to the local police," Tony said. "I'm just trying to clear some things up."

"Why would Alison want to kill LaDonna?"

Bret had him there. Tony hadn't had time to come up with a motive for LaDonna's murder. But he wouldn't be much of a G-man if he let a little thing like that stop him.

"Are we done now?"

Julia asked the question, but Tony continued to study Alison. He was fascinated by how shaky she appeared. "Where's your husband tonight?" he asked.

She looked startled. "He's in Mexico on business."

"How did he get there? What airline?"

"I don't know. He didn't mention it."

He debated telling her that her husband hadn't flown out on any scheduled flight with a commercial airline based in San Diego. Nor had Tony found any record of a private chartered flight. He also debated telling her that her husband may have fucking deserted her, but that would set off alarms, and he wanted to get to Villard first. "When's he coming back?"

"Soon— I don't know. He was supposed to be back tonight."

"I'm going to want to talk to him."

Her eyes changed. It was weird, like fire burning through blue clouds. If he'd ever seen that before he didn't remember it.

"I'm sure you do," she said, "but unless you're here to charge me with something, he doesn't have to talk to you about anything—and neither do we."

Tony grinned. He couldn't help himself. She was kicking him out of the house the way she'd kicked him off the boat. He saw Julia coming for him, and knew he was about to be escorted out. He was far from done with these people, but he could save the rest of the fireworks for later. None of the suspects except Alison, but he didn't have to let them know that.

"There will be an investigation," he said, looking at all three of them. "You can count on that. No one is to leave town for any reason. You've heard the old expression, you can run but you can't hide. Believe it."

Julia reached for his arm as if she was going to forcibly escort the uncouth lawman from her home. Tony grabbed her by the wrist, clamping down hard enough to stop her in her tracks.

He loved the shock that rolled through her cosmetically enhanced features. Nothing equaled the thrill of power—not sex, not booze or drugs. The food chain had just upended itself, and this woman was nothing but a tasty morsel. He wondered how that felt to a person of her stature. Probably not much different than it felt to a peon like him. There were a few things that actually did level the playing field.

Birth, death, taxes—and this.

"I know where the door is," he said. "I'll show myself out."

Marnie stood out on the bedroom balcony with the cell phone pressed to her ear. She'd come out here hoping for better reception. She'd been trying ever since Bogart left to get through to Andrew, but he wasn't answering. His voice mail had kicked in the first few times she'd called, but the menu hadn't given her the option of leaving a message. Now she was getting an automated response telling her the person she was calling was unavailable. After that the message cut off and she was disconnected.

She flipped the phone shut, deeply frustrated.

Not being able to leave a message was almost as bad as not being able to talk to him. He wouldn't even know she'd been trying to reach him. She couldn't tell him about LaDonna or find out when he was coming back, and she was worried that something had happened to him.

About an hour ago, she'd pressed the panic button on the cell phone, trying to connect with the detective he'd hired, but no one had responded. She hadn't seen anything of Sanchez since that morning. Bret may have sent him away, and Marnie didn't even know if Sanchez *was* the detective.

She'd thought she was isolated in Oyster Bay, but this was worse. She felt cut off from everything and everyone. She couldn't reach Andrew, couldn't talk to the people around her. There was nowhere to turn for help, and she had no idea what was going on with the search for her grandmother, or if anyone was even searching.

She went back inside, tossed the phone on the bed and contemplated the liquor cart, wondering what she might take to slow down her madly racing mind.

Glenfiddich, Absolut, Bombay Sapphire, Casa Noble Blanco.

Her sense of despair grew as she scanned the labels. She'd read books on wines and spirits to prepare for this trip, but right now she barely knew one from the other. No booze, she decided. No pills, either. She couldn't sleep her way through this.

A wave of disbelief hit her, rocked her to the core. LaDonna was dead? Marnie couldn't believe it. It was impossible to grasp that her friend had been murdered—and even more surreal that she'd fallen from Satan's Teeth, just as Marnie had.

No, not fallen. LaDonna hadn't fallen. She'd been shot and then pushed from the cliffs, and for some reason Bogart thought Alison did it.

Marnie turned to look at the nightstand. The gun! Andrew had left her a gun. Relief flooded her as she opened the drawer and saw that the pistol and the bullets were there. It didn't look as if anything had been touched. Thank God.

She sagged to the bed and leaned forward, palms pressed to her throbbing forehead. She was overreacting. The situation couldn't be anywhere near as bad as her mind was making it out to be. Still, she couldn't seem to push away the feeling that things were closing in on her.

When she looked up, she caught a glimpse of herself in the armoire mirror. She looked like a transient, wild-eyed and crazy, and yes, maybe a killer who pushed people off cliffs. Worse, Tony Bogart had seen her looking exactly like this.

The nightstand clock told her it was midnight. Andrew had been gone twenty-four hours, and given what had happened since he'd left, Marnie couldn't wait any longer to hear from him. Bogart had promised an investigation, and as much as she might want to think he'd been bluffing, she didn't dare let herself think so. She had to calm down and start reasoning her way through this mess.

She left the bed and went back out to the balcony. No cell phone or panic buttons this time, just the cool, bracing air and the deep quiet of midnight. Within moments she had realized that she didn't need sleeping pills or booze. What she needed was coffee. She had work to do and it might take her all night. Neither her own cell phone nor the one Andrew left her were set up for the Internet, and so she would continue to search the old-fashioned way, in the phone book. She had already gone through the hospitals and nursing homes in San Diego County, but could easily have missed something.

It had become imperative that Marnie find her grandmother. She was worried about her health, and that was reason enough. But it was more complicated now. Marnie's situation had escalated, and she was just beginning to understand how grave things were. She had to find her grandmother to assure herself that she was safe, but she'd realized it was mutual. Josephine Hazelton might be the only one who could save Marnie now.

"Vending machine coffee in the age of Starbucks?" Tony muttered. "Isn't that against the law?"

Gamely, he put several quarters in the slot, hit the buttons for coffee with double sugar, no cream, and watched the paper cup drop and fill, anticipating all the robust flavor of a bag of sawdust. This wasn't his first trip to the San Diego County Sheriff's Office, and it wasn't his first experience with this coffee, probably from this exact machine.

That was back when he was a punk-ass kid. He'd never been charged with anything, but twice in his teens he'd been picked up for fighting. Finally, he'd figured out there were easier ways to deal with difficult people. You didn't have to lay a hand on them, just play with their heads until their brains liquefied and ran out their ears. He'd gotten good at liquefying brains, but every once in a while a man needed some instant gratification.

"Hey, Bogart!"

Tony turned to see Vince Connelly coming toward

him. He'd been the detective at the LaDonna Jeffries's crime scene last night, and Tony had shown up this morning specifically to track Vince down and get an update. Not that Connelly owed him one. Tony was an eyewitness, not a member of the investigative team, but it was a courtesy from one law enforcement officer to another, one agency to another.

Vince punched Tony on the arm, hard enough to hurt. He was a big guy in all ways, tall and thick with salt-and-pepper hair and an ebullient personality. He was also the county's hotshot homicide detective, and he didn't let anyone forget it.

Tony didn't punch him back, although…

Vince was the rookie deputy who'd caught Tony fighting all those years ago. He'd lectured him, embarrassing him in front of all his friends, and then let him go. Twice. Big fucking man, Vince was. Tony had hated him back then the way he'd hated all authority figures. There'd been no bonding between the troubled teen and the law enforcement officer. And time hadn't changed the hostile feelings all that much on Tony's part.

He figured it was mutual.

Fortunately, he was essential to Vince's case.

"Let me get some of this stinking stuff," Vince said, kicking the vending machine, "and then, if you can fit me into your busy schedule, I'd like to show you some of the forensic evidence we've collected."

"All the time you need," Tony said. The man was a raving dickhead. Punch his arm? Tony should have laid him out right there, but he wanted to see that evidence.

Vince got his coffee, and as they walked back to

his office, he sipped from the cup and greeted people by name, as if he were the office's ambassador of goodwill. But Tony could feel the aggression rolling off the man. He was a bully, even when he smiled at people. They *had* to smile back or be on Vince's shit list. That was the implication.

"We got something interesting, *Agent* Bogart," Vince said as they entered his office. "How the hell did you get into the FBI?" He chuckled and went to his desk.

"Same way everyone else does," Tony said evenly. "Let's see what you got."

Vince grabbed a large manila folder, from which he pulled out several clear plastic evidence bags, and spread them out on the desk.

"Recognize any of this stuff?" The bag he picked up and handed over had a small navy-blue button in it.

Tony studied it for several seconds. More than anything the color seemed significant. The button had clearly been torn from a piece of clothing. An image of Alison's dazed expression—and her missing navy-blue cardigan sweater—flashed into his mind.

He looked up at Vince, his gut twisting. "Yeah, I do."

27

Rebecca knocked on Julia's door, carrying a tray of coffee, juice and fresh fruit. Julia was expecting her, so Rebecca nudged the door open with her hip and backed in, carefully balancing everything.

"Incoming," she called, noticing that Julia was still in bed in her silk pajamas, absorbed in her reflection in a hand-held mirror.

"Put the tray on the table by the chaise," Julia directed without looking up. "Any luck with those flights I asked you to check on?"

"To Mauritius? It's a twenty-four hour trip, you know."

"Rebecca, I didn't ask how long it took. I asked—"

"I know what you asked," she stated. "I can get you connections through DeGaulle. It depends on when you want to go. This is a pleasure trip, right?"

Rebecca had never heard of the exotic island off the coast of South Africa until this morning, when Julia asked her to check on flights, and she was more than curious why her boss would want to go to the ends of the earth—or anywhere—right now.

Julia sighed. "I don't know about pleasure. I just need to get away, and Mauritius is sublime, although probably deadly hot this time of year. Could you check on that?" She glanced up from the mirror. "There was a murder on the cliffs last night. Did you hear? The police were here asking questions. Well, not the police. It was that thug who used to sneak around with my daughter, thinking I didn't know. He's an FBI agent now if you can believe."

Rebecca felt a strange sensation in the pit of her stomach. It was like a leaky faucet dripping into an empty sink. Anxiety. She told herself to keep busy. She set the tray on the table and began turning cups over and arranging things. Julia was still peering at her face in the mirror and tweezing the fine hairs above her lip, one by one. Crazy woman. Why didn't she just get the hair zapped with a laser? She could afford it.

"Bret told me about it." Rebecca poured a cup of coffee and added artificial sweetener and nonfat creamer for Julia. God forbid she put a calorie of food in her bony body, other than pinot, of course. "He said Tony Bogart asked each of you to account for your whereabouts."

"Yes, he did. Can you imagine? Luckily, we were all in the media room, watching the Padres, except Alison, who wasn't feeling well. Is she up yet? I'd like the entire family to meet here in my room this morning. We need to make sure our stories match, just in case."

"Just in case of what?" Rebecca had to set down the coffee before she spilled it. A sudden rush of giddiness had made her unsteady. Afraid she might hyperventilate, she consciously slowed her breathing. Who would have dreamed it could feel this good to witness the implosion? She also felt racking guilt and remorse, which was probably why she couldn't stop her legs from shaking. But the thought of the Fairmonts getting sucked into a criminal trial and a big juicy scandal was just too delicious.

"I don't trust the law—or the media—in these things," Julia said. "They're always out to get their betters, as my mother would say."

Especially when the "betters" were as obnoxious about it as Julia.

"Bret's up," Rebecca told her. "Alison may be out taking a walk. I knocked on her door this morning, but she didn't answer."

"How odd." Julia looked up from the mirror. "Walking again? That's so not Alison. Did she leave a note?"

"I didn't find one. It sounds like you're worried about her. Was she okay last night?" Rebecca tried to sound concerned, but she really didn't give a damn about any of them anymore, including Alison. Maybe she just knew too much. The Fairmonts were like wormy fruit; the rotten stuff was deep in the core where you couldn't easily see it, but that didn't make it any less putrid.

"Of course I'm worried," Julia said impatiently. "People are being murdered and fingers are being pointed at my family!"

Rebecca changed the subject. "Do you want anything besides coffee?" she asked. "Orange juice? Some fruit?"

"No coffee. I'm jittery enough already. I can't even pluck my damn facial hair."

"You specifically *asked* for coffee."

"I shouldn't have. Let Bret have it. Or you drink it."

"I've already had my coffee— Julia, what are you doing?"

"Trying to get these last hairs. They're driving me crazy."

"Let me help," Rebecca said, rushing over to her. "Julia, stop. You're bleeding. That's your skin you're plucking."

The doorbell sounded downstairs, and Rebecca glanced at her watch, wondering who it could be. It wasn't even nine o'clock.

She grabbed the tweezers from Julia's fingers, knowing the woman would be furious, and headed for the bedroom doors. "I'll get the bell," she called back.

Rebecca got no farther than the hallway. Bret had already answered the door and now he was bounding up the stairs. He grabbed Rebecca's hand and dragged her with him back into Julia's bedroom.

Julia threw off the bedcovers and got out of bed. Blood oozed from what looked like small nicks above her lip.

"What's going on?" she asked Bret.

"The police are here," he said, "two of them. They have two warrants, one to search the house and another for Alison's arrest. Apparently there was an eyewitness to the murder last night."

Rebecca gaped at Bret, realizing as she saw the tense white line around his mouth that it was true. He was terrified. Julia was, too. She looked about to crumble. This was beyond anything Rebecca had imagined when she'd been secretly orchestrating the Fairmonts' downfall. This was awesome.

Marnie heard a horn blaring and glanced in her rearview mirror. It was the guy right behind her, driving the fancy sports car. Apparently she wasn't going fast enough, because he was waving at her and making what looked like obscene gestures.

Probably a smart-ass teenager who thought he owned the road.

"Back off!" she yelled, knowing he couldn't hear her. He wanted her to speed up or get out of his way. No way was she going to do either in this traffic. It was the middle of summer, and she was on Pacific Coast Highway, heading south toward San Diego. Several of the nursing homes on her list were in this direction, but the PCH was jammed with beachgoers and tourists.

The blaring horn pissed her off, and she slowed down. Let him go nuts back there. A jolt shook her car, causing her seat belt to lock. The horrible sound of crackling metal told her he'd hit her. What was he doing?

Another jolt shook the car. Again? If only she'd put the gun Andrew had left her in her purse. She pulled over to the side and stopped, searching through her bag for her cell phone to call the police. The guy hadn't hit her hard, but she had no idea who she was dealing with. If he drove on by, at least she'd be able to get his license number.

Someone was banging on her car window. She turned and saw Bret's face looming close to the glass.

"Why the hell don't you answer your phone?" he shouted at her. "I've been calling you every five minutes!"

She hit the button to roll down the window. "Are you sure? The cell hasn't rung." She flipped it open to check it, and then realized he was talking about *her* phone, not the one Andrew had left her. She hadn't even turned hers on. She wasn't expecting any calls, except from Andrew.

"Have you heard from Andrew?" she asked Bret. "Is that why you pulled me over?" Something else dawned on her as she stared at him. "How did you find me?"

"You left the phone book lying open on your writing desk. It had a bunch of rest homes circled. I figured I'd go right down the list. What the hell are you doing?"

She'd left the phone book open. God, that was idiotic, almost as stupid as not turning on her phone.

"Never mind," Marnie said. "What do you want?"

Bret seemed to be taking a moment to catch his breath. "The sheriff's office has a warrant for your arrest for LaDonna's murder. They probably have an APB out for you right now. I'll drive you down to the courthouse. Mom's going to meet us there with an attorney."

"No—"

"Alison, it'll be all right. You *have* to come with me."

Marnie's first impulse was to bolt. She wasn't that far from the Mexican border. She could hit the gas and speed off. Bret might have a faster car, but he didn't have her determination or her gut fear.

She couldn't let him take her down to the courthouse. They would discover who she really was, and God knew what would happen when that bomb exploded. She had no idea how it would affect her or Andrew, who knew nothing about this. She might never find her grandmother.

Her hands tightened on the wheel. She could see

the bones through her flesh, and her knuckles were a ghastly dead white. What was she going to do? *And where the hell was Andrew?*

Marnie pulled over to the curb in front of the San Diego County Courthouse, cut the engine and got out of the car. She'd refused to let Bret drive her over, but had agreed when he insisted that she meet him in front. He'd offered to park her car while she spoke with Julia and the attorney—and he'd lectured her about not taking the situation seriously.

He was acting just like a brother would in a crisis, she realized.

Bret had told her to look for Julia and the lawyer on the courthouse steps. Marnie saw people clustered around, but she didn't see Julia, or Bret, for that matter. He was probably still parking his own car. Marnie had seen the huge parking garage as she drove up.

"Alison! Over here!"

Julia rushed down the steps with a tall, distinguished man in tow. Marnie went around the car to meet them.

"This is James Brainard." Julia presented the attorney with a graceful wave of her arm. "He's a brilliant criminal lawyer, and we're so lucky he could take your case. He understands that you're being framed by a jealous ex-boyfriend, and that this is about revenge, nothing else."

"An ex-boyfriend who just happens to be an FBI agent," Marnie reminded them.

Brainard extended his hand to her. His grip was solid, and she liked his demeanor. It gave the impression of gravity and concern.

"I've met with the prosecutor," he told her, "and she's agreed to a speedy arraignment. We're already on the court docket for one o'clock, so once we have you processed, we'll go straight to the hearing."

"Processed?" Marnie asked.

"Booked." He seemed slightly apologetic for having to use the vernacular. "They'll take fingerprints and mug shots. You'll be searched. It's not pleasant, but it has to be done if we're going to post a bond today and get you out of here."

Fingerprints. Once they had Marnie's they would discover she wasn't Alison. She had no choice but to go along with it, however. Brainard was promising her that she would be out on bail before the day was over, and that might buy her a little time. Enough, she hoped, to reach Andrew and find her grandmother.

"Can't you do all that?" Julia was asking the attorney.

"All what, Julia?" Brainard looked annoyed. "They don't want my fingerprints. They want Alison's."

"She will get out on bail, won't she?" the older woman persisted. "They're not going to put her in jail?"

"It's all right." Marnie had to make her stop. Julia's pleading tone was making her feel terribly claustrophobic.

Brainard spoke directly to Marnie. "The prosecutor's going to ask that you be held without bail. That's her job, but I've spoken with her and she won't go to the mat on this. She'll agree to bail, as long as it's high."

"How high?" Marnie asked.

"I don't expect it to be under a million. They want to be sure you don't try to flee."

Stunned, Marnie glanced at Julia, who whispered that that was fine.

"Now for the bad news," Brainard said.

"I thought that *was* the bad news." Marnie listened in silence as the attorney told her a crime team had searched the house and found a gun in her nightstand.

"They claim it was recently fired, but can't prove it was the murder weapon. They're waiting for lab results."

Julia gripped Marnie's hand, squeezing much too hard. "What were you doing with a gun in your room?"

"I've never touched it," Marnie explained. "Andrew left it for me because he was worried about my safety. I was nearly hit by a terra-cotta pot that someone dropped from the balcony at Sea Clouds."

Julia gasped. "You didn't tell me that! When did it happen?"

Marnie tried to explain, but Brainard intervened, cupping Marnie's elbow as if he intended to take her away and never bring her back. She wished he would!

"Julia, will you excuse us?" he said. "I want to talk to my client for a minute." When he had Marnie far enough away, he spoke in low tones. "I know you've never gone through this process before, but I have, many times. Let me handle everything, all right?"

"Of course."

"The only thing I want you to do in the courtroom is plead not guilty to the charges, and look the judge in the eye when you do it."

"All right."

"And one last question. Have you told me everything? I don't like surprises, Alison. I can't be your attorney if you're holding things back."

Marnie felt as if she were going to be ill. This was the moment she'd been dreading. How could she possibly proceed any further with this without telling him?

Marnie stood before the judge. Numb with shock, she heard the bailiff read the two counts against her. She was being charged with her own murder? Somehow Tony Bogart had convinced the district attorney's office that Alison Fairmont had pushed not one but two people off the cliffs, Marnie Hazelton and LaDonna Jeffries.

She was not being charged with Butch Bogart's murder. Apparently there wasn't enough evidence.

"Do you understand the charges?" the judge asked Marnie. When she nodded, he said, "How do you plead?"

The lawyer's words rang in her head, but she found it impossible to look the judge in the eyes. "Not guilty to both counts," she said to the table.

The judge turned to the prosecutor, a fortyish woman with a determined set to her mouth and a nasal voice.

"Do you have reason to believe that Mrs. Villard poses a threat to flee if released from custody?" he asked her.

"Your Honor," the prosecutor said, "she's not even a resident of the state. Yes, I believe she poses a flight risk. I'm requesting that bail be denied and that she be held in custody pending trial."

James Brainard rose to protest, and Marnie realized he had long gray hair, pulled into a ponytail at his nape. Maybe it was her state of mind, but that caught her off guard. It didn't seem to match his dignified mien or his immaculate dark suit.

"Your Honor," Brainard said, "Mrs. Villard is the

daughter of Julia Fairmont, an exceedingly generous and well-known philanthropist and a long-standing member of this community. Mrs. Villard poses no flight risk, and we're asking that bail be set at a reasonable amount."

Marnie listened with an odd kind of detachment as the prosecutor and her attorney mentioned amounts of money that were staggering to her.

At last, the judge banged his gavel. "The bail is set at three million dollars. A bond can be posted with the clerk of courts."

Brainard protested, but His Honor wouldn't budge. Alison Fairmont was going to pay through the nose for her freedom.

Marnie didn't say a word. Julia and her attorney had made it very clear that she shouldn't do anything except declare her innocence.

"Court is adjourned," the judge announced.

He rapped his gavel again, and Marnie Hazelton was a free woman, maybe for a matter of hours.

Tony was caught off guard when Alison turned and faced the gallery. Shock must have drained the blood from her face. Her lips were bluish and her skin looked as thin as parchment, but with her hair flying everywhere and her eyes as big and dark as bruises, she was breathtaking.

He still loved her. Christ. That was reason enough to send her to death row. She was killing people, apparently because they were inconvenient. She'd killed him when he became inconvenient, and she'd gotten away with it. He didn't need convincing that this was the right thing to do. It *was* right.

Her eyes searched the gallery. He felt a weird jolt as they found his. She seemed to be imploring him to explain, as if she didn't understand why he'd done it. Tony felt something hot flare in the pit of his gut. Not anger, guilt.

He watched as they led her out, and the uneasy feeling persisted. Her family would pay the bail bond and have her out in an hour. They'd already hired her a big-name defense attorney. The county would have a fight on its hands putting Alison Fairmont in jail, but Tony couldn't get her bewildered expression out of his mind.

What he needed right now was a firing range and his .40 Glock. That would clear his head.

He went over the evidence in his mind as he left the courtroom. After witnessing LaDonna's murder, he'd begun to see how it all could have come together. He'd concluded from the anonymous calls and the hair barrette he'd found that Alison had pushed Marnie Hazelton, and then she'd bribed LaDonna, who was on the beach that night, to keep quiet. Alison's disappearance from the yacht was probably intended to be an incredibly clever alibi, but somehow the plan had backfired, and she'd been injured badly enough to require plastic surgery. Her husband may or may not have been in on it. That wasn't clear to Tony, but Alison must have panicked and killed LaDonna to make sure she didn't talk.

Pay attention, he told himself. *Focus on what has to be done.*

Six months ago Alison defended herself against Butch's retribution and then covered up her brutal crime by eliminating Marnie, the only witness. Tony had some promising forensic evidence to corroborate the second crime, and he was an eyewitness to her deadly attack on LaDonna. But one significant mystery was still unsolved—the identity of Tony's voicemail snitch. Someone had placed those anonymous calls to his cell, and that person was vital to the case. His informant's testimony at the trial might be the only way to make sure Alison didn't escape justice. Tony also had to find Andrew Villard. His disappearance was just too convenient. The bastard was up to something.

28

"Alison, you're not drinking? It's delicious." Julia picked up the bottle of California chardonnay they were having with the salmon Bret had just barbecued for dinner. "Are you still upset about this afternoon?"

Marnie could hardly bring herself to answer the question, it was so ridiculous. Julia and Bret were acting like this was just another dinner at Sea Clouds. She didn't know whether they were in denial or delusional.

"Why would I be upset?" she said. "It was only two charges of premeditated murder. It could have been so much worse."

Her sarcasm was evident. She was too much on edge to try and pretend otherwise. She'd been waiting all afternoon for word that the prints didn't match. There was no way to explain away evidence as concrete as fingerprints, which meant the lid would blow once everyone knew she wasn't Alison. But the call hadn't come—and the waiting was terrible.

She needed to talk to Andrew. She still hadn't been able to get through on the phone, and he hadn't called. Meanwhile, she was struggling to convince herself that something hadn't happened to him. Even the sheriff's office was making inquiries, and she didn't know how much longer she could hold them off.

"Well, excuse me," Julia said, clearly miffed, "for bailing you out and getting you the best criminal defense lawyer money can buy. If you want to take that attitude, go right ahead. I'm going to stay positive."

"Me, too," Bret said, grinning over the top of his wine glass. He winked at Marnie. "But don't you change, sis. I like it when you're a nasty little bitch."

Marnie ignored him. There wasn't much else you could do with Bret, and she'd begun to think of him as annoying but harmless. Andrew's absence felt far more sinister than Bret's presence. At least Bret was making an effort to be supportive in his own weird way. He'd offered to cook tonight when Rebecca went to her room, saying she didn't feel well—and he'd suggested the three of them have dinner on the terrace, where it was quiet and cool.

Marnie drew her cardigan sweater around her shoulders. She'd showered and changed into a simple cotton sundress with a matching sweater when they got back from court. It was getting a little chilly now, but otherwise dinner on the terrace had been a good idea.

A pink mist lay over the sea, and the sun was as red and round as a pomegranate. She might have enjoyed the view under other circumstances.

"I appreciate everything you're doing," she assured Julia. "I really do, more than I can say."

Julia smiled and gushed, "Darling, it's going to be fine. You've had a terrible time, I know, but try not to make it worse."

Marnie nodded. Agreeing was probably the only way to get Julia to stop being so insanely upbeat. She'd taken on the role of cheerleader and she seemed determined to make Marnie believe that the lawyer she'd hired would have the case thrown out in no time. That's how good he was and how flimsy the county's case was.

Marnie guessed this was typical of families during tough times, and especially the wealthy. They drew together and closed ranks. But it went against everything in her own nature. Given the choice, she would have pulled away from the group and taken cover, alone. It was what she knew. The Fairmont family *esprit de corps* felt dangerous to her, especially since she wasn't part of this family, and that bombshell might be revealed at any minute. The phone could ring and it would all be over.

She almost wished it would.

"Wine?" Julia said, lifting the bottle.

"Sure." Marnie held out her glass and Julia rose to fill it. Maybe she'd just get drunk. It seemed to work for everybody else.

"What do you hear from the hubby?" Bret asked.

Marnie continued to ignore him, proud of herself for not taking the bait he kept dangling. He knew she hadn't heard from Andrew. He was just twisting the knife. She flaked some salmon with her fork, moving it around on her plate. The bite or two she'd had was delicious, but she had no appetite at all.

"Maybe I should take something up to Rebecca," she suggested. "She must be hungry."

"I'll do so later," Julia said. "That way I can have a little talk with her. I'm afraid she's taking this badly, even worse than we are. Of course, the Driscolls always soldier through—and we all have Driscoll blood, don't we?"

The soldiering-through part sounded like a quote from Julia's mother, Eleanor. It was interesting how often Julia quoted the person she supposedly hated. Marnie knew from her own experience that Alison's relationship with her mother was complicated. Surely Julia's relationship with her own mother was about more than hatred.

"Would it help if I spoke to Rebecca as well?" Marnie asked. "If it's me she's worried about I could reassure her."

"That would be very nice, Alison. By the way, you didn't answer your brother when he asked about Andrew. And I heard you tell that detective—what was his name, Connelly?—that you hadn't heard from him."

Julia just wouldn't shut up tonight.

"You understand that if he doesn't show up soon," she continued, "the officials will surely start searching for him. If you have some way to reach him, it might be a good idea."

"Don't you think I'm *trying* to reach him?" Her voice cracked with frustration, and she took a moment to calm herself. "I'm sorry," she said. "It's the stress. I've left messages for him daily, including an emergency message on his pager. I'm sure he'll call soon."

She prayed Julia would let it go. Marnie had reached the point where she didn't believe Andrew was going to call—she should have known he wouldn't keep all those ridiculous promises he'd made about protecting her and finding her grandmother. He hadn't even answered his messages. She'd actually had moments of thinking it would be easier if something terrible had happened to him. At least she would know he hadn't run out on her.

She touched her throat, slammed by the realization that he had her penny ring. She'd insisted he take it with him. With that awareness came the horrible sinking feeling that she was lost. Truly lost. What an idiot she'd been, getting caught up in the sex they'd had and offering him the only thing she really valued. *What an incredible idiot.* She was in this alone, and once she'd been exposed, the Fairmonts would turn against her, too.

She had an appointment with James Brainard first thing in the morning, but that would have to be re-scheduled. Marnie had something else to do, and it couldn't wait.

Andrew stood in front of the grainy television screen, watching news footage of Marnie trying to avoid reporters outside the county courthouse. Sur-rounded by Fairmonts and her top gun attorney, she looked lost and bewildered and defiant. He'd seen that look before. It didn't bode well for her—or anyone else.

The local news media had broken the story, de-scribing her as the mysterious, reclusive heiress who'd had a near-fatal boating accident and a miracle resur-rection six months ago. They reported the multiple plastic surgeries to restore her face—and the pictures they flashed of Alison before the accident, looking art-lessly blond and beautiful, were quite a contrast to the feral, dark-haired woman shown here.

Andrew hit the mute button. Only he knew who the mysterious heiress really was—and only he could get her out of this unholy mess. But if he did, it was all over—for both of them. He and Marnie had invisible slipknots around their necks, at either end of the same rope. One wrong move now would be their last.

He glanced at the well-stocked wet bar, and his throat tightened, burned. He wanted a drink. It would solve nothing, except to push away reality, but right now that didn't sound half-bad.

He was back in Mirage Bay, staying at the beach house rental he'd arranged before he left for Mexico. He'd hoped he wouldn't need the hideaway, but had wanted to be prepared. His trip to Baja had been a trap to flush out the mastermind who'd tried to frame him, and who may have committed a string of murders, including pushing LaDonna off the cliff.

Andrew still believed the trap would have worked, but he'd had to abandon the plan and return to the States when he got word that LaDonna had been murdered and Marnie was the chief suspect. The police were all over Sea Clouds by the time he got back, and Andrew couldn't go near the place. If his cover was blown, whatever chance he had to help her was blown with it. He had to lay low, and unfortunately Diego Sanchez, Andrew's eyes and ears while he was gone, had been kicked off the premises by Bret.

Diego couldn't even stake the place out without risking discovery by the local law or Tony Bogart. So Andrew was doing his own stakeout. The rental beach house was on a bluff behind Sea Clouds, and from his vantage point, he could watch the nightmare unfolding, but there was nothing he could do. *And it was only going to get worse*. She'd been charged with her own murder, and there was no way to prove her identity. Even he couldn't do it. There were no records. There never had been.

When she'd agreed to take on Alison's identity, he'd searched for Marnie Hazelton's records, but hadn't found any. That's when he'd discovered, through newspaper accounts of Butch's murder investigation, that the sheriff's office hadn't found anything on her, either. Except for sporadic school records, Marnie Hazelton didn't exist. She didn't even have fingerprints.

They'd questioned her grandmother, but she'd stuck to her story about finding a baby in a basket, even when they'd threatened to report her to Child Protective Services. She'd told them Marnie had been home-schooled off and on because her deformities had made her a target, which explained why her school records were sporadic. She'd also claimed to have provided Marnie's medical care. The cops got nowhere with Josephine Hazelton, but apparently they'd decided not to prosecute a distraught elderly woman whose child was missing.

Andrew hadn't understood the lack of records, and still didn't, but at the time it had made his work easier. Now it blocked his path at every turn. If he tried to convince the county prosecutor that she wasn't Alison, he would expose them both to charges of murder and fraud—and the real killer would go free.

Alison Fairmont might have a chance of beating the charges with Brainard as her attorney, but could Marnie Hazelton beat the charges against her? She'd admitted to killing Butch, but there was only her word that it was self-defense. Worse, she would lose all credibility when they found out what she'd done. She was the woman who'd conspired with Andrew Fairmont to defraud Julia. No one would believe their motives. It would look as if they were after the trust fund and had killed Alison to get it.

Jesus. It just got worse and worse. Andrew felt like a car skidding on wet pavement, brakes locked. There was going to be a collision no matter what he did.

He looked up to see his face plastered all over the screen. The mute button brought the sound blaring back—and Andrew winced. He'd had the volume up, trying to catch every word. The news was repetitive and sensationalized, but it was his main source of information right now.

An insert popped onto the screen. A deputy from the sheriff's office was addressing a reporter's questions about the case.

"The suspect's husband is Andrew Villard," the deputy said. "The family says he went on a business trip and hasn't returned. Even the suspect doesn't know how to contact him. Obviously, we're very concerned about Mr. Villard's whereabouts. He's not a suspect yet, but he's definitely a person of interest—"

Andrew clicked off the TV. His task had just gotten monumentally more difficult. He was no longer anonymous. Every Joe Blow out there knew what he looked like and could turn him in.

The bar called to him. It whispered and cajoled. He'd noticed a bottle of Dewars, which he could almost taste. He hadn't had a serious problem with booze since he'd quit, but this craving *was* serious. It was bad.

He turned away. Out of sight, out of mind.

Marnie's attorney *might* be able to get her out of this, but Andrew couldn't take that chance. His only hope of getting her out of the frying pan without tossing her into the fire was to hunt down LaDonna's killer. Unfortunately, his main suspect had no reason to have killed LaDonna and plenty of reasons not to. And if Andrew believed Bogart's eyewitness testimony, Alison was the murderer.

Andrew knew Marnie hadn't done it, which left him with two possibilities: the real Alison wasn't dead, or, more likely, someone wanted the police to *believe* she wasn't and had turned to murder. Tony Bogart and his vendetta against Alison came to mind first. Payback seemed to be Bogart's purpose in life, and with his knowledge of forensics, he was well equipped to set her up for a fall. But unfortunately, so did several other suspects, including Julia and her boy toy, Jack Furlinghetti.

Andrew had learned about that relationship through Diego Sanchez, who'd been keeping an eye on the Fairmont family. Furlinghetti was trustee of the fund established by Eleanor Driscoll, and his clandestine relationship with Julia could mean the two of them were conspiring to keep Alison from getting the fifty million. What better way than to frame her for a murder and lock her up for life? But Diego hadn't been able to come up with anything concrete, and now Andrew was hamstrung. Worse, he was out of time before he'd started.

He walked out to the deck that had a view of the ocean and Sea Clouds just below him. The cover of trees allowed him to observe the place without being seen, and everything looked deceptively quiet right now. Even the press had taken a break. But he was just in time to catch the blood-red sun as it sank into the ocean, staining the water a deep crimson. If he'd been a believer in signs, he would have said that this was a bad one. Worse than bad. He would have said that someone else was going to die.

29

Marnie checked the rearview mirror again, making sure no one was following her. She'd slept very little last night. Her head was full of thoughts and desperate plans, but she'd had to wait until this morning to follow through on any of them.

It was early, 6:00 a.m., and the traffic was light enough that spotting a tail shouldn't be too difficult. She wasn't as concerned about Bret or Tony Bogart as she was the sheriff's office. The arraignment had been held yesterday afternoon, but evidently they still didn't know she wasn't Alison. She'd thought those fingerprint records were all computerized and could be accessed within minutes.

It was hard to imagine what was causing the delay, but she had to act before they did. It was crucial that she get to the Springdale Convalescent Home before the police, or anyone else, got to her.

She may have located her grandmother.

Having had no luck locating Josephine Hazelton, Marnie had started over, this time using her grandmother's maiden name, Clark. It was a fairly common name, and Marnie had located a Josephine Clark on the second call. She couldn't be sure it was the right one, but that's where she was headed now, praying that she could find the place. According to the directions she'd been given, it was a half hour inland, in a little town called Billingsly.

Marnie had never had a driver's license of her own, but Gramma Jo had let her drive their old station wagon into town, and Marnie had never been stopped. Now, she was using Alison's license, of course, but Andrew had insisted she take driving lessons in Long Island before he'd let her out on the road. Marnie could remember begging Gramma Jo to let her get a license when she turned sixteen, but something had always come up, and Gramma Jo had never gotten around to taking her for the test. For some reason, she hadn't wanted her to have that license, but Marnie had never figured out why.

Marnie found the door to room 220B wide-open, but she couldn't see beyond the short hallway. "Hello?" She spoke softly, not wanting to startle anyone, especially her grandmother, if this was her room.

No one answered, but Marnie couldn't leave without making sure. When she got beyond the hallway she was stopped by the sight of a silver-haired woman sitting at the window. She seemed to be absorbed by the hummingbirds visiting a hanging feeder.

Her grandmother didn't have silver hair, but something prompted Marnie to speak anyway. "Josephine Hazelton?"

The woman turned, and Marnie was startled to see her grandmother's iridescent blue eyes and rounded features. "Who is it?" she asked. "Come out of the shadows where I can see you."

Marnie was almost afraid to move into the room. She hadn't expected it to be Gramma Jo. Her hair had always been long and naturally curly. She'd worn it tied back, and she'd been graying for years, but now she'd gone almost white.

Marnie wondered if her disappearance could have caused it. She didn't know how to explain what had happened, but she'd decided to confess everything—and hope to be forgiven. Maybe she should hope to be believed.

"It's me." That was all Marnie managed to say as she walked into the room and hesitated by the bed, wondering if she would see any sign of recognition now that she was standing in natural light from the window.

"You?" Josephine Hazelton peered at Marnie, fear in her expression. "What are you doing here?" Her eyes were so piercingly focused that Marnie could feel their heat. She had been recognized, but did her grandmother think she was looking at Alison or Marnie?

"You get out of here," Josephine whispered. "You have no business coming to this place."

"Please, let me tell you who I—"

"Get out!"

Marnie reached for her throat, for the ring that she'd worn every day since her grandmother had assured her it was good luck. The ring was gone. Andrew still had it. But the need to touch it was a reflex—and one that Gramma Jo well knew.

The older woman saw the gesture and fell silent. Her brow furrowed and within moments her fierce expression began to crumble. Her hands came to her mouth, prayerlike, and slowly, agonizingly, her eyes filled with tears.

She shook her head. "No, it can't be. Marnie? What's happened to you?"

"God, so much."

She studied Marnie's dark hair, her eyes and her anguished smile, and then pressed her fists to her chest. This was her child. Her shoulders sagged. "Come here," she said. "Come to me."

Marnie crossed the small room and dropped to her knees beside her grandmother's chair. "*I'm sorry.* I couldn't tell you I was alive. I couldn't tell anyone."

She took Gramma Jo's hand, fighting to keep her voice under control as she went back through the events of the last six months. She started with Butch's attack, sharing everything she could remember about that afternoon and what had happened afterward, including the way Andrew found her on the rocks, their arrangement, and the real reason they were in Mirage Bay. It was difficult, and she had to stop at times because silence seemed the only way to deal with the emotions that welled up, but her grandmother listened with a calm acceptance that felt like more than Marnie deserved.

As Marnie told her about all the surgeries and her long recovery, she had the strangest feeling that Gramma Jo already knew about what she was describing. "Had you heard that I was alive?" she asked.

"No, I knew nothing," the elderly woman said. "They told me you'd jumped from the cliffs after you killed Butch. I think they were trying to get me to admit that I'd seen you kill him. I told them the truth. I wasn't home. I was down at the flea market. I also told them that Butch *deserved* to die for making your life so miserable."

Marnie was reluctant to talk about what had happened in the last forty-eight hours, but she had little choice. Gramma Jo might be the only one who could help her now. But just as she feared, her grandmother reacted with horror when she told her about La-Donna's murder and how the police had charged Marnie with two counts of homicide.

It took Marnie some time to convince her that she would be all right. She had a plan. It could only be used as a last resort, but at least it was a plan.

"What will you do?" Gramma Jo asked. "They can't try you for your own murder."

"They can unless I prove who I am. Marnie Hazelton doesn't exist, except for school records that prove nothing. There's no birth certificate, no social security number, no driver's license, no fingerprints on file, no paper trail of any kind."

Gramma Jo's nod was tentative.

"They fingerprinted me yesterday," Marnie said, "but apparently they still haven't figured out that my fingerprints and Alison's don't match."

"What about Butch's murder? Won't you be charged with that if they find out who you are?"

"Yes, probably, but if it comes to that, I'll say I was defending myself. Everyone knows how he stalked me."

Outside, the gray sky had grown dark. A storm was brewing, and the lack of light cast a pall over the small room. As Marnie got up to turn on a table lamp, she heard breakfast being announced over the PA system.

"Would you like me to walk with you to breakfast?" she asked. She took a moment to look around the room, which was sparsely furnished with a bed, a television and a chair. It was more like a hotel room than a place where someone could make a life. And it was nothing like her grandmother's ramshackle cottage where the two of them had lived such a crazy, and often wonderful, patchwork quilt existence.

Concern for her grandmother washed over Marnie. "What are you doing here? Are you ill?"

"No, I'm fine. I blacked out at home one day, and when I went to the doctor he said my blood pressure was too high. I was getting forgetful and confused, couldn't remember to take my meds. I needed some help is all, and this seemed like a good place."

"So you came here on your own? Found it and arranged it? What are you doing with the cottage? LaDonna told me you asked her to keep an eye on it."

Gramma drew in a breath. "Marnie, never mind that right now. You came here to tell me what really happened, and to unburden yourself. And now I need to do the same."

Something in her grandmother's tone caused Marnie's heart to hesitate. "Why would you need to unburden yourself? You haven't done anything."

"Please do your old grandmother a favor," the other woman said, "and remember that you kept a secret from me that broke my heart. I've thought about you every day since you disappeared, and prayed that you were all right."

"I'm not likely to forget it. I hate what I had to do…but why are you asking that of me?"

"Because I am about to tell you a terrible secret, one that's much worse than yours, and I pray to God you can understand and forgive me. Human beings aren't noble, Marnie. We compromise, we do what we have to, and then we live with the guilt. And if we're any good at all, we spend the rest of our lives trying to make up for what we did."

"What did you do?" Marnie asked.

Gramma Jo looked out the window again. "You know that I've always worked with natural medicines. Years ago, before you came to me, I created a herbal brew that could bring on a woman's period."

"You mean if she was late?"

"Technically, it was more like a morning-after pill. It had to be taken before a period was missed. Anyway, word got out, and I had women flocking to me. I was nervous about the safety issues, but these women were all so desperate that I couldn't refuse them."

"So you sold them this brew?"

Marnie had become aware that her grandmother was worrying the button on her cuff, as if trying to get it fastened. But it already was buttoned, and Marnie wanted to plead with her to stop.

"No, I gave it away," Gramma Jo said. "No one had any problems, but I worried that harm might come of it, so I stopped. I quit altogether—and then I had a woman show up at my door, crying and hysterical, saying she'd made a terrible mistake. She was married, but she'd had a fling with some drifter. She offered to pay me any amount of money to give her a dose of the brew."

The button came undone. Marnie reached over and stilled Gramma Jo's frantic fingers. "Let me," she said.

"I didn't take her money," Gramma said, "but I gave her what she wanted, and that was *my* terrible mistake. She'd lied to me. She was already pregnant, three months along. She came back the next day bleeding and in severe pain, but there was nothing I could do for her. We both thought she'd miscarried, but months later, she discovered she was still pregnant."

Marnie felt an icy draft, but it had nothing to do with the stormy day. It was dread.

"She came back to me and begged me to raise the baby. Me! A crazy old woman." Gramma shook her head, silvery hair flying from the loose bun she wore. "She said her husband would leave her and take her children away. It sounded bizarre to me, but she was distraught, and the more she talked the more I came to believe her.

"She'd managed to hide her pregnancy until quite late, and then she'd gone into seclusion somewhere. Her family thought she was traveling in Europe, something to do with a charity art auction, I think. No one knew about the pregnancy, and she didn't intend to go home until after the baby was born."

"What did you do?"

"I let her stay and I assisted her through the delivery. The baby was born alive and healthy, but—"

Marnie wanted to stop her. She had some preternatural sense of what was coming.

Gramma voice's was raw with regret, pain. "The baby was born with deformities, and the woman—the mother—she couldn't handle it."

"Deformities," Marnie echoed. "Of course, the herbal brew." She touched the curve of her throat where the birthmark had been, and a vivid picture of her own contorted face screened through her mind.

The lopsided features and misaligned teeth. She'd looked like a monster.

"Who chose the name Marnie?" she asked.

"The mother did. If there was any significance to the name I don't know what it was."

"Who was she, my mother?"

"Julia Fairmont."

"What?" Marnie's voice went high with disbelief. Shock buzzed through her, stinging shock. This was the last thing she'd expected to hear. She was related to Julia? No, not just related, but her *daughter?* Marnie Hazelton was the product of a fling with a drifter and an attempted abortion. What a sickening twist of fate. She didn't know whether to hate Julia or to pity her.

No, she did know. She hated her.

Still, she had to ask. "Did she ever come and see me? Did you hear from her?"

"She sent a check every month, and thank God. It was the only way we got by."

"Good of her," Marnie said bitterly. That was the least the bitch could have done, and she couldn't have sent very much, given how they lived.

"And she's paying for this place," Gramma Jo said.

"Hush money."

"Yes, probably. But you're in trouble now, Marnie, and Julia Fairmont has the money and the contacts to help you."

"I don't want her help, not *now*."

"Marnie, if there's a record of your birth, Julia will have it. I wrote something up for her with height, weight, all the details I could think of. She may have destroyed it, but you should find out. Talk to her, tell her everything."

"Gramma Jo, couldn't *you* tell the court who I am? You raised me."

"Of course, but I can't prove anything, and they have no reason to believe me. I'm not your birth mother, and I'm not Julia Fairmont. You need her help, and she owes you that much."

Marnie nodded, but she wanted nothing from Julia. She wasn't sure she could even look at the woman who'd done something so reckless and then refused to take responsibility. She'd disposed of Marnie like trash.

Marnie didn't say anything, because she didn't want to upset her grandmother, but she knew exactly what she was going to do.

30

As Marnie drove up to Sea Clouds she saw the van of a local television station parked outside the gates on the far side of the entrance. There was a second van and an SUV that looked as if they were media-related as well.

Some of the people milling about appeared to be part of the television crew, and Marnie recognized the statuesque chestnut-blond female reporter from the local news. The rest had cameras with impressive zoom lenses, and some looked suspiciously like tabloid reporters.

Did Mirage Bay have paparazzi?

Either something newsworthy had just happened at Sea Clouds, or word of Alison Fairmont Villard's murder charges was bigger news than Marnie could possibly have imagined. There'd been TV crews at the courthouse when she left yesterday, and she'd wondered how they could possibly have known about the arraignment. Someone had to have tipped them off, possibly Bogart, although she didn't know how that would help the case against her.

Marnie pressed the remote button, and the crowd spotted her as the gates opened. Several men rushed toward her, trying to cut her off. It was difficult not to hit anyone, but she had no intention of being trapped. One man came close enough to kick her fender as she veered away from him and sped through the gates. Her heart did a painful slam-thud.

Jerk. What was that all about?

She wheeled around the side to the wall of garages rather than park in the portico, where she would be exposed to the photographers. The gates closed automatically, but she couldn't see if they'd shut quickly enough to keep the reporters out. Fortunately, the garage was secure, and she made sure the door was down before she got out of the car.

A moment later, she rushed into the kitchen, where Rebecca was busy preparing lunch. "Where's Julia?"

Rebecca glanced over her shoulder, her hands in a colander full of the spring greens she was rinsing for salads. "You mean your mother? She's upstairs in her bedroom, getting ready to go out. Alison? Is something wrong?"

"The barbarians are at the gate," Marnie called back.

Julia was standing in front of the bedroom mirrors when she burst into her room unannounced.

"What's going on outside?" Marnie asked. "There are TV crews."

"There you are, darling. Come here." Julia, nonplussed, held out her hand to Marnie, who didn't take it.

"Did you hear me?"

"Of course." Julia's eyes were glittery, her voice brittle. "Now, come *here*. I think we should have our picture taken together, don't you? A mother-daughter portrait? We haven't done that since you were little. Shame on us!"

"Mother-*daughter* portrait?" The idea was abhorrent, but Julia seemed oblivious to the disbelief in Marnie's tone. Marnie wanted to slap her, but had the feeling Julia would shatter like crystal. She was dressed to go out, in a chic three-piece summer suit with a bustier top. But her hair was too stiff, her makeup too perfect and masklike. It reminded Marnie of armor.

Julia clicked across the marble floor in her sling-back heels and slim skirt, clasped Marnie's hand and dragged her back to the mirror. "See?" was all she said.

Her voice was throaty, and her eyes filled as she gazed at their reflections in the mirror. Marnie's hair was Medusa-like and Julia's smile was flash-frozen. Not your ideal mother-daughter pose, but the resemblance was there. Now Marnie knew why. She also knew they were both in trouble. Something was terribly wrong here.

"There's a news crew outside," Marnie said, determined to be heard this time. "Did something happen while I was gone?"

"The police came this morning. It was the CSI unit—you know, like the show your brother enjoys so much. They searched your room again and then went through our garbage cans. They found something of yours and took it with them, a piece of your clothing, I think."

Dear God. Marnie hadn't noticed that any of her clothing was missing. This wasn't the time to question Julia in depth—or to confront her about the daughter she'd abandoned. But Marnie had no more choice now than she'd had with Gramma Jo. She was out of time. They were *all* out of time.

"What exactly did they find in the garbage," she asked, "and how did it get there?"

"I don't *know*, Alison. I wasn't allowed out there. They said I was obstructing their search. They escorted me back inside, and told me to stay out of their way, in so many words."

"Was Bret here? Does he know what happened?"

"Your brother suggested that he and I take a walk on the beach the way you do so often. It was pleasant."

Pleasant? "Is Bret here now?"

"No, he's gone on an interview for an editorial position with a men's magazine. Can you imagine? If he gets the job, he'll be moving to New York. He says it's something he's always wanted to do. Things have a way of working out for the best, don't they? The family has always been lucky that way."

Marnie stared at her in disbelief. Julia's strange, vacant smile was starting to make her feel ill. "I don't understand," she said. "Why aren't you taking this seriously? I've been charged with murder. I could go to prison, death row."

Julia sighed. "Now you're being dramatic. You're not going to jail, not for one second. Your attorney won't allow that."

Marnie didn't waste time arguing. People like Julia believed money could solve anything, because too often it could. The ones who had it bought what they wanted from the ones who didn't, a sad legacy of the American Dream. But throwing some money at the right attorney wouldn't solve this one. It was hideously complicated.

"Everything's going to be fine," Julia said.

"No, it isn't. You need to sit down. I have something to tell you."

Julia blinked. "Can't it wait? I'm on my way out to lunch, and I desperately need the distraction."

Marnie stepped in front of her, effectively blocking her way. "No, it can't wait. Sit down. Did you hear me? *Sit down now.*"

A glimpse of the real Julia surfaced as she glared at Marnie. For a second, her eyes seemed to flare with the tiny red dots of an overexposed photograph. She was angry, enraged. Good, now they might get somewhere.

"I'm sitting." Julia plunked down on the chaise by the windows, opened her Gucci bag and took out her makeup case. "Hurry up," she said, opening her compact to check her face in the mirror.

"I didn't kill LaDonna Jeffries or Marnie Hazelton."

Julia tidied up her lipstick with the nail of her little finger. "Of course you didn't kill them. I never thought that. No one thinks that. You're completely innocent. The charges are ridiculous."

"I am innocent, but not for the reason you're thinking." Marnie hesitated, wondering how to soften the blow, but realizing there was no way. And why should she? Had Julia ever softened the blow for the child she didn't want?

Anger churned in Marnie's gut. "I didn't kill LaDonna because she was my best friend, and I didn't kill Marnie Hazelton because I *am* Marnie Hazelton."

Julia looked up from the mirror. Her lashes quivered. "What did you say?"

"I'm not Alison. Your son has been sniffing around and hinting at that since Andrew and I arrived." She saw the glimmer of desperation in Julia's eyes and hesitated, still struggling with the need to protect her from the truth. "Bret was right. I'm not her."

"What in the world are you talking about? Are you all right?"

Marnie came very close to laughing. "God, no, I'm not all right, but I'm better than I have been for quite a while now." A part of her wanted to stop. Clearly, Julia would let her go on with the charade, and might even encourage it, but Marnie couldn't. Even though it would expose her—and Andrew—to grave consequences, it had to be done. Andrew was gone. Marnie had to accept the possibility that he knew what was going on and had run out on her. It might even have been intentional. He had some grand plan, and Marnie was never anything more than a pawn. At any rate, he wasn't here, and she had to protect herself, whatever that took.

Julia didn't interrupt once while Marnie described the meeting she'd just had with her surrogate grandmother. Julia listened as silently as Gramma Jo had, but her face and body were knotted. She had none of the older woman's calm acceptance, only icy gray eyes suffused with disbelief and denial.

"I know what happened in my grandmother's cottage twenty-two years ago," Marnie said as she finished. "You were pregnant, but not by your husband. You were desperate, and people do terrible things out of desperation— I know that, too. I've been desperate myself."

She went on to tell Julia everything she remembered about February second and what had happened since. No details were held back, no matter how difficult they might be to bear. She needed to shock the other woman into hearing her. But by the time Marnie was done, Julia had gone from disbelief to defiance. Her face was pale with outrage and her hands were clenched.

"Why are you here?" she demanded. "And what do you want from me? If you think you're getting your hands on Alison's trust fund, think again. I'd hire a hit man before I'd let you see a cent."

Julia's outrage was contagious. It burned in Marnie's soul like hellfire. She wanted to strangle the woman with her bare hands. How dare she rail at her and make accusations?

Julia was up and out of her chair. Her designer bag clattered to the floor and she threw the mirror on the bed. "Do you understand what you've done?" she said. "You conspired with Andrew to deceive me in the cruelest possible way. You pretended to be Alison! You made me believe my daughter was alive. You gave me *hope*."

Marnie's throat tightened. She heard the pain in Julia's voice, but whatever compassion she felt was gone before it had any chance of expression. Her own voice dropped to a lethal whisper. "I *am* your daughter. Do you understand what you've done to *me?*"

The anger became horror. Julia's mouth went slack. She looked away.

Marnie wondered if Julia had ever thought about anything except in terms of its impact on her. She seemed congenitally incapable of empathy and she'd passed that trait on to her son. It made Marnie deeply regret that she was related to these people in any way. She'd stubbornly wanted to believe that Alison might be different, but now she was sure that her half sister was as sick as her family. They were corrupt. All of them. Emotionally corrupt.

When Julia finally looked up, it wasn't to apologize or explain. "Did Andrew kill her?" she asked. "Will you tell me that much?"

"I don't know," Marnie admitted. "At this point I don't know where he is or what he's done. I swear."

"Then what is it you want? You're here, telling me this story. You must want something."

Marnie had a moment of wishing that she could walk out and never say another word to this woman, but she had her grandmother's caution in her head—and the fear of what would happen to Gramma Jo if Marnie went to jail. She wouldn't have the money to stay in that dismal place.

"I'm not a cold-blooded murderer," Marnie explained. "Butch attacked me, and I acted in self-defense, but the authorities aren't going to believe that. I'm not even sure they'll believe I'm Marnie Hazelton without proof."

"How can *I* possibly help you with that?"

"There are no fingerprints on file for me, no records. It's like I don't exist. My grandmother said she made up a certificate when I was born and gave it to you. Do you have it?"

Julia's face went pale with shock. "You can't be serious. Do you realize what will happen if you reveal that you're my daughter? What if the media found out?

Can you imagine the scandal? The Fairmonts and the Driscolls have been involved in philanthropy and public service going back decades. They're good people, *fine* people. Do you expect me to throw all that away?"

"You threw *me* away," Marnie said. "Too bad you weren't able to get rid of me. Then you wouldn't have any of this messiness to deal with."

Julia strode over to a console holding a tray with three crystal decanters of liquor, all in shades of amber. She filled a highball glass nearly to the rim, and after she'd drunk half of it, she banged the glass down.

"We're done talking," she said.

"Done?" Marnie felt a moment of paralyzing fear and indecision. Julia was throwing her out? Her fate lay in this woman's hands. Marnie would have no legal counsel without Julia, no support. She had no money of her own, except what was in her wallet. It was all Andrew's. She had to make Julia understand how important this was. Scandal was nothing compared to what Marnie was facing.

"How can we be done?" she said. "What am I supposed to do?"

"I don't care what you do. My life is in ruins. Get out of my house and leave me alone to deal with that."

Marnie nodded. As swiftly as panic has risen, anger flared, to burn it back. Julia had never cared about her bastard daughter, and there was nothing Marnie could say or do to make her care. Julia's fancy world was the only thing that existed for her, and Marnie had never fit there and never would. Julia had tried to abort her, and when that failed, she'd abandoned her. Marnie understood that women were sometimes forced to make terrible choices. She'd had to take a life to defend her own. But Julia had turned her back on a helpless infant, apparently because she couldn't stomach the sight of the deformities that she'd caused with her carelessness.

"I was just leaving," Marnie said. Throw herself on Julia Fairmont's mercy? Not a chance. She turned on her heel and walked out of the room. She was done with this heartless bitch and her family. Done.

Marnie had the suitcases out and was weighing her options when she heard a sharp rapping sound.

"Can I speak with you?" Julia called through the door.

Marnie turned from the balcony window, where she'd been watching the half-dozen people who were still at the gates, despite the fact that the sun was going down and it would soon be dark.

Julia at her door couldn't possibly mean anything good.

Marnie went to open it and saw that she had come with what looked like a peace offering, a tray of food.

"Rebecca said you never came down for anything to eat today," Julia said. "You must be starving. I put this together for you."

Marnie gave the crab leg and marinated asparagus salad a skeptical glance. "You did this? I saw Rebecca cleaning the greens."

"Excuse me? I can put a salad together."

"I'm not hungry," Marnie said, but her rumbling stomach gave her away.

"Of course you are," Julia said. "Let me in. I need to talk with you about our conversation today. There may be a way we can work this out for everyone's benefit."

Wary, Marnie stepped aside and let her in. Julia set the tray on the coffee table by the fireplace.

"Help yourself," she said, "please. I'd like you to. I can talk while you eat."

Marnie was still uneasy about any plan Julia might have to work things out, but her noisy stomach won. She sank onto the couch and bent over the tray, trying not to wolf her food. The crab was luscious, rich and moist, the asparagus crunchy and the dressing had a citrus tang. "This is wonderful."

"I'll tell Rebecca," Julia said with a shrug. "She made it."

"I thought so." Marnie dug into the repast, eating with relish. The probability that she was being poisoned had just lessened.

Julia wandered around the room, discreetly checking things out and apparently giving Marnie some time.

Finally Marnie could stand it no longer. "What did you come to talk about?"

Julia couldn't quite manage a smile. She was clearly emotional as she spoke. "I'm sure Alison is dead, and I suspect Andrew did it. I've always believed it. He had the motive and the opportunity. But I've been thinking about that, and I realized something. Andrew may have taken one daughter, but he gave me another."

Marnie put her fork down. What in the hell was she talking about?

"I want you to be my daughter. I want you to be Alison. You've already transformed your entire life for just that purpose. There's no reason you shouldn't continue. It would be such a good life—and one you deserve, after everything you've been through."

"Continue being Alison?"

"And my daughter."

"What about Andrew? How does he fit in?"

"You'll have to make that decision. To be blunt, I'd like you to consider leaving him. I don't think you're safe with him, even here. A man who would replace his missing wife with another woman would do *anything*. But that's up to you. I'll go along with whatever you decide."

"And what would I have to do?" She hesitated, then echoed Julia's own words. "You're here. I'm sure there's something you want."

"I want you to go through with the trial, let James Brainard defend you. There isn't a chance in the world he won't get you off. He doesn't believe they'll pursue the second charge. There's no evidence, and he's sure he can beat the first one."

"And if he does win, and I'm exonerated?"

"The trust is yours. More than fifty million dollars, all of it yours, with no one the wiser. I ask only that you never reveal your real identity to anyone, but especially not to Bret. I have my own reasons for asking that. And, of course, I want us to have an ongoing relationship. There's so much I can offer you, so much I can teach, and I'd consider it my chance to make up for…everything."

Marnie barely had to think about it. Andrew was gone, and she'd decided before they came to Mirage Bay that the money would complicate her life more than anything else. If the Fairmonts were any example, that was painfully true.

"I wish I could do it, but I can't," she said. "I know it would make everything so much simpler."

Julia stiffened. Obviously she wasn't used to be rejected. "Why can't you do it?"

Marnie was actually surprised that Julia didn't understand. "I don't want to live my life as someone else, having to lie and pretend and struggle to remember my lines. No amount of money will ever make that okay. No matter what I'm going to be faced with, I'd rather confront it head-on. I know who I am, and maybe it isn't much by your standards, but at least I can trust it, and by my standards, that's everything."

Without a shred of animosity, Marnie added, "No offense, Julia, but I don't know who the hell your daughter Alison is."

Julia heaved a breath. "Take some time to think about it, please."

"I don't need to think about it."

"Fine, then prepare yourself to deal with *this* head-on. I'm firing your attorney and revoking the bail money. Good luck, *Marnie.*"

She barely skipped a beat before dropping the next grenade. "Oh, and by the way, James called this afternoon. He tells me the gun they found in your drawer is definitely the murder weapon—and the crime lab was able to match a button found at the crime scene to a navy-blue cardigan sweater—yours—that was stuffed in the trash behind the house." She smiled. "He says the prosecutor is talking about the death penalty. Of course, they're bluffing, but then again…you never know."

Marnie's stomach turned over with violent force, threatening to expel the crab salad. She sat back on the couch, breathing, praying she wouldn't puke. Julia played a ruthless game, but Marnie shouldn't have been surprised at that, or at anything she would do. The woman had a lot to lose.

Julia started for the door, hesitating when she saw the bags Marnie had hauled out of the closet. "Suitcases?"

"I'll be out soon," Marnie assured her. "Give me an hour, no more."

"The press is still outside. They'll see you leaving with your bags, and it will cause an uproar. I'm not just thinking of me, really. I'm considering you, too. They'll stalk you and make your life miserable."

She had a point, especially considering what had happened when Marnie drove in. "What are you suggesting?"

"Stay here until things calm down. And don't tell any of those vultures who you really are. If you won't keep our secret for yourself, then do it for me."

"Why," Marnie asked, "would I do anything for you?"

"Because I'm your mother."

"You never were and never will be my mother. I owe you nothing."

Hurt shadowed Julia's expression for just a fleeting moment before her angular face turned hard. "As you wish," she said, and left.

31

Tony surveyed the contents of the vending machine with a jaundiced eye. If he was looking for flavor he might as well go with bottled water. He fished some quarters from his pocket, fed them into the slot, and moments later he was sitting in Vince Connelly's office, nursing his bottled water and waiting for Connelly to get his wide-load ass off his land-line phone. He hadn't even acknowledged Tony with a nod and that was just plain rude.

At last the detective hung up the receiver. "An interesting turn of events in the LaDonna Jeffries case," he said, looking like the cat that had the canary by its tail feathers. He was practically licking his chops. "That was the prosecutor. James Brainard is no longer Alison Villard's attorney."

"Who's replacing him?"

"No one. Ms. Villard will have to hire her own attorney or use a public defender. It seems mother and daughter had a spat and mother has withdrawn her financial support, including a request to revoke the bail bond. But that's not the best part."

Connelly sipped carefully from a steaming mug of what looked like real coffee. Apparently there was an employee lounge somewhere around, and no one had bothered to tell Tony.

"The prosecutor's office thinks they have another reason to revoke bail."

Tony set the water down. *"Really?"*

"The morning after the murder, she was in her car heading south on the San Diego Freeway when her brother caught up with her and convinced her to turn herself in. It may have been a flight attempt. Plus, now there's news footage of her trying to run down a reporter."

"I guess that leaves you no choice," Tony said.

Connelly grinned, obviously thinking this was the case that would get him the media attention—and the promotion—he so richly deserved. "I guess it doesn't."

He muffled what sounded like a giggle, and Tony felt queasy hearing it. Men who carried guns should never be allowed to giggle. It was unseemly.

Tony hated the guy, and it would give him great pleasure to be the monkey wrench in Vince Connelly's machinery. But Tony also hated Alison. Seemed it came down to a question of which one he hated more. Not as easy a decision as the bottled water.

Marnie groped for the remote while she was still lying in bed, half-asleep. She'd heard TV news could be addicting, but that was a gross understatement when your own life was flashing before your eyes. It had to be like shooting heroin. She had the television on before she lifted her head off the pillow.

Last night's local news had shown video of her trying to drive around the reporters at the gate, and it had made *her* look reckless and crazy, despite the crowd surging at her. After watching it, she'd gotten hooked trying to find other stations with a more balanced version. She'd listened carefully to each word of commentary, hoping to hear something condemning the paparazzi-type onslaught, but it was the same footage on every station and the same raised eyebrows by the news anchors.

Now she was a double murderer *and* a bad driver.

She propped herself up with pillows, wincing at the brightness slicing through the glass doors. The sound that groaned out of her was closer to despair than laughter. Yesterday's clouds seemed to have passed. Too bad, actually. They suited her mood better than blinding sunlight.

She could hear activity downstairs, which was probably Rebecca in the kitchen. Marnie wasn't going to subject herself to Bret and Julia this morning. Maybe Rebecca would take pity and bring a cup of coffee up to her.

All Marnie could find were the usual morning talk formats and game shows as she clicked through the stations, which was probably a good thing. Maybe her fifteen minutes of infamy had passed with the weather. She had spent the night trying to figure out how to prove her identity without involving Julia or Andrew, but it didn't seem possible. Without Julia's cooperation, Gramma Jo might be her only choice, but Marnie hated the idea of putting her through that, and as her grandmother had pointed out, there was no guarantee anyone would believe her.

Marnie's greatest concern was Gramma Jo's health. Julia might have been paying the bills, but she didn't give a damn about Josephine Hazelton. Marnie wanted her grandmother safely back in her cottage, where she'd lived her whole life. But sadly, Marnie couldn't even help herself, much less Gramma Jo.

Every fiber seemed to ache as she sat up and swung her legs out of bed. But at least her body brought a comforting sense of familiarity. She didn't always recognize her reflection, and it was bizarre to be trapped in someone else's life, in their identity. Possibly she should just turn herself in. They must have figured out the prints didn't match by now. That would prove who she wasn't, but she still couldn't prove who she was, and she had no way to explain taking Alison's identity without involving Andrew… although protecting him should be her last concern right now.

Her feet touched the icy marble floor, and for an instant she wasn't aware of anything except the almost painful cold. She crossed the room, intending to open the balcony doors, but a sparkle of light from the liquor cart caught her attention.

She'd left the earrings there.

Those are the Villard diamonds. They're cursed, you know.

Marnie wondered how anything so beautiful could be evil, but the gems' lavish perfection *was* slightly sinister. They gave off a blushing light of their own, and the yellow diamond border had an aura-like glitter. Nearly constant movement in their depths made them seem alive.

She had to put them away, but she wasn't exactly anxious to pick them up. Curses were nothing but superstition, she told herself as she scooped them up, quickly returned them to their black-velvet box and tucked the box in a drawer of Andrew's jewelry case. They were his now, for better or worse.

That accomplished, she crossed the room with a sense of relief and threw open the balcony doors, enjoying the warmth that flooded in and the quiet outside. There were no reporters stationed at the gate. Maybe the furor was over.

As she entered the bathroom and turned on the faucet, she heard an announcement of breaking news. Half listening, she splashed some cool water on her face and grabbed the hand towel. The only thing she caught was a reference to a body washing up on shore. She couldn't hear what shore or any of the other details. Curious, she walked back into the bedroom, drying her face with the towel.

On the screen was a helicopter shot of a deserted beach. The headline running across the bottom said that the remains of a body had been found on a deserted beach in the Baja Peninsula. The next shot showed a crew of investigators going over the scene and the insert was a photo of what might have been the remains.

The female commentator said the body was a woman's and blond hair and black fibers had been found, but no identification had been made.

Blond hair and black fibers.

Marnie thought immediately of the photo journal she'd found on the boat, and all those snapshots of Alison, the ones Andrew said he was comparing. She'd been wearing a black bathing suit. Of course, millions of women had blond hair and wore black bathing suits, but how many of them were lost at sea?

Marnie stared at the screen long after the special report was over. Her head was still buzzing, and she hadn't heard why the discovery was receiving national attention, but she couldn't talk herself out of the possibility that this was about Alison. Marnie needed to talk to Andrew, but he still hadn't called or returned any of her messages. She had also never heard from the P.I. he'd supposedly hired.

Outside, the entry gates creaked and clanked. It sounded as if they were opening and a car was driving into the compound. She could hear the engine noise. Her heart began to race, and she ran for the balcony doors with the unreasonable hope that it was Andrew coming back.

What she saw as she burst out onto the balcony was two patrol cars and an unmarked sedan driving through the gates. Marnie's heart froze. No one had to tell her why they were here or who they'd come for.

From the window of her third floor bedroom at Sea Clouds, Rebecca watched the deputy sheriffs take Alison away in handcuffs. Apparently the county felt that six men, four in uniform and two wearing suits, were required to apprehend one slender, dazed woman.

Rebecca assumed the men in suits were detectives assigned to investigate the case, and she actually felt a stirring of sympathy for the woman being led away like a sacrificial lamb. Nothing that would change Rebecca's mind about what she herself had done, but still, she was human. Alison wasn't any worse than the other two, just convenient. If Rebecca had had her choice, the deputies would be taking all of them away.

Bret was a practicing sociopath, and Julia hadn't even come out of her room when the law arrived. Rebecca had let the men in and shown them to Alison's room, and then she'd gone to Julia's door and knocked. Julia had shouted at her to go away, said she wasn't well. Rebecca had figured she was drunk, and left her alone. She hadn't bothered going to Bret's room. She was fairly certain he hadn't come back the night before. He probably had some new girlfriend to torture.

The deputies had let Alison get dressed, but she looked like a gypsy in the black prairie dress she wore. Her hair was flying loose and uncombed, and her feet were bare. Rebecca wondered if it was shock or defiance that had made her dress like that. She also found herself wondering what Alison had been like before the surgery. It seemed to have changed everything but her looks.

At least the media was nowhere around. There would be no witnesses to this part of the slaughter, except Rebecca herself, and her guilt was already subsiding. She had convinced herself that what she was doing was necessary for survival. She was taking advantages of the opportunities that came her way, and she'd been taught by the best—the Fairmonts themselves.

The prints were a perfect match.

Marnie sat on a concrete slab in a holding cell, wearing a jumpsuit the color of neon-orange roadwork signs, and waiting for the public defender the court had appointed to represent her. She'd been locked up all morning, and all anyone would tell her was that his name was Paul Esposito, and he would show up when he showed up. It was a little different than the last time she'd been booked.

James Brainard had already withdrawn from the case, claiming Alison herself had fired him. That was bullshit, but Marnie couldn't very well argue the point. Nor could she tell the female officer who'd fingerprinted her for the second time that the prints couldn't possibly match.

They *did* match, both times. A mix-up once, perhaps. Not twice.

The prints on record for Alison Fairmont matched Marnie's—and it only got worse from there. The CSI team had found Marnie's sweater, missing a button, in the garbage at Sea Clouds, and the crime lab had matched the sweater's cotton thread with the residue on the button and with the fiber they'd found under La-Donna's fingernails. LaDonna had apparently pulled the button off while she was struggling with her killer.

And now Marnie was being framed for her murder. But that wasn't why the court had revoked her bail and ordered that she be incarcerated. Someone had convinced them she was a flight risk. Probably the same person who was trying to frame her: Tony Bogart.

Marnie was convinced of it. How difficult would it be for a law enforcement officer to set someone up? Tony knew exactly what he was doing, and he wouldn't rest until he'd avenged himself on Alison. Either whatever Alison had done to him had turned him into a monster, or he'd been one all along. It ran in his family. Butch had been crazy-mean, and Marnie had heard the rumors about Butch and Tony's mother, how she'd tried to kill herself with them in the car.

Marnie rose from the slab and roamed the small

cell like a zombie. Nothing felt real, least of all her. None of the Fairmont family had been there when the police handcuffed her and took her away. The house was still, and she hadn't seen any sign of Julia, Bret, or even Rebecca. It was as if they didn't exist.

Marnie touched her throat. It was a reflex, but it always felt as if she'd been caught in a net when she realized nothing was there. It was a hot, suffocating feeling. Her best hope now was that the body found in Mexico would be identified as Alison's. If she could endure this cement cage and stay quiet a little longer, perhaps she wouldn't have to prove anything. It would be done for her.

Bret wasn't in his room, but Julia knew something was going on when she saw the open dresser drawers and the clothing laid out on his bed. There were two summer suits hanging on the valet stand, and he'd pulled several pairs of shoes out of his closet.

He was leaving. "Bret? Bret! Where are you?"

She found him in the kitchen on his cell phone, madly talking to someone. He gave her a thumbs-up as she entered the room, and mouthed, *"I got the job."*

He was beaming as he talked on the phone. Julia couldn't remember seeing him so happy, and her heart ached at what she had to do.

"I need to talk to you," she whispered, using rudimentary sign language to get her meaning across.

He nodded and said his goodbyes to whoever was on the other end of the line. Even before he'd hung up the phone, he began to eagerly fill Julia in on the details of his new job on the magazine, which included moving to New York.

"One of my frat brothers from U.S.C. lives in Manhattan," he told her. "He's going to let me stay with him until I find a place of my own. That is *so* cool of him. It's almost impossible to find housing in Manhattan. I've already started packing, and I have a flight…" His head tilted quizzically. "What's going on? You don't look overjoyed about my good news."

"Bret, I'm thrilled about your job. Really, I am, but you'll have to push back the start date. We have a crisis, and I need you here in California."

He threw his arms up in exasperation. He opened a cabinet and slammed it shut, nearly breaking the glass panes in the door. "You can't keep doing this to me. You constantly nag me about not working, but every time I get a job you sabotage it. I *want* this job. I deserve it, for Christ's sake."

He turned on his mother, seething with anger and hurt. "It's Alison, right? Rebecca told me the cops came and got her. She's the fucking crisis, as always."

"No, it isn't Alison. *She* isn't Alison. Bret, you were right about her."

His glare turned suspicious. "What are you talking about?"

Julia desperately wanted a drink to stop her voice from shaking, but she'd given up booze an hour ago. She was done with it. No more booze, no more pills. Somehow she had to get through this sober.

"Sit down," she told him, no longer pleading. He was the only family she had left that she could—or would—acknowledge, and he was going to stay with her because that's what family did.

Bret's face furrowed with frustration, but he hoisted his butt onto the island countertop and listened, brightening only when she told him about the imposter in their midst. Julia described Andrew and Marnie's deception in great and gory detail, starting with Butch's attack on Marnie and ending with the confrontation with Marnie yesterday. The only thing Julia left out was the part about her indiscretion years ago and the tragic result. That she could never admit. That she would take to her grave.

Bret wasn't quite as glum by the time she'd finished.

"I *knew it* wasn't Alison," he said softly.

"How could you have known? She was so like your sister," Julia said.

"You were oblivious to all of it." Bitterness crept into his tone. "You wanted to believe Alison had returned from her watery grave and that you two could hug and make up and all would be forgiven."

"I suppose so," Julia said, just as glad he thought that was the only reason she'd blinded herself to the obvious. It always surprised her how naive and gullible men could be about women.

"You haven't heard the worst, Bret. I'm going to need your help with damage control. This Marnie Hazelton person is crazy. She's making outrageous claims, and they're all untrue."

"What kind of claims?"

"She's trying to extort me into helping her get out of the murder charges. When she told me who she really was, she also threatened to say that she was my illegitimate daughter. Isn't that absurd?"

He shook back the blond curls that were forever tumbling onto his forehead. "Why would she do that?"

"She claims there's no other way to prove she didn't commit the crimes that her alter-ego, Alison, has been accused of. Marnie Hazelton could hardly have killed herself, but she swore to me that she has no way to prove her identity. She made up some ridiculous story about having no birth certificate or any other records. She wants my financial support, of course, but I'm *not* going to be blackmailed."

Julia couldn't tell by his puzzled expression whether she'd convinced him or not. "Bret, please stay. I don't know whether your sister's alive or dead, and I can't lose all my children at one time."

Still silent, he gazed at the floor.

"Bret?" she repeated.

Julia was startled when he slid off the counter and came over to her. He pulled her into his arms and gave her a hug that was completely unexpected. Tears stung, catching in her lashes and threatening to turn into a flood. She couldn't remember the last time he'd done that—just swept her into his arms and hugged her—and she really wanted to remember, for some reason.

"I'll talk to the magazine's editor and see if I can get more time," he said, his arms locked around her. "I'll tell him there's a family crisis. He'll figure it out for himself when the news hits the papers."

Julia shuddered. "I'm trying not to think about the media." She hugged her son back, thanking him profusely, and hoping this nightmare didn't put his new job in jeopardy.

In truth, Julia wasn't at all certain Bret could help her—or that anyone could. But she was going to fight to the bitter end. Deny deny deny. No matter what they tried to accuse her of, and she was certain the media would accuse her of everything from Butch Bogart's murder to her own daughter's disappearance, she would deny it all. She would wear black and comport herself with the dignity of a grieving mother, because that's what she was. She would behave as only Eleanor could have behaved in a situation like this, because she had no other choice. There was nothing left to hide behind now except the family bond, even if it was an illusion. She was a Fairmont only by marriage. By blood she was a Driscoll, and she would go down a Driscoll.

She imagined Eleanor was sitting up in her grave and howling by now. Julia didn't know if it was with approval or rage, and to her surprise, she found that she didn't really care. It was a good feeling, not caring. It might be the only pure and honest feeling she had.

32

Marnie sat across the interview room table from her court-appointed public defender, wondering if the ink was dry on his diploma from law school. Paul Esposito was a twenty-something kid who clearly had no interest in her or her case, and did not want to be there. As far as she could tell, his only goal was to close her file as quickly and as permanently as possible, even if that meant throwing her to the lions.

"The prosecutor's talking death penalty," he said in the tone of someone discussing inclement weather. "I think she'd come down to life without possibility of parole, if we played her game."

"Life, that's a long time."

Paul shrugged, and Marnie realized irony was wasted on him. Probably *any* effort to enlist Paul to her cause would be wasted. Of course, he thought he was dealing with Alison Fairmont, whose case had all but been crushed by incriminating physical evidence and no financial support. But he probably wouldn't have cared if he'd known who she really was.

"And what is her game?" Marnie asked him.

"We plead guilty to the first count, and they reduce the second to manslaughter. I'll hold out until they drop the second charge. There isn't enough evidence to make it stick."

"And I spend the rest of my life in maximum security?"

"It's better than death row." Paul shrugged again. Someone should tell him that was bad for the posture.

"You're sure? You've been on death row?" Why did she bother?

He closed her file and slipped it into his briefcase, all nice and tidy. Out of sight, out of mind. She'd been relegated to lifelong storage, as far as he was concerned. As far as everyone was concerned.

"Can I tell the prosecutor it's a deal?" He actually looked hopeful.

"Let me think about it." She wasn't going to make his day when he'd just tanked hers—and probably all the rest of her days. And she wasn't letting him out of here that quickly, either.

"I have a question," she said. "I saw a report on the news yesterday morning about the remains of a woman's body that had washed up in Baja."

"Yeah, I saw that, too." Paul closed his briefcase and straightened his tie. "Apparently they weren't able to identify the remains. Her teeth had been broken out. They couldn't tell whether by accident or foul play. Lousy way to go."

Marnie didn't respond. It felt as if the ceiling had crashed down on her, and she could hardly hold up her head. Her disappointment was profound, and Paul Esposito had noticed. His hand was frozen on his briefcase, and he was watching her with more interest than he'd shown the entire meeting.

"Why did you ask about the body in Baja?"

Marnie shrugged. It was her turn. "Nothing specific. My husband's down there on a business trip, and I was a little concerned." She let it go at that, but apparently she'd triggered something she hadn't intended to. Paul's attention was now riveted on her.

"Ms. Fairmont, when is your husband coming back? Was his business trip in any way related to your case?"

Was Andrew coming back would be the better question. Now that she had Paul's attention, Marnie realized there might be an opportunity to use the resources of the public defender's office to find Andrew. If she said the word, would this man send out the dogs? But Marnie wasn't ready to make that decision. She was still thinking about the consequences to Andrew, and even to Julia.

It felt as if she held both their fates in her hands, and there were no good choices. It was one thing to try and save her own life, but could she live with herself if she had to destroy others to do it? Did she owe Andrew or Julia anything? No, she didn't. In theory, the answer was easy. But in reality it was much more complicated.

Julia's raw desperation was vivid in Marnie's mind. She seemed to urgently believe that acknowledging an illegitimate child would destroy her life—and maybe it would, given the rarefied life Julia led. Possibly she would be shunned, a social outcast. Marnie wondered if there was more to it.

Maybe she should have bargained with Julia. She could have insisted that Julia get Gramma Jo out of that dismal nursing home, return her to her cottage and pay for whatever outside care was necessary. That wouldn't be too high a price, would it? Marnie would spend her life in jail, but have the comfort of knowing her grandmother was back at the cottage, safe and secure, *if* she could trust Julia to do that. And then there was Andrew. Maybe Marnie should have found her own private detective to track him down. Or insisted on going to Mexico with him. Better yet, demand he not go at such a difficult time.

Too many maybes. She couldn't decide now. She couldn't even think. "My husband is due back in a couple of days," she said, keeping it vague.

"And what about the prosecutor? What do I tell her?"

"I need time."

"Sure, whatever." He got up to leave, signaling the deputy, who'd been waiting by the door and would take Marnie back to her cell.

A short time later, locked in for the night and staring at the tray of cold slop that was her dinner, Marnie wondered if there was any way out of this trap that she herself had helped set. She was still reeling from hearing that the remains couldn't be identified. Even if she told Paul Esposito who she was and confessed to Butch's murder, there was no way to prove it.

Alison's fingerprint records must have been switched. Andrew seemed like the likely culprit there, but he hadn't bothered to tell her what he'd done, and Marnie had no records. Before he could make the switch, he would have had to obtain Marnie's fingerprints from Marnie herself, and without her knowledge. Possibly when she was in the hospital, unconscious.

The thought made her queasy. Would an innocent man have gone to such lengths to insulate himself from murder charges? Worse, not even DNA, the most basic and irrefutable method of identification known, could help Marnie prove her identity now. A DNA test would only confirm that Julia was her mother—and be taken as proof positive that Marnie, who looked like Alison, plus had all of Alison's identification, including driver's license, social security number and fingerprints, *was* Alison.

No one would believe her. Ever. Nor would they believe Gramma Jo, who had always been seen as eccentric and would now be dismissed as senile, Marnie was sure.

She crouched down, staring at the unrecognizable food and wondering how hungry she would have to get before she could eat it without gagging. She'd always thought of herself as a fighter. She'd survived an abortion attempt, a near drowning and a lifetime of scorn and hatred. But it felt as if there was no way to survive this. She didn't know who or what to fight. She couldn't even prove her own existence.

As a kid there'd been times when she wondered why she'd been born. It sounded self-pitying, and she wasn't proud of those black moods, but she had honestly felt like a cosmic joke. The very same question came to her now. Why had she been born? To end up like this? She knew that some lives were visited with more pain than others, but she didn't understand how that worked, how pain got dealt out. How much was enough? An eternity? Because that's what it felt like she was facing now.

She wouldn't even be allowed to live out as herself the time she had left. And bizarre as it seemed, after years of longing to be someone else, she would rather have been the way she was, deformities and all.

But for some reason the most confounding question was Andrew. The only man who had ever professed to care about her had vanished. He could be dead, for all she knew. She almost wished he was, because the possibility that he was alive and responsible for this nightmare was unbearable.

Eventually, she lay down on the cement's unforgiving surface and prayed for sleep. She didn't want to think anymore. There were no solutions. Exhaustion took her in and out of the fitful struggle. She couldn't seem to stop wrestling, but at some point in the night, all that changed. Out of her hopelessness came an answer. And it was Paul Esposito who'd given her the way out.

As she sat up in the darkness, she heard for the first time the other inmates' shouts and obscenities. She wasn't alone in this cell block. She caught the stink of urine and the clanging of objects against the steel bars. She let the chaos into her consciousness for a moment and then tuned it out again. Survival.

The only one who cared about her was Gramma Jo, an aging woman who now needed to be cared for herself. Marnie really only had one choice. She would make a deal. No, two of them—one with Julia and one with the prosecutor. All she had to do was confess to the crimes she'd been charged with, and it would be over. Why prolong the pain and uncertainty? That way at least she would have some control over her life. It would be settled.

She had no desire to be a martyr. She didn't want

to sacrifice herself or anyone else. This was the least of all the possible evils, and it was the only way she knew to ensure that the woman who'd raised her, and taught her everything she knew about strength and survival, would survive herself. That much was in Marnie's power, she hoped.

She touched her throat, knowing the chain wasn't there—and that she would find some way to exist without it. She had to. From now on she would make her own luck, her own way. And it was time to start.

"Guard!" Marnie called out. She went to the bars and shouted until the female guard finally appeared.

"I want to talk to my attorney again," Marnie told the woman, "as soon as possible."

"Julia?" Rebecca's voice came over the intercom in Julia's office. "It's a Paul Esposito for you. He says he's Alison's attorney."

Julia looked up from the letter she was writing. She set down the pen, her eyes riveted on the phone. She'd never heard of Paul Esposito, and she couldn't imagine why he was calling unless Marnie had decided to accept her offer. There was one other unthinkable possibility. Marnie was going public with her maternity claims.

"Julia? Are you going to take the call?"

"I have it," she said, picking up the phone. "Hello? Mr. Esposito?"

The attorney got right to the point. "Mrs. Fairmont, Alison has asked me to let you know that she plans to plead guilty to both charges."

Julia couldn't believe it. "Alison knows my conditions. There's no need for her to plead guilty to anything. I can still provide her with the best legal defense team in the country. Tell her that."

Esposito cleared his throat. Had she actually offended him?

"I'll pass that on," he said, "but it's not why I'm calling. Alison has made up her mind about the plea, but she's asking something of you."

Julia's palm was sweaty against the receiver. "What?"

"She's asking that you move one Josephine Hazelton back to her home in Mirage Bay and provide for all her needs there. I have the terms and conditions in writing and I can fax them to you for your signature, if you agree. They're quite straightforward, and I'm sure you'll find them fair."

He paused, as if to let her absorb the information. "Can I fax you the agreement?"

"Yes, of course. I'll have my assistant give you the fax number."

As she hung up the phone, Julia realized that she was free and clear. Relief washed over her. It almost made her dizzy, but there was no real joy in the feeling. If anything, she felt oddly bereft.

Five days. Marnie marked time by scratching tiny pieces of cement against the large slab she slept on. Four crude lines and a diagonal slash. She'd had no visitors, no word from anyone in that time, other than Paul Esposito, who'd come by to tell her he was trying to get her change-of-plea hearing moved up. Right now it was still two weeks away. Esposito had also given her a signed document from Julia, who'd agreed to provide care for Josephine Hazelton until her death.

She'd accepted all of Marnie's terms, and they had been considerable.

Marnie wanted the cottage renovated and redecorated, according to her grandmother's wishes. She wanted Gramma Jo moved back and all her care provided, including a live-in companion and a home health care nurse as necessary. Julia was to pay any medical bills, plus provide all creature comforts— living expenses, a generous monthly allowance, an annual vacation.

Julia had agreed to it all and offered to throw in James Brainard for Alison's defense, but Marnie had refused. Why would she need him now? Everything was settled, and Marnie was at peace with her choice. For her, all the questions had been answered. Paul Esposito had promised to see that Julia followed through with the agreement, and he'd also arranged for Marnie to call her grandmother.

Over the aching lump in her throat, Marnie had told Gramma Jo that she had a surprise for her, and that she should be mentally preparing herself to go home soon. Marnie couldn't resist giving away that much of the surprise. Gramma Jo had broken down and cried. They'd both cried, and Marnie had hoped she could always hang on to the sweetness of those feelings.

Gramma wouldn't let Marnie go without asking her if she'd talked with Julia. Marnie had assured her that was part of the surprise, but she'd begged off answering any more questions, and then she'd made up a story about having to take a short trip with Andrew, so she wouldn't have to explain why she couldn't come visit. That conversation would come someday, but not now. Marnie wanted as much time as she could steal to savor the idea of her grandmother's return to the cottage with no shadows darkening that vision. It was the only thing keeping her alive right now.

She took a tiny pebble of cement and began to scratch out another day. Now there was nothing for her to do but wait.

"All rise," the clerk intoned as the judge, robed in black, assumed the bench. The clerk called the case of the County of San Diego versus Villard, read off the case number and the charges—two counts of murder in the first degree.

The judge turned on his microphone and spoke into it. "Mrs. Villard, your attorney tells me you want to change your plea to the charges against you?"

"I do, Your Honor." Marnie rose to her feet and stood at the defendant's table with Paul Esposito next to her. The judge had a fatherly look and a warm manner, but Marnie wasn't getting her hopes up. She had liked James Brainard's looks, too. "I'm pleading guilty to both charges."

The judge slipped on a pair of reading glasses and scanned the papers in front of him. "Not so fast, Mrs. Villard," he said. "Some things need to be covered before we get to your change of plea. Do you understand the charges that have been brought against you?"

"I do," Marnie said, uncomfortable with the way the judge was peering over his glasses at her. She just wanted this over.

"You understand that you have been charged with two counts of capital murder," he said, "and that the penalty for each count could result in the imposition of the death penalty, or in the alternative, a life sentence at a maximum security prison?"

Marnie stated that she did, and he continued asking her questions that stressed the gravity—and finality— of her decision. She answered in the affirmative to every question, robotically nodding her head. Yes, she understood.

"Thank you, Mrs. Villard. Now, would you please explain to me why you want to do this? You're young. You have your whole life ahead of you. Why not go through the trial process?"

The question stopped Marnie. She wasn't sure how to answer him. It had taken her an entire agonizing night to make the decision, and she'd been living with it for days. But how did she boil all of that down to a few words that would make sense to this godlike figure in a black robe?

Paul Esposito glanced at Marnie, as if to encourage her. She could feel the heat in her face, the dampness at her temples. Her skin was breaking out, and Paul must have seen it, too, because he spoke up immediately.

"Your Honor, Ms. Villard wants to pay her debt to society, and changing her plea is the first step. She has great remorse for what she's done and is willing to do whatever she can to make it right."

"Thank you, Mr. Esposito," the judge said with a raised eyebrow and great forbearance. "I'd like to hear that from Mrs. Villard herself, since she's the one whose life and liberty is at stake here."

Marnie understood that her attorney was trying to help her, but he'd gotten it completely wrong. He'd never asked her reasons, so he couldn't possibly express them for her. Worse, her struggle to come up with an answer was making her wonder if she'd made the right decision. This *was* her life and her liberty, as the judge pointed out. Maybe she wasn't ready to give it up without a fight.

She tried to speak, but couldn't get the words out. A strange sensation of numbness was invading her extremities. It was almost as if she were balanced on Satan's Teeth again. It would all be over once she jumped, and she wanted that, the freedom of nothingness, the release from pain. But her legs wouldn't move, her arms wouldn't move.

A tremor ripped up her spine, unlocking her. Feelings flooded her, and suddenly she was awash in sorrow and loss, consumed with rage at the unfairness of it all. "I just want it to be *over*," she said. "The alternative is unthinkable."

The judge frowned. "What alternative, Mrs. Villard? Can you tell me what you mean?"

Esposito spoke up again. "Your Honor, my client was very clear with me about what she wants. She may be having trouble expressing herself, but she fully understands the consequences of her actions and—"

The sound of a door banging open behind them interrupted the attorney. Marnie turned, half expecting to see Tony Bogart stride into the courtroom. If anyone would want to see Alison self-destruct, it would be Tony. But she didn't see him anywhere.

Stunned, she realized it was a woman who'd entered. Julia Fairmont? What could she possibly want? Marnie's first reaction was apprehension, but it evaporated the moment she realized there was nothing Julia could do to her now. Marnie was beyond being hurt by anyone.

"She's an imposter." Julia actually pointed her finger at Marnie. "She isn't, and never was, Alison Fairmont. My daughter is still missing, and I believe she was deliberately pushed from her husband's—Andrew Villard's—yacht." Julia spotted the bailiff coming toward her and began frantically waving her hands. "Wait, let me finish!"

Marnie wondered if she was having a breakdown. Her hair was disheveled, and she looked desperately out of control, at least for Julia.

The judge rose to his feet as the bailiff hooked her by the arm, clearly intending to eject her.

"Let her stay," the judge said. "I want to hear what she has to say."

Esposito spoke up again, addressing the bench. "Who is this woman—and why is she being allowed to interrupt the proceedings?"

The judge silenced him with a look. "This is *my* courtroom, Mr. Esposito." He directed his next question to Julia. "Please approach the bench and tell the court your name and your relationship to the accused."

Julia straightened her linen suit as she came forward, aligning the jacket and skirt. She combed a hand through her hair and then looked up abruptly with a tiny, nearly invisible shudder.

"I'm Julia Fairmont of Mirage Bay," she told the judge, "and the accused was living in my home, and pretending to be my daughter. She lied, deceived and took advantage of me, and if that isn't a crime worthy of capital punishment, it should be."

Julia's bitterness rang throughout the room. She probably would have continued to rail about Marnie's duplicity if the doors at the back hadn't crashed open again.

Andrew Villard entered the courtroom, and Julia fell quiet. Everyone fell quiet. Marnie had to lean against the table to steady herself. Her head was spinning. Had he found a way to force Julia to come forward?

"Excuse me, sir," the judge said, "are you a party to this proceeding?"

"I'm the accused's husband," Andrew explained.

"In that case, take a seat." The judge waved him toward the defendant's side of the gallery. "Mrs. Fairmont, would you be good enough to sit down until I call you. Are any other family members expected, or can we get on with this hearing?"

Julia stayed where she was, planted in the aisle in the middle of the courtroom. "Your Honor, that man isn't the accused's husband. He's Andrew Villard, my daughter's husband, and the accused is *not* my daughter."

The judge leaned forward, locking Julia in his sights like a sniper with a rifle. He clearly had no interest in Andrew at that moment. "The only person in this courtroom charged with a crime is Alison Fairmont Villard," he informed Julia. "Mrs. Fairmont, if the accused isn't your daughter, who is she?"

"Her real name is Marnie Hazelton." Begrudgingly, Julia added, "And she didn't kill anyone, except perhaps Butch Bogart."

The judge peered over his rimless glasses. "Unless I'm mistaken, Marnie Hazelton was one of the victims in this case."

"You're not mistaken," Julia said, "but unfortunately the county prosecutor's office was when they charged her. The accused *is* Marnie Hazelton."

Julia produced two documents. The first was a handwritten record of Marnie's birth, dated twenty-two years ago and signed by both Josephine Hazelton and Julia Fairmont. It listed Marnie's vital statistics at birth, her weight and height, and it detailed her disfigurements. It also had rudimentary hand and footprints, done in what looked like black ink.

According to Julia, Gramma Jo had prepared the document and insisted that Julia sign it, but had agreed to let Julia keep the only copy. For reasons she didn't explain, she had not destroyed it.

Marnie was amazed to hear Julia confess aloud that she'd had a baby out of wedlock, and that child was the accused, Marnie Hazelton. Marnie wondered what it had taken to make her come forward with that. Probably threats of death and dismemberment, she imagined. By Andrew?

The judge didn't want to hear the details of Julia's indiscretion. He urged her to come to the point, and she quickly produced the second document, a standard-looking birth certificate, also with hand and footprints.

"This is the official birth record of my missing daughter, Alison Fairmont," she said. "Your Honor, even if someone has tampered with Alison's prints in the criminal database, no one has touched these. This certificate has been in a safety deposit box since she was born."

The judge ordered Julia, the two attorneys, the court clerk and the bailiff to the bench. After a hushed conference, he rose and announced that court would recess until that afternoon, but no one was to leave the courthouse.

"We're fortunate to have an excellent forensics lab within the county complex," he told the gallery. "The hearing will reconvene as soon as the documents have been verified as authentic and the fingerprints analyzed."

In an ominous tone, he warned that if the certificates were valid, but the prints didn't match, he intended to dismiss the charges.

Four hours later his Honor did exactly as he'd warned. Over the prosecutor's furious objections, he threw the case out, saying the lab's findings were enough to convince him that the defendent was not Alison Fairmont-Villard. He remained firm even when the prosecutor argued that while Marnie Hazelton could not have murdered herself, she could have killed LaDonna Jeffries.

"The person charged with that crime is Alison Fairmont-Villard," the judge reminded the court, "and there is no one by that name in this courtroom. If the district attorney's office intends to charge Marnie Hazelton with a crime, then the necessary steps should be taken. Meanwhile, she's free to go. I'm releasing her on her own recognizance."

"No!" The prosecutor was swift and shrill. "Your Honor, it's imperative that Ms. Hazelton be held until we can determine what she's done."

The judge fired back. "What's imperative is this. Next time you charge someone with a capital crime, counselor, *get the right person*."

The prosecutor was clearly seething with frustration. She said nothing, but her glare spoke for itself. She fully intended to come after Marnie, but for now, there was nothing she could do but accept the judge's decision.

Julia ducked out of the courtroom without a word to anyone. Marnie found the presence of mind to thank Paul Esposito and ask him to give her a moment to catch her breath. Paul agreed to wait outside, and as he turned to go, Andrew was there.

Marnie didn't know what to feel or think as she looked at him. She was blank, still numb from the ordeal, and shaking. Even his appearance confused her. His slacks and shirt were immaculate, straight off the rack of some designer boutique, but his skin was devoid of color. His face was as gray and burned-out as ashes.

He reached into the pocket of his shirt and drew out the gold chain she had given him. "You seem to need this more than I do," he said, offering it to her.

Marnie was startled at the icy chill of his hand as she took back her good luck charm. She studied the copper ring, she realized what had just happened. Julia had made sure that she exposed Andrew today, and now he would probably become the object of another investigation into Alison's death, if she was dead. And who knew what he might be facing if the prosecutor decided to press charges? Someone had to have altered or switched Alison's fingerprint records, and who had a better reason?

Marnie had no idea where he'd been, but she was just beginning to understand what it might have cost him to show up at this hearing. His face was gaunt, as if he hadn't eaten or slept in days.

At least he'd had his freedom, she told herself. Fiery anger burned the back of her throat. She had no idea what to say to him. None.

Fortunately, he articulated the emotions she couldn't.

"You must want to shoot me," he said, his voice low enough that only she could hear him. "Give me a chance to explain before you pull the trigger."

Marnie had heard him, but she still couldn't respond. She moved around him, her heart aching. She was throbbing with some emotion she couldn't describe. It was too much for her, all of it, too much to take in. What she wanted now, the only thing she wanted, was to walk out of this courtroom, out of the courthouse, and see for herself if the sun was still shining.

33

So *this* was where he'd been?

Marnie made no attempt to hide her shock as she registered the quaint beauty of the beach house Andrew had used as his hideout. The Cape Cod design had decks overlooking the ocean and a warm, rustic interior. It was hard not to fall in love on sight with the cedar shake walls, the comfortable plaid couches and the old-fashioned wood-burning fireplace.

"Can I get you something?" Andrew gestured toward the kitchen, part of the great room they'd just entered. "I could make you an omelet. The food couldn't have been very good."

"The food in *jail,* you mean?" Her tone was too sharp. The protective numbness had worn off, leaving her raw and exposed. She was angry that he'd abandoned her, angry that he'd left her to twist in the wind, *angry that he hadn't saved her sooner.*

"Marnie, you can't think I wanted you to go through that."

She cut him off with a toss of her head. "So this was where you were—a perfectly charming beach house, while I was locked in a cement bunker, choosing between swill and starvation? *Good food?*

Andrew, I was in hell, facing my life and my death. What were *you* doing?"

"Trying to get you *out* of that cement bunker." He walked to the wet bar, opened the refrigerator and took out a can of Red Bull.

"Are you going to explain yourself?" she said.

He popped the top and took a deep pull of the drink. The can stayed locked in his fist as he set it down, his back to her. "The original plan was to flush out a killer. I set a trap to see who would take the bait. But I had no way of knowing that LaDonna would be murdered and you'd get arrested. I just needed a little more time."

"Well, excuse me if I inconvenienced you." She wanted to slap him. All of the emotion that had been dammed up by despair was flowing out of her, and she couldn't seem to hold anything back.

He turned and leaned against the bar, his arms folded. "I brought you here to tell you everything. Honest to God, I did. Are you going to let me do that?"

She folded her arms, too. "Start with the change-of-plea hearing. How did you know about that? It can't have been coincidence that you showed up in that courtroom at that moment."

"I had Diego Sanchez checking the court calendar on a daily basis. He's the detective I hired to keep you safe while I was gone. Unfortunately, Bret took a dislike to him and kicked him off the premises, but Diego came through in other ways. His contacts within the criminal court system let me keep track of what was going on with you."

"So you knew I was in jail, charged with two counts of murder?"

"You're going to hate me for this, but at some point I realized you were safer in jail than at Sea Clouds. I needed the time to hunt down LaDonna's killer, and I wanted you safe, Marnie. I had to rethink everything when I found out about your change-of-plea hearing. I couldn't figure out what the hell you were doing, but I knew I had to get you out of there before you pleaded guilty to anything."

"How did you get Julia to the hearing?"

"Simple blackmail. I searched her bedroom suite and found your birth certificate in her wall safe. That was enough to shake her down. I also insisted on a copy of Alison's birth certificate for comparison."

"You knew where to look for my birth certificate?"

"I'd been through the room before and found the safe in the closet. I'd also noticed that she had certain months circled on her calendar, and the initials *B.C.* with an arrow pointing to the letter *S*. I put it together that the months were the numbers in her combination." He lifted a shoulder. "You can imagine my shock when I discovered she was your biological mother. I thought she was going to kill me with her bare hands when I confronted her."

Marnie had no trouble imagining his shock, or Julia's. But something else was troubling her. She wanted to know more about the trap he'd set for the killer. Ever since he'd mentioned it, she'd been grappling with a question.

"Was I the bait for your trap?" she asked him.

He seemed genuinely shocked. "No—hell, no. I'd had a plan in the works for months, long before we came to Mirage Bay."

She listened quietly as he admitted that the concert

had only been a small part of his reason to go to Baja. He'd chartered a private plane and made the trip to finalize the details of his plan, which included the remains that washed up on shore. They were not Alison's, he explained. He'd paid off an assistant in the *oficina de juez de guardia,* the local coroner's office, to have the body of an unclaimed drowning victim found on the beach.

"It was risky," he acknowledged, "but the goal was to flush out the person who had the most to gain from Alison's death. Obviously, that's the same person who tried to frame me."

"And may have killed LaDonna? You think they're all connected."

"I do." He shrugged. "But everything changed when you got arrested."

Marnie realized that he'd had to abort his plan and expose himself to prosecution to show up at her hearing. Julia wouldn't rest until he was indicted for Alison's murder, and there could be fraud charges. It wouldn't surprise Marnie if Julia launched a civil suit for damages because of their plan to deceive her, but Marnie had no assets. It was Andrew who would pay if Julia won.

"Who altered Alison's fingerprints?" she asked.

"I had that done months ago, after you and I entered into our arrangement. I'd taken a set of your fingerprints while you were in the hospital. I didn't know if you were going to regain consciousness, and I had to find out your identity. Diego did a search for me, but he never found a match. Later, I had him switch your fingerprints for Alison's."

"How did he do that?"

"Diego doesn't give away his secrets, but he did tell me the only fingerprints he found for Alison besides her DMV record were in a local police database. She had a traffic accident when she was a teenager that resulted in a driving offense. To change the prints required some hacking, I'm sure, but nothing like breaking into the FBI's database."

Marnie wondered what happened to people who altered fingerprint records. Andrew was probably in much greater jeopardy than she was.

It was all beginning to sink in, and it was very frightening. She let out a huge, pressured sigh, remembering the horror of the last few days.

"Andrew," she whispered, "in the name of everything that's holy, why didn't you pick up the phone and give me a call to let me know you were all right? Do you know what it did to me, not knowing?"

She averted her eyes as tears threatened. She didn't want him to know how vulnerable she felt, still.

"I couldn't call without putting you at risk," he told her. "Diego had time to search Sea Clouds before Bret kicked him out, and he found bugs all over the house. Someone had wired the place, but Diego couldn't remove them without alerting whoever had done it."

Marnie could hardly believe it. "Why would anyone bug Sea Clouds?"

"No clue, but he found devices in every room he checked, including our bedroom."

She still couldn't accept Andrew's rationale. "You could have told me the real reason you were going to Mexico. You didn't know the house was bugged then."

"Marnie, you were worried about the dangers of a

rock concert. What if I'd told you I was trying to trap a killer? I couldn't take you with me, and I couldn't have gone, knowing I was leaving you in torment. I'm not trying to frighten you, but we could be talking about a serial killer. Whoever killed LaDonna may have killed Alison, and possibly even Butch—and trust me, it won't stop there. *Somebody* needs to stop this freak."

"Do you have any idea who it is?"

"I have suspects, lots of them."

She began to speculate aloud. "Julia, maybe? Bret? He just broke up with LaDonna. Tony Bogart? Maybe he killed her and then reported her murder."

"It could be any one of them, and if LaDonna was murdered for the sole reason of framing you—or rather, Alison—then the list of suspects widens. There's even a kinky estate attorney that Julia's screwing around with."

"Really?" Marnie was more than a little curious about that, but it had just dawned on her that Andrew had missed some names. "I can think of a couple more people to add to your list," she said.

"Who?"

She shook her head, quelling a nervous, exhausted smile. "Make me that drink first. And some food, dear God in heaven, make me that omelet you promised!"

As Marnie watched him pull things from the refrigerator, she wondered what kind of omelet he had in mind. Mandarin oranges and feta cheese? It should be interesting. She also wondered why he was so sure Alison was dead. He hadn't included her in his list of suspects, but Marnie had never been convinced she wasn't alive.

* * *

Marnie closed her eyes and took a long, slow sip of her Cristal champagne. This was not actually nirvana, she told herself. It just felt like paradise, compared to everything else.

The doors to the deck of the beach house were wide open and a balmy ocean breeze gently ruffled her hair. The gulls cried as they soared and dived, feeding on fish. In the distance, dazzling white sails belled in the afternoon winds. The blue-and-gold seascape that stretched out before her was beautiful, and for once, she was actually enjoying the view.

She touched the ring that hung around her neck. There was little in her experience that allowed her to grasp what Andrew had done. He'd sacrificed his plan, his chance to exonerate himself, and possibly his freedom for her. Crazy as it seemed, it would have been easier to believe that he'd run out on her. That would have made more sense, because this felt like a miracle, and miracles didn't happen to people like her.

She turned just enough to see him stretched out on the couch, his bare feet up on the rattan coffee table and an iced drink in his hand, looking surprisingly relaxed. He'd changed into khaki shorts and a flowing silk shirt after their talk, and then he'd opened the Cristal so they could celebrate.

At the moment, she was so madly in love with him it was sickening.

Fortunately, she understood the feeling as an aberration. She was no more in love with him now than she had been at twelve or thirteen. Then, it was a fantasy. Now it was relief, loneliness and gratitude.

Not love, not nirvana; it just felt like that compared to jail and Sea Clouds.

She wondered how much time they had left, and then she pushed the thought away. Impulsively she said, "It's such a beautiful day. Do you think we could go for a sail? I've never been out in a sailboat."

"Never?" He dropped his feet to the floor and set his drink down. "Seriously? We have to remedy that at once."

His smile was wide, his teeth a flash of brilliant white, and as he rose from the couch and walked over to her, Marnie felt her heart shift in a very odd way.

What is going to happen to us?

She was avoiding the question. They both were, but it had been hanging in the air between them since they'd left the beach house. Marnie moved out of the beating sun and into the shade of the canopy over the wheel, closer to Andrew, who was at the helm, guiding the sailing yacht toward San Diego.

She'd asked Andrew to drive her over to see her grandmother before they went out on the boat. Gramma Jo had taken one look at Andrew and asked if he was the surprise she had mentioned. Marnie had blushed and said that yes, he was quite a surprise. She'd also heard herself promising to get Gramma Jo out of that place, without knowing how she was going to do it. There was no chance Julia would be involved. But it was a promise Marnie intended to keep.

Questions could wait, she decided. This was an adventure, a respite from the world and serious talk. Questions were irrelevant when you had an ocean of water beneath you and an ocean of sky above.

Andrew had suggested they dock at one of the marinas in San Diego and have dinner that evening, another of his brilliant ideas. Marnie had even brought along a sexy little sundress for the occasion. They were celebrating her freedom, and it was important to celebrate well. She had no idea how long it would last, and very soon they would need to talk seriously about what they might be facing in the way of criminal charges, and how to deal with it. But for now, they would go where the wind took them.

Andrew spotted her to his left, and his gaze swept over her in a very physical way. Perhaps it was a male reflex, but the look was nakedly interested. He caught himself and smiled. She was wearing one of the bathing suits he'd packed. The silky two-piece was a decent fit, except for the top. She was fuller there than Alison, and possibly he'd just realized that. His only other opportunities to compare had been fast, heated, and at very close range.

Not like today. This was a slow trip, leisurely. They could go only as fast as the ocean breezes would let them. The land was to their left, the open sea to their right, and they were headed due south. Maybe they would just keep going.

Blue waves crashed against the bow, scattering liquid diamonds. She could taste the salt spray on her tongue. "I know why you love this," she said. "It's glorious."

His hands rested lightly on the wheel. "I'd go insane if I couldn't get out on the water."

She could hear the conviction in his voice. He actually meant it, and that concerned her, because there was nothing she could do to ensure that for him. If he'd really been her husband, he would have reached for her, and she would have gone to stand beside him. But they hadn't touched other than when he'd offered a steadying hand as she came aboard. It was almost as if they had never touched.

"Do you want to take the wheel?" he asked.

"Yes." The boat rocked as she went to join him. *Yes, she did.*

He stepped back, giving her access, but he stayed behind her as she slid between him and the teak and stainless steel steering mechanism.

"What do I do? This boat is huge."

"Technically," he said, "it's a yacht."

Laughter fizzed up. "Is that supposed to be helpful?"

"Someone once described sailing as half ecstasy and half abject terror," he told her. "You decide."

"It feels like freedom to me," she said without hesitation. She tried the wheel, surprised at how sensitive it was, even to the lightest touch. Odd that a caress was all it took to control such a huge vessel. It was a lesson some CEOs and politicians could learn.

"Do you think she's still alive?" Marnie asked him. The question came with no preamble, but he seemed to know what she meant.

"Someone pushed LaDonna off that cliff, and according to Bogart, the perp looked just like Alison."

"Why would she do it?"

"To get rid of you, I'd guess."

"All she had to do was come forward and expose me."

"Ah, but then she couldn't get *me*. If Alison were alive, I would no longer be the prime suspect in her death. She's a mastermind, Marnie, as cunning as she is seductive. She befriended Regine for the sole purpose of getting rid of her."

Marnie studied him. "Do you have any proof of that?"

"Nothing that would hold up in court. Alison didn't show her true colors until after we were married. That's when she started pressuring me to get her a record deal and to let her open shows for some of my big names."

"But you didn't?"

"I couldn't. She had no fire, no stage presence. I tried to tell her, but she went nuts. She shrieked obscenities and accused me of sabotaging her because I was still in love with Regine. She ransacked my office, destroying everything she could find of Regine's, records and posters, smashing awards. It was childish, but I could see how destructive she was."

Marnie was trying to imagine the Alison she'd idolized flying into a rage that way. "What do you think actually happened the night Regine died?"

"Alison played bartender, and I believe she put something in the drinks. That would explain why I passed out and why Regine drowned, probably with a little *help*. Autopsies are rarely done on accident victims. Obviously Alison knew that. She also knew exactly how long she'd been away from the pool, talking on the phone, which seemed odd."

Marnie wanted to ask what he would do if Alison was alive. Given how he felt, she couldn't imagine he would ever want her back. But she also sensed his obsession with her, his churning conflict, and she didn't understand it. Either he did want her back or he wanted her dead, but he wanted something.

Once again, Marnie forced the gnawing doubts from her mind. She couldn't go there again, no more gut-wrenching questions. She had no idea how much time she and Andrew had, but she didn't want to waste any of it. As the silence built, so did another thought that had been on her mind since they got to the beach house.

"What's going to happen to us?" she asked him.

His sigh could be heard over the noise of the sails. "I wish to hell I knew."

His hand dropped over hers on the wheel, and the unexpected contact set fire to her imagination. Every sense flickered and lit. She could feel the sun-baked deck beneath her feet and smell the damp musk of wet canvas. But mostly, it was the tactile sensation of his palm, his flesh, that she responded to.

He moved closer, hot against her shoulder blades. She leaned back until they were touching. Full contact. Her breathing trembled. It was thrilling to be so close. And bizarre that it could be so powerful.

"I know what's going to happen to us," he said.

She tipped her head to look up at him. "What?"

He turned her around and kissed her. "This."

The boat rolled beneath them. Marnie fell against the wheel, and it began to spin. Andrew caught her around the waist and clamped a hand on the wheel at the same time, fighting to steady it. He pulled her against him hard, and she felt the air expel from her lungs.

It was strange to be held so tightly. She was pinned by his arm, and his thigh had slipped between her legs. He was trying to brace them both, but the intimate contact was wildly stimulating. She softened against him, melting, moaning in her throat.

They rocked that way until the seas calmed, and he kissed her again. His mouth was luscious, as smooth and strong as good liquor. She could get drunk on him. She *was* drunk.

His tongue breached her lips, sliding along the side of hers. It made her wild, that feeling.

"You kiss like a woman who means it," he whispered.

She nipped him. "I do. Mean it."

The ocean swelled, lifting the bow. She lost the fit of his mouth for a second, and moaned. She wanted it back.

"This *yacht* of yours is coming between us," she complained.

"We can't have that." He drew back to look at her, and his face changed as he saw her limpid eyes and passion-swollen lips. He touched her mouth and felt its wetness. He knew immediately what that meant.

"Nothing is going to come between us," he said. "Give me a minute?"

She nodded, and he left her to go the pilot house, mysteriously saying that he had to make some adjustments. When he came back, he clasped her hand and started toward the companionway that led to the lower deck. "You're coming with me," he said.

Apparently he'd accomplished what he wanted with the wheel.

"Who's going to steer the boat-uh, yacht?"

Some time later, as she lay next to him, dozing and pleasantly spent, she noticed a darker, richer light filling the windows. Absently, she realized the sun was setting.

"Should we go above?" she asked him.

He cupped her breast as he was pulling her to him. "Not quite yet."

She met his advances with a hissing sound—and a kiss that felt as if it could explode like firecrackers on a string. Suddenly they were rolling again, slipping and sliding. She stopped him, but had to catch her breath before she could talk.

"How are we doing, timewise?"

"If we wind up in Mexico we'll know we missed our dinner reservations."

They made love again, coupling in the near dark—and Marnie couldn't imagine how sailing could be half abject terror. It felt like ecstasy to her. Her only fear was that it would end.

At two in the morning, they were jarred awake by bullhorns. Someone was yelling that they were about to be boarded.

"Stay here," Andrew told her. "It's the Coast Guard."

34

When Tony Bogart checked his voice mail that afternoon, he found a message from Andrew Villard. Tony listened to it with a smile. Villard was being held without bail on murder and fraud charges, and he wanted to talk. Since he wasn't actually married to Marnie Hazelton, he could testify against her, and by the sound of his message he was ready to make a deal to save his own skin.

Tony sipped iced coffee, basking in the glow of his latest coup. He was parked in his Corvette outside a Starbucks. He had the ragtop down and life couldn't get much better. Finally he had the bastard where he wanted him, down on his knees. Alison had eluded him, but he'd tagged Villard, and that was almost as good.

Almost.

He hit a couple buttons and surrounded himself with music—cool, soothing jazz, designed to drown out bad vibes. But his sense of satisfaction evaporated anyway, gone before he'd finished his coffee. Marnie Hazelton was in jail, awaiting trial for the murder of his little brother, but Alison was still out there. Somewhere. Haunting him, taunting him. There wouldn't be closure for Tony Bogart until he'd dealt with *her*, with Alison. She would live on until he saw her dead and rotting body with his own eyes.

And if it wasn't Marnie in the guise of Alison who'd killed LaDonna Jeffries, then who the hell was it?

By nightfall a thick, dank fog had settled over the coastline, and the woman who picked her way through it was disheveled and exhausted. Her hair was matted and stuck to her head like yellow brambles. Her face was a grid of white scar tissue. She looked like a vagrant, but she knew exactly where she was going and what had to be done.

Tonight an old score would be settled. There would be no more betrayals, no more bloodshed. She would be avenged. Everyone who had been hurt would be avenged.

Through the mists, the house on the cliff glowed like a medieval fortress. Her legs burned with fatigue, but she climbed relentlessly, guided by the lights. The small, sharp-edged object she held cut into the skin of her palm. It was a key to the house, and when she entered, she would announce herself, and the lady of the manor would gape at her in shock. That lady was her mother.

Bret Fairmont was entertaining himself with his online porn collection when he heard the door to his room open behind him. "Who's there?" he said, without bothering to close the screen.

"Surprise." The answer was soft and raspy. "Look what the tide washed up."

The familiar voice caused the skin on the back of Bret's neck to prickle. He swung around and sprang out of his chair. The woman standing not ten feet from him looked like a skid-row vagrant. Her gallows grin revealed cracked lips and rotten teeth. Her skin was pimply and pitted. Still, he recognized her immediately—or who she was *supposed* to be.

It was the same woman he had up on his computer screen, but this one looked as if she actually had drowned and floated back up to the surface.

He began to laugh. He couldn't help himself. "Let me guess…Alison? What is this? Some kind of sick joke?"

"No, my *brilliant* brother." Her grin stretched into a grimace. "It's no joke. Your master plan failed. But then you were up against me. You never stood a chance."

His plan? This *was* sick. Bret couldn't decide whether to throw the imposter out himself or call the police. "Who the hell are you? No, fuck, I don't *care* who you are. Who put you up to this?"

She reached into her grimy clothing, as if to scratch herself, and the stench she gave off made Bret's stomach turn over. He broke out in a sweat, fearing he was going to be sick as she pulled out an automatic weapon.

"You're supposed to ask where I've been all this time," she said. "Isn't that what a brother would ask a sister who'd been missing for six months?"

"My sister is fucking dead. Now get out of here—"

Laugher ripped out of her. Sharp and savage, it nearly pierced his eardrums. Jesus, who was this bitch?

"Ask me where I've been, you *asshole!*" she shrieked. "Ask me!"

He covered his ears, protecting them. "Where have you been?"

She sucked in a breath, as if to calm herself, but her knuckles were white against the trigger of the gun.

"I was waiting for the right time," she said, "and this is just about perfect, wouldn't you say? I got rid of Andrew and his weird little girlfriend, and now there's just you left."

Bret still didn't believe she was actually Alison, but he was going to play along, anyway. The psycho bitch had a gun. Besides, he wanted to know who was screwing with him now. Andrew and Marnie Hazelton were behind bars, but someone was messing with Bret Fairmont's head. Was this another one of his mother's crazy ploys? Why would she do it?

"Where's Julia?" he demanded. "Our mother— where is she?"

"She's downstairs, pouring herself a drink, a big one. She knows all about our plan, Bret."

"Our plan? Which plan was that? There are so many."

Her dark eyes glittered. "The plan to fake my death and split the trust-fund money."

Sweat drenched him. No one had known about that but Alison. The Alison who was actually dead. He hadn't told another living soul about their scheme to get around that fucking morals clause.

"How could our mother know about that?" he asked her.

"I told her, you idiot."

"No way. This plan you're talking about," he said,

speaking as casually as he could, "*our* plan—it wouldn't work. The trust-fund money goes to the next surviving female. That's the way our grandmother set up the trust. It wouldn't come to me under any circumstances."

"Bret, for Christ's sake. You're talking to me, *Alison.* You know as well as I do there's a provision in the trust that says the money goes to you if I should die without female issue. I guess Mom never intended to tell you about that, even after she thought I was dead and the money *should* have come to you. She really doesn't give a shit about you, does she, baby brother?"

Bret knew about the trust's actual line of succession only because Alison had told him about it six months ago, when they came up with their plan. But how the hell did this woman know? "Who told you about the succession? Julia?"

"No, *I* told you that—six months ago. I broke Mother's silly code, opened her safe and found the papers. That's when I came up the plan, which would have worked if you hadn't gotten greedy and fucked it up."

She repeated the nine-digit combination to his mother's safe, and Bret's stomach heaved. He really was sick then, all over himself. Wretching and coughing, spewing up the remains of his dinner. He wished she would shoot him.

"You are fucking *not* Alison," he said, wiping his mouth on his sleeve. The stink was unbearable, worse than hers. "I watched her drown. I saw the current sweep her away. She's *dead.*"

That laughter again, slicing at him like razors. She wouldn't stop! The bitch was trying to blame him for the screwup, but the goddamn plan had been Alison's idea, and no one could stop Alison once she got a hair up her ass. She actually thought she could jump off Andrew's yacht in a storm and make it look like he'd pushed her.

She'd done all the prep work earlier that day, gone down to the boat, hidden the life jackets and loosened the lifeline. She was a strong swimmer and she'd researched the currents. Plus, she'd stashed an inflatable device in the lining of her cover up, but she'd totally overlooked the fatal flaw in her plan: her rat-fink little brother, Bret.

He was supposed to wait in a skiff in a protected area on the far side of the reefs where the currents would carry her. He was also supposed to throw her a lifeline and pull her in before she was swept out to sea. Poor stupid Alison. Why would anyone split a trust fund when he could have it all?

"I told mother about the rest of it, too," she said. "How we tried to frame Andrew for my death, how you were able to get an insurance policy on me, using just the phone and the fax, pretending to be Andrew."

"That's insanity," he whispered. "Why would you tell her any of that?"

"Because I want her to understand why I have to kill you." She reached into her putrid layers of clothing again and drew out a silencer for the gun, a modern gleaming high-tech silencer.

"Are you totally psychotic?" Bret hissed. "There are witnesses downstairs. She knows you're up here!"

He covered his ears, terrified she would start shrieking again. This couldn't be Alison. This was too insane even for her.

"Are you forgetting Mother's obsession with me?" she pointed out. "She'd never turn me in, no matter what I did, especially if I did it to you. She hates you now, anyway. You left her precious daughter for dead."

He believed that. His mother *would* feel that way. "What do you want from me?"

"I'm giving you a choice. Either confess or I'll shoot you through the heart where you stand. That's assuming you have a heart."

Now he wanted to laugh, but he didn't have the strength. "Nice try, Ali*suck*, but a coerced confession won't stand up in court."

She let out a ghoulish cackle. "You should live that long! You're not going to make it to court, genius. I just want to hear you confess. I want to hear you grovel."

She pointed the gun dead at him and fired. The computer screen exploded behind him, and Bret dropped to the floor, covering his head and cowering. She continued firing until she'd pulverized the machine, and then she reloaded.

"You're next, asshole. You're next!" Her shriek nearly split his eardrums. *"Talk!"*

Bret crouched in abject terror. If this was Alison, he had no doubt that she would shoot him—or that their mother would protect her. That's exactly how it would go down. If it wasn't Alison, he didn't have a clue what kind of crazy he was dealing with. But now he did want to know who she was. *And he wanted to live.*

"What do you want to know?" He'd decided to talk about anything, everything, give her what she wanted. It would buy him some time until he could figure out a way to turn this around and kill her. He would make it look like suicide, or even self-defense. Christ, it *was* self-defense.

She prodded him with a question. "You double-crossed me because you wanted the fifty million for yourself, right?"

He sighed. "That was the original plan, but you came back from the dead—or someone who looked like you did—and I had to regroup."

"Regroup?"

Bret was still crouched down, but he'd spotted a pile of photographs. They were of Alison, and they'd fallen to the floor when she was firing. They were almost within reach. He shifted and groaned, as if his legs were aching.

"I sent Andrew a front-page story about your disappearance, marked up with a threatening message, to motivate him to get you back to Mirage Bay," he told her. "Anonymously, of course. I also left Tony Bogart several anonymous voice-mail messages to make him think you'd killed Marnie Hazelton. It was working until LaDonna told me the imposter *was* Marnie."

"What was the point of framing the imposter?"

"To expose her. I wanted to prove she wasn't you. Getting her out of the way brought me one step closer to the money. Then, all I had to do was finish the job of framing Andrew for your death."

He swallowed back the urge to laugh, afraid he'd sound as psycho as she was. "It would have been a slam-dunk, sis. What jury wouldn't convict Andrew of murder after they found out that he had his girlfriend pretend to be you? What more proof would they need that he was after the money?"

"And now Marnie's in jail and LaDonna's dead."

He wasn't admitting to LaDonna's death, even if she shot him in the balls. When LaDonna had told him the imposter *was* Marnie, he'd quickly come up with a plan to deal with both women. LaDonna was out of control anyway. She'd become so jealous and possessive that she actually snuck into Sea Clouds during Alison's reception to spy on him. Somehow she got herself trapped on the third floor and came up with the bright idea of dropping a pot on Alison to create a distraction so she could escape.

LaDonna had to be sacrificed in order to frame Marnie, who had a motive to kill her because LaDonna had discovered her true identity. He didn't care whether or not Marnie took the wrap. He just wanted her exposed as an imposter without exposing himself.

When he'd searched the guest room he'd found sleeping pills, as well as the gun Andrew had left in the nightstand drawer. He'd used the pills to drug his mother's and Marnie's drinks the night of the Padres game, and he'd TiVo'd the second half of the game while he was out on the cliffs. Bogart had scared the shit out of him, but Bret had been too fast for him. He'd been too fast for everyone until tonight.

Bret massaged his thigh and inched closer to the pictures. As long as he was confessing his sins, he might as well reveal another one to his she-wolf of a sister.

"I had a video camera hidden in your room for years." He taunted her with the singsong voice he'd used when they were kids. "I created a Web site devoted to porn shots of you. You're a star, Alison. There are millions of men out there beating off to your pictures."

"*Bret,* that's the nicest thing you've ever done."

She laughed, and that was the moment he believed her. She *was* Alison. His sister wouldn't have given a shit about being the object of men's masturbation fantasies. She would have dug it. God, what a slut she was. What a nasty, unrepentant slut. He could almost love her for that.

"You never could resist a picture of yourself." He grabbed the snapshots and flung them at her.

She ducked as the pictures flew into her face. In the confusion, Bret sprang up and rushed her. There was a fight for the gun, and a shot rang out.

Bret felt a fire split his skull. It felt as if his brains were pouring out, but consciousness stayed with him for another second or two. As he slumped to the floor, he stared up at the woman who'd shot him. She was right. He had no chance against her in this life.

Darkness came at him like a hammer. But there was no pain as his eyes drifted shut, and his parting thought was a sweet one. Every man deserved a second chance, and Bret Fairmont would get his. He would be waiting for his sister, Alison, in the lowest level of hell.

A two-man SWAT team burst through the French doors that led to the deck, and at the same time, Tony Bogart came through the bedroom door. Andrew was right behind him.

One of the SWAT team knelt next to Bret's body and checked his vital signs. "He's dead," the officer said. "Our sniper got him."

His sister, who thought she had shot him, sank to her knees and stared in horror at the blood that was oozing from Bret's head wound. Andrew lifted her into his arms and turned her away from the gruesome sight.

She *was* Bret's sister, but she wasn't Alison. It was Marnie, posing for one last time as the woman she'd always wanted to be. The sting operation had been Andrew's idea, and his call to Tony had been to bargain—dropped charges in exchange for his and Marnie's cooperation in a sting operation to get the real killer, Bret.

Andrew had also found the details of the trust fund's succession in the safe in Julia's dressing room. He'd gone to Mexico, thinking it was Bret who would take the bait and come down to identify his sister's body. But LaDonna's murder had brought Andrew back to the States before the trap could be sprung— and it had thrown him off Bret's scent.

Bret had no motive to kill LaDonna, unless it was to frame Alison, and that made no sense. To claim the trust, Bret needed Alison dead, not rotting in jail for the rest of her life. What Andrew didn't know was that Bret had discovered Marnie's true identity. LaDonna had told him. The girl who made one mistake after another with men had made her last one.

Marnie was grateful not to have to watch as the emergency techs took Bret away. She honestly didn't know how she felt about her brother. There was revulsion, of course, considering everything he'd done. But it was more complicated than that. She felt pity, too, and sadness. Maybe in time she would sort it out.

Time was what she needed, she realized as she met

Andrew's concerned gaze. She touched the penny ring, aware that she had never been more grateful not to be Alison Fairmont. Perhaps she'd had to go through the ordeal of the last months to realize how much she'd loved her life and her grandmother and everything that was Marnie Hazelton. She would take that knowledge with her as she faced the future, and if she ever had children of her own, she would do her best to teach it to them.

She had a realization as she looked down at the outline on the floor where Bret's body had been. He may have thought he could get away with letting his sister drown. He may even have felt justified because of the way she and her mother had treated him over the years. But obviously he'd never heard the old saying that Marnie had learned from her grandmother all those years ago, and had seen for herself in the depths of the ocean as she looked down from Satan's Teeth.

When you give things to the sea, be it trash, woe, prayers or wealth, the sea remembers.

35

"Just put me in a hospital," Julia said, worrying the emerald-and-diamond ring on her finger, "and give me drugs, please. Strong drugs. Knock me out for a month, at least."

The psychiatrist Julia had found through a friend sat in a high-backed chair next to hers, slowly nodding his head. He was large and bearded, a pleasant-looking man who reminded Julia of Sigmund Freud, and he'd been nodding sympathetically from the moment she entered his office.

"You've been through a lot," he said, his tone soothing. "You just lost your son in a horrific way, your daughter is still missing, and now you're dealing with this adult child, born out of wedlock."

Julia's heart felt heavy enough to crush her. She'd gone to the media room last night to watch a Padres game in honor of Bret. She'd sat in his chair, drank a beer from a plastic cup and wept through the entire game, wondering how she had so totally lost touch with her son.

Julia pulled a handkerchief of fine Irish lace from the breast pocket of her blouse and blew her nose. The doctor waited patiently until she'd composed herself.

At least he seemed to understand how badly she hurt, that she *could* hurt.

"Is there anything else you haven't told me?" he asked.

She thought a moment, trying to find her way through the fog of pain. "Yes," she said suddenly, "there's my *former* assistant, Rebecca. I just learned she has a six-figure contract with a big publisher to write a tell-all book about the prominent families she's worked for. The Fairmonts will be featured, of course."

Julia stuffed the hanky in her pocket, not caring if she wrinkled it. "The double-crossing bitch bugged our house. I'll see her in court, I swear."

The anger felt good, she realized. Cleansing energy coursed through her, and she took a deep, calming breath, trying to remember if there was anything she hadn't covered. She didn't see the need to tell him that she had inadvertently kept Rebecca from bugging Marnie and Andrew.

He knew about Andrew's grand plan to have Marnie pose as Alison, but to be fair she'd also told him about Bret's insane maneuvers, including his plan to let his own sister drown and then frame Andrew for her murder. Julia had also had to admit that her son had dressed up in his sister's clothes and killed LaDonna Jeffries. That had been terribly hard. It had all been terribly hard.

But it had surprised her that one of the most difficult things to confess was the affair she'd had over twenty years ago. She'd explained that her mother had discovered it, but instead of confronting Julia, Eleanor had gone to her husband. Eleanor and Grant had plotted together to catch her with her lover, and

Grant had confronted them. He'd paid the man off right in front of her, forcing him to choose between the money or Julia. The man had taken the money, of course. And Julia had known exactly what she was worth to her lover *and* her husband.

She'd never forgiven Grant for that. She hadn't felt a moment's sadness when he died. She'd actually thought she might never feel sad again, over anything, anyone. She'd been wrong.

"How do you feel about Marnie?" the doctor asked. "Let's go back to your decision to have Josephine Hazelton raise her."

"I feel guilt, of course. I'm eaten alive with guilt. Always was. I can't hear a baby crying without losing it. I see a fire, even in a fireplace, and I think it's a sign that I'm meant to burn in hell for what I did."

She hesitated, aware that these were the memories she'd been trying to block for two decades. "I named her for the Marnie in the Hitchcock movie. I really don't know why, except that I love the name. I couldn't tell the world about her for obvious reasons, but I didn't abandon her because I was ashamed of her. I was ashamed of *me,* and horrified at what I'd done to her. The sight of her, even the thought of her, sent me to a terrible place."

"Do you have a relationship with her now?"

"No, and I'm sure she wouldn't want one."

"Would you?"

"I don't want to sound impossibly corny, but how could I expect her to forgive what I can't? There's no defense for what I did. If there's a competition somewhere for the world's worst parent, I must be in the running."

She tried to adjust her wedding set, but couldn't make it sit right. Why hadn't she just taken it off after all these years? Why was she still trying to make it right? "Couldn't you just hospitalize me?"

Tears burned like acid, and this time she couldn't easily stop them. There was no composing herself with a deep breath, no anger to energize her. She bowed her head and cried. The doctor said nothing to comfort her, but she could see compassion in his expression when she finally took a breath. "I'm sorry."

He shook his head. "You have nothing to be sorry for, certainly not your feelings. Julia, where do you think you got your poor parenting skills?"

The hanky was soaked and stained with her eye makeup. She would have to throw it away. "Shit, I don't know. My mother, I suppose."

"Your mother, indeed. She wins the worst parent award by a mile."

"Really? And I grew up thinking she was perfect, everything I should aspire to be."

"What a shame," he said softly. "You had a mother who had no clue who you were and never bothered to find out. Eleanor's obsession with doing good was about ego gratification. Her moral standards were a way to measure others and make them less worthy than her, including her daughter. She professed to want to make the world a better place, but she couldn't take care of one little girl. She was too wrapped up in her own needs."

He sat forward, as if to make sure Julia heard every word. "Your mother was a failure as a human being, but she was never able to acknowledge that. She couldn't look at herself for who she really was. You, Julia, are more woman than she ever was."

Julia was shocked at the doctor's bluntness, but knew it was exactly what she needed to hear. Even the trust fund, Eleanor's legacy, punished anyone who didn't meet her standards.

"My obsession with my looks, even to the point of plucking every little hair?" she asked him.

"You were trying to meet her standards in the only way you still could. You'd failed all her other tests, so you struggled with physical perfection. I'm speculating, of course. You'll have to decide if that answer feels right for you."

Julia allowed herself a moment to try and digest it all, but it was too much. Some of what he was telling her she'd always known, even if not consciously, but other things he'd said were a revelation. She could never have imagined herself as more woman than her vaunted mother.

"Shall we set up another time to get together?" the psychiatrist inquired politely.

Julia took a moment, but finally shook her head. "I don't think so. Thank you, though, you've been a great help. And no offense, but I know what I need to do."

"What's that?" he asked.

She managed a smile as she picked up her bag. "You wouldn't approve."

Tony Bogart pulled to the curb, parking down the street from his dad's heavily fenced stucco house. This wasn't a police maneuver. Tony was embarrassed at the outright flamboyance of his rental car. His dad would take one look at the sleek red Stingray and ask him how he got to be such a fucking big shot, and it wouldn't end there. He'd probably go into a tirade.

Tony figured this was easier. He didn't want any fights with the old man. He'd tracked him down only to let him know that Butch's murder had been solved. Not that justice had been done. In Tony's opinion, it hadn't. Because she was key to the prosecution's sting operation, Marnie had gotten off with a slap on the wrist. But at least she'd owned up to what she'd done to Butch. She'd confessed.

It took Tony only a couple minutes to get to his dad's place. Once he'd jimmied the lock on the chain-link fence and let himself in, he saw the run-down condition of the small, one-story house. His dad had sold cars for as long as Tony could remember, but he could be retired by now and living in reduced circumstances. Not that the Bogart family had ever had a lavish lifestyle.

Tony knocked on the front door and heard someone inside bellow, "Stop making that fucking noise!"

"Dad? It's me, Tony. I need to talk to you." He tested the knob and the door opened.

"Get the hell inside and shut the door," his father snapped.

Tony entered the bare-bones living room, feeling as awkward as a kid when he met the old man's questioning glare. His father was sitting in an upright recliner, watching something on an old nineteen-inch television set with rabbit ears on the top. On the table next to him was an empty long-neck beer bottle, a rotary dial telephone and the remote. There was not another stick of furniture in the room.

"Are you okay?" Tony asked. "It's been awhile." He didn't add that his father had never bothered to give him his new address when he moved away from Mirage Bay.

The old man lifted a shoulder, as if to say it wasn't important.

Already Tony could feel his blood rising. It didn't take much. He really did hate his father's cold indifference. *Hated it.*

"Butch's killer confessed to the crime," Tony said, wondering why he'd bothered to come. "It's a local woman named Marnie Hazelton."

"I know," his father said.

"You know she confessed?"

"I know it was Marnie Hazelton."

Tony nodded. "Yeah, it's probably been on the news. Sounds like they're going to let her off with a slap on the wrist, when they should be throwing away the key. Christ, she stabbed him *seventeen times*. That's not self-defense. That's something else."

"It's rage," the old man said. "It's hatred. She didn't have that kind of hate in her."

Tony felt something go soft and slimy in the pit of his stomach. It wasn't a good feeling. He focused in on his father. "Did you know her?"

The old man looked up, his face as hard and eroded as the rock reefs in the bay. "Well enough to know she didn't stab him seventeen times. I did that."

Tony stepped back, bracing himself against the wall. There was nowhere to sit, and his legs wouldn't hold him. "You don't mean that, Dad. Butch was your boy. You loved Butch."

His father sat forward, crossing his arms over his legs as he stared down at the floor. "I never said I didn't love him."

Tony's throat felt like it was lined with rust and corrosion. Somehow he managed to ask his dad to tell him what had happened.

"I got a call one day from one of Butch's friends," his father said. "The kid was worried that Butch was headed for trouble, said he was obsessed with some girl, but in a bad way, harassing her, stalking her."

"Marnie?"

The old man nodded. "When the kid told me the girl's name, I didn't believe him. I knew who Marnie Hazelton was, everybody did. She was deformed. I laughed and told the kid that Butch would never be interested in a freak like that. I told him somebody should put the ugly slut out of her misery, and if it was Butch, more power to him."

He exhaled heavily. "Butch heard me say it, and we had a good laugh. We were kidding each other. It was a joke, that's all. People don't really do things like that."

"Like what, Dad?"

"Like kill a girl because she's ugly."

Tony slid down the wall to the floor and sat there in stunned silence. He didn't know what to say. It sounded as if his father had unknowingly provoked Butch into the attack on Marnie.

The sound of the telephone being dialed brought Tony back. "What are you doing?" he asked his father.

"Calling the police. Butch was alive when I found him in the pool. Just barely, and he was a raving maniac, but he was alive. The girl was unconscious on the ground, and he was trying to get to her with the pitchfork, trying to get enough leverage to kill her. When I heard the filth coming out of his mouth—about the girl, even about his own mother—I picked up the pitchfork and clubbed him over the head with it."

His voice was giving out, and he seemed to sag forward with every word. "Even that didn't stop him, nothing could. I had to kill him to shut him up."

"You killed him to shut him up? What was he saying?"

"He was saying I told him to kill the ugly slut and put her out of her misery. He was saying I told him to do it. I had to shut him up. *I had to stop him.*"

Tony could hardly grasp it, a father stabbing his beloved son repeatedly. Where did that kind of blind rage come from? But his father had already said it. From hatred, the kind that sprang from ignorance and fear.

"What happened to Marnie?" Tony asked.

"At some point I realized she was gone. She must have come to and made a run for it. I had a hunch she'd gone to the cliffs, and that's where I found her."

"You followed her?" Had his father killed Marnie, too?

The old man closed his eyes. "I was too late."

"She'd already jumped?"

"She didn't jump. The rocks gave out from under her. There was nothing I could do."

Tony sat there in silence and let his father call the police. He knew the howling ache inside him would never go away. He also knew that he came from a family where insanity reigned, and he couldn't possibly be fit to serve in the FBI or any other organization that protected people. He was insane, too. All the signs were there—the guns, the firing range, the obsession with Alison, the intermittent explosive disorder. He was sick. It was a virus he'd caught from the man crumpled in the chair across from him, and it had infected Butch, too.

Eventually Tony got himself up off the floor and stood by the window, waiting for the police to get there. His father had collapsed like a rag doll. He was mumbling something about Butch's mother, how she shouldn't have done it, and even though he needed comfort, Tony knew his old man would never accept it from him.

Tony could predict his father's future, and it was endlessly bleak. He had no clue about his own. If he didn't stay with the FBI, what would he do? End up in a recliner, sobbing his heart out over the lives he'd wrecked, the children he'd ruined? End up alone? In jail?

As the patrol cars rolled up and he watched the officers get out, Tony realized that something had happened here this morning, something besides the hopelessness of his father's situation. Tony had learned how easy it was to fuck up a kid. Even hatred masquerading as humor could do it. Butch had been eager to please his father. All kids were at some point, and that was when it could all go wrong.

Tony drew a breath and felt the aching in his chest flare into his throat. He was never going to be a preacher or a counselor or even a nice guy, but he had learned something, and maybe there was a way to put it to use. At least when he dealt with kids who were hell-bent on death and destruction, he would understand where things might have gone wrong for them, where their eagerness to please might have been twisted into something else, something sick.

"Maybe all is not lost, Bogart," he heard himself

saying as the deputies pounded on his father's door. "Maybe you could make a halfway decent G-man someday."

Julia knew she looked hot in her peony-pink slip dress, and she was tremendously pleased with herself. She had a rendezvous with Jack Furlinghetti, and he was meeting her right here in her own home. She clutched the prescription bottle hidden in her hand, excited at the prospect. What could be more delicious than that?

Her breathing tight, she waited for the sound of his footsteps on the stairs. She'd left the gate and the front door unlocked, and told him to meet her in her suite of rooms. She could hardly wait.

Just as she was giving her head a little shake to wake up her hairdo, she heard a telltale creak. "Jack!" She gushed his name as he entered the room, wearing a trench coat that nearly touched the floor. She knew exactly what was under it.

He raked her body with a hungry gaze. "You look beautiful, Julia."

"So do you, Jack. Nice coat."

"I'm going to fuck your brains out, Julia."

"You're such a charmer, Jack. Could it wait until I take control of the trust away from you?"

Jack's grin evaporated. His eyes got dark and shiny. "I don't think so, Julia."

She produced the pills, waggling them above her head. "I do, Jack."

When he realized what they were—his illegal prescription drugs—he began to laugh. "Are you blackmailing me? *Me?*"

"No, I wouldn't dream of it. This is just insurance. I want my mother's trust fund money, Jack, and I'm going to have to insist that you fork it over."

"You can't have it. Take me to court. You'll lose."

"Yes, perhaps I would lose a court battle, but Marnie wouldn't. She's my daughter, Jack. My blood daughter. She's my one surviving child, *and* a female. She's next in the line of succession, all nice and legal."

Jack began to sweat. "But she killed someone, didn't she? The morals clause—"

"Actually, she didn't. Butch died at the hands of his own father. Tragic story. I just read about it in the paper this morning."

Julia jiggled the bottle again, making sure the contents made lots of noise. "These little red pills are my insurance that Marnie's slate will remain clean. She's clean as a whistle, do you understand? And if that doesn't convince you, I have some interesting pictures of you and your hairy derriere on my cell phone. I'm sure the partners at your law firm will love your black leather jumpsuit."

His smarmy smile had vanished. He was starting to look like a man who had envisioned his financial fall from grace, and Julia had never seen a more beautiful sight. As trustee he would have continued to control the fund, pay his own exorbitant fees from it and eventually drain it dry.

She glanced at his trench coat and gave him a bawdy wink. "You should have worn your shirt, Jack. The one you're about to lose."

Epilogue

Three months later

On one side of the continent, a group of marine biology students, diving off the shoals of the Channel Islands, discovered the skeletal remains of a woman's body and called 911. That same week technicians from the county coroner's office in San Diego identified the remains, based on dental records. Alison Fairmont Villard was no longer a missing person. Her fate: death by drowning.

That same week, on the other side of the continent, in the Long Island home that Marnie and Andrew shared, the wheel of fortune had turned in the opposite direction. A home pregnancy test confirmed that Marnie's queasiness wasn't the flu. She and Andrew were bringing a new life into the world. A Christmas wedding was planned. Julia Fairmont had already RSVP'd her regrets, saying that she didn't want to cast a shadow over the happy event, but that her wedding gift—the Driscoll trust—would give full ownership and control to Marnie. And Marnie would not be without family. Josephine Hazelton, the only mother she'd ever known, would give her away.

New York Times bestselling author

DEBBIE MACOMBER

It was the year that changed everything...

At fifty, Susannah finds herself regretting the paths not taken. Long married, a mother and a teacher, she should be happy. But she feels there's something missing in her life. Not only that, she's balancing the demands of an aging mother and a temperamental twenty-year-old daughter.

In returning to her parents' house, her girlhood friends and the garden she's always loved, she discovers that things are not always as they once seemed. Some paths are dead ends. But some gardens remain beautiful....

Susannah's Garden

"[A] touching and resonant tale."
—*Booklist*

Available the first week of May 2007 wherever books are sold!

New York Times bestselling author

RACHEL LEE

A SINISTER PLOT TO SEIZE POWER IS ABOUT TO PLUNGE EUROPE INTO A NEW HOLOCAUST...

After the assassination of the German chancellor, the security of Office 119 is torn by the multitude of threats facing Europe and its people. Now time is running out. Agent Renate Bachle must do everything and anything to stop a conspirator willing to push nations to war and scapegoat an entire race in a bid for deadly power.

THE JERICHO PACT

"A highly complex thriller...deft use of dialogue."
—*Publishers Weekly* on *Wildcard*

Available the first week of May 2007 wherever paperbacks are sold!

MIRA®

www.MIRABooks.com   MRL2416

A compelling new book in the
VIRGIN RIVER series by

ROBYN CARR

John "Preacher" Middleton is about to close the bar when a young
woman and her three-year-old son come in out of a wet October
night. A marine who has seen his share of pain, Preacher knows
a crisis when he sees one—the woman is covered in bruises. He
wants to protect them, and he wants to punish whoever did this
to her. Paige Lassiter is stirring up emotions in this gentle giant of
a man—emotions that he has never allowed himself to feel.

SHELTER
MOUNTAIN

"A beautiful romance entangled with passion and intrigue."
—*New York Times* bestselling author Clive Cussler

Available the first week of May 2007
wherever paperbacks are sold!

Journey back to Valhalla Springs with
a new comic romance mystery by

SUZANN LEDBETTER

Halfway to happily ever after…probably.

Hannah Garvey, the resident manager of Valhalla Springs, an exclusive retirement community, is convinced she has this love thing all sewn up. She's engaged to David Hendrickson, the hunky Kinderhook County sheriff, and thinks the future looks pretty rosy—until one of Sanity, Missouri's most esteemed citizens becomes the county's latest homicide victim.

Meanwhile, Delbert Bisbee and his gang of senior gumshoes are driving Hannah nuts, digging dirt where they don't belong. Literally. And no matter what they unearth, there's just no halfway about it…life has a funny way of happening when you're making other plans.

Halfway to Half Way

"A crowd-pleasing, lightweight whodunit filled with unabashedly wacky characters."
—*Publishers Weekly* on *Once a Thief*

Available the first week of May 2007
wherever paperbacks are sold!

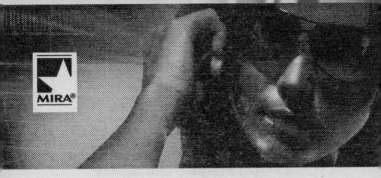

Enter a new reality in this sexy thriller
by acclaimed author

GENNITA LOW

Chosen to be the ultimate secret operative, Helen Roston
has become the most dangerous woman in the world.
Two years of training and she's now ready for the final phase, a
risky combination of virtual reality and a mind-altering serum.

Helen's final test is a challenging mission, picked by the other
government agencies whose candidates lost out to her.
To succeed she has to put herself completely in the hands of her
mysterious and faceless "trainer," a man she's not sure she can trust.
But all of COS Command are counting on her. She cannot fail.

VIRTUALLY HIS

"A gritty, powerhouse novel of suspense and intrigue."
—Merline Lovelace, *USA TODAY* bestselling author
on *The Protector*

Available the first week of May 2007
wherever paperbacks are sold!

www.MIRABooks.com

REQUEST YOUR FREE BOOKS!

2 FREE NOVELS
FROM THE ROMANCE/SUSPENSE
COLLECTION PLUS 2 FREE GIFTS!

YES! Please send me 2 FREE novels from the Romance/Suspense Collection and my 2 FREE gifts. After receiving them, if I don't wish to receive any more books, I can return the shipping statement marked "cancel." If I don't cancel, I will receive 4 brand-new novels every month and be billed just $5.49 per book in the U.S., or $5.99 per book in Canada, plus 25¢ shipping and handling per book plus applicable taxes, if any*. That's a savings of at least 20% off the cover price! I understand that accepting the 2 free books and gifts places me under no obligation to buy anything. I can always return a shipment and cancel at any time. Even if I never buy another book from the Reader Service, the two free books and gifts are mine to keep forever.

185 MDN EF5Y   385 MDN EF6C

Name _____ (PLEASE PRINT)

Address _____ Apt. #

City _____ State/Prov. _____ Zip/Postal Code

Signature (if under 18, a parent or guardian must sign)

Mail to **The Reader Service:**
IN U.S.A.: P.O. Box 1867, Buffalo, NY 14240-1867
IN CANADA: P.O. Box 609, Fort Erie, Ontario L2A 5X3

Not valid to current subscribers to the Romance Collection,
the Suspense Collection or the Romance/Suspense Collection.

Want to try two free books from another line?
Call 1-800-873-8635 or visit www.morefreebooks.com.

* Terms and prices subject to change without notice. NY residents add applicable sales tax. Canadian residents will be charged applicable provincial taxes and GST. This offer is limited to one order per household. All orders subject to approval. Credit or debit balances in a customer's account(s) may be offset by any other outstanding balance owed by or to the customer. Please allow 4 to 6 weeks for delivery.

BOB07

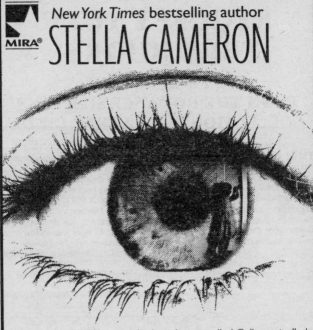